The Blossom Festival

Western Literature Series

a novel

University of Nevada Press   Reno, Las Vegas

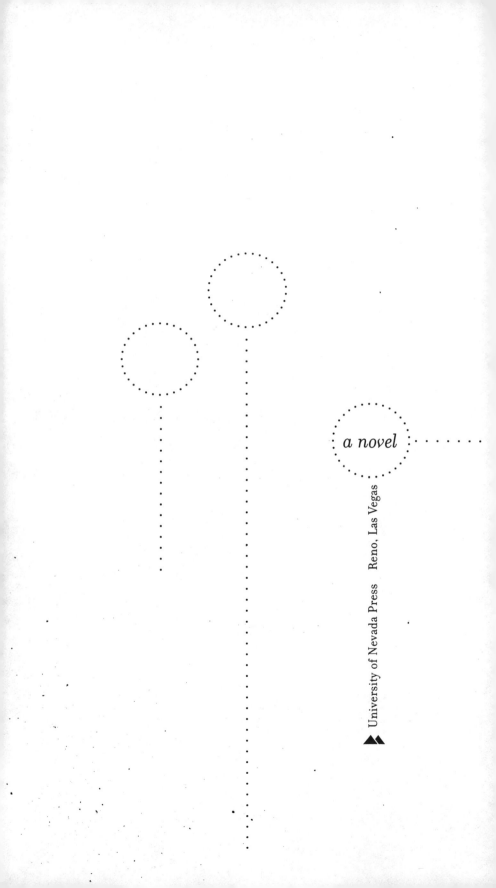

The Blossom Festival

Lawrence Coates

Western Literature Series

University of Nevada Press, Reno, Nevada 89557 USA

Copyright © 1995, 1996, 1997, 1999

by Lawrence Coates

Manufactured in the United States of America

Design by Carrie Nelson House

Library of Congress Cataloging-in-Publication Data

Coates, Lawrence, 1956–

   The Blossom Festival / by Lawrence Coates.

p. cm. — (Western literature series)

ISBN 0-87417-337-X (pbk. : alk. paper)

I. Title. II. Series.

PS3553.O153B58   1999   99-25314

813'.54—dc21   CIP

The paper used in this book meets the requirements of
American National Standard for Information Services—
Permanence of Paper for Printed Library Materials, ANSI
Z39.48-1884. Binding materials were selected for
strength and durability.

The following chapters were previously published in
somewhat different form. "Cherry Rain" originally
appeared in *The Long Story* 13 (Spring 1995); "The Fairy
King" in *Tailwind* (1999), a publication of Southern Utah
University; "Southland" in *Santa Clara Review* 81: 3 (May
1994); "A View from the Tower" in *Writers' Forum* 21
(1995), a publication of the University of Colorado at
Colorado Springs; and "The Year of the Rooster" in
Connecticut Review 29: 2 (Fall 1997).

07 06 05 04 03 02 01 00

7 6 5 4 3

For my mother and father

The branch here bends beneath the weight of pear,
And verdant olives flourish round the year.
The balmy spirit of the western gale
Eternal bears on fruits untaught to fail;
Each dropping pear a foll'wing pear supplies
On apples, apples, figs on figs arise;
The same mild season gives the bloom to blow,
The buds to harden and the fruits to grow.
—Pope's *Odyssey*

. . . .

God may consent, but only for a time.
—Emerson

Contents

one : Lone Hill

The Last Game   November 11, 1920

They played ball on a dirt field that sloped up toward the
railroad embankment in right field and dropped off beyond left field into a ravine. They always called it the Southern Pacific Field, because the railroad owned it. None of
them thought it had ever been called anything else. Leafless
fruit trees marked the foul lines, but the boys could not
have told if the field had once been an orchard before the
railroad bought and cleared it. They didn't know if it had
once served as wheat field for Yankee, or grazing land for
Spaniard, or vineyard for Franciscan, or, in times past, a
seed meadow where Ohlone women walked and gathered
and greeted each clump of trees and each large rock by its
true name. The boys played in the endless present of the
game, hit and ran across a field created, they had no reason
to doubt, especially for them.

Harold Madison, the oldest and tallest of the players, watched a ball crack cleanly in the air toward him in left field. He circled in, the ball a high white mark in the dark sky, then knew in an instant he'd misjudged. It was over his head. He spun and ran with his back to the field, but he saw the ball land beyond him, bounce twice, and disappear into the ravine.

"Damn," Harold swore automatically. He hung his glove on the foul-line tree and spidered down to find the ball. The sides of the ravine were slick and leaf-covered, and putty-colored trees curved in toward the creek at the bottom, and everywhere the air smelled wet and rotten.

Then he stumbled over some rock and ash—a dead hobo fire—and he heard a noise.

"You lost something? Or just lost."

An old man with leaves tangled in his hair grinned at Harold from across the creek. He held the baseball up, and Harold saw that the man was missing three fingers. Stumps, dirt-grained as old carrots, played across the seams.

Overhead, a freight train pounded slowly across the railroad bridge that leaped the ravine.

"Can I have the ball back, mister?"

"So, you *did* lose something," the man said. Harold figured that this was another crazy logger or teamster, left over from the lumbering days. The last redwood had been brought down the hill nine years earlier, when he was seven, and some men had never quite caught on anywhere else. They wandered through the prosperous valley like graying ghosts, and Harold had always been told to leave them be. They were dangerous, people said. Strays.

"What did you lose?" The man's yellow teeth showed in his smile.

"The baseball."

"*This* baseball?"

"Please, mister." Harold didn't want to get any closer to him.

"Ho, ho, ho. *Please!*" He laughed, then threw the ball across the creek to Harold.

"Thanks." Harold turned and scrambled up the hill, and he heard the old man behind him.

"See you around, sport."

The trees thinned and the sky grew lighter as he reached the edge of the ravine, and the air was colder and cleaner, without the damp rotting smell. He pushed off one last tree and clambered up to the playing field. The other boys were waiting for him.

Paolo, the shortstop, waved for the ball.

"Come on. Rain's coming."

Harold signaled thumbs-up and threw in to Paolo, and their makeshift diamond grew alive again with game chatter. But Harold looked up to the sky, and he knew this would be the last day for baseball. Time was passing. After this holiday, the days would grow short and the rains would come frequently, turning the field to mud. This was Armistice Day, two years after the war, and he and the others, standing on the field under the gray sky, had decided to skip the flags and parade and speeches in San Jose and play one last time together.

Now the old man had taken him away from the game. He looked back to the ravine, half afraid he would see him rising out of the leaves, rank and enormous. He saw there instead a picture from his memory, a day in October, some years past.

From the yards a track switch clacked into place and a train whistle blew.

2

Southland   October 1912

When the man stopped them all on the way to school, Harold
knew it was something he'd been waiting for, expecting almost, for a long time.

The man stepped out suddenly from behind a wagon. He
must have been crouched down there on the gravel road,
listening for their voices. But when he stood before them
with his arms outstretched, thin and towering, he looked
like the egret Harold had seen on the sloughs near Alviso,
stretching out its neck and wings just before pulling into
flight.

He was dressed like a railroad man. He wore overalls with
thin black and white stripes, and a matching striped hat, and a
bright-red bandanna around his neck that moved a little when
his Adam's apple worked up and down.

His dark eyes picked over the boys, ignored the two girls

in the group. He glanced quickly up and down the road, then turned again to sifting and sorting the boys.

Slowly he brought his arms together and aimed his two big hands at Harold's chest.

"Harold?" He dropped down to one knee so that his eyes were on a level with the children's.

Everyone drew back a little from Harold except his best friend, Benny.

"Yeah?" Harold said.

"Do you remember me?"

"Sure. 'Course I remember you."

"Do you want to go on a trip with me?"

"On a train?"

"That's right. On a train."

"Harold?" Benny tugged at his sleeve. "Who is it?"

"It's my dad," Harold said.

"No, it isn't. You don't have a dad."

"Harold." The man looked all around again. One darkish tooth showed in his smile. "Come on over here."

Harold looked at Benny to see what he thought.

"Come on, Harold," the man said. "Don't be scared."

Benny bit his lip. But Harold walked forward, and the man grabbed him under his arms and placed him on his shoulders. He stood up and lifted Harold suddenly six feet off the ground.

Harold grabbed a fist of hat and hair to keep his balance. With his other hand, he waved at his friends.

"Now," the man said. "You don't want Harold to get in trouble, do you?"

"No," they all chorused.

"I'm Harold's Poppa, and I'm taking him on a trip. But when the teacher asks you where Harold is, you just say he's sick. Okay?"

"Isn't that lying?" asked a little girl.

"No," the man said. "It's just helping out a friend. That's what you want them to say, isn't it, Harold?"

"I guess so," Harold said.

"Well, let's skedaddle on out of here."

The man gave a little hop and began to walk with long quick strides toward the Southern Pacific yards.

The chill air spanked against Harold's face as he rode, and he felt his cheeks tingling. "Poppa?"

"Yeah?"

"Where we going?"

"Down to the Southland, where the orange trees grow. Down where you can hop a big red car from the Pacific Electric and be at the beach in an hour."

"Is Mom coming too?"

The man laughed.

"Your mother never liked trains much."

They walked into a gravel-lined ditch, then through a break in a wooden fence. Suddenly, tall iron engines and painted boxcars were all around them, and Harold breathed in the sharp smells of burning diesel, dripping oil, steam, and soot. The man took a watch out of his pocket and snapped it open. Then he slowed his walk a bit.

"You see the steam coming out up there?" He pointed to a gray curl lifting up at the head of a line of cars. "That's our engine."

They walked past the black cylindrical tender to the front of the engine. Harold thought he'd never seen something so big seem so alive. A deep sound rumbled down inside the engine, and puffs of smoke and steam escaped from the stack and around the pistons, as though the machine were breathing. Oil gleamed where the silvery connecting rods attached to the driving wheels. There was a brass bell above the boiler, and a narrow catwalk alongside it with lots of handles and levers painted red.

"See the number?" the man asked.

A thick metal plaque under the headlight was painted with the same heavy silver paint as the connecting rods.

"Twelve," Harold began. "Six. Nine."

"Why, you know your numbers."

"'Course. We learned that in first grade!"

"Madison," a voice called out from the cab. "How about getting your hind end up here and getting to work."

"What time you got?"

"We're not due out for another five minutes, but damn it all if I'm going to keep doing two men's work."

The man lifted Harold off his shoulders and placed him on the first rung of the ladder.

"Scramble on up there, Harold."

As he climbed step by step, Harold could see the inside of the cab. Big round brass gauges with white faces, a glass tube with water in it encased in wire, a large gear-toothed quadrant connected to a lever. But after Harold looked around once, he didn't take his eyes off the large, frowning man sitting in the engineer's seat on the right side of the engine.

The engineer stared at him, rubbed the white crop on his jaw, and then spit out the window.

"So you're Madison's kid, eh?"

Harold watched his father haul himself into the cab, then nodded.

"Yes, sir," he said.

The engineer spit again. "Well, God help you."

His father moved to the seat on the left side. "Where's the needle?"

"The needle's right where she should be, at two hundred. And you've got half a glass of water. You think I forgot how to fire?"

"Harold," his father said. "I need you to hide yourself right under my seat there. Don't touch anything. And don't peek your head out. We don't want anyone stopping us from making our trip."

Harold nestled under the fireman's seat on the left side of the engine. There was only room in the cab for him, his father, and the frowning old engineer. He wasn't sure why his mother wasn't coming, but he was afraid that if he asked, his father might not take him along. And since his father had left, he had been wanting only that—to be taken along.

"All right, Madison," the engineer said. "Let's take her down to Los Angeles."

He leaned out the side of the train, gave a wave of the hand, and slowly pulled back on the throttle. Harold felt his father shift around as well. The sound of the engine changed, as the steam that had been venting was directed down to the cylinders. The engine breathed deeply, exhaled, huffed forward slowly. It paused to gather behind it the string of cars, boxcars, grain cars, caboose, then strained forward, breathing faster now, a loud rhythmic push of fire and water into steam into motion.

Harold felt inside this sound, the big booming breathing of an engine pulling down the track. It was the sound he heard at railroad crossings, or with a bunch of other kids at the S.P. yards when they tried to put a penny on the tracks and not get caught, the sound he heard out the window late at night, distant, fleeting, soon gone. He always heard it passing him by, growing louder and closer, then trickling off and disappearing. And he always said, *My father works on the railroad.* Silently, if his mother was around. Quietly, too, if too many other boys were near, boys who no longer believed him. Out loud if he was alone. The railroading was what he loved most about his father.

Now the rush of steam surrounded him, and the wheels moved under him, and his father was by him, above him, showing him the way.

Across the cab, the engineer pulled down on a lever. The great steam whistle roared.

The train was past Coyote in the long, dry, southern Santa Clara Valley before Harold was allowed out from under the seat. He climbed up on the green leather cushion. His father was leaning out the left-hand side of the engine, looking forward, and Harold poked his head out beside him. The hot air rushed by his cheeks at forty-five miles an hour, and he watched the plume of smoke fall back horizontally over the top of the cab. The hills to the east were smoothed and round, still burned golden brown by summer.

His father leaned in to check the gauges, and Harold drew back in with him. "Poppa? What do they grow here?"

"Nothing. It's too dry. Now you keep an eye on the stack there, and I'll show you something."

He knelt down and loosened the metal port over the firebox. "We call this the peephole," he said. When he opened it, the fire sucked in a howl of air. He quickly took a large scoop of sand from the tin box at the rear of the cab and shoved it into the roaring blaze. Within seconds, the plume of smoke from the stack changed from a whitish blue color to cinder black, twisting against the bright sky. Some of the soot loosened by the sand fell from the plume and floated back down into the cab.

He bolted the peephole back down while Harold watched the changing smoke. "You like that?"

The engineer brought himself back inside the cab. "Madison." He had to shout to make himself heard across the cab. "You're a damned fool."

"What do you mean I'm a damned fool?" Harold's father yelled back. "Didn't you tell me that if I wanted to see the boy, I should go get him?"

"I only told you that because I was tired of your bellyaching. If I'd have thought you'd really do it, I'd have never told you to."

His father took a look down the track, then popped back in. "But look at the kid," he shouted. "He's never seen anything but a prune orchard."

Both Harold's father and the engineer put their heads and shoulders outside the cab, then came inside again.

"You think his mother's not going to track him down?" the engineer bellowed. "You think that bimbo you're shacked up with in Echo Park is going to take care of him? What are you going to do when he needs his nose blown, or his temperature taken?"

"All right," he roared back. "So I don't have it all thought out yet."

"Poppa?"

"Yeah, Harold."

"I have to wee."

His father and the engineer looked at each other, then broke into laughter. The engineer said, "There's something else you don't have thought out yet."

His father said, "Okay, you want to go the same way the men do?"

Harold thought for a moment. Then he nodded.

"Thatsaboy. Now get your wiener out, and I'll lift you up."

Harold looked from his father to the engineer, then he turned away from them and unbuttoned his fly.

"Better not play with that thing too much," the engineer called, "or it will never grow."

"Don't pay any attention to him." His father picked Harold up and held him standing on the sill of the window. The wind rushed by, and Harold looked down at the blur of rail ties passing fifteen feet below him.

He held himself with both hands.

"Be sure you aim downwind," his father instructed.

Harold tried, but something froze up inside him. The endless rounded hills, the sun, the dry air, the beat of the steam engine, and he was out on the edge and he couldn't go.

"Poppa," he said.

He heard his father's voice behind him, low and sure. "Don't worry. I've got you. You're with me now."

Harold felt himself relax. Felt himself let go. And suddenly, the yellow water flew and scattered horizontally in the rushing air alongside the engine.

"Okay, Poppa," he said.

His father lifted him down and let him button his fly. "Good boy," he said.

The train highballed past dark fields of cut wheat, littered with chaff and stubble, and began the long, slow climb along the Salinas River. When they drew near Greenfield and King City, his father had Harold hide under his seat. But as soon as they were past, his father let him sit by the window again. The hills changed gradually. In the folds of straw gold, stands of trees now clustered, green bunches following a creek line down toward the valley.

His father was often beside him, watching down the tracks with him. Then he would duck back inside to check his fire.

"Keep an eye on things for a sec, Harold," he'd say.

"Okay," Harold would answer.

When Harold tired of being out in the wind, his father explained things about how the engine worked. Riding an engine was like riding a long load of dynamite. As long as you kept the right amount of water and the right amount of fire, the pistons would move the connecting rods, which would move the driving wheels. But if you let the water level fall, you were asking for trouble.

"You see this water glass?" He pointed to the glass tube inside the wire cage. "The bottom of the glass is three and a half
inches above the crown sheet, the top of the firebox. As long as
you keep that crown sheet covered with water, you'll be making
steam. Let the water level fall and the crown go dry, and you'll
have an explosion."

"Wow," Harold said.

"Or else melt a safety valve, like Soft Plug Lenny did. You
make a mistake like that on the railroad, they never let you
forget it."

The engineer brought his head in, and Harold's father
called, "You remember him?"

"Who?"

"Soft Plug Lenny."

The engineer looked at his gauges, then frowned at Harold
and his father. "You really think talking engines to him is going to make him forget his mother?" He turned to spit out the
window. "How old are you, anyway?"

"Almost eight," Harold said.

"And who do you like better, your mother or your father?"

Harold looked up at his father. "Both," he said.

The engineer shook his head. "You got to choose."

"No, you don't," his father said.

"Ha," the engineer said.

They saw a train order signal swing up its black and white
arm just north of the long grade, and they slowed down into
the next town. Harold hid under the seat, and his father adjusted the dampers and the oil to keep the fire down. The
wheels under the train were turning slowly still, another half
turn, another quarter turn, until finally the engine sighed to a
halt.

The engineer gave Harold a look, held his finger to his lips,
and then hopped out of the train. His father stayed in the cab
and leaned out the window. Harold heard him talking to some
men outside.

"What's the news? Anybody get killed?"

"Cinder bulls ran a couple of Wobblies out of town last week.
That's about the only excitement we got."

"Nothing else on the wire?"

The engineer climbed back into the train. "No posse yet," he said in a low voice.

"So what's the deal?"

"Grain spill in the mountains between here and Los Angeles. The big hooks have already cleared the wrecks, but there's grain all around."

"For Christ's sake."

The engineer leaned out the cab, waved his arm, then pulled the throttle back. The engine again gathered up the weight of the cars behind it and moved slowly forward.

When the train cleared the station, Harold's father brought him up on the seat. Harold looked at the gauges as he'd been shown, then checked the level of water in the glass. Everything was in order, so he put his head out the window with his father.

"Poppa? Why did we have to stop?"

"We got a grain spill in the San Gabriels up ahead. What do you think that means?"

"I don't know."

"Well, it means that everything within fifty miles that likes to eat grain is going to be all over the tracks. Can't highball it through there, or we might get derailed by a bear."

Harold looked to see if his father was joking. "By a bear?"

"It's happened before."

"I like bears."

"Bears are a pain in the ass. If they slow us down too much, maybe there *will* be a posse waiting for us."

The train was climbing steadily now. The smooth-shaped golden hills gave way to sharper slopes, bristly with Monterey pine. The sun was past its peak, tumbling down to the west, and the pine was dusky green in the low light.

The train was still some miles away from where the grain spill was reported when the engineer began to ease up on the throttle. He nodded at Harold's father, who adjusted the dampers and the oil flow, cutting down the fire. Harold leaned out of the cab, looking for the bears.

"Are we almost there, Poppa?"

"We got a ways to go. But it takes a long time to slow down a train. Hey, chief. What are you going to slow her down to?"

"Five miles an hour. That ought to let them get out of the way."

"We going to be able to make up any of that time?"

The engineer shrugged.

The train climbed through a deep cut in the hills. Pine rose tall on either side of the track, covering the slopes and allowing only a filtered horizontal sunlight to penetrate. Harold had his head out of the cab while his father was busy with the fire. The tracks seemed to go on forever into the green light, forever curving into the tall woods.

Suddenly, Harold saw them. Before the engineer or his father, he saw the husky, shaggy shapes playing in the half-light. There were eight or ten in all, rolling with each other, pawing slowly through the thick needles mixed with grain. One bear lazed on its back, stretched a right forepaw toward the roof of the forest, and watched unconcerned as the train grew closer.

Two bears had their heads right down between the ties of the tracks. They picked carefully in the cracks with their long claws, flicked their pink tongues out. Then they sat and chewed something from their paws, tilting their heads sideways.

Harold looked at his father, still concerned with his fire, and the engineer on the throttle. Then he climbed up on the windowsill, all by himself this time, and leaned out.

The train was crawling through the woods, and he was out in the open air, under the trees and light, going toward the bears. They sat with their big round rumps nestled on the duff, and they turned their heads toward him as he neared. They seemed to smile, a long, welcoming smile stretching down their muzzles.

Harold saw the two bears still blocking the tracks, and he remembered what his father had said. He leaned forward and began to shout.

"Get out of the way! Go 'way, bears! We have to go to Los Angeles!"

His father looked up. "Holy Christ, Harold!"

The bears already alongside of the track lolled back on their haunches to watch the train go by.

Harold felt a big hand grab his belt and drag him back inside the cab, but he could still see the bears in front of the train. They stopped pawing between the ties, and one rose up on its hind legs and faced the engine. Its reddish coat glistened in the late sun, and it stood upright on the tracks with its forepaws close to its body. The bear's mouth yawned open.

"Hrrrnhaah. Haarwhngh."

Then it stooped back down to all fours, and both bears stepped unhurriedly out of the way and joined the group on the side.

"Did you see them move, Poppa?" Harold asked. "They moved like they heard me."

"Damn it, Harold, don't you ever do anything like that again." His father shook him a little. "You hear?"

Harold looked over at the engineer. *Who do you like better?*

"Don't look at him, look at me. Never again. Okay?"

"Okay, Poppa."

"Bears are a pain in the ass. When you're railroading."

The engineer turned and spit out the window.

The train came down from the mountains onto the wide Los Angeles plain, running through dark, silent orange groves, by isolated farmhouses. Harold had to hide when they pulled half an hour late into the S.P. yards in East L.A., but his father soon told him that the coast was clear and lifted him down from the train. They walked with the engineer past men unloading boxcars into trucks, moving around empty cars with a pusher, lubricating and repairing machinery. No one seemed to notice them at all.

Just outside the main gate, a white-haired woman in a black car opened the passenger door and let the engineer in.

"I never drive," the engineer said. "Do enough of it at work. I always let her drive. You need a lift?"

"Shirley should be coming along on a streetcar, and we'll go out for a bite to eat."

"Sure." The engineer looked at Harold. "Good luck, kid."

The car pulled away, and Harold looked down the wide, dark street. He didn't see any headlights coming for them.

"I'm hungry, Poppa."

"Okay, Harold. We'll just wait a little while longer."

Harold turned back and rattled the fence. In the yards, large black shapes moved incessantly to and fro, becoming suddenly yellow when they passed under a light. His father paced back and forth.

"Poppa?"

"Here she comes, Harold."

A large, sleek streetcar rolled up outside the fence and came to a stop at the gate. As Harold watched, men in caps and overalls piled off the car, carrying canvas bags. Railroad men, like his father, going out to work.

There were no women on the car, and Harold's father cursed. Then he grabbed Harold by the hand.

"Okay, Harold. We're going home."

. . . .

The first thing Harold saw in the Echo Park apartment was something scuttling across the kitchen floor when the light came on.

"Look," he pointed.

His father tapped it lightly with his foot and swept it to one side.

"Just a cockroach."

He went to the icebox and looked inside. "Well, sport," he said, "we got a problem. I got beer here, but no milk." He cracked off a bottle cap with the opener bolted to the wall; the cap fell neatly into the trash.

"That's all right." Harold climbed up on a stool.

His father found some cans of pork and beans, some tuna fish, and a bottle of Heinz ketchup, and he put them on the counter. In the bread box on top of the icebox, there were some bread heels.

"Tell you what," he said. "I'll heat us up some pork and beans, and I'll make toast out of the bread. That won't be so bad, will it?"

"No," Harold said. "Poppa, where's the bathroom?"

"Right there. We have our own bathroom in this place. Don't have to go down the hall." His father struck a match, lit a cigarette, and then touched the match to a burner.

Harold picked his way around a pile of dirty clothes and pressed the light switch in the bathroom. The light glanced off dozens and dozens of little bottles. Tiny jars, vials, and fancy prismatic glass containers covered the counter around the sink. They were lined up, in pink, pale blue, green, behind the toilet, up on a shelf, along the windowsill. Harold opened the medicine chest and found more bottles.

He picked up a red one carefully, as though it might shatter in his hand, and sounded out the label.

"Ee-ow dee toy-letty."

It didn't make much sense to him. He undid the cap and poured a little bit into his hand. It looked just like water, but it smelled thick and sweet.

"Perfume," he said. "Phooey!" He washed his hands with soap and water and wiped them on a towel hanging over the edge of the tub.

In the kitchen, his father was taking the bread off a metal stand over the rear burner. "Toast is done," he said. "And the beans are hot. You hungry?"

"Yeah!"

His father opened another beer, spooned the beans into two bowls, and laid them on a board that hinged down from the wall and served as a table. Then he pulled up a stool, and Harold did the same. "I put a little ketchup in with the beans while I was cooking them," he said, "and a little sugar, too. That's what makes them good."

Harold dipped the toast into the beans, let it sit long enough to soak up some juice, and then took a bite.

"It's good," he said. He swallowed a spoonful after chewing a couple of times, then took up another spoonful. His father patted him on the back.

"You want to try some beer?"

Harold looked at the bottle, thick, heavy, and brown. "Sure."

"Go ahead."

Harold took the bottle in both hands and tilted it back. It tasted funny, and the bubbles tickled his nose, but it wasn't bad. His mother always made it seem bad when she talked about it.

"You like it?"

"Yeah, I like it."

"Well, go ahead and finish it." His father took down a square bottle from the cupboard and poured an inch into a glass. "I'm going to have a little bit of the real stuff."

After dinner, he cleared off a place on the couch for Harold to sleep and gave him a pillow and a blanket. Harold didn't have to get undressed. He didn't even have to brush his teeth or wash his hands.

"You'll be all right on the couch for tonight, won't you, sport? Tomorrow we'll figure out what to do."

But Harold couldn't reply. As he lay down, the voice grew distant, and through the bars of his eyelashes he saw his father's face float up from him and turn away.

. . . .

Angry voices cracked through the dull hum of dream, and a glass shattered. Harold woke up to a light flaring on.

He stood, still half asleep, and walked toward the light. The angry voices sounded like something he'd heard before, something he heard every night in his sleep.

He saw them now, male and female, colossal. His father and a woman, face to face, framed by the kitchen door. "I'm a do-right kind," his father shouted, "but damn it, Shirley, you drive me crazy."

"You want me to sit around and darn your socks, waiting for you? Take care of a kid? I didn't come out to Los Angeles to sit around."

The woman was holding the square bottle like a club, and Harold's father stood over her with his fists clenched like white hammers. Harold knew they were fighting because of him.

"I've got a good mind to haul off and slap you silly."

"You wouldn't dare, damn your eyes."

Harold stepped between them, just at the moment his father was raising his hand. He turned to the woman, wrapped his arms around her legs, and buried his face in her skirt.

Above him, a shrill of laughter.

"Look at the kid, willya? Look at the kid."

"What a pain in the ass," his father said, sounding suddenly weary.

Harold held on tight. He smelled the same strong perfume he'd found earlier, but it smelled different now, better, mixed with the smell of this woman's body.

"Look at him. He don't want you to hurt me."

"Leave us be, Harold."

His father's hands grasped him around the waist and pried him free.

"This is grown-up stuff."

. . . .

Two days later, Harold and his father got off a Pacific Electric car at the S.P. passenger terminal. They had taken the Venice Short Line down to the beach and spent the day riding on the Ferris wheel, the Giant Dipper, the Bamboo Slide, and the Rolling Barrels. Afterward, they walked out on the pier and Harold ate a hot dog while his father watched the ocean. Harold had an ice cream cone, too, and he could have had two ice cream cones if he'd wanted. That's what his father said.

When they left the pier, his father bought a wicker basket packed with two oranges and two jars of orange marmalade, wrapped round by a souvenir dish towel with a picture of an orange grove.

"That's a gift for your mother," he said.

His father had slept past noon the morning after they arrived, and Harold had wandered alone in the still apartment, hungry and empty and afraid to wake him. The only food he found in the kitchen was the can of tuna, but he couldn't find the can opener. In the bathroom, half the bottles of perfume were gone, and the other half were smashed and shattered in the trash. Harold spent time playing with the pieces of glass, trying to put them together like a puzzle, until his father finally staggered up and took them out to eat at a cafeteria.

That night, his father left him alone again, telling him he was going to find Shirley and bring her back. Harold had trouble falling asleep in the dark apartment, and when his father came back alone, Harold watched him with slitted eyes while he kicked at furniture and glared at his son. Harold thought he had done something wrong, and he lay very still and quiet.

The next morning, his father woke up in a good mood, went out, and returned with eggs, bacon, potatoes. While he fried up breakfast, he told Harold that they were going to head down to the S.P. hall and see what runs were on the board.

"We going on another train ride?" Harold asked.

"In a way."

"If we see bears again, I'll know what to do."

"Yeah?" his father asked. "What?"

"Go right through them. Pain in the ass!"

His father laughed.

The S.P. hall was on the east side, near the yards. It was large and low-ceilinged, with cold tile floors and hard benches, and a few men who looked like Harold's father smoked and talked, and their voices sounded hollow in the space. At one end of the hall, a large and scarred wooden board made from tongue-and-groove pine had the names of trains tacked to it. Harold stood close to his father and listened to him read the litany of names low to himself, each train an adventure: the *Lark*, the *Owl*, the *Coast Daylight*, the *Starlight*, the *Golden State Limited* . . .

Then they walked over to one of the benches, and Harold watched his father slowly roll a cigarette. When he licked it and lit it, he turned to Harold, and his dead tooth showed in his smile.

"I telegrammed your mother this morning. Told her I was going to have to send you back."

"How come?" Harold asked.

"'Cause I'm a train man, can't you see?"

"So?" He felt himself beginning to cry, and he tried not to, or he'd lose his father forever.

"So I can't take care of a kid."

"Why not?"

"Why not?" His father began to look impatient. "Because I'm heading to Chicago in two days, *that's* why not."

"I'll go with you."

"Shit." His father pulled angrily at his cigarette. "You can't.

Not 'til you're a man yourself."

"But I already did."

"If I could've counted on that bitch Shirley . . . but you can't depend on anyone."

His father scratched his face.

"Listen, Harold. You sorry I'm a train man?"

"No," Harold said. "I tell the other kids you work on the railroad."

"Yeah?" His father sounded pleased.

"That's what I say. 'My father works on the railroad.'"

"I'll be damned." His father looked up at the ceiling, looked over at the job board. "That don't change things, though."

. . . .

Now they went through the low, red-tile-roofed passenger terminal and out onto the platform where Harold's train waited. His father nodded to the conductor and helped Harold up the first step into his car. When he'd settled Harold into his seat and placed the wicker basket in the rack overhead, he sat down next to him.

"I'll tell the conductor which stop is yours. And your mother will be there waiting for you, so there should be no problem. Here." He fished out a silver dollar. "Put this in a safe place."

Harold dropped it into his shirt pocket and buttoned the flap.

"That's money for food along the way. But if you buy a sandwich, make sure you get change from these sharpers. A sandwich should go for ten cents, tops. Okay?"

"Okay," Harold said.

The train whistle blew once, and his father stood up in the aisle. He patted Harold on the back.

"Did you have a good time?"

"Sure."

"Good." His father patted him on the back once more. "Well, see you around, sport."

When the train pulled out of the station, Harold watched his father through the window, waving at the departing train. He watched until his father had blended in with all the others on the platform, one by one lowering their arms and turning to leave.

Then he turned forward, trying to look out the window as he had looked out the cab a few days earlier. When the train climbed into the Coast Range north of Santa Barbara, he began to watch for bears again.

But there were no bears on the way back. They had all disappeared.

3

. . . .

Lone Hill   June 1920

In that year, the warm summer's sun ripened the prunes in
the orchards that covered Santa Clara Valley.

The prunes grew thickly in the trees, thick as bunches of
grapes. They grew round and sweet, and changed from a
dark-green color to a dusky, silvery shade of purple. As they
ripened, their weight spread the branches of the trees, part-
ing the leaves and allowing the sunshine to filter through.
They basked in the sun, and sometimes grew so heavy that
props had to be placed to keep the branches from breaking.

Then, in their own time, they fell from the tree to the
ground. Ripe and full, they broke from the fragile stem that
had held them and nourished them. First one dropped, and
the tree shuddered slightly. Then several dropped, from the
many fruit-bearing branches of the tree. In the course of a
few days, prunes ripened and dropped throughout the or-

chards, and spread out in a circle around the tree trunks—silvery, dusty nuggets of fruit.

Each row of trees would be picked four times, to gather the fruit that had just fallen at the peak of ripeness and to allow the fruit that remained on the tree to ripen and fall in turn.

When the prune harvest began that year, Harold had just turned sixteen and finished the last year of school he would attend.

. . . .

Harold lived with his mother on the Ida Valley Ranch, where she helped in the kitchen at the big house. Harold's father hadn't been heard from since he put Harold on the northbound train. His mother spoke of him seldom. But once she'd said he'd either struck it rich or been killed by an exploding boiler. Either way, she didn't expect to hear from him again.

When Harold was nine, he scraped the large drying trays that the fruit would be placed on to bake under the sun before shipping. Later, he went out with the older men to prune the trees, and learned to handle the shears and the knife. Then he began to take on heavier work in the packing house or the drying yard. But as he grew into the work of the ranch Harold wondered about his father, who had once been part of this life and who had left it behind.

During the second picking that year, Harold found himself working a row of trees in the Lone Hill section beside Betsy Moreberg. Lone Hill was an isolated piece of high ground beside the San Natoma–Los Gatos Road, in the corner of the orchard furthest from the packing houses. Shorty, the foreman, might come there only twice a day with the tractor to pick up the full boxes, drop off empties, and punch their cards, once for every full box.

Betsy and Harold worked rows parallel to each other, advancing tree by tree. They gathered prunes off the smoothed earth with both hands and piled them into large galvanized buckets. When the buckets were full, they carried them down to the stack of boxes at the beginning of the row and emptied them there. Two very full buckets were needed to fill one box.

The ground under each tree had to be picked clean. That morning Shorty had said, "I want you out there, Harold, 'cause I won't be out to Lone Hill much. But I know I won't have to tell you not to leave any fruit on the ground to rot."

Harold looked over at Betsy when he finished a tree and saw that she was still working. She was a strong picker. Not as fast as he was, but he liked the way she swept her pale arms across the ground. When Shorty had called out for one or two more pickers for Lone Hill, Betsy's hand fluttered up, and she looked around to see if anyone else was coming.

Harold bent beside her and began to shovel prunes into her bucket.

She smiled at him. "You don't have to give me your prunes, Harold."

"I don't mind. I want you to keep up with me."

He picked with both hands, moving in a circle around the trunk.

"It's more fun if we're together."

When the buckets were full, he picked them up to carry out to her stack of boxes. She smiled again at him. When she bent back to work, he watched her hips move under the loose cloth of her skirt.

They moved on to the next tree. Every so often, he saw her hold handfuls of fruit up to her nose and inhale deeply. Then she dropped most of them in her bucket, wiped the dust off one or two against her blouse, and popped them between her lips.

"Betsy," he said, still picking, "what are you going to do with your fruit money?"

"Buy things for school. And something nice to wear, if I can. I want to buy a butterfly skirt and spectator shoes."

"What's a butterfly skirt?"

"One of those with lots of pleats. You know."

"Oh. One of those." Harold didn't know what spectator shoes were either, but he didn't want to ask. "Why do they call it a butterfly skirt?"

"Maybe because it makes you feel like a butterfly? Dancing and light."

She stood up and moved her arms like wings. Harold nodded.

"Miss Anderson wears them all the time," Betsy said. "I'm going to take geometry with her next year. She said I have the perfect kind of mind for geometry."

Harold had been watching the back of Betsy's head in school for years. She sat in the front of the class, solved problems on the blackboard that almost nobody else got right, and always turned in her homework on time, written neatly on unlined paper. Harold sat in the back and was hardly ever called on. When he did go to the blackboard, he usually made some mistake, and Mrs. Quinley made him stand there while she corrected his errors for the rest of the class. He never knew where to put his hands while she erased his large, awkward numbers and chalked in her own with lightning speed. Sometimes he put his hands in his pockets, and sometimes he clasped them behind his back. Once, he looked down at his shoes while she corrected his work, and she caught him with her quick blue eyes.

"Harold, this is mainly for your benefit," she'd said.

Harold took his two buckets back to the boxes, then joined Betsy under the branches of her tree.

"But it's nice not to be in school now," Harold said. "Don't you think?"

"I love being able to be outdoors," Betsy said. "You're lucky, Harold."

"You think so?"

"You get to be out here all the time, while Papa keeps me cooped up."

"Yeah," Harold said. "But I don't get to go back to school next year."

"Really?" Betsy sounded surprised, though they both knew that the numbers of students fell off in the last two grades at high school.

"I'm going to be working here at Ida Valley. Going to be a full-time man." He knelt down again, picked up a few prunes from the ground, and put them into Betsy's bucket.

"My mother needs me," he added with some bitterness.

"But you're doing right, Harold."

"You think so?" Harold saw that Betsy was listening carefully, and he suddenly wondered what would happen if he tried to kiss her.

"You can be proud of yourself."

"Hmm." Harold looked over the rows of trees in leaf, the round fruit that lay across the swelling land of Lone Hill. "We won't see each other much after this harvest. You won't pick fruit next year. You'll be too busy. Too old."

"Too cooped up," Betsy said.

"Too educated," Harold said. "You'll be too smart to be picking prunes off the dirt."

"No, I won't." Betsy sounded hurt. "I'd rather be making things grow like you than finish high school and just keep house for my father."

"You'll do more than that."

Betsy shook her head. "Don't think so."

"Sure you will."

She shook her head, picked up a prune, and began to brush it against her blouse. Then she dropped it to the ground again. Harold turned to her and saw that her eyes were bright and wet.

"Hey." He reached out and took her hand, surprised at the softness of her touch, sure that his own hand felt like sand-paper to her. He looked at her arm, bare below her rolled-up sleeve, warm and round, the color of ripe peaches. He squeezed her hand as gently as he knew how.

She pressed his hand in return, more firmly than he had pressed hers.

Harold found a prune with the flower still attached. He held it out toward Betsy in his open palm.

"Here's the kind of prune you should eat in the orchard," he said. "It will get graded out, because the skin is scarred from where the flower stuck. But still, it's just as sweet."

With his thumb, he brushed off the shriveled flower, which broke away at its brittle stem.

"Do you want to try a sweet-and-sour?" he asked.

"Okay."

"Here. Don't bite down on it yet."

They stood up, and she took the prune and put it in her mouth. Then he bent down and grasped her around the hips and lifted her up through the branches of the tree. She was among the green leaves and the thick, round fruit, and he let his face sigh into her skirt.

At the very tip of a branch, she found a prune that wasn't too green and wasn't too ripe, and she plucked it and put it in her mouth.

"Okay," she said.

He lowered her down. She chewed the two prunes together, letting the juices mingle on her tongue.

"Sweet-and-sour," he said.

She closed her eyes. She was still in his arms, and there was no one else around. He leaned his head at an awkward angle and kissed her.

. . . .

Half an hour before sunset, Shorty turned his tractor and trailer up to the Lone Hill section, chewing on an unlit cigar. He frowned when he saw how many trees Harold had picked; the stacks of filled boxes were not as high as he had expected, and Harold and the girl had only finished three and a half rows.

He pulled the trailer up alongside the boxes and blew a whistle, and Harold and the girl stood up from where they were stooped over. Shorty noticed that the young man picked up all the buckets, both the girl's and his own, before coming to the trailer. He also observed that the two of them walked closer together than they needed to.

Shorty began to pile the full boxes onto the trailer, and Harold fell in beside him without a word. Betsy stayed to one side to watch. She found something very beautiful in the way Harold picked up a fifty-pound box of fruit and swung it in one motion into place on the trailer.

Shorty finished off one stack, pulled the unlit cigar out of his mouth, and aimed it at Harold. "What happened today, Harold? You used to be a ton-a-day man. Now it looks like you barely topped forty boxes between the two of you."

Harold paused slightly, then resumed work. "I don't know, Shorty. It just didn't seem to go so fast today."

"Anybody'd think you spent your time lollygagging around instead of working." Shorty began again to move the boxes of fruit onto the trailer. He added, "That's not the way a full-time man should work. Especially if he's got enough upstairs to be foreman someday."

Harold didn't look at either Betsy or Shorty. "You're right, Shorty," he said.

"There's no room for slackers during the harvest. You've only got a few days to get the fruit off the ground, onto the dry yard, into packing boxes, and off to the market."

Shorty chewed on his cigar. Harold continued to load boxes without looking at anyone.

"It took a long time to build up the Ida Valley name, but you've still got to earn it every season. One load of substandard produce, and the buyers won't trust you for years."

"I know, Shorty," Harold said.

"Maybe you'll climb the ladder and have your own farm someday. Then you'll know just what a good name means, and you'll sweat blood to keep it."

The last box was loaded, and Shorty asked, "All right, whose card do I punch for these boxes?"

Betsy and Harold looked at each other, and then Harold spoke. "Just punch each of our cards twenty-two times."

"Half and half?" Shorty nodded. "I'm going to have to get a few more pickers out onto Lone Hill, I can see that."

· · · · · · ·

Harold and Betsy rode on the trailer down Lone Hill toward the packing house, sitting with their backs against the full boxes of fruit. As Shorty had acidly pointed out, with only forty-four boxes, there was plenty of room for passengers.

Harold sat by himself to one side of the trailer, with his knees drawn up to his chin and his arms wrapped around his legs.

Betsy scooted over closer to Harold and touched his knee.

"Harold," she said, "aren't you happy?"

Harold sat like a lump. "Nobody criticized you," he said.

They rumbled past row after row of trees, darkening in the twilight.

"It doesn't matter so much for you how many boxes are picked," he said. "It's piecework. But I'm supposed to be better than twenty-two boxes."

"That doesn't make any difference about whether you're happy or not."

"No?"

Harold looked down toward his shoes.

"It was like being in math class again, me being cut down and you watching. And I should know what's what out here."

She grabbed his arm. "Harold, I don't care what he thinks. I need to know how you're feeling."

She was looking at him intently, her face drawn and troubled, and he realized somehow that she asked whether he was happy in order to discover how she herself felt.

He thought about kissing her that first time, her mouth filled with warm, seeded fruit. Then spending the rest of the day half in work, half in play, chasing around the trees and wrestling each other to the ground. He thought of the wild feeling when their bodies were suddenly pressed together, a feeling that seemed bigger than the work of the orchard. He wanted to keep that feeling, explore it, walk all around it, and step right into the middle of it.

He took Betsy's hand.

"Yes," he said. "I'm happy."

Her face changed with his, softened, brightened with a smile.

"Look," she said.

The shallow depression they rode through was in shadow, cut off from the sun now by the tall crest of the Coast Range. But behind them, down the straight row of trees, they could see the top of Lone Hill. The hill floated brilliantly in the distance, an isolated, sunlit rise of land amid the darkness. The crowns of the trees were painted gold, full in leaf and heavy with fruit, and perhaps the sweet scent that surrounded them was from that part of the orchard, there where the prunes still caught the sun.

They drew further away with each slow, inevitable turn of the tractor's wheels.

4
. . . .

The Well-Kept Home   June 1920

At the end of the school year, Miss Anderson had stopped Betsy in the hall. "Have a wonderful summer," she said. "I'll look forward to seeing you in the fall."

"Thank you, Miss Anderson. I mean, I will too."

Her teacher smiled. "You know, Betsy, you're so good at algebra, you should be a math teacher yourself."

The principal, walking down the hall, had overheard Miss Anderson. He stopped and added, "Certainly. You should go to college and be a math teacher."

Betsy felt herself blushing. "But my father needs me."

"You don't have to go far. The teachers college in San Jose. Just a streetcar ride away. Tell him that," the principal said.

"Yes, do," Miss Anderson said.

But she hadn't told him anything yet.

Betsy walked up the back steps of her house after picking fruit. She always used the back steps. The front entrance was reserved for her father and his guests, and the less it was used, the less she had to polish the oak floorboards. Ernest Moreberg was a house builder, and he always said that a well-kept home was the best advertising he could have, better than any shingle he could hang out. When people saw the shining wood joiner work in the front hall, and were served coffee by Betsy in the front parlor, and could look out at the orange tree in the front yard through the lace curtains in the bay window, he didn't have to do much selling. They were already sold.

She saw by the dishes in the kitchen that her father had found the cold chicken pie she had left for him. He was neat in all things. The dishes were piled up in a tidy stack waiting to be washed. She found her father sitting in the Morris chair in the parlor, smoking a short-stemmed pipe, with a magazine open on his lap.

"Hello, Papa," she said. "You comfortable? Anything you need?"

"You're home late," he said.

"It was such a beautiful day," she said. When he looked at her, she added, "We worked almost to twilight."

"Let's see your card."

She handed over the punch card, and he looked at it slowly, drawing on his pipe and exhaling.

"Twenty-two boxes. You'll be able to buy all the things you want for school next year, if you keep this up."

"Miss Anderson said I should buy something smart. To work in an office or a bank in San Jose next summer."

Ernest shifted his weight, and the Morris chair creaked at Betsy.

"She said it would be good to have some work experience. Some job where I worked with numbers."

Ernest asked, "Who is Miss Anderson?"

"My algebra teacher."

He clicked his teeth against the pipe stem.

"I told you about her. My favorite teacher."

"A job like that would take you too far from home," he said.

He held out the punch card, slightly bent now, and said, "I'm fine. You should go wash up."

She took the card and turned away. She hadn't told him what Miss Anderson had really said. That work experience would look good on her college application.

The sink in the bathroom was spotless, smooth white porcelain, bright by her own scrubbing hands. She washed with a large yellow bar of soap, washed off the sticky traces of fruit that clung to her hands. Then she washed and dried her face, and she looked at herself critically. There seemed so little to love. Her cheeks would always make her look chubby, no matter how much she weighed. Fat cheeks, she'd once told her friend Anna, were the curse of the Morebergs.

She stroked the skin of her face and remembered. Harold had kissed her there. And there. And there. She touched her lips with the tip of a finger.

Before she washed the dishes, she knocked on the door of her mother's room.

"Come in, Betsy," said a thin voice.

Her mother was sitting at her dresser, wearing a long white robe, and the air in the room was close and heavy and smelled of lilac water. She looked at Betsy with large black eyes in a narrow face. One loose rope of milky hair lay across her neck.

Betsy closed the door behind her and sat on the edge of the bed.

"Was it nice today? Tell me about it."

"We worked in a section called Lone Hill today."

"I know where that is. Tell me about the trees and the sunshine, and the people you worked with."

"There were lots of people there," Betsy began.

"Children?"

"Children. Whole families. Some of the boys and girls were playing tag around the trees until the foreman came and made them stop." Betsy tried to remember something from other harvest days. "Then one boy was groaning because he'd eaten too much fruit, and his mother took him away, saying he wasn't going to get any ice cream."

"Boys are so greedy. They always want more than is good

for them. But I always liked the taste of just-fallen fruit my-self."

"I had a sweet-and-sour," Betsy said.

"How was that?"

"It was . . ." Suddenly Betsy couldn't remember anything except Harold's warm breath, coming closer to her. She knew he was going to kiss her. Then his lips touched hers, and the taste and feel of him was mixed up with the taste and feel of the sweet and sour fruit on her tongue.

"It was sweet and sour," she finally said. "And I picked twenty-two boxes!"

Her mother coughed into a handkerchief. "Your father will be glad of that."

Betsy waited.

"He's a tightfisted Dane, tight as a tick, and he wants you to work to save the buying of clothes for you come September. That's the only reason he's letting you out of the house. Stingy. Among other things."

When the kitchen was clean and everything ready for the next day, Betsy went to her own bedroom and put on a blue nightgown that went down to her ankles. She folded up the white crocheted bedspread, turned back the smooth, clean sheets, and got into bed.

Her father was moving unquietly by the door. She drew the covers up to her neck and settled in with a rustle.

He came in beside the bed and brushed her hair back with his large, square hand. Then he bent down and kissed her forehead.

"Good night, daughter," he said.

His breath was heavy as he left the room.

Betsy turned on her side and looked out a window. The shadow of a tree branch fell diagonally across the panes of glass. There were so many things she hadn't said yet, couldn't tell her mother or father right now. But she was certain that wonderful possibilities were going to open up for her. She had seen them, in the orchard.

She rolled over and thought about Harold.

5

. . . .

Mrs. Madison   July 1920

When her husband left, Mrs. Madison took the only respectable work that was available for an uneducated woman—
cooking and cleaning for a woman better off than herself.
She found a place with the Roberts family on the Ida Valley
Ranch, and they let her and her son live in the small house
that the first Roberts had built when he settled in the Santa
Clara Valley during the wheat-farming days. Mrs. Madison
was as satisfied as she could be, and nobody in San Natoma
thought she had a right to anything more, not when she
hadn't been able to hold on to her man.

She still felt her hands clench when she thought of her
son being stolen from her for three days. She was sure
Madison had done it just to spite her. She didn't think that
he cared at all for Harold. She just imagined her husband's
railroading voice, talking in engine cabs, and boardinghouses,

and saloons: That woman did *this* to me, and that woman did *that* to me. What can I do to *her?* And then realizing that the worst thing he could do would be to take her son away.

During the days Harold was gone from her, she went to the constable and even to the police in San Jose. She was polite and patient and she wanted to scream. She explained to them that she knew who the kidnapper was, she was sure of it. The heavy-lidded men smoked and looked interested until she told them that the criminal was the boy's father. Then they settled back in their chairs, looked amused, and said they expected it would all work out in the long run. When she insisted, they said they might check with Southern Pacific to see if her husband still worked for them and where he might be living now. But they weren't sure if it was time to bring in the law. She left wanting to spit on the big shoes they propped on their desks in front of her face.

When Harold came back on the train, he'd given her a trashy basket with oranges and cheap marmalade in it and told her it was a gift from his father. She threw the basket down on the platform and trampled it under both feet. People stared, and her son backed away at the crack of glass. Then she flung the crushed basket under the steel wheels of a northbound train that was just pulling out.

Mrs. Madison wasn't sorry she'd been so angry in front of Harold. Maybe it crushed whatever good feelings he had for his father. If Madison himself had shown up, and especially if he tried to apologize, she would have done the same. Sometimes she thought about her husband arriving unexpectedly and apologizing for everything, and about her proudly refusing to accept a thing from him, while Harold watched and admired her. But she never had the chance.

. . . .

Mrs. Madison was kneeling in her herb garden when her son walked in from the orchards, slapping clouds of powdered earth off his overalls with both hands. She finished clipping some sprigs of rosemary, admired their tiny blue flowers. Her hands felt thick and dusky with the herb's aroma. Then she sat back on her heels and squinted up at Harold, tall beside the falling sun.

"When's dinner?" he asked.

"Soon as you change your clothes," she said.

Harold shook his head. "I'm working the dry yard tonight. Double days."

"Just wash your face and hands, then." She held out her hand, and her son helped her to her feet. "Lamb stew tonight, with white beans."

"Kitchen of the big house?" Harold asked.

"Uh-huh." Mrs. Madison looked down at the walkway of brick that curved between the mint and the mother-of-thyme, and at the squares of beaten earth where she could kneel to gather and tend. She liked the herb garden. She thought of it as her own, just like her son.

"It would be nice if you'd build me a little bench seat out here," she said. "I'd like to have a place to sit."

"Like the Lion Bench in the Robertses' rose garden?" Harold asked.

"Nothing so fine," she said. "I get tired of spending the whole day on my feet or on my knees, that's all."

"Maybe after the fruit is shipped," he said. They walked toward the back door of the big house.

"Just someday," she said.

. . . .

The kitchen swelled with the clouds of steam coming from black dutch ovens of stew, and Mrs. Madison ran from the dining room, where the Roberts family was eating, back to the kitchen, where her son ate at a square table. She tried to get him to take thirds, because he was working tonight, but he pushed his plate away and took out his sack of Bugle Boy and some papers.

"Mrs. Madison." One of the Robertses was calling from the dining room.

"Coming," she replied. "Harold, please don't smoke up here."

"I'm not smoking," he said. "I'm rolling a cigarette. I'll smoke outside."

"You shouldn't smoke anywhere. It's idle, and a waste of money."

Harold pushed his chair back from the kitchen table and grabbed his cap from the peg. "Mr. Roberts smokes cigars."

Mrs. Madison wanted to say that his father had smoked too and look what happened to him. But she didn't know what happened to him. She only knew what had happened to her—abandoned and working in someone else's kitchen.

"Mrs. Madison," the voice called. "Could you serve the coffee, please?"

Her son was standing in the doorway, halfway in and halfway out, waving at her with his cigarette in his hands.

"Harold," she said, "stay. I don't mind what you do."

He took two steps back into the kitchen and kissed her quickly on the cheek. "I'll be back late."

"Harold," she said.

The door slammed.

"Don't slam the door."

And he was gone.

She leaned back against the hot stove and bit down on a corner of her apron, thought about making a pie that night.

"Mrs. Madison!" they called from the dining room.

. . . .

Harold stopped halfway to the dry yard, just beyond the eyes of the big house, and took a few large wooden kitchen matches from his shirt pocket. He stuck one foot on a log and drew a match sharply up the taut denim along his thigh. It didn't light, and he wore off most of the phosphorous before he threw it away in disgust.

The second match hissed into flame against his leg on the first try, and he looked at it happily. This was something he had seen the older hands on the ranch do. He held the match up to the smoke he had rolled and puffed until the end glowed red and it was well lit, then he exhaled through his nose.

He hadn't been smoking openly for very long. At school, he and some of the boys his age used to walk around with their Bugle Boy in their shirt pockets, and they let the little red drawstring dangle in the open, as a sign of their secret. They smoked in the boys' room, or under the stands near the stadium. But now that he was through with school, ready to work with the full-time men, he didn't see any reason to keep his smoking a secret.

He took a deep drag and looked at the sun. Still half an hour of light left, and the work in the dry yard wouldn't start until after dark. Shorty always said that during the day too much dust would be kicked up and settle on the fruit. All the packing and handling of Ida Valley prunes was done at night after the dew fell, to keep the dust to a minimum.

He held the butt end of the cigarette to the front of his pants, as though he had a stiff one with a smoldering tip, and he laughed out loud.

"I'm hot," he bragged. "I'm hot."

Betsy was coming to see him, late that night, in the lye shed. He'd told her on her last day of picking that she would have to sneak out if they were going to see each other. When she said yes, he thought he knew what that meant, thought she did as well.

He felt himself growing large inside his pants, and he pressed a hand down on the denim. He thought that he was huge, enormous, big enough to go right through anything, big enough for the world.

6

. . . .

The Lye Shed   July 1920

The lye pot fumed in the dimly lit shed. The great cast-iron
pot, round as a pumpkin and heated from below by a blue
gas flame, sent wisps of acrid vapor into the night air. The
vapor caught in the light for a moment, gossamer white
above the churning black surface, then disappeared into
the sky.

One of the group of shadow-faced men gave the pot a stir
with a huge wooden paddle. The lye solution swirled, and a
white foam appeared at the center. Then it resumed its
smooth but unquiet aspect.

The man with the paddle nodded, and a large metal basket of freshly picked fruit was swung over the pot on a
counterweighted arm. The basket was lowered slowly into
the pot, and a low hissing sound was heard, while the acid
attacked the thin-skinned fruit. Then the basket was raised

again, swung over one of the three-by-eight drying trays, and dumped out.

Two men with gloves worked quickly, spreading the fruit out on the tray, leaving enough space for each prune to be baked thoroughly by the next morning's sun. Then they heaved another flat on top of the first one, ready for the next dripping metal basket from the lye pot.

. . . .

Shorty put down the paddle and smiled. These were all good men. Now that the lye pot was going, they would continue to work at a good pace, dipping and spreading the fruit on the trays until they had stacked them ten high in the dry yard cars. He kept the older men here, because this was not the heavy work. Men like old Tom, who had thick streaks of gray in his wiry beard. Tom had come down from the hills after the last of the redwoods had been cut down and the last seven-horse team had hauled lumber under ringing bells through the main street of San Natoma. He'd asked Shorty for a place at Ida Valley, and Shorty said, "You know, we're making trees grow here, not cutting them down."

"If it's a man's work, I can do it," Tom said.

Shorty didn't have to ask whether Tom had any family, or would be satisfied living in the common house with twenty-four other men. Tom was the kind who named himself after the place he worked. He had been a Bank Mills man; now he'd be an Ida Valley man. Shorty took him on, and today, some eight years later, he was working with the older men, steady as a rock.

Shorty kept the young bucks, proud of their strength, on the yard itself. When the dry yard car was stacked full, two of the younger men walked it out into the field. The car had a small railroad truck and ran on metal rails, and two men were enough to control it. They pushed it forward from either side of the stack, while the wheels clacked around the curves.

The dry yard was an open space of fifteen acres, crisscrossed by electric lines sagging between fourteen-foot-high poles. At the lowest point of each arc of line, a single light bulb hung nakedly and lit a circle of ground around it. Prunes had to stay out in the sun some four days before they were ready to be packed. The lye cracked the skin to allow the juice to bake off, and the sun did the rest.

Shorty followed this stack of trays out into the yard, and he smiled again when he saw Harold, the youngest in the field. Harold was trying to prove himself by being the first to reach for the top tray of fruit. Shorty remembered Harold as an eight-year-old, scraping drying trays, leaving holidays. Shorty had pointed out the places where dried fruit still stuck to the tray. "There's a holiday. There's another. And another. Christ, it looks like Chinese New Year here." The boy had started to puddle up, and Shorty said, "It's not something to cry over. It's something to improve." And he'd patted him on the back.

He would never say this to Harold now, but Shorty was pleased to have him as one of his men, and to know that he would have him for years to come. Some men had been known to borrow money, get their own eight to ten acres to farm, climb the agricultural ladder. He didn't think this was beyond Harold. But it was bad to tell a young man that you thought too much of him. It would only give him a big head.

Shorty had known Harold's father. Madison had come down from the mountains like Tom. He'd run the steam donkey that hauled logs up the skid road to the mill, and he left when he saw the lumber beginning to thin. He knew better than Tom that the string was going to run out. At Ida Valley, he worked for a year side by side with Shorty and was known as a smart but complaining sort of man.

"No way for an honest man to get rich anymore," he said. "Used to be there was always free land just over the hill."

"Who says you got to be rich?" Shorty asked.

"Who says I don't?"

Madison used to go down to Gold Mountain laundry on payday and play tickets for the lottery the Chinese ran over in San Jose. He never managed to get all eleven right, never managed to hit the jackpot. And if he did "beat the China-man" for a few dollars, hitting five or six characters, the money never stayed in his pocket for long. It would go to one of the saloons in San Jose, not far from where he collected his winnings. His wife never saw any of that money, that was sure.

Then Madison took his knowledge of steam and hooked on with the railroad. A couple of years later he disappeared for good.

Shorty looked around at the acres of trays with fruit drying, and he breathed in the warm, sweet smell that filled the still evening air. Madison had never realized that the real riches were right here, in staying on the land and working through the lean years, always looking forward to the harvest.

He hadn't meant to be too hard on Harold that afternoon last week. But Harold had to learn that a man couldn't be playing grab ass when there was work to be done. It was as simple as that. Shorty didn't care if it was this girl, or some painted lady in San Jose. The work came first. He wanted Harold to be like he himself had been when he was young, and the talk seemed to have done the trick. Hadn't Harold made his forty boxes, fifty pounds a box, every day since?

At the end of this harvest Shorty planned to take Harold away from his mother, who did nothing but spoil him, and have him move in with the rest of the full-time men. Then he might finish growing up.

. . . .

Jax took a box of Abba Zabbas out of his shirt pocket and emptied some of the candies into his mouth. He nudged Harold. "Look who's coming."

Harold saw Shorty walking beside the new car of trays coming down the tracks.

"Dollars to donuts, Short Stuff will have something to say," Jax said.

The two men stood on either side of the top tray, lifted it off the stack, and edged sideways until they were clear of the tracks. The trays were heavy now, spread with fruit still full of juice, and awkward to handle. In a few days, after the fruit had dried, the trays would seem light.

"Let's keep it level, there," Shorty hollered. "We don't want any frogs on the yard."

"What did I tell you?" Jax said. "I knew he couldn't come down here without yapping."

Harold looked up to Jax because he had been in the war and had seen combat in France. Harold's closest contact with the war had been Jax's letters from the front, printed every week in the *San Natoma Star*.

> And then 4:35! Zero! The time to begin. Oh, boy, you should have seen the way that platoon went over the top—as pretty a line as ever you saw. I could hear the sergeant swearing like a demon at them—"Right dress there, you dirty lousy doughboys, right dress, or I'll drill your damned feet off when I get you back in camp!" And so we went on, with a rolling barrage to clear the path, like nothing could stop us.

Harold felt it was kind of an honor to be working with the town's war hero, even though he didn't understand Jax's attitude toward Shorty. Jax thought that bosses existed mainly to make his life miserable, and he sometimes threatened to pick Shorty up and see how far he could throw him. But nobody bothered him about his attitude. Even Shorty let him be, because he was a veteran.

They lugged the tray over to the edge of the dry yard and lowered it down, bending at the knees. Shorty always demanded they fill the flat from the furthest point on in, to avoid kicking dust onto the fruit. Then they pushed the end up flush against the previous row and walked back for another tray.

Harold had worked especially hard since Shorty chewed him out, and even though the foreman had given him no praise, at least he hadn't criticized him anymore. That seemed to be the most you could expect from Shorty. If you did a job well, you were only doing what you should be doing.

He thought he was working himself back up in Shorty's eyes. But if the foreman had known that Harold was seeing Betsy, he'd probably have said that if Harold had enough energy for such horseplay, it meant that he wasn't putting enough horsepower into the ranch.

Harold and Jax went to the new car, next to where Shorty

stood, and lifted off the top tray. Then Harold began walking toward the flat at a faster pace than usual. Nobody was going to be able to say he wasn't putting enough into the ranch.

"Whoa, there," Jax said. "Where's the fire?"

· · · · · · ·

Shorty looked over the flat at night. Like a patchwork quilt of fresh, drying fruit, pieced together out of three-foot-by-eight-foot slabs, extending out to the distant tree line. Under the spaced circles of light, the newly placed fruit looked dark and wet and shiny. The fruit of two days ago was already puckered, no longer reflected the light. Day after tomorrow, they'd bring it in to the packing house.

"Let's try and turn right in," he told the men, "so you'll be worth something tomorrow."

It was near midnight, but the air was still soft and warm. Harold found himself alongside Jax, who asked him if he wanted to have a drink over at the common house.

"No," Harold said. "I'd better head home. On account of my mother."

"On account of your mother, huh?" Jax smiled strangely. Harold thought for a moment that Jax somehow knew that Betsy was going to try to see him tonight.

Jax paused and looked right overhead. "See that star, twinkling all alone up there?"

Harold followed Jax's gaze up and saw a bright star almost directly above them.

"That's Vega," Jax said. "Brightest star in the Northern Hemisphere."

"It's pretty," Harold said.

"A French whore showed that to me, from a rooftop in gay Paree."

Harold looked at him, not sure if his leg was being pulled.

Jax smiled again. "Go on home. Your mother will be worried."

· · · · · · ·

Halfway home, Harold doubled back to the dry yard. The electric lighting above the flat had been cut off, but he was able to guide himself by the light of a waning half-moon—that, and the smell of the fruit itself. Acres of ripe fruit, lying out with its skin cracked, on a warm still night. Harold could have closed his eyes and followed his nose back to the flat.

Cautiously, he followed the tracks into the lye shed, where earlier that evening the great pot had churned and fumed. The shed was completely dark. He reached out with one hand and felt the heavy cast iron, still warm from the night's work.

Harold stood still. "Betsy?" he said.

There was no answer.

He leaned back and felt a post bite into his back. He wished he had a cigarette. Suddenly, he realized he was getting hard. He reached down and hefted himself. Big enough, he guessed, though now he wasn't sure how big it was supposed to be.

"Betsy?" he said again.

He wondered whether Betsy's mother was awake and moving like a ghost through the house. Or maybe her father had decided to board up her window and nail shut all the doors to keep her inside. He wondered how long he had to stay before he could leave. The idea of suddenly leaving brought a shudder of relief to him. But he had to stay long enough that he could be sure he was leaving because she had failed to show, not because his bones felt as fragile as glass.

"Harold," a voice whispered.

Harold pushed himself off the rough post and felt a flower bloom in the pit of his stomach.

"Here. But be careful. I brought something for you."

The voice was coming from the other side of the lye pot. Harold felt his way around, keeping one hand on the rough cast iron. A low laugh retreated in front of him. He walked around in the dim light, following the laugh, gradually increasing his pace until, half running, he caught hold of Betsy's hand.

"Got you." Her hand in his made him feel reckless, and he squeezed it hard.

"What did you bring me?" he asked.

"Open your mouth," Betsy said.

He opened his mouth and closed his eyes.

"Wider."

Harold obeyed. He felt something flaky and sugar-coated on his tongue, and he bit down. Still warm, sweet fruit and sugar and juices, butter-flaked crust just barely crunchy on top.

"Pie," he said with his mouth full. "You baked a pie."

"My father thought I baked it for him," she laughed. "He was surprised I was making a pie, because I usually don't do any baking when I'm working the harvest. But I really made it for you. All the time he was eating, and saying he was glad I decided to bake, I knew I was going to bring you the best piece. He had the first piece, but I saved the best piece for you."

Harold gobbed the pie into his mouth, looking at Betsy. Her face and body were indistinct in the half-light. Harold suddenly felt proud, proud that she had come here because he was here, and had baked something for him. When he finished, he licked his hands and reached for her. She took one hand, but she wanted to walk outside, and he let himself be led out onto the flat.

Under the moonlight, they didn't look at each other. Betsy turned her head a little away from him, as though she didn't want to be looked at too closely, as though she were afraid she wasn't pretty. Harold watched his feet pacing slowly. He felt her hand in his, but she seemed far away. The crickets were singing inside of his head, confusing him, and he suddenly thought that if he looked at her, he would again see the back of her head in math class, telling him he was wrong.

"I wish I didn't have to sneak out," she finally said.

"Was it hard?"

Betsy shook her head. "I know when my father goes to sleep. He kisses me good night in bed every night, then he goes to sleep himself."

"He kisses you good night?"

"In bed. Every night."

"To make sure you're there," Harold said.

"I don't like it," she said. "And he says something under his breath every night when he goes out. I asked him what it was, and he said it was a prayer. But my mother said it was a curse to keep me sealed up in the house."

"He's an old creep," Harold said.

"You're not afraid of him, are you, Harold?"

"Not me."

They made a broad circle under the close branches of the prune trees and came again to the edge of the dry yard. The glistening trays of fruit were breathing out a heavy perfume, and they walked along the metal tracks through the center of the yard, dizzy with the sweet air. Harold felt her lean into him.

"We won't always have to sneak around," she said. "Will we, Harold?"

"Of course not." Harold felt himself getting hard again. He bulged against his fly, plain as an elephant. He didn't know what she would think if she looked down, so he pointed to the sky.

"See there? That bright star all alone? That's Vega, the brightest star in the Northern Hemisphere."

She leaned her head back to look at the pretty star, and left her neck long and lovely and exposed. Harold bent into her neck and kissed her there.

"Let's go into the lye shed," he said.

"What we're doing is all right, isn't it, Harold?"

He remembered how, when he had been a little withdrawn, she had needed him more. "Don't you think it is?"

"Well, if we love each other, it's all right. Right?"

"Then it's all right. Come on."

Betsy went before Harold up the ladder from the dimness of the shed floor to the perfect darkness of the loft. When he saw her skirt disappearing before him, he wanted to embrace it and hold on to it forever, and he also wanted to run away. But the boards creaked and the horse blankets in the loft flopped, and he followed her into the loft.

There were too many arms and legs, too many hands and lips. Harold thought he was fumbling with the front of Betsy's blouse, when suddenly he felt her hands guiding his hand onto her breast. It was so soft and tender, so firm and stiff that he couldn't remember anymore why he was there or what anyone had ever told him about what to do. Everything tasted like salt in the darkness, everything tasted like salt mixed with the acrid smell of lye and the sugared smell of drying fruit. When she touched him, she told him she loved him, and he said he loved her too, but just then he was wondering where to put his knees, where to put his hands, how to ask her about things he didn't know, was this how it was supposed to be, did this feel right, should I do this now? He was tumbling around with her, feet were somehow where heads should be. Then, finally, he felt gigantic, and he couldn't remember what Betsy's face looked like.

. . . .

Harold walked quietly up the back steps into the kitchen of the small house. He didn't want his mother to wake up and see what time he'd come back. It could lead to questions he wasn't yet ready to answer, or lies he would rather not tell.

When he turned on the small wall light in the kitchen, he saw the pie. It was waiting for him, a twinkling disk, a sparkling, cinnamon-dusted wheel on the scarred kitchen table.

Harold recognized the pie as being exactly the work of his mother's hands. The way the upper crust rose and fell, crisp and browned in places but never burnt. The three precise cuts she had made to let the steam rise, always in the same place, always with a very sharp knife. The two crusts joined together with a serrated border, blunt indentations just the size and shape of thumbs, his mother's thumbs, working patiently around the pie pan.

The pie was whole, entire, untouched. The first piece was for him, and the best piece was for him. All for him, as long as he was hers. He wished suddenly he had someplace else to sleep that night.

A small note was folded under one edge of the pie. Harold picked it up and held it to the light.

Dear son:
I know you worked hard tonight, so I thought you deserved a little reward. Have as much as you want.

Mom

He crumpled up the note, took a long knife from the knife block, and cut a large wedge of pie. Then with a spatula, he slipped the wedge onto a plate. His mother's piecrusts never stuck to the pan.

Harold studied the large piece of pie, the cherries dense and dark.

He went to the kitchen garbage can, peeled back a layer of garbage with his hands, and slipped the wedge of pie in. Then he covered it up again carefully.

The next morning, he would be sure to take out the garbage before he went to work. That would please his mother.

7

The Butterfly Skirt   September 1920

Betsy walked down South First in San Jose and looked in all
the store windows. Every ten steps, she saw somebody she
knew. She said hello to Miss Twilling outside of Blum's, and
waved across the street to Jack and Mike, two boys in her
grade, and ran across Pam Allison smiling at black shoes
with bows and a red sale tag, shining just on the other side
of the plate glass. Downtown to the Valley, the merchants
said. People from all the little towns in the Santa Clara Valley were here, spending a little more freely just after the
harvest.

Betsy had always enjoyed September shopping with her
fruit money. But this year was different. She wasn't sure what
to buy to prepare to be a full-grown woman, which she supposed herself to be, now that she was in love. In love with
Harold.

It was still a funny kind of love because it was hidden, and it wasn't always wonderful. Harold was nice before and ready to run off afterward, even on that first night, when she was so hurt-feeling inside and knew from talks with the girls that she would have to use a cold vinegar douche when she got home. She was confused when he was anxious to leave so soon, and she found that the only way to hold him was to promise to meet him again. She always had to want him. Then he stayed in love with her.

Betsy felt her face flush suddenly, and she turned into the cool of Prussia's Clothing. The entranceway was high and white, and a brass chandelier with electric lights hung down over the central aisle. She heard the hushed rustle of wool and silk on all sides, the whisper of money and recognition, telling her that shopping here meant something mysterious and important. She felt heavy as she walked further into the store. All the women shopping here were older than her, but they stepped lightly with the sense that they were in their place.

She came upon a pair of mannequins coolly wearing the butterfly skirts she had been wishing for. The two smooth, suave faces looked past her, and the store whispered around her. Something about being a woman resided here, it whispered, in the hush of wool and silk and money.

She stepped forward, suddenly bold, and took the hem of one skirt between her fingers. A saleslady in gray serge came up like a sentry and smiled with her teeth.

"Would you like to try something today?"

The price tag flipped over shamelessly between Betsy's fingers, and she knew if she bought the skirt here, she wouldn't be able to afford anything else.

"I'm still deciding," she said, dropping the skirt.

"They carry skirts like these at Hart's. And at Blum's too. Maybe more in your size."

The saleslady smiled in a way that made Betsy back up a step. She turned to retreat when she saw Miss Anderson herself sitting over in the shoe department. The math teacher beckoned to her, and Betsy went to her side as though pulled by a string.

Miss Anderson handed a pair of smart black pumps back

to another saleslady. "These aren't quite right. Do you think you could show me those in the same size. Those." She pointed.

"Of course." The lady took the shoes and whisked away. Miss Anderson turned to Betsy.

"Has your summer been fun?"

"Oh, yes, Miss Anderson."

"Well, I'm glad I'll have you in my class again next week. You'll like geometry. You have the perfect kind of mind for it."

Betsy didn't know exactly what it meant to have the perfect kind of mind for geometry, but it sounded wonderful.

The saleslady came back with several pairs of shoes, and Betsy stayed while the math teacher tried them on. She asked Betsy's opinion as she walked up and down in front of a mirror. Betsy tried to judge, but everything Miss Anderson wore looked beautiful. Her teacher finally asked the saleslady to wrap up one pair for her and decided to go on to another department.

"See you next week," she said.

Betsy walked out onto bright, shadowless South First Street. The mannequins behind the windows at Prussia's seemed distant, reserved, and she walked further up the street to look at the displays at Blum's. She couldn't afford the kind of shoes Miss Anderson had bought, but if she shopped around and sacrificed something else, she was sure she could buy a butterfly skirt. And someday, when she had married Harold, when she was a math teacher herself and he stood on his own orchard land, when she was a full-grown woman publicly and proudly, she would be able to enter Prussia's with a light step and point with her finger and say, *Those.*

All her possible purchases were still jumbled in her head when she turned into Woolworth's to buy her pads of paper and pencils and erasers. She could postpone making any final decisions as long as she was in the five-and-dime.

The store was filled with neat aisles, each holding long metal bins, or pegboards, or stacks of boxes, brimming with all the little items necessary for daily living. The paper section was just past sewing notions on the right. When Betsy turned the aisle, she saw Anna Gundersen and her mother inspecting a blue folder. Shopping bags from other stores sat at their feet.

For a moment Betsy felt jealous of them. They looked so comfortable together, so content to be shopping together. She was sure they had discussed the different combinations of skirts and blouses, colors and styles, and thought about how to take advantage of the bargains they had found. Betsy's mother never went shopping with her anymore.

"Betsy!" Anna said when she saw her. "Come here, I've got something to tell you."

Mrs. Gundersen smiled fondly at the two girls. "Why don't you go over to O'Brien's for a soda? Take the bags. I'll meet you there in a little while."

"Okay?" Anna asked Betsy.

They crossed the street from Woolworth's to the soda fountain and ordered a root beer float and a cream soda. Anna wouldn't tell her the news until they had properly sat down, which made Betsy think it was important.

"What's the news?" she asked when they were finally at a table.

"Miss Anderson is going to get married," Anna exclaimed.

"Really?" Betsy's voice rose. "Who?"

"To a man she knew in high school, who works in a bank in San Jose now. They didn't see each other for years while she was away at college, but when they met again, it was love at first sight."

"That's so perfect," Betsy said. "Did you hear if they had a date set?"

"I don't know, but if I were her, I would get married in June, after school is out. You can have such wonderful flowers at a June wedding."

"She's so lucky," Betsy said. "I saw her today in Prussia's."

"You were in Prussia's?"

"Just to look," Betsy said.

"You know who I saw today?" Anna asked. "Jack Widmark."

"Did he go away for the summer?"

"To his grandma's in Wisconsin. He's much taller than he used to be."

"He was always kind of awkward," Betsy said.

"He's pretty cute now."

"Really?"

Betsy sipped at her root beer, suddenly confused. Boys she would see again in school jostled in her mind with Harold and the man who would marry Miss Anderson. She knew that Harold was going to begin working full time, and she thought that was a good thing. It made him less of a boy, and so her less of a girl. But he still seemed far from the equal of the man in the San Jose bank.

"Wouldn't you like to have a piano in your home someday?" Anna was asking.

Betsy nodded. She felt her face flushing again.

"So what clothes are you going to buy for school?" Anna asked.

"It's hard to decide."

"Do you want to see what I got?" Anna was already opening up her packages.

"Sure," Betsy said quickly to cover up her confusion. Anna looked at her funny.

. . . .

Betsy turned around once in the front parlor, and the butterfly skirt swirled up gracefully.

"See?"

"Very lovely."

She turned around again, and the pleats of the plaid skirt spread apart and lifted the hem into the air, then settled back down sharply into place.

Lillian Moreberg smiled.

"Very lovely, indeed," she said.

Betsy loved to model clothes for her mother. She drew her out into the front room, where it was lighter than in the shaded bedroom, and bounced in and out wearing her new purchases. If her mother no longer went shopping with her, at least she would comment on what she'd bought.

Betsy wore a red blouse smooth as water tucked into the top

of her skirt. She drew her finger along a line of red in the plaid that matched the blouse.

"Do you think it makes me look mature?" she asked.

"You're becoming a woman," her mother said.

Betsy smiled. That was just what she'd hoped to hear.

"Miss Anderson has one like this."

"Does she?"

"In a different pattern of plaid. But she never spins around so fast."

Betsy spun around again for her mother, and the skirt flowed outward. When she saw her mother smile, she kept spinning, faster and faster, until the skirt swirled in a horizontal disk, and her legs were completely exposed.

The front door slammed.

Betsy stopped turning, and the dress fell back down over her.

Ernest Moreberg's square figure appeared in the entrance to the hall.

"I built this room," he said, "so that you could sit in it. Or knit in it. Or serve coffee in it. I didn't build it so that women could dance, in full view of God and the neighbors."

Lillian stood up. "And if women would dance, where would you have them do it?"

"Not in this house I built."

"Do you think you can lock her away in a dark closet her whole life?"

Ernest glared at her. "I'll keep her safe. Safe at home if I need to."

Betsy stood to one side, watched her parents face each other. Then her mother bent over and coughed.

"I'm feeling poorly," she said. "Don't bother to bring me anything for supper."

She walked back to her room, leaving Betsy alone with her father.

"I'm sorry," Betsy said. She felt that the argument was her fault.

Her father looked her up and down, and raised his blunt hand.

Betsy bowed her head in front of him. This was what she'd been taught to do. Accept the punishment if she had been bad.

Then he lowered his hand, sharpened it into a sign pointing at the skirt.

"Take that thing back," he said. "Get the money."

. . . . . .

Alone, Betsy picked up her bags and parcels and took them back to her bedroom. There she unpacked everything and spread it all out on her bed, to see everything she had bought once before it was all packed away in drawers and closet.

She spent some time matching clothes and colors. Then, making certain the door was closed and the curtains drawn, she took off the butterfly skirt and laid it down on the bed as well. It was the piece of clothing that made her look most like a full-grown woman, most like a math teacher, most like all the people she wanted to become.

She ran her hands up and down her bare legs. She shivered. Was it this? Was it because her father couldn't believe he possessed anything unless it was guarded under lock and key in a house he had built? He didn't want the neighbors to see his daughter, and he hadn't wanted anyone to see his wife. Was this why her mother had grown thinner, lost her birdlike beauty, withdrawn into a darkened room? Because he only knew one way to treat all things—the same way a miser treats gold. And at the end of years of being always pushed back into the house, her mother had given up and remained there, to spite her father with his own desire?

Carefully, Betsy put the butterfly skirt back in the bag from which it had come. She put the red blouse in the bag too. She didn't want to be the cause of more trouble.

She thought she had already broken free from her father, although he might not know it. Harold would soon be a full-time man and able to stand up for her. But the steps between where she stood and where Miss Anderson resided were long and dark. In her mind she could see the teacher, standing high above her, with a perfect faceless man by her side.

8

. . . .

Full-Time Man   October 1920

Shorty decided to give it one more try.

"You have to realize," he said, "that it will be good for Harold. To live with the men he'll be working with. It's the only way he'll really learn how this ranch runs."

Mrs. Madison's eyes were shining with tears.

"Listen," Shorty said, "it's not like I'm going to take him away by force. Mr. Roberts himself said it was a good idea. But let Harold say what he thinks."

He turned toward Harold, who sat as though paralyzed between the two, not speaking and not looking one way or the other.

"Harold," he said, "what do you think?"

"Don't answer him, Harold," Mrs. Madison said.

"Why not?" Shorty asked. "Let him have his say."

"He doesn't have to. I know what he wants. I can see it in his eyes."

"Then why can't he just say it?"

"Because I don't want him to," Mrs. Madison said. "I'll let him go off and live with the men, if that's what he has to do. I want him to. I want him to work hard and earn his place here at Ida Valley. But I don't want to hear him say that he wants to go away from me."

"Harold," Shorty asked directly, "what do you say?"

"Harold," his mother cut in, "you love your mother, don't you?"

"Sure I do," Harold answered his mother.

"Your father always said he worked on trains because he loved me. He was gone all the time to earn money for me because he loved me. Then, one day, he was gone and never came back."

Mrs. Madison stood up from the table. "You two go ahead and eat. Go on and eat, your food is getting cold. Eat together and talk. You'll have lots to talk about that I won't be interested in. Important business. I'll come back later when it's time to clean up."

She put her own plate on the sideboard and walked slowly out the door.

The two men sat in silence for a time. Shorty said, "Sometimes I'm glad I never married."

He carved off a piece of meat and began to chew it vigorously, and he added a forkful of beans to his mouth before he'd finished the meat. Then he noticed that Harold wasn't eating.

"Harold," he said, "you sorry you're moving over with us?"

"No," Harold said. "I want to."

"Good." He pointed toward the food on Harold's plate with his knife, and they both began to eat.

. . . .

On the first Monday of October, Harold left his mother's small house and walked to the long, one-story lodge between the packing house and the barn where the full-time men lived. Shorty handed out jobs for the day at breakfast, so Harold came over early. He found the men clumped around the gas stove spooning up burgoo and pouring coffee from a blackened pot. They all knew him, and they made room for him at the stove. But Harold noticed that everyone was a little bit more distant, a little less warm than when he'd been just a kid helping out.

Shorty came in halfway through breakfast, helped himself to coffee from the stove, and stood at the head of the table. The men continued to eat while he talked, steadily piling food into their mouths.

"First off," Shorty said, "Harold's moving in with us. I figured I'd let him bunk with Jax."

Harold looked at Jax a little too eagerly. The older man regarded him noncommittally, and Harold looked down. Shorty continued on about the start of pruning, cleaning out snags, and cutting broken branches. On the way out of the lodge, Jax fell in beside Harold.

"You got the upper bunk and the lower two drawers," he said.

After a day's work in the orchards, Harold moved his clothes from his mother's house. His mother wanted him to stay for supper, but he thought it would look bad if he spent too much time with her. The men ate at a long redwood table, with benches on both sides. Harold hung back and let everyone sit before him, so he wouldn't make the mistake of taking someone else's spot. But while he was eating, he reached too far for the salt and dragged his sleeve near old Tom's plate. The ex-lumberjack quickly seized Harold's wrist; his grip cut like an iron manacle.

"I remember a time when somebody reached across my plate," he announced to the men, standing up and holding Harold's wrist aloft. "It was in '04, when I always had an ax handy. All that pup brought back was a nub."

Harold watched the men laugh. Jax laughed at him too. Then Tom let go of his wrist, and Harold moved his hand to get the feeling back in it. He sat quietly during the rest of the meal and made sure that he asked for anything that wasn't in front of him.

After dinner Harold climbed into the upper bunk in the space he shared with Jax and lay down to test the mattress. It was thin, and he could feel the canvas sag under him. The ceiling was long-grained redwood, so close overhead he could smell it. He could hardly remember another night he'd spent away from his mother's little house, except for the few days when his father had carried him along to the south.

He suddenly wanted to talk to Jax about it, and he climbed down and went to the common room. But Jax wasn't there. Some of the older men were playing pinochle, but Harold knew he shouldn't ask them. He had to be self-sufficient. He rolled a cigarette and smoked by himself, then he turned in alone.

Jax was out until late nearly every night. Harold met Betsy some evenings, and once he ran into his bunkmate on the way back to the lodge. Jax was walking slowly on the road and singing carefully to the sky.

Douce France
Beau pays de mon enfance
Je te garde dans mon coeur.

He stopped singing when he saw Harold, and they walked together in silence toward the lodge. When they entered their cube, Jax reached down and took a bottle from under the foot of the mattress. He tipped it back after pulling the cork, then shoved it at Harold.

"Have a drink," he said.

Harold took a cautious swallow from the dark, smooth bottle. The liquid tasted of leather, and gave his mouth a funny, dry feel. He clicked his tongue against the roof of his mouth.

"Dago Red," Jax said. "I buy it from some Italians up in the hills. Like it?"

"I don't know."

"When you need it bad enough," Jax said, "you will."

He took back the bottle and sat on the edge of the bed.

"Out seeing your mother?" he asked.

"No," Harold said.

Jax smiled and took another drink. "Nothing's better than

love," he said. He jammed the cork back in the bottle with the heel of his hand and stowed it again at the foot of the bed. Then he lay down and rolled over, his back to Harold.

Harold sat still for a moment. He wasn't sure if he should take what Jax said seriously or not. Slowly and quietly he began to get undressed. He had thought that Jax might be impressed by it, impressed that Harold had a girl, and that she came out at night to see him; but now he had the feeling that Jax knew all about Betsy, knew where he'd been and what he'd done. And he had the feeling that Jax had been to a more exciting place than the lye shed. He had been to a place filled with strong flavors and sounds that Harold wanted without knowing what they were.

. . . .

On a Friday in mid-October, the men knocked off work early and gathered around the back door of the big house. The door opened wide, then shut again, and Shorty was standing at the top of the steps, an unlit cigar working in his mouth. He carried a sheaf of envelopes in his right hand, bound by a silken cord.

One by one he called out the names of the men, and they shuffled through the crowd, or snaked an arm forward for the pay envelope with their name on it. Some of the men could neither read nor write, but all had learned to recognize their name in the elegant script from Mr. Roberts's own hand.

"Harold," Shorty called.

Harold came forward, and the foreman looked him in the eye when he gave him the envelope.

"See that you keep earning it," he said.

Harold ran his hands over the envelope. The paper was a grainy, creamy-white color, and it felt stiff and textured. On one side was his name, in flowing black India ink—"Harold Madison." The flap was completely sealed, and for a moment he didn't want to rip it open; the envelope looked so beautiful and unsullied that he wanted to wait and use his mother's letter opener. But finally, with as much care as he could, he slipped a finger under the flap and tore one end of the envelope open.

The check dropped out, larger than his hand. Once again, his name in the same flowing hand, under the large printed name of San Natoma State Bank. And at the bottom of the check itself, the name of Mr. Roberts, his own signature. Harold was important enough for Mr. Roberts to sign his checks.

"First paycheck, eh?"

Harold found Jax standing next to him.

"After a while," Jax said, "the only thing you'll look at is the numbers, to make sure they didn't shortchange you. Don't ever trust a boss all the way."

Harold looked at Jax for a moment. Then he looked back down at the check. It was true that he hadn't looked at the sum. For fruit picking, he'd always been paid in cash. This was the first time he'd had a check made out to him.

After they were paid, all the men washed up, changed out of their work clothes, and talked about where they would go that evening. When Harold stepped outside with his check neatly fitted into the pocket of a crisp denim shirt, he saw that Jax was already strolling down the road toward town. Harold had promised to have dinner that night with his mother. He also had a date to see Betsy late in the evening, if she could sneak out. But he decided to follow Jax, just for a little while, to see where he was going.

He trailed along behind Jax, not so close as to be noticeable, and turned after him onto Lumber Street. Jax didn't stop at the bank; he didn't stop at the station, either. He wandered easily along the new cement sidewalk, said hello to those who greeted him, patted a pair of horses tied up outside the drugstore, then passed by the white Memorial Arch on the village plaza. Harold wondered how far he was planning on walking, when he disappeared into a drab storefront on the outskirts of town.

Harold walked close enough to see the faded sign above the door: GOLD MOUNTAIN LAUNDRY AND EMPLOYMENT AGENCY— CHINESE LABOUR PROVIDED. The door to the store was open, but the inside was so dark that he couldn't make out what was in there. He had never set foot in any of the few Chinese establishments in San Natoma. Ida Valley didn't use non-white workers, and he'd been given to understand that Chinese laundries were unhealthy and that men spit on the clothes while they ironed them.

As he peered in, Jax suddenly came to the edge of the shadow and beckoned to him. "Come on in. I saw you following me."

Harold hesitated for a moment. But he wanted to see where Jax spent his time, so he went in after him. The walls of the laundry were of old dark-stained wood, and a low counter crossed the width of the building. Behind the counter sat a Chinese man with lines of gray in his hair, dressed in a coat and tie, and wearing a short-brimmed hat. Six ironing boards winged down from one wall, and a younger Chinese man was putting a cold iron on a charcoal stove in the center of the room and picking up a hot one. From the back came the sound of wash water sloshing in large iron tubs.

Jax smiled at the two Chinese men and sat down on the counter.

"Pok Kop Pew," he said.

The two men exchanged glances. Jax looked at them angrily.

"He's all right. What do you think he is, the constable? His name is Harold Madison, he works at Ida Valley with me, and he's all right."

"Mad-sonn." The old man looked slowly at Harold, and pronounced his last name in a long, whistling exhalation. "I knew your father."

"What?" Harold asked.

The man behind the counter smiled a little. "I knew your father."

"What do you mean, you knew my father?"

The old man nodded. Jax stirred impatiently.

"Just give me the Pok Kop Pew," he said.

The Chinese man looked at him with resentment. Then he drew out a small piece of paper with a grid of Chinese characters on it. Some of the numbers had been blackened out with a single brushstroke.

Jax pulled a similar grid from his pocket, with a different set of characters brushed out. He compared the two grids for some time, moving his lips. Finally he looked up in satisfaction.

"Five right," he said. "You owe me two bucks."

The old man pursed his lips and perused the two sheets of paper with great care. After a time, he took a long-handled brush from behind the counter, dipped it into a pot of watery ink, and gracefully made a mark in the corner of Jax's sheet. He kept the sheet and handed over two single dollar bills to Jax.

"You play again?"

Jax shook his head. "I don't feel lucky right now."

"You?" He turned his gaze on Harold.

"No, I . . . I don't know how," Harold stammered.

"Go on, if you want," Jax said. "All you have to do is pick out nine or so figures. And it's only two bits."

The old man offered him a sheet of paper with eight rows of ten characters. Feeling foolish, Harold checked off things at random with a pencil until the old man made a sign. He took back the grid, then dexterously made two copies with his brush. He kept one and gave the other back to Harold.

"Your father. He play all the time." A short giggle.

Harold stuffed the ticket hastily into his billfold. "Can we leave, Jax?"

"Sure." They stepped from the dark store into the bright sunshine and blinked while their eyes adjusted. Then they headed back up Lumber Street.

"The main game is in San Jose," Jax said. "But Hop Kee will take your bets for you. And he's always played square with me."

"Do you think he really knew my father?"

"Could be." When they came to the station again, Jax stopped and looked at Harold.

"You want to go into San Jose? We can see my brother and get our checks cashed."

Harold looked at the clock above the drugstore. There might be enough time to ride into San Jose and get back in time for supper.

"Sure," he said.

A single red car ran between San Natoma and San Jose in the middle of the afternoon. Jax and Harold had no trouble finding a seat on the north side, away from the sun. They sat on a polished wooden bench, quiet and waiting, until the electric motor began to whine and the train slowly started forward.

Jax looked out the window at the power line describing shallow arcs between the wooden poles that lined the track. "My brother," he said over the rattling of the car, "is to be married."

"Yeah?" Harold said.

"He's the pride of the family, the light of our parents' eyes. He has a job at a bank, the Bank of Italy. One of the few non-Italians working there, in fact. And he's going to marry a schoolteacher, which makes everything just about perfect."

He kept quiet for a time, as Harold watched him look out the window. Then he spoke again. "I was the pride of the family once."

"During the war," Harold said.

"Yes. During that dirty war."

In San Jose, they found the Bank of Italy, San Jose Branch, on a busy corner downtown. A mahogany counter angled out into the tiled lobby, and a low fence of opaque beveled glass stood above the counter, broken by teller windows with brass bars. Jax bypassed the lines in front of the tellers and went to where a half door separated the lobby from the business area.

"Hey, Albert," Jax said.

A man in a suit turned toward the voice, and Harold stared. It was as though Jax had suddenly tricked himself out in different clothes and was now sitting behind a desk. Harold looked again at Jax beside him and at the man who looked just like Jax on the other side of the counter.

Jax grinned. "Twins," he said. "We're twins."

Albert came to the door and said, "Hello, Howie."

"Hi, Al. How'd you like to change this into money for me?" He showed him his check. "And while you're at it, how about doing the same for Harold here? He just started at Ida Valley."

"You're sure you don't want to put some of this away? You've still got an account on the books."

"Cash," Jax smiled.

Albert turned to Harold. "You want to open an account? Do it for you in no time."

"I guess I want cash too," Harold said.

Albert grimaced. "I don't know why you're giving this young man the wrong ideas," he said to his brother.

"There's nothing wrong with my ideas. They just aren't your ideas."

"Have it your own way," Albert said. He took both checks and gave them cash, after explaining to Harold that checks had to be signed on the back.

When they stepped outside, Harold asked, "Where you going now, Jax?"

"To have a drink. Want to come?"

"In a saloon?"

"Where else?" Jax was already striding toward the east side of town. Harold had to walk swiftly to keep up. He had never been much off South Main Street in San Jose, and after a short time, he felt he'd have trouble getting back to the station. Jax noticed him looking around, and he stopped at a corner.

"There's nothing says you have to come, you know. If you're worried about home, maybe you should leave now."

"I want to come," Harold said. "I've got my own money, too, that I earned myself."

"You would have gone over to France with us too, if you'd had the chance."

"Sure thing."

"Come on, then," Jax said. "I'm not one to tell you that the ranch is the whole world."

He turned down a narrow street with Harold following, and he spoke over his shoulder. "It might be better than the whole world, though."

They pushed open an unmarked door and entered a small vestibule scarcely the size of a phone booth, with another door, painted red. Jax pushed open this door into the sound of a woman laughing.

The air in the saloon was red and murky from cigar smoke and heavy fringed curtains, and a large woman draped in red laughed and spun around as though music were playing. Jax shouted at some poker players grunting in the corner to give him a seat when one opened up, and then he steered Harold to the bar. The bartender was dressed in a white shirt, a vest, and a black bow tie, and he had a knife scar running diagonally across his left cheek, so that the bottom half of his face seemed a bit askew.

"Either some pre-Prohibition bourbon, or something Canadian," Jax said. "The real stuff, now. This is Harold's first time here."

"First time, eh?" The bartender pulled a bottle from behind the bar and rubbed his scar with his thumb. "How old are you?"

Surprised, Harold said, "Sixteen."

"Sixteen, eh. Sorry. It's illegal to serve you alcohol." He poured a shot for Jax and left Harold's glass empty.

Harold looked around him at all the women and men drinking, and he turned back to the bartender. "What do you mean? This whole place is illegal."

Jax and the bartender both broke up in laughter. "Welcome to the Coosctown Saloon," the bartender said and poured the whiskey.

Jax lifted his glass. "Down the hatch," he said.

They both drank in one motion, and Harold grabbed for a glass of water.

Then a little kid with an evil grin came and tugged on Jax's sleeve. Harold turned to get a good look at the kid and saw that it was really a very small man with bandy legs and a face that looked fifty years old.

"Hey, Larry," Jax said. "You want to run out and grab me a box of Abba Zabbas?"

"Sure thing, Jax, sure thing." Little Larry took the dime Jax flipped him and scuttled away.

Another woman sat down two stools from Harold and looked carefully at him. Her body was as straight as a boy's, and she wore a green dress that looked like a sheet wrapped under her arms. When Harold looked back at her, she moved one stool closer to him.

Larry ran back into the saloon like a drunken sailor, waving the box of candy. "Here you go, Jax, here you go."

Jax ripped off the top of the box and emptied some of the licorice pieces into his mouth. He looked over at the poker table and counted six hats still hunched over the cards. So he winked at Harold, then leaned back against the bar and looked down genially at Larry.

"Larry, is it true you used to be in the circus?"

"That's right," Larry said. "The Greatest Show on Earth. That's me."

The thin woman moved down another stool so that she was next to Harold. "Don't listen to him." She stroked Harold's arm. "Buy me a drink instead."

"Don't you like Larry's stories, Bella?" Jax asked.

"I hate them," she said. "Hate them, hate them, hate them. Come on, baby? Buy me a drink?"

Harold didn't know what to do. Jax winked at him again, which didn't tell him a thing. Larry continued on in a melancholy voice, as though talking to himself. "The circus. What a wonderful time. Then they kicked me out."

"I know who you are," Bella said to Harold.

"Yeah? Who am I?"

"You're Sugar Jake."

"Sugar Jake? Where do you get that from?"

"From your Sugar Jake." Bella slipped her hand between Harold's legs and left it there. "Come on?"

Harold nodded to the bartender, who poured a drink for Bella. Jax was still talking with Larry. "So why did they kick you out? Harold doesn't know."

Larry looked down at his shoes. "They kicked me out because of my peedle," he said.

"You're a liar," Bella spit at him. "Everything you say is a lie."

"I have a ten-inch-long peedle," Larry said. "And all the girls wanted to do it with me. All the girls, they wouldn't do it with anybody but me."

"It's not true," Bella said. "It only looks big because you're small."

"So they kicked you out because of that?" Jax asked. "Were they jealous?"

"Yeah, jealous, that's what they were." Larry sighed deeply.

"They thought that if they got rid of me, the girls would want to do it with them again."

"I'd never do it with you," Bella said. "And you can't say I have, either."

"Did it work?" Jax asked. "Did they do it with them again?"

"I don't know. They kicked me out, and I came to California. Maybe some of them are still waiting for me. Maybe Julie is still waiting for me. She said she would never want to do it with anyone but me."

Bella was working her hand further up between Harold's legs. "Don't listen to him, Sugar Jake. He's as full of shit as Christmas turkey."

"Don't call me Sugar Jake," Harold said.

Jax tilted his box of candies over his mouth and began to chew. "What's wrong with being called that?" he asked. "Nothing's better than love."

"Jake was my father's name."

"Ohh." Jax waved the bartender over. "Hey, Giancarlo. When you had your other place, before the saddest day of all, did you ever know a guy named Jake Madison?"

The scar-faced bartender rubbed his chin. "Jake Madison?" Harold thought he saw some message pass through the looks exchanged by the bartender and Jax. "Sure," the bartender said slowly. "But it's been years since I seen him."

"Did you like him?" Jax asked.

"Sure. He was an okay guy." When the bartender spoke, the two halves of his face seemed to move out of joint. "He was a lot of laughs around the bar. We all liked him."

One of the rumpled hats stood up from the poker game and joined them at the bar, smoking the butt of a cigar. "Your father was very well liked around here," he said in a raw voice. "Very well liked."

Harold still felt Bella's hand clutching at him. He didn't know whether any of this was true. But he had never been around people who had known his father, and who liked him and spoke well of him.

"Does anybody know where Jake is today?" Harold asked.

Nobody at the Goosetown Saloon wanted to talk about the

whereabouts of an absent man. They shook their heads one by one as he looked around. Then Larry piped up, "You know, a lotta guys went to Signal Hill when they brought in oil down there. That's what I heard."

"You think he might be there?"

"I don't know," Larry said. "I wish I was. But they'd probably kick me out of there, too."

"Come on," Jax said. "We're going to drink a toast to Jake Madison. And Harold's going to pay for it."

The bartender was already filling glasses all around. Bella dug her hand into Harold's thigh. "I knew you. I knew who you were."

"Did you know my father?"

"Sugar Jake. I recognized you."

Jax raised his glass. "Here's to Jake Madison. To everybody's father, wherever the hell they are." They drained their glasses, then passed a schooner of beer from hand to hand for a chaser. As soon as Harold put his glass down on the bar, the bartender refilled it.

Jax went over to the poker table and left Harold alone with Bella and Larry. Harold bought Bella another drink. "Did you really know my father?" he asked.

"Sugar, you know I did."

"Hey." Little Larry tugged on the leg of Harold's pants. "You want something? You want something?"

"What did he look like?" Harold asked.

Bella looked at him wisely. "You don't know, do you?"

Harold shook his head. His mother didn't keep any photographs, and the face of the train man faded every year. He could remember the pin-striped overalls and knotted handkerchief, and the dead tooth in his father's smile remained sharp and clear. But he couldn't bring to his mind his father's face.

"Well, at a younger age," Bella said, "he probably looked a lot like you do now."

Harold nodded. It was what he'd expected to hear, but also what he wanted and needed to hear.

"You want something? You want something?"

Bella leaned close to Harold and whispered in his ear.

"Come with me, and I'll show you something your father saw."

Harold looked around. Jax had settled in with the slouched hats at the poker table, and the large woman in red was dancing alone. She was laughing.

"You want something?" Larry asked.

To feel what his father had felt. To know what his missing father had known. Harold took Bella by the arm and twisted her off the stool.

"Come on," he said.

"Sugar Jake," she said.

9

Knock on the Door   November 1920

Reverend Walters lifted his head from the book he was reading. He sighed, stood up from his soft leather chair, and went to the office door. It was his Saturday morning visiting hours, but he'd hoped nobody would need him today.

Sometimes, he didn't want to be bothered by the members of his congregation. Sometimes, he simply wanted to sit and read one of his older books of theology, one of the books from divinity school. When he read these old books, the earth seemed to stand still, and the stars and planets revolved around it in perfect harmony. Men and women loved one another, toiled for their bread and were thankful for it, raised their children to fear God and hope for salvation, grew older in peace and contentment, and were grieved by their survivors. Life was a perfectly straight path, leading to a perfectly known goal. Things were in balance. The world was good, and completely comprehensible.

He'd answered a call in California some ten years ago, leaving behind a cold, narrow congregation of Lutherans in Minnesota. He had been attracted by the rich agricultural region and the promise of a growing congregation. But he'd also sent away for brochures from the local improvement associations, which described the never-ending warmth and sunshine, and the beautiful forests and coastline, and the rich soil. One brochure, titled "Valley of Heart's Delight," carried a verse from Homer on the first page, a verse that he pondered.

> Each dropping pear a foll'wing pear supplies
> On apples, apples, figs on figs arise;
> The same mild season gives the bloom to blow,
> The buds to harden and the fruits to grow.

Surely, he'd thought, this was where man could be happy on Earth.

In the time since then, he'd found that men and women in the sunlit fields of the West still desired things they did not have, still were restless and discontent, still were troubled by unanswerable questions of how best to live, how to raise their children and care for their spouses, how to grieve for a loved one, how to face death themselves.

Then the war came and cropped off some of the best of the youth. Mrs. Shipley, whose boy was killed in France, came to him almost every week. He had long since run out of comfort for her, but they could sit together, and he would repeat words for her, and she would nod, and understand, and still not be able to accept it.

In public, he found he was expected to mix a message of civic optimism in with his preaching. The Valley was rich, and going to get richer. Fruit prices were good, and going to get better. Population would increase, towns would grow, homes would be built. We were all on the right path, and all we had to do was stick with it.

And somewhere, between the counseling of remorse and despair he did in private, and the facade of boosterism he put up in public, Reverend Walters discovered that he himself would never marry, never take a wife or bring children into the world. He would only be able to sit in his study and read his old books of theology, to find everything intelligible, round, and harmonious, to hear the fabled music of the spheres.

. . . .

He opened the door and saw Jennifer Anderson there, dressed in gray, wearing a proper hat. Not one of those new ones that swooped down over one eye. Jennifer was, by some accounts, to be married.

Reverend Walters smiled. This interview perhaps could be a pleasure, if it had to do with her marriage. It was only rumor thus far, and of course people had a way of talking, but this would not be upsetting for his reading, his thoughts, his quiet hour in the study.

"Jennifer," he said, "a bee has been buzzing your name in my ear."

The young teacher smiled briefly. "I wish I were here about myself, Reverend. But I'm not."

Then he looked past her and saw someone else, sitting very small in the corner chair.

The reverend couldn't keep the surprise from his voice.

"Betsy," he said.

. . . .

"Betsy!"

It was Saturday and his daughter was nowhere to be found. Ernest Moreberg searched through the rooms of the house and then went to the back porch.

"Betsy!" he called again.

There was no answer.

Normally on a Saturday morning, Betsy would be dusting the shelves, polishing the oak furniture, cleaning the glass windows with ammonia, and finally sweeping the floor. Sometimes she also baked something, if cleaning didn't take too long. But today, when Ernest was having friends over to play cards and wanted the house to be neat as a pin, Betsy had left without telling him.

Back in the house, he poked his head inside his wife's

room. She sat in front of the dresser, wearing a long white robe.

"Did Betsy say she was going somewhere?" he asked.

Lillian coughed into a handkerchief. She didn't answer, and Ernest inched the door shut behind him.

He roamed through the house once more, as though he thought Betsy was hiding from him. Then he went to the kitchen and began to cut the bread and cheese he wanted to have ready for his friends. The pumpernickel bread he liked was dark and dense and shaped like a brick, and he cut slices thin as laths with his sure carpenter's hands.

The back door rattled, and Finney, the newspaperman, called out, "Anybody home?"

"Come in," Ernest said.

Finney walked in and looked around keenly. "How come you're working in the kitchen, Ernest?"

Ernest shrugged. "Wife's sick. Daughter's out right now."

"Huh," Finney said. "That's women for you."

Ernest nodded. He separated off another fragrant slice of bread and wondered where his daughter had gone.

. . . .

When she tells the story, she knows that every step she has taken has led her in exactly the opposite direction she had thought to take, and it's absolutely clear to her that she hadn't meant to do a thing, that she just wanted someone to love her, that she never did what she really wanted to, never has done what she wanted, never, never.

He gets his first paycheck, and she waits for him for hours, in the loft of the lye shed. First she thinks he's had an accident and is close to dying somewhere. Then she thinks he's forgotten about her and is still eating at his mother's. Then she thinks he doesn't care about her because he's in love with someone else. She thinks and can't understand, and she finally climbs down from the loft, walks back home alone, and climbs through her window and into bed. And she understands that she has no way to get a message to him, nobody she can trust to set up another time and place.

She doesn't see him, and she doesn't know who to tell. She doesn't want to tell anyone else. She doesn't want to tell anyone. It's only something that hasn't happened, she tells herself, hasn't happened yet. It might begin any day, in which case she shouldn't tell anyone. She feels her breasts and belly, tries to judge whether she feels sore or swollen, more or less like other months, she sleeps uneasily in hopes of the silent signal that it has come, and always checks her nightgown and her underwear for the spot of blood, the blood that would mean she doesn't yet have to tell anyone what she's done.

One week passes, and then two weeks. Time takes on a different meaning for her. School has started, and everybody except for her seems caught up in an eternal present, a daily spin of classes attended and homework and party planning and maybe a movie in San Jose. But for her, each day is like the tick of a clock counting down to zero.

Then she sees him across Lumber Street, walking with another man. She waves at him, and he waves back and keeps walking. She has to cross the street to catch up with him.

She calls his name, and he turns around.

"Can I talk to you?" she asks.

The other man, a tall, leering fellow called Jax, walks on a few paces.

"It's harder to see each other now," she says. "Than during harvest."

"Yeah," he agrees. "Especially because I'm working full time now."

She can see in his eyes, hear in his voice, he doesn't mind that it's harder to meet. He likes it. And she can't tell him just then.

"Do you want to?" she asks. "Soon?"

"It's not that I don't want to. It's just that I'm working all day long, and I'm tired at night."

She doesn't say a thing about doing schoolwork herself, and then cooking and cleaning and marketing and washing clothes. She doesn't mention it. She only makes him agree to a day and time they can meet.

The two men walk away from her, and she hears Jax laugh nastily.

He doesn't miss that meeting, he doesn't miss any more

meetings. She holds on to him when they meet and doesn't want to let him go. But she doesn't tell him that she feels like she is slipping over a cliff, slipping a little further every day. He isn't quite ready, the moment isn't quite right, it doesn't seem like he loves her quite enough yet.

Anna, her friend, talks about the boys in high school, the boys who are seniors and would go on to college. One or two of them seem to her to be "quite sophisticated." If Betsy told her, Anna wouldn't consider him sophisticated in the least, would perhaps be critical. And Betsy can't bear to hear anyone say, "How could you?"

Her mother, she's sure, would give no comfort or counsel, would only find her dilemma a reason to tell her how terrible her father would be when he found out.

Finally Miss Anderson notices her. Miss Anderson is beautiful and smart, and is a math teacher, and is going to be married to Albert Jackson in June. She asks her why she's having trouble concentrating on geometry, when she'd been one of the best students the previous year. Asks her if she's well. And Betsy tells her everything. Everything except who.

The first thing is to visit a doctor. Miss Anderson will borrow her fiancé's car—yes, she knows how to drive—and take her to a doctor in San Jose. She will be home in San Natoma only an hour later than normal, so she won't have to explain anything to her parents yet.

The next thing, Miss Anderson decides, is to visit Reverend Walters. Her parents will have to be told, the boy will have to be told, his parents will have to be told, everything will have to be worked out. But she can't decide the best way to do all that, and perhaps the reverend can. Betsy sits in Reverend Walters's study and tries to tell her story. When he asks her a direct question, she raises her head; there is some hope, after all, in the name.

"Harold," she says. "I love Harold."

. . . .

"Harold," Paolo called.

A small crowd of people had gathered in front of Paolo's house on a still, sunlit Saturday afternoon, and Paolo waved Harold to come join the fun.

His old schoolmate grinned conspiratorially. Harold saw on the back of a truck a large redwood winepress, five feet in diameter, and a number of barrels on the ground, some already full and some empty and waiting. Two Italian men with their shirts off stood on either side of the press and grasped the long wooden levers to turn the screw.

"Bravo, bravissimo!" shouted some of the women.

The two men pulled in tandem, and their backs popped with ridges of shiny muscle in the sun. They caught their breath and then pulled again, and a stream of grape juice came down the spout, twisting and falling like roseglass into the barrel.

"Bravo!"

Then Paolo grasped Harold by the hand and led him into the circle as the two men jumped down from the truck. Paolo took a moment to loosen his shirt, and a gold crucifix shone from his neck. Harold loosened his shirt as well, and the two mounted beside the press. At a sign from Paolo, Harold took the smooth oaken shaft into his hands, braced one foot against the heavy redwood planks of the press, and pulled.

"Ecco i ragazzi!"

Harold felt that he and Paolo had moved the press further than the two men before them, and he smiled triumphantly. The lever did not move easily; it felt like they were forcing the wooden disk down onto a solid cake of rubber. Yet little by little, they gained a half turn of the lever, and then a whole turn, as the roseate liquid continued to trickle into the waiting barrel.

"It's easier at the beginning," Paolo said, blowing.

"We can go for a few more pulls," Harold said.

They took up the lever again, braced their feet, and pulled until their legs straightened out. Sweat broke out on Harold's brow and back, and he took his shirt completely off for the final few pulls, his pale skin contrasting with Paolo's olive.

"Bravo, l'americano."

One last pull, and they jumped down to shouts of acclaim and appreciation, and two more men climbed up to take their place.

Paolo gestured with his head and led Harold out of the circle. Harold recognized the constable, a big Irishman named Mallory, looking on with the rest of the crowd. He looked a question at Paolo, who shrugged his shoulders.

"He's not going to bother us," Paolo said. "He knows an Italian can't live without his wine."

Behind the house, Paolo brought out his sack of tobacco, and 'he and Harold rolled cigarettes. They lit up from a match Harold struck along his pants leg, breathed in the smoke with appreciation, and felt the perspiration drying on their faces.

"It's too bad you won't be in school this year," Paolo said. "We could use you in the outfield."

"Santos isn't bad," Harold said.

"He can run, but he can't hit. Not like you, anyway. You hit a couple balls last year that went a mile."

"You guys will do all right without me."

"Well, you probably wouldn't have time for baseball, any-way. Not with all the running around you do now."

Harold had reported in great detail his visit to Goosetown, changing certain things that didn't fit so well, such as the way he'd passed out afterward in the little room, or the talk he'd had about his father. The woman became more beautiful in his telling, younger. Paolo had been very impressed, and wanted Harold to take him there as soon as he'd gotten to-gether a little money. He even said he would get money out of his father's wallet if Harold would take him there. Harold was vague on promising to take him, because he didn't think he could find his way back there without Jax, and they probably wouldn't go again until next payday.

He hadn't told Paolo about Betsy. He hadn't told anybody about Betsy. It wasn't something he could brag about. Betsy was still with him, folding him in her arms as though she would never let him go.

Until she was in the past, he couldn't speak of her.

"Listen," Paolo said, "we're getting up a game for Armi-stice Day, at the Southern Pacific field. One last game be-fore winter. Can you play?"

"Paolo . . ." Harold warned.

Paolo's father, a short, paunchy man dressed in work

pants and undershirt, came up behind Paolo and cuffed him on the side of the head.

"What did I tell you about smoking?" he said.

"Ah, Papa . . ."

"If you smoke, you don't do it at the house. When you're grown up, then you can do what you want."

"But, Papa, you smoke."

His father cuffed him again. "Don't talk back to your father."

"It's Harold's tobacco."

"Harold," Paolo's father said. "He can do what he want. He's big now."

"I'm sorry we smoked, Mr. Pirelli," Harold said.

"Well." Paolo's father turned toward Paolo.

"I'm sorry, too, Papa."

"Well, that's better." He put a hand behind Paolo's neck, drew him closer, and kissed him roughly on the forehead.

"I wanted to give Harold a glass of wine," he said. "Since he helped with the pressing."

"Sure thing," Harold said.

On the front porch, Mr. Pirelli's face crinkled into a grin as he pulled the cork from a heavy dark-green bottle.

"From last year," he said.

He poured three thick tumblers half full of red wine and handed one to Harold and one to Paolo. Then he held his own glass up to the sun; the wine turned glowing crimson.

"Sometimes," he said, "you got to check for sediment."

They sipped the wine. Harold enjoyed the taste that seemed to flower inside his mouth.

In front of the house, another load of grapes had been dumped into the press, and two more men pulled on the handle.

"Bravo!"

Paolo's father smiled.

"Where I come from," he said to Harold, "we been making wine for a thousand years."

"Ah, Papa, he doesn't want to hear about that."

"You, be quiet. What do you know what he wants to hear or doesn't want to hear." He turned back to Harold. "A thousand years. A little town in Chianti, called Castello in Montefiori. It's on top of a hill, where an old castle used to be from the Middle Ages. Stone streets, just wide enough for one horse and cart to get through. And all along the side of the hill, down from the town, we grow the grapes."

He sipped his wine and shook his head.

"This wine is good," he said. "But not like the wine from Chianti."

"Why did you leave, Mr. Pirelli?"

"Why did I leave?" He smiled again. "My momma and poppa, they liked the bed too much. You two, you're too young still to understand that."

Harold said, "I'm not too young."

"Ha," Mr. Pirelli laughed. "Maybe you're not too young to know what a woman feels like. But you're too young to understand what *I'm* talking about. I had three brothers and six sisters, and there was no room for us all in Montefiori. I was the second-oldest son. It was my place to leave and try my luck in the New World."

The two men on the back of the truck paused while others wrestled a full barrel away from the press and replaced it with an empty one.

"One brother and sister come over with me. Maybe I send for the youngest sister, too, if she wants to come. But now, I got babies of my own, you see." He reached out and mussed up Paolo's hair.

"Ah, Papa." Paolo rearranged his hair, and his father took another sip of wine.

"The land here is good," he said. "Maybe too good for the best wine. But maybe we'll make wine so good as in Chianti, if we try for a thousand years."

The two men on the back of the truck pulled, and their upper bodies glistened, and the juice poured into the barrel.

"Bravo!"

. . . .

Alone in his study, Reverend Walters shivered.

The sun had gone behind a bank of clouds outside, and the study now seemed chill and dark. The shelves, the vases, the teapot, all held a grayish cast in the diffuse light.

The reverend thought about making more tea. But it would be such an effort to take the pot to the kitchen, and put on water to boil, and clean out the tea sock, and the pot, and measure out more tea, and pour boiling water, and then wait five minutes for it to steep. It would be such an effort, and it was all so petty and vain.

He had talked with Betsy a long time, while Jennifer Anderson listened. He didn't talk about sin, or leading an upright life; if she had come to him before anything had happened, he would have given her those speeches, speeches on the satisfaction in resisting temptation and the pleasures of a righteous life. But now he talked about the cross we have to bear, and the strength God sends to help us bear it. He told her not to resent this child, but to accept it, as a gift from God, that He would aid in finding a place for.

Betsy tended to nod in agreement when he said these things. But Jennifer was much more practical. She demanded to know what they were to do, whom they were to tell and how, and what he, Reverend Walters, could do to help. Finally, he felt forced to agree to talk with Betsy's parents and Harold's mother. Jennifer, in turn, agreed that it was up to Betsy to talk to Harold himself, before the reverend talked with the parents.

Then he asked them both to kneel and pray. He prayed aloud in the melodious voice that was so effective in the pulpit. He asked God to bless and help this troubled child, give her strength to withstand her afflictions, and guide her to a better life. He asked that her parents' hearts be softened and that they accept her with love and understanding. And he asked that he himself be given wisdom, to be able to comfort and counsel and guide all the troubled parties in this vale of tears.

When they'd gone, he walked around and tried to decide whether he'd said anything at all that was new, anything at all that he hadn't said already many times before.

He didn't think he had.

He picked up the book he'd been reading; then he put it down again without opening it. He thought about writing something himself—a sermon, a meditation, a book—and he looked at his writing desk. His pen, a blotter pad, and a sheaf of foolscap waited for him. He gazed at his desk for some time.

Finally, he sat down in his soft leather chair and looked out the window at the grayish half-light.

A knock on the door.

He stood up. It was still his visiting hours, and he couldn't hide just yet.

Mrs. Shipley was dressed in somber tones. As she had been every week, since her son fell in the Ardennes.

"Come in, Mrs. Shipley," Reverend Walters said. "I'll make you some tea and we'll talk."

10

· · · · · · · · ·

The Last Game   November 11, 1920

Jax spat on the toe of his shoe.

Harold, sitting on the top bunk, looked down.

Jax brushed the spit into the smooth patent leather until it completely disappeared. Then he began to buff the shoe with an old velvet rag.

Harold worked some neat's-foot oil into his glove. "You sure you don't mind?" he asked.

Jax grinned cynically and spat on his other shoe.

The veteran was in full dress uniform. The tie he wore was straight and knotted sharply, his uniform coat was bloused over a white webbed belt, and the creases in his pants were crisp and starched. Over his left pocket, two rows of heavy bronze and silver medals hung from bright cloth ribbons in green and blue and magenta. The medals swayed slightly as Jax patiently continued to brush the shoes.

"Because I could go late to the game," Harold continued. "I could go into San Jose with you for the parade and then play baseball afterward."

Jax shook his head. "Don't miss your game for anything like an Armistice Day parade. The only reason I'm going is because my mother stayed up last night cleaning and ironing everything. That and the fact that there'll be a lot of good whiskey at the hall afterward. The old-timers who fought in Cuba still have a lot of the good stuff laid by. Real Scotch."

He gave a few more strokes with the buffing rag, took the trees out from his shoes, and slipped them on with a shoehorn.

"I hate Armistice Day," he said. "Every time I see people standing along a street waving flags, it makes me wish I had stayed with French Jane and never come home."

. . . .

Against a darkening sky, Harold swung two baseball bats around in a slow circle.

The score of the game had long been forgotten. They didn't play to win, but only for the sweet endless feeling of the game, running for a fly hit far to the left, or feeling the bat hit the ball squarely, and then the round of jogging out into the field or back to the plate to swing the bat, the always new chance to play.

And yet, as it grew late and more boys thought about their suppers growing cold, all agreed that there was to be a last inning with a last out. Harold stood near the plate, windmilled his bats, and hoped he'd have one more swing. There were two outs and a man on first; he watched the batter beat the first pitch foul. Harold was supposed to eat with his mother that night and if the game went on much longer, he would be late. But he hoped to be able to hit once more, maybe drive in a run, and not have the frustration of being stranded on deck.

The pitcher wound up again and threw, and the batter swung. Harold cursed at the soft sound of a pop-up, twisting into right field.

The right fielder waved his arms, warning others away from the ball. Then suddenly he put both hands over his head and cringed. He'd lost sight of the ball in the gray sky, and it fell untouched in front of him. By the time he recovered the ball and threw it in, there were runners on second and third.

Harold smiled and threw one bat aside and stepped up to the plate. He took a few practice swings, then cocked his bat. He decided to swing at the first pitch, no matter where it was, just swing and drive the ball and run, and burn up his chance all in an instant.

The pitcher rocked back and threw the ball, a straight hard fastball on the inside part of the plate. Harold turned on the pitch, felt the sweet, almost shock-free sensation that meant he'd hit the ball squarely. He turned as he ran to first and saw the third baseman leap into the air. The ball streaked over his head and landed safely in left field.

Harold rounded first base as one runner crossed the plate. He'd gotten a hit, driven in a run, and now maybe he would have a chance to score himself.

Then he saw the runner from second trying to score as well. Harold had hit the ball so hard that it went to the left fielder on one bounce. Now the left fielder threw the ball in to the shortstop, who relayed it to the catcher, and as Harold watched in disbelief, the runner was out by ten feet.

The game was over. In one body, the players on the field began to jog in toward home plate, leaving Harold alone, standing between first and second.

A few members of his team were abusing the runner who had tried to score, especially the boy who would have had a chance to hit. The runner looked toward Harold and shrugged.

Harold began to walk in slowly. A voice seemed to whisper in his ear, an old voice, loveless: "You lost something?"

. . . .

A few of the boys remained standing under a tree near home plate after the rest had scattered. They rolled cigarettes, laughed, talked over parts of the game, trying to keep it alive, trying to keep the feeling of the group and the game together for a moment longer before they would have to split up and find their way to their separate homes.

Harold told the story of his visit to Goosetown one more time for those who hadn't heard it. One or two of the others pretended to have had similar adventures, but nobody really believed them. Harold was the only one in the group who had quit school and was working full time.

As the twilight grew thin, they promised in shouts to play together again soon, or if the weather turned bad, in springtime of next year. And they ran, each in his own direction, toward the light and warmth of home.

Harold was heading toward Ida Valley when one of the boys caught him from behind. This was a boy not really of their group, and Harold had been surprised to see him staying behind, hanging on the edges and listening. He'd also noticed that the boy had given him a few funny looks while he was telling his story.

"Harold," the boy said.

"Yeah."

"I'm Bobby Gundersen, Anna's brother. You know—Anna, Betsy's friend?"

"Yeah? What about it?"

"I've got a message for you, from Betsy."

Bobby pulled an envelope from his hip pocket, creased and dirty but still sealed, and gave it to Harold. Harold recognized the neat, precise lettering.

The younger boy looked at him curiously.

"Well? Aren't you going to open it?"

"I'll open it when I'm good and ready to open it," Harold said. He wished this kid with the big blue eyes would leave so he could have a moment to think.

"My sister said that you were supposed to open it up right away."

"Well, I don't give a rat's ass for what your sister said. Now why don't you get lost?"

Harold turned his back on Bobby and began to walk again. After a moment, he heard footfalls running in the opposite direction.

He stopped and opened the envelope. Inside was a single sheet of paper.

Dearest Harold:

Please meet me at Lone Hill tonight at six o'clock, after the game. It's important.

Love, Betsy

"Damn it." Harold crumpled the message in his fist. He was supposed to be at his mother's at six o'clock. And Betsy thought she could just tell him to come and he had to come, as though he didn't have a life of his own.

His mother had been making his life difficult as well, always trying to take over his free time with invitations to dinner, or little projects that he alone could do for her. And if he begged off, she tried to find out what else he was going to do. It had gotten worse since he missed dinner with her that night and hadn't provided any explanation; he'd hoped that spending this evening with her would keep her quiet for a while.

It's important. Maybe he should just catch an interurban into San Jose, try to find Jax, drink some of that good Scotch, leave both of them flat.

But he turned and walked toward Lone Hill.

. . . .

The trees were dark and dormant. The fruit had long since fallen, and the leaves were taken away by an early chill and rainstorms. The branches of the trees, bare and twisted, reached many-fingered toward the lowering sky.

Harold walked up the swelling land, crushing dead leaves softly under his feet. On top of Lone Hill, the trees looked like a line of naked skeletons, pointing at him. He told himself to think of the pruning, soon to take place. Pruning, when the trees slept even more soundly. To shape each silent, leafless tree, so that it could support the blizzard of blossoms, the leaves, and then the heavy purple fruit that would come, would surely come with the summer.

The trees still looked strange and disturbing.

A figure detached itself from one dark tree trunk, came out of the tree itself, and ran at him. He opened his arms, and then he felt Betsy's arms wind tightly round him, and her head against his chest, her body pressed against his as though she wanted to grow into him.

Her head was buried in his chest, and he could hardly make out what she was saying. The trees breezed insistently about them, and she was sobbing and talking at the same time. He tried to loosen himself from her, but every time he moved away, she tightened her grip.

"What are you saying?" he asked. "What about your father?"

"No, no." She wouldn't lift her head to look at him.

"Your father?" Harold asked. "My father?"

"No, no. You're a father."

Your father. You're father. You're your father. "What do you mean?" He shook her a little so she would look at him. "What do you mean?"

"I didn't want to tell you, because I wasn't sure." Her up-turned face was pale as a single flower petal.

"Sure about what?"

"I love you, Harold."

"Betsy . . ." He felt himself get hard, as though he wanted to sink himself inside her. Then he thought of the woman who had called it his Sugar Jake. He almost laughed aloud, until Betsy's fingernails dug into his back.

"You have to protect me, Harold."

"From what?"

"From my father," she said.

"What's he done now?"

"Nothing. He doesn't know yet."

The trees waved bone-thin arms at them.

"So he doesn't know," Harold said. "So why?"

"Don't you understand?"

"Understand what?"

"You're going to *be* a father." Her body pressed into his. "I'm going to have a baby. Your baby."

Harold heard the wind chuckle, and he felt her holding his body down. He understood. He was standing on a high place, where sudden vast landscapes opened to the eye. Back-ward and forward in time, an infinite distance he could see. Back through his mother's bitter years, he saw his father ex-plode into his life, grow huge as colossus, then suddenly van-ish, while his mother's daily bitterness continued. He saw schooling end and full-time man begin; and every step he had taken to grow himself had brought him right here, to this place. He looked forward and saw his mother leaning upon him more heavily every year. And Betsy, through the part of himself she held within her, rooted him down. He suddenly saw her as one more skeletal tree, and the hilltop was the scene of a dance he could never leave. He was weighed down here, he would die here.

Betsy was crying. She rubbed her wet face against him, as though she would burrow into him, as though she would plant herself inside him, inside his body, in the middle of his heart.

"Stop crying, Betsy."

She held him fiercely. He didn't like the way her arms bent around him, the way her flesh creased and swelled at the elbows.

"Please stop crying. I have to go soon."

"Promise me," she said.

"Promise you?"

"Promise me. Promise me."

"Promise you what?"

"Promise me everything."

"All right," Harold said. He couldn't bear to stay there a minute longer. "All right. Everything."

Betsy hugged him close, then relaxed her grip.

"Meet me here tomorrow night, so we can talk?"

"All right," he said. "I promise."

She kissed him, squeezed his hands, released him.

"Tomorrow night," she said.

"Tomorrow night."

They walked down Lone Hill in opposite directions, but after they'd gone ten yards, they turned back to wave. He saw her hand, waving through the branches of the dark, many-fingered trees.

. . . .

"Harold," his mother said.

Harold looked up from his empty plate.

"Do you want some more coffee?"

"No. Thanks." He looked down again. His mother pursed her lips.

"Are you feeling well, Harold? Should I take your temperature?"

"No. I'm okay."

She came over and laid the back of her hand on his forehead. He drew his head back from her touch.

"I'm okay, I said. I'm just a little tired."

"I'm not sure if they're feeding you well over there. You look a bit peaked."

"It's nothing," Harold said. "They feed us all right."

"But not as good as home."

Harold felt his mother leaning over him. He let his breath out slowly.

"Of course not." He stood up slowly, careful not to scrape the chair legs against the floor.

She smiled. "It's always so nice when you come for dinner, Harold. You've gotten so big now, just in the last few months. But for me you'll still be my little boy."

. . . .

Harold walked the dark way alone back to the lodge. Every leafless tree reminded him of Lone Hill, every tree reminded him of Betsy. He wanted to hide in the lodge, away from everything and everybody, and not hear her voice or his mother's voice holding on to him.

A lamp was still burning in his cubicle. He found Jax there, sitting on a stool, scrabbling over the makings of a cigarette. His hat and tie were gone, his uniform was caked with mud from where he must have stumbled on the way back, and his medals were tangled on the unbuttoned coat.

"Jax." Harold pushed his hands away from the scattered tobacco and papers.

Jax started, lifted up his pasty face, thin lips.

"Come on, Jax. We got to get you into the bunk."

Jax gripped Harold's arm. "Listen. Don't trust them. When they tell you this is the world, don't trust them."

"Come on, Jax." Harold put his arm around Jax's back and lifted him to his feet.

"Over the top," Jax muttered. "The world has been made safe for democracy. Buy paint."

"Okay, Jax. Easy does it."

"Don't trust a single one of those bastards. When they tell you . . . Not a goddamned one. When this oughta be the world."

"Okay." Harold eased him down onto the bed and let his

head fall back onto the pillow. Then he hoisted the dead legs off the floor and began to take off the shoes.

"Nothing could stop us. Nothing, nothing could stop us."

"Okay, okay."

Harold unbuttoned the coat the rest of the way and took a moment to straighten out the medals. Cold disks of silver and bronze, bright striped ribbons, and a somber purple heart.

He drew a blanket over the ex-soldier.

"Go to sleep now, Jax."

"I was the pride of the family." Jax covered his eyes with his fists. Then he began to beat himself on the head, and Harold had to grab his wrists to stop him.

11

· · · · · · ·

Beat the Chinaman   November 12, 1920

Jax was still asleep.

Harold watched him sleeping, lying on his back with his eyes closed and the blanket draped over him, still and silent as a soldier's statue, sleeping forever on top of a carved tomb.

He watched for a long time. Waited for Jax to arise, somehow transfigured, again the clean straight soldier of the previous day, sharp creases in his pants, crisply starched shirt, hat worn at a military angle, two rows of medals bright and glorious.

The blanket moved slowly up and down over Jax's chest. A tiny movement, barely visible. No sign, no words of guidance from the sleeping man except those of last night.

This isn't the world. This oughta be the world. Don't trust them.

Around noon, Harold slipped out the back of the common house.

He went toward the Southern Pacific field, stood near where home plate had been yesterday, and studied the railroad tracks. The sky was low and dark, and a sneaky wind pulled at his jacket.

He had a vague idea of heading for Southern California, the Alamitos or the Signal Hill fields he had heard about, to look for work on the oil rigs. It was the kind of place his father might be, even if little Larry didn't know what he was talking about.

But he didn't really know how to get to Los Angeles, and he didn't know where the oil fields were from there. He didn't know how to look for work in an oil field and didn't have a clue what the work involved. And he didn't have much money to make a start.

He didn't know how to hop a train, either. There were always some hoboes around the tracks, like that old man in the ravine yesterday, especially when it was cold back East. But he didn't know how they went about finding a spot on a train, and there wasn't much choice if he wanted to go all the way to Southern California.

Once away from Ida Valley, away from the orchards, he didn't know much of anything.

He shouldn't try until it was dark, anyway, he decided. That would give him time to figure out if he really wanted to go or not. He went back into town, thought about killing time in one saloon that Jax had shown him.

When Harold crossed the village plaza, he heard a bicycle bell chirp behind him. He turned and saw the younger Chinese man from the Gold Mountain Laundry rolling toward him on an old paperboy bicycle. The man, dressed in a denim jacket and denim trousers, had a tight grip on both handlebars and pedaled with great concentration, intent on keeping his balance. Behind him, a huge bundle of clean wash, wrapped in brown paper and tied with string, was lashed crosswise to the bicycle rack, sticking out two feet in each direction.

He stopped pedaling when he saw Harold and glided up

to him, finally coming to a halt by skidding his shoe along the ground.

"Hey, you," he said. "You are a lucky man."

"What do you mean?" asked Harold.

"Yeah. You are a lucky man." The Chinese man didn't seem to understand that Harold had asked him a question.

"You mean I won something?"

"You are a lucky one in Pok Kop Pew."

"This? You mean this?" Harold dug into his pocket and pulled out his billfold. The ticket with the graceful brush-strokes was still there.

The man nodded in agreement. "Very very lucky."

"How much?"

"I don't know. You go see at the laundry."

"Okay. I'll go there right now."

"Okay. Okay." He pushed off with his right foot, wobbled a bit, and then continued down the street, pedaling cautiously, with the unwieldy bundle threatening at any moment to cause him to fall.

Hop Kee smiled when Harold came into the laundry, still holding the ticket in his hand.

"Mad-sonn. You win."

"How much?" Harold asked. "How much?"

The old man held up his hand for patience, opened a drawer, and pulled out a piece of paper. "Last month," he said. "But I have the paper. I know you will come back. I'm an honest man."

He spread his grid on the counter next to Harold's creased sheet and carefully ran his hand over the two sheets, moving his lips, counting silently. The pattern of brush marks was similar on both, nearly identical.

"A lot of money?"

The old man counted the figures three times before he looked up.

"Eight right. That make two hundred dollar."

"Two hundred dollars?" That was months of work on the ranch. "Give me. Give it to me."

Hop Kee looked disappointed at Harold's haste. He pursed his lips, took out his brush, and made a small mark in the corner of Harold's ticket. Then he stood up and carefully straightened his suit and tie.

"You wait here," he said.

Harold watched him disappear through a dim doorway behind the counter. For a moment he thought that the Chinese man was trying to escape with his money, and wanted to follow him into the back room. But Hop Kee returned a minute later, a sheaf of bills in his hand.

He stacked the money bill by bill on the counter, forbidding Harold to take it until the entire sum had been counted and counted again. Then, after Harold had grabbed the money and stuffed it into his shirt pocket nervously, he smiled.

"You play again?"

"No, I—I think I'm leaving town."

"Ah," the old man said wisely, "just like your father."

"What do you mean?"

"Just like your father."

"What do you mean, just like my father?"

"Your father win big time. Ten right. Then he leaves town. Never see him again."

"How much is ten right?" Harold asked.

"Big time. One thousand dollar."

"My father left town after winning one thousand dollars?"

Hop Kee smiled and shrugged his shoulders.

"Jesus Christ, you're sure?"

"You play again?"

"You're sure, aren't you? You're telling me the truth."

Hop Kee gradually lost his smile; he looked gravely at the young man.

"I'm an honest man," he said. "I tell the truth."

"I just can't believe it."

"You play again?"

"No, no."

Harold walked through the door into the face of a quickening south wind. Dust rose in gusts and drifted in the hazy air, and leaves kicked horizontally along the road. He suddenly knew that his father had loved the main chance, the big gold mountain, more than anything or anybody. When he'd had the chance, he'd grabbed it with both hands and let everything else go. Now Harold had the main chance, as pretty a chance as ever his father had.

The two hundred dollars lay like a large cold hand next to his heart.

. . . .

Reverend Walters sat in a straight-backed chair in the front room and watched Ernest Moreberg carefully light a short cigar.

The two men were alone. Reverend Walters thought it usually better to have both parents present and the child absent; if one parent was too emotional, the other could usually moderate the situation, better than he could. And it was best to let the news sink in before they saw their child again. Especially in the case of an only daughter.

But Lillian Moreberg was sick and didn't feel strong enough to leave her room. So he would have to broach the subject with Ernest alone.

Earlier, Reverend Walters had gone over to the house where the full-time men stayed, to ask Harold in for counseling. But all he had found was a filthy, unshaven man lying in a bunk, stinking of alcohol. The man told him to go peddle his product elsewhere, he wasn't buying any today. Then he rolled over and belched mightily.

Now Reverend Walters sat across from this square-shouldered Dane, an immigrant, quietly drawing in a puff of smoke. Ernest was going to wait for him to begin, that was clear; he had asked to come, and Moreberg had admitted him, and now it was up to him to state the purpose of his visit.

He cleared his throat. "I wanted to ask you if you had noticed anything unusual in the way your daughter has been behaving."

"No," Moreberg said slowly. "My daughter has been fine. She's had to cook and keep house since my wife has been ill, but she has never complained. There was one afternoon last week when she came home late, but she said she had to help her friend Anna with some schoolwork."

"You love your daughter, don't you, Mr. Moreberg?"

Moreberg looked at him, suddenly hostile and suspicious, and Reverend Walters realized he'd taken the remark for an insult. "Because your daughter is going to need all your love now," he hurried on. "She's going to need the love of a strong, kind father, one who can judge what is right and wrong, but also one who can forgive when need be. Forgiveness is a quality much more divine than judgment."

"Say what you mean, Reverend."

"I mean, your daughter came to see me last week."

"Why?"

"Your daughter's in trouble, Mr. Moreberg."

The reverend tried to be direct. But he saw from Moreberg's face that he didn't understand the expression in English.

"Why did she go to you and not to me?" Moreberg asked. "What kind of trouble?"

"Your daughter," Reverend Walters said, "is going to have a baby."

The blunt, heavyset man bolted upright. He crushed out his cigar and then walked around and deliberately drew all the curtains in the front room. The room darkened, and he turned toward the reverend, thick hands tense at his sides.

"How could she do this?"

"You have to learn to forgive," the reverend said.

"How could my daughter, who I work for, and raise, and provide a home for—how could she do this to me?"

The back door opened and shut. Both men heard it, but Moreberg realized what it meant a second sooner than the reverend, and he stalked toward the kitchen.

"Mr. Moreberg, wait."

Betsy saw her father walk into the kitchen followed by the reverend, and she knew he had been told. Her father stood in front of her and folded his arms across his chest.

"Mr. Moreberg," the reverend said.

"Well?" Moreberg addressed his daughter.

Betsy quickly ducked around her father and ran into the dining room. Moreberg stood still, dumbfounded, then wheeled and ran after her. Reverend Walters followed. Betsy looked around, then skipped into her mother's room and locked the door.

Moreberg rattled the doorknob, pounded on the door.

"Open up," he shouted. "Open up and put another knife into your father's heart."

"Mr. Moreberg," the reverend said. "Acceptance. Forgiveness."

"If you'll excuse me, Reverend, I'm talking with my daughter."

He beat on the door until it rattled in its frame.

"Poisonous," he shouted. "Poisonous as a nest of vipers."

"Mr. Moreberg, come away from the door, or she'll never come out." Reverend Walters took Moreberg by the arm and tried to lead him away. Three steps from the door, Moreberg broke away and barged back into the door with his shoulder. The door bent and held, and he bounced back and fell to a seat on the floor.

"I've hurt my shoulder now. Do you hear? I've hurt my shoulder." He stood up and let the reverend take him away, rubbing his arm.

"You have to talk with her."

"And what have I been doing?"

"Gently," Reverend Walters said. "Gently."

The door opened a crack, and then Betsy sprang out and ran into her own room. Moreberg charged after her, but she managed to close and lock the door. He rattled this door too, but it wouldn't budge.

"I built this house too well," he said. "Betsy! Betsy!"

They both heard a creaking sound, and Moreberg stopped shouting. "The window," he said. "She's going to climb out the window!"

He raced outside, followed by the reverend, and saw some clothes fly out the window. He reached the spot before she could climb out, grabbed the sliding window, and slammed it down. She tried to raise it once, but he slammed it down again. Then he turned to Reverend Walters.

"Guard the window."

He ran back inside. The reverend stood stupidly by the window for a moment. He looked inside, and saw that Betsy was walking back and forth, fully clothed. He didn't know why he expected her to be naked. He felt himself blush, and he quickly went back inside.

Moreberg was roaring. "Harold?"

"Harold," came Betsy's voice through the door.

"I'll show you Harold." He took the doorknob in both hands and wrenched it off. The door swung open, and he reached in like he was reaching into the icebox and pulled his daughter out by the hair.

Betsy butted her head into her father's belly. He staggered back, but kept hold of her hair and struggled with her across the floor.

Then Lillian Moreberg appeared in the room, fantastically dressed in a fringed purple shawl with flower patterns, a hat with flowers growing out of it, impossibly tall, impossibly thin, white hair flailing about her shoulders. She struck her husband's arms with her small, pointy fists.

"Let her go," she shrieked, "let her go. She's the only one alive in this house."

Moreberg released Betsy's hair to take his wife's wrists in his hands and stop her from attacking him. Betsy, free from his grasp, pounded her fists a few times on his back until she saw he wasn't defending himself. Then she collapsed against a wall.

Moreberg stood close against Lillian, his large hands around her thin, fragile bones.

"You see," he said to Reverend Walters. "You see what they do to me? You see what they make of me?"

"Lord help us," the reverend said.

"Harold," Betsy said.

"Lord help us all."

· · · · · · · ·

A light broke the early-evening darkness.

"You going somewhere?"

Harold turned and saw a train agent, dressed in blue with a gold badge, carrying a bull's-eye lamp.

"'Cause if you're going someplace, you sure picked a dumb place to wait."

The agent played the light over Harold, resting it for a moment on his face. Harold felt ashamed of his thick boots, his overalls and canvas jacket, his plaid shirt.

"Why, you're just a kid, aren't you? You running away from home?"

"I don't know."

"You don't know?" The agent laughed out loud. "Well, you don't know shit from beans, do you? You don't know the first damned thing about train yards, for one thing. Anybody looking at you would think you'd never been off the farm before."

Harold almost spit out that he had two hundred dollars on him, to shut the agent's mouth, to prove he wasn't a kid. But he kept quiet, deciding that the first chance he got, he'd buy some different clothes.

"I ran away from home once. Ended up going back a couple days later, half starved. But I found out I liked trains, so it wasn't so bad."

A smile crossed the agent's face in the dim, reflected light.

"You want to catch a train, you don't wait here in the yard. You wait alongside the tracks, just outside the yard, under some cover. And you don't sneak on until the train has just started to move. Or they'll catch you, and send you home to your momma. You got that?"

"Yeah," Harold said.

"You got any idea in hell where you're going?"

"Sure I do," Harold said defensively. "The Southland."

"Well, there's your train." The agent took a watch from his vest pocket. "She's leaving in twelve minutes. Outside the yard, okay? You'll find a handle."

"Okay."

"And, kid—good luck."

The agent laughed again as he walked away. The kid would probably throttle him if he knew that he'd been sent on a train to San Francisco, only fifty miles north. But if, as the agent suspected, he would be back in a few days' time, it was better that he didn't go so far.

. . . .

The train started slowly out of the yards, rolled along the northern edge of the ball field. One by one, the cars swept by the fruit tree that marked the left field line, each car moving by a little faster as the engine picked up steam, each car marked with the name of a distant city: Seattle, Santa Fe, Denver. Like rafts on a great, swelling river they passed, following the current downstream, never to return.

A dark car with a darker opening in the center loomed up, and the young man broke from the tree. The train picked up momentum. He scrambled up the gravel embankment and ran alongside the moving car, raced the train in his heavy boots.

For an instant he was moving at the same speed as the car. The steam whistle blew, and the train surged forward. He reached for the edge of the opening and found something to grasp.

He leapt. His feet left the ground, and he swung inside the opening, disappeared from sight.

The train crossed the bridge, high above the dank ravine, and left San Natoma. The steam whistle blew again, heading north.

two : The *Coast Daylight*

12
. . . .

The *Coast Daylight*   May 10, 1933

In that year, the last Interurban train ran from San Natoma to San Jose, and the tracks were torn up and sold for scrap. San Natoma Avenue was widened and repaved and painted with a broken white line; it rolled now between orchard land toward the largest city in the Valley, a long straight line, tar black and glistening under the sun.

A Jordan motorcar drove toward San Jose under the quick, cloudless heat. On either side of the road, orchards formed a broad green canopy twelve feet above the Valley floor. The blossoms had fallen, and new leaves had just unfolded to cup the sun. Under the trees, the soft green shade of plum and apricot spread out in all directions, an inviting shade of crisscrossed leaves and branches, fecund with the first tiny swellings of fruit.

But the narrow black line the Jordan drove on was set

apart from the shade of trees. The road touched on the orchards, yet remained separate from them, as of another world, breathless and sun-beaten.

. . . .

Halfway to San Jose, the Jordan pulled into an Associated Gas Station. Paolo Pirelli came out of the small glassed-in workshop, wiping his hands on a rag he pulled out of the hip pocket of his overalls.

"Hello, Betsy," he said. "You're looking nice."

"Just fill her up, Paolo, and don't bother about the oil and water. I've got to meet a train."

"That doesn't surprise me, dressed as pretty as you are." Paolo took down the nozzle and walked to the back of the car.

Betsy had been at this station many times before because she liked supporting the business of somebody she had known in school. But she seemed to see it differently today. It was small but clean. The tools around the workbench were all hung in place, matching the painted outlines on the wall behind them, and a little sign that hung in the window read, PLEASE—NO TOOLS LOANED. The buildings and the pumps were all freshly painted yellow-green, with red trim, and other signs read, FREE AIR AND WATER, and USE ADCO MOTOR OILS. Any puddles of oil were promptly spread with sand and swept up, so that customers could get out and stretch their legs if they felt like it, without soiling themselves.

The station was a good little business, and Paolo had a future in it because he worked at it. It was the kind of thing Harold could have started, if he had stayed.

Betsy knew that Harold and Paolo had been friends. But she hadn't quite known Paolo well enough at the time to ask him if he knew where Harold had gone. Afterward, it had seemed useless, senseless, too late. And now, especially now, when decisions had been made and everything was about to change, when she was determined to stick to the path she had laid out for herself, she tried hard to keep from even thinking of asking about him.

"That will be a dollar eleven, Betsy."

Betsy looked into her change purse, counted out the change carefully, and placed it in Paolo's hands.

"So how's business, Paolo?"

"I'm keeping the mortgage paid, keeping bread on the table. That's about as best you can do these days."

"And how's Christina?"

Paolo smiled. "Cooking up a storm, doing her best to give me a little paunch." He slapped his belly with both hands and jiggled it up and down. "I don't know how she does it, taking care of two little kids."

"Well, give her my love. And I'll stop in for gas whenever I'm this way."

"Will do, Betsy. And thanks."

Betsy pulled back onto the hot, mocking road. Even with the window open at twenty-five miles an hour, the inside of the Jordan was oppressive. The shade of the trees ran beside her like water, never quite lapping onto the blacktop where she had to drive.

At a stop sign, she took off her hat and placed it on the seat beside her, then unpinned the tortoiseshell barrette that held her hair in a bun. She ran her fingers along her temples and let her hair spill down across her shoulders and shook her head. She felt cooler instantly. But she knew she would have to arrange herself when she got to the station. Loose hair would look too young. She didn't want to look the way she had twelve years ago, not to meet this train.

When she put the car in gear again, her hair spread out behind her, snapping and fluttering in the breeze like an unfurled banner.

In front of the Southern Pacific station in downtown San Jose, she was sure that her hair was hopelessly windblown. She hurried up to the glazed brick portico, where an old conductor smoked a cigar. The conductor smiled under his broad white mustache, stained yellowish in the center by smoke, and was already reaching for his watch chain when she came up to him.

"When does the *Coast Daylight* come in from Los Angeles?" she asked.

He chewed on his cigar a bit, consulted the heavy brass watch. "She's due in twenty minutes."

"Only twenty minutes!"

The conductor smiled at the hat and barrette she held in one hand, the snap purse she clutched in the other, the disheveled hair.

"There's a waiting room for ladies inside," he said. "Why don't you freshen up in there? Whoever-he-is won't mind, anyway."

The main waiting room was cool and high-ceilinged; knots of men stood around waiting for the train, smoking pipes or short cigars. A few men sat on the polished wooden benches, reading the afternoon paper. When Betsy walked in, she felt the newspapers rustle after her, and she quickly exited under the sign that read LADIES.

The ladies' waiting room was small, but there was a full-length mirror where Betsy could smooth her dress and rearrange herself. She brushed her hair, but there still seemed to be something windblown about it, some stray hairs that refused to stay down. She gathered it all as best she could into the barrette and hoped that the hat would cover the rest.

Another woman was also pinning up her hair. "Do I look all right in back?" she asked.

"You look fine," Betsy said.

"I'm meeting my husband," the woman said. "He's been in Los Angeles for a week."

Betsy smiled.

She sat on one of the benches from which she could see into the main waiting room. The air out there was bluish and hazy. All the men seemed distant, frozen in position with pipe or newspaper or watch in hand, still as painted figures in a mural.

Then, as if at a common signal, everyone was in motion. The men sitting down folded their newspapers under their arms and stood up, other men stubbed out their smokes in tall, sand-filled ashtrays, bags and suitcases were picked up, and everyone began moving in the same direction.

"The *Coast Daylight*, Now Arriving On Track Number Three."

Betsy walked through a tunnel to the platform where the train would arrive. People filed out from the stairway and spread out under the corrugated metal canopy that shaded the platform. Porters brought out the bags of the passengers who were boarding, and conductors repeatedly warned people back from the edge.

She chose a pillar to stand beside, and she waited. The train was already moving slowly when it came into view. The brakes hissed, fell silent, then hissed again as two dark-green engines rolled smoothly past, followed by the mail car. Then the passenger cars arrived, rows of rectangular windows filled with faces, smiles, waving hands. The people waiting on the platform scanned the windows to catch the soonest possible glimpse of their passenger. One newspaper boy held up the afternoon edition of the *Mercury*, ready to peddle it to the people just arriving, and a man held a tray of cigarettes and cigars. The train moved slower still, yet delayed indefinitely the moment when it would come to a complete and final stop.

Then, as if by magic, conductors popped out of the doors and lowered the collapsible metal steps, a final loud hiss was heard from the brakes, and the train ceased moving.

Passengers streamed off the train, exchanged hugs or handshakes, or went directly to the tunnel. Betsy held back from the crush of people meeting the train. She thought she would recognize him, but she wanted to be sure. And she wanted to be able to watch him, for just a moment, before he saw her. The walrus-mustached conductor directed people to their cars. The woman from the waiting room was embracing a man in a dark-blue suit; the man's hat was tipped back, and he was smiling. Passengers for Oakland or Sacramento hurried up the stairs.

Then the crowd parted, layer upon layer of passengers and conductors and vendors melted away, and a thin youth in an ill-fitting suit appeared at the telescoping end of a long human corridor. The boy's suit was short in the sleeves and too broad in the seat, and as he fidgeted in the heat, his bony wrists showed below the cuffs and his pants began to droop and bag.

He had two cardboard suitcases beside him, and while he looked around at the faces of strangers, he touched the bags with his feet to make sure they hadn't walked away. He tugged awkwardly at his collar, obviously uncomfortable, yet unwilling to take off his tie.

Betsy could see, bright and clear, every move he made. There was something endearing in the way he hitched up his pants and tucked in his shirt and tugged down his sleeves, something lovable in his awkward movements, something especially lovable in his lanky frame, long face, pointy chin, wide-set eyes. She was sure. This was the one she was waiting for, the one she'd been waiting for for so many years, the one she hadn't seen since he was born. This youngster wearing the poorly fitted suit, with the tie too tight and afraid for his luggage, this young man was Peter, Pete, little Petey. This was her son.

. . . .

Peter kicked the suitcase.

"Darn it," he said.

The old conductor approached him. "You sure you have the right station, son?"

"The *Coast Daylight* to San Jose," Peter scowled. "So where is she?"

"Who is it's supposed to meet you?" The conductor looked at him curiously.

Peter shot a defiant glance at the old man. "Forget it," he said.

"No need to have a chip on your shoulder, son."

"I'm not *your* son." He pulled down the cuffs of his coat and hitched up his pants again. He hated this suit. The people he had lived with had promised him a new suit after he turned eleven, for his confirmation at the community church. But when the moment approached, the woman decided to just alter one of her husband's old suits for him. She hadn't done a very good job, and all the while Peter was on his knees in front of the altar, he was ashamed at how foolish he looked. The girl next to him had a new dress, and he was sure this was the first time she had worn it. She didn't have patches sewn on to hide threadbare elbows.

When he tasted the bread soaked in wine, the reverend had noticed tears in his eyes.

"Bless you," the reverend said. Peter was surprised at the wine's sudden bitterness.

Now, ten months later, he was wearing the same suit, altered once again for the way he'd shot up, and altered once again badly. The woman had commented how smart they'd been not to buy a brand-new suit in the first place. A waste to spend good money on clothes until he settled down. But she'd told him to be wearing the coat and tie when he met his mother. He had to create a good first impression.

He picked up his suitcases, turned toward the tunnel, and he saw her. He recognized her immediately, standing by the pillar. Every year, at Christmas, he'd received one photograph of her. She always wore a nice dress in the photos, stood on a front porch, or beside the decorated tree, or in front of the china cabinet, beautiful dishes behind thick leaded glass. One photograph every year, to keep under his pillow, and study, and handle until the corners were chewed and the image cracked with white paper creases.

This is your mother who loves you, they said. When Peter was young, he looked at the photos with wonder. Somewhere, someone he'd never seen or couldn't remember loved him, cared for him, watched over him.

Later, he began to note the difference between the abundance displayed in the photos and the constant penny-pinching in the household to which, it seemed, he'd been banished through no fault of his own.

He recognized his mother. But she was so small, barely taller than he was. He'd always imagined her gigantic, with long white arms that could fold him into herself. Not a neat, average woman in a tidy blue dress and hat, walking toward him on a train platform.

This is your mother who loves you. This average person was his mother, who had kept him waiting for years, who'd kept him waiting today once more, waiting on the platform.

"Peter." She reached out to touch him. He shied away from her hand and dropped his suitcases. Then he loosened his tie and unbuttoned his collar and stood a step away from her.

"Where have you been?" he asked. His arms dangled awkwardly at his sides.

13

· · · · · · · ·

Off Visiting Relatives   1921

"Where have you been?" her son demanded.

She had been "Off Visiting Relatives."

When Betsy was five months pregnant, her father drove her early in the morning to the train station. They waited out on the platform; Betsy sat on a hard wooden bench while Ernest stood and looked around uneasily. Then they boarded a slow local train and rode four hours south to the small town of Paso Robles.

They talked very little on the trip. But once Ernest turned to Betsy and said, "Remember now, you're off visiting relatives. In Minnesota. That's what I'll be telling everybody, so that's what you'll have to say."

Betsy looked out the window at the flat layer of clouds.

"You should like it there," he went on. "Lord knows, it isn't cheap, so it should be nice. I'll have to hire a housekeeper while you're gone. I can't depend on your mother for anything."

Betsy nodded.

"It will be very dear, paying for your mistake. I don't know how many houses I'll have to build to pay for it. But I'm glad to do it. That's a father's place, to take care of his children no matter how much it costs."

"All right," Betsy said. "All right. I'm grateful." She covered her ears and looked away from him.

The matron, Mrs. Barker, met them at the Paso Robles station. Short and square-shouldered, she wore a plain gray shift and had her hair pulled back severely with a black ribbon. She walked right up to them, as though she had learned to recognize immediately those bound for her institution.

"Mr. Moreberg?" she said. "And this must be Betsy."

Ernest took Betsy's grip to the car and saw her in. "Can't go out there with you," he said. "I'm catching the next train back."

Mrs. Barker took Betsy to a two-story house surrounded by trees and lawn and a high iron fence. It was a house once owned by an old Californio family, a family who had measured their land in leagues and lived with easy profligacy from game and cattle and the labor of Costanoan vaqueros. They built this house in town after the sparsely settled land had passed from Mexican to American rule, then saw their land chipped away by squatters and fraudulent surveyors and taxes, though most went to the very lawyers whom they paid to be their defenders. The house itself was sold at last to pay debts, and the old family seat, once a place of ease and generous hospitality, came to be a place for the pale daughters of Lutherans to hide their bodies and their shame.

Mrs. Barker unlocked the gate, drove through, and locked it behind her. The big iron key moved the bolt with a solid, well-greased click.

"This is the Abundant Life Home for girls," Mrs. Barker said. "Your home for the next four months."

Betsy looked up at the house and saw that all the windows were shuttered.

Mrs. Barker took Betsy into what once had been the formal dining room. Four girls about her age sat at a long wooden table with sewing baskets and balls of yarn and crochet hooks spread out in front of them. They all looked up at Betsy, and she saw that they were all dressed exactly as Mrs. Barker was, in gray shifts with black hair ribbons.

"Betsy, this is Margrethe, Kate, Gretchen, and Lissa." She walked behind the girls as she spoke their names and touched each one lightly on the head. Betsy noticed how Margrethe swelled out in front.

"Yes," Mrs. Barker said. "Margrethe will not be with us much longer. But she'll be a better person when she leaves than when she came."

The girls nodded, but remained silent. When Betsy went with Mrs. Barker up the stairs, she heard voices begin low and insistent behind her.

They went into a single room with a narrow bed and a painting of Jesus praying at Gethsemane hanging on the wall. "This will be yours," Mrs. Barker said. "You can change clothes here. Have you moved your bowels today?"

"What?" Betsy asked.

"Have you moved your bowels today?" Mrs. Barker repeated. "If you haven't, I want you to go to the water closet at the end of the hall and try. Then try again tomorrow right after breakfast. We're very strict about this."

She closed the door as she left. "When you've changed, go down and join the other girls."

Betsy found a loose gray shift hanging in the closet. There was plenty of material for it to expand as she did. She put it on and looked for a mirror, but there was none in the room.

She went downstairs, and the other girls made a place for her. "Do you know how to crochet?" Margrethe asked.

"Sure," Betsy said.

"Good." Margrethe passed a ball of yarn and a hook over to her.

Betsy picked them up and looked at them. "What should I make?"

"It doesn't matter," Margrethe said. "'Idle hands are the devil's tools.'"

The girls all giggled low, except for Lissa, who looked over at the door to Mrs. Barker's quarters.

"It doesn't matter what you make," Gretchen said. "You may think you're making something for your lad, but I'll swear that she takes and sells everything in town."

"Where are you supposed to be?" Margrethe asked.

"Off visiting relatives," Betsy said. "In Minnesota."

"That's like me," Kate laughed. "I'm supposed to be visiting relatives in Omaha. And Lissa is supposed to be with her grandma in Pasadena."

"I wish I *were* there," Lissa said.

"I'm supposed to be studying," Margrethe said. "Back East."

"Studying what?" Betsy asked.

"I don't know. Just studying."

"How far gone are you?" Gretchen asked.

"Five months," Betsy said.

"Really?" Gretchen looked at her. "Well, a slack before a pack. How did you get caught?"

"What do you mean?"

"I mean, didn't you try anything?"

"Well, I tried, you know, with vinegar after every time."

"You should hear what Lissa tried," Gretchen said.

"Oh, Gretchen," Lissa said.

"Go on. Tell her."

"Well, he said that if I just lay there quiet and didn't get too excited, nothing would happen."

"Anybody who'd take a man's advice for *that* . . ." Margrethe shook her head.

"I didn't try anything," Kate told Betsy. "I wanted to have a baby so I could get married."

"You still believe he would have married you?" Margrethe asked.

"He *will* marry me," Kate said.

"You believe that?"

"He's going to come and get me out of here, too."

"You're getting out the same way I'm getting out. After you've lost a few pounds." She patted her belly.

"We'll see," Kate said.

"When I get out of here in a few weeks, you'll still be here for a few months."

"We'll see, I said."

Margrethe laughed harshly. "If you trust a man to do anything that's not his pleasure, you're a fool."

Suddenly the door opened, and Mrs. Barker was looking at them.

"I don't see any needles knitting, or any clothes being sewn. Idle hands are the devil's tools."

Lissa held up her needles to show she had been working. The other girls slowly picked up their handiwork. Mrs. Barker paced up and down behind them, touching them briefly on the shoulder.

"If you were talking about men," she said, "the only man you ought to be thinking of is the Lord. It's He who is the acknowledged head of *this* household."

She picked up the sleeve of the sweater Margrethe was knitting, felt it between thumb and forefinger, then let it drop.

"On the other hand, there's no reason to give up on a husband. You all can still find a man who will cherish you and be on his knees before you. There's a man out there waiting for every one of you."

Betsy bent her head to her crochet and felt Mrs. Barker walking heavily behind her. The only man she could think of waiting for her was her father. Waiting until he didn't have to pay a housekeeper.

"And that's all the more reason to keep sewing," Mrs. Barker said. "A good hand with a needle and a good hand in the kitchen will keep a man better than a pretty smile."

She stood and watched them work in silence. Then she added, "You're all proof of that, aren't you?"

She went back into her quarters. Lissa was near tears, but Gretchen wore a crooked smile.

"That's the way it is here," she told Betsy. "A bowel movement every day, and the Lord every hour."

On Tuesday, Doctor Rolly came to give the girls their weekly examination. He walked in with Mrs. Barker, red-faced and smiling, and greeted the girls by name.

"Hello, Margie, Katie, Lissa. Gretchen, did you miss me?" He patted Gretchen's arm.

"Get your hands off me, you old goat," Gretchen said.

"Ho ho ho," Doctor Rolly said. "Ho ho ho. What a nice group of girls. And you must be Betsy."

"Yes, doctor," Betsy said.

"Well, I'm glad you're here. Ha ha. Even if you're not. Have you been eating your prunes?"

"She's up to four a day, Doctor Rolly," Mrs. Barker said.

"Wonderful, wonderful. Good work." He rubbed his hands together. "Now Margie, why don't you come upstairs first, and we'll see when you get to leave."

Mrs. Barker went up with Margrethe and the doctor, and Gretchen leaned over to Betsy.

"The doctor's a goat," she said.

"He's terrible," Lissa said. "I wish Doctor Leland were here."

Kate picked up her knitting and smiled to herself.

"Don't you get any choice?" Betsy asked.

Gretchen shook her head. "He delivers you, along with one nurse and Mrs. Barker. And he doesn't like to give chloroform either."

When Margrethe came down, she told Betsy to go on up. Mrs. Barker met Betsy in the hallway, handed her a specimen jar, and pointed down the hall. Betsy filled it and carried it back up the hall toward the large master bedroom that had been converted into the Lying-in Room.

Doctor Rolly was dressed in a white gown and wore a surgical cap, and a silver circle like a Cyclops eye grew out of his forehead. Mrs. Barker stood to one side with a notebook open in her hands. The doctor motioned Betsy to the bed, then pulled on a pair of long rubber gloves and raised a surgical mask over his face.

"Lay down, Betsy, lay down and relax," he said through the mask. Betsy felt a rubber sheet under the cotton. A table stood to the right of the bed, with a pitcher and a basin and open glass jars filled with long metal instruments.

"So, my dear," the doctor first began to palpate her abdomen through her clothes, "any twins in your family? Accidents in childbirth? Insanity? All normal, eh?"

Betsy felt his hands working in a circle around where, she thought, her baby was. She didn't know how to answer, but decided that anything she said would jinx her baby.

"Normal," she said. "Normal."

He took a white sheet from the table and draped it over

Betsy's lower body. "Now, darling, please put your knees up. That's a good girl." Betsy felt him spreading her dress from her, felt his eyes on her, felt the sudden cold touch of the stethoscope, but she couldn't see what he was doing.

He reached for an instrument that looked like a pair of ice tongs. Mrs. Barker stood ready with the notebook. Betsy felt two metal fingers touch her on either side of her hips. He was measuring her.

"Intercristal, twenty-nine centimeters. What wide, lovely hips," he said.

That night, while Betsy lay in her bed, she ran her hands over the same places the doctor had touched, prodded, measured. Then she felt, she thought, the tiny fluttering of a bird inside her. She first had felt this several weeks ago, just before her father decided it was time to send her away. Then it had stopped, and she thought that her father had scared it away, killed it. But now, here it was again, fluttering inside her.

There was a quiet knock on the door. Betsy put on a robe and found Kate standing in the hallway.

"Do you want to talk?" she whispered.

Betsy lit a candle, and they sat together on the bed. Kate told Betsy about the man she loved, and how he was going to come and help her escape. "I sent word to him," she said.

"How?" Betsy asked. "Mrs. Barker reads everything before it goes out."

"The boy who delivers groceries." Kate smiled. "I winked at him and slipped him a letter to send. Margrethe doesn't want her baby, can you believe that?"

Betsy shook her head.

"I want mine. You want yours too, don't you?"

"I want to keep mine," Betsy said. "But I'm not sure why."

"Because you love it," Kate declared.

"I just want to be able to decide something again," Betsy said. "For myself, *and* for the baby."

"Don't you have anyone you want to write to?" Kate asked.

"The boy ran away," Betsy said. "Left town, left his ranch. Left me."

"I'm sorry."

"Baby's all I've got."

"I'm sorry," Kate said again.

On Sundays, the girls left the home to attend church, which was only two blocks away, on the town plaza. Nobody was excused unless they were in their eighth month. Wednesday evenings after dinner, they were required to join in a prayer circle, presided over by Mrs. Barker. The first week, she had them read aloud from the Fifty-first Psalm.

Wash me thoroughly from my iniquity,
   and cleanse me from my sin!
For I know my transgressions,
   and my sin is ever before me.
Against thee, thee only, have I sinned,
   and done that which is evil in thy sight,
so that thou art justified in thy sentence
   and blameless in thy judgment.
Behold, I was brought forth in iniquity,
   and in sin did my mother conceive me.

Mrs. Barker made it crystal clear how the text applied to the girls, their past conduct, their future lives. When they all understood that the Bible was talking to them, she ended with a prayer of her own making.

"O Lord," she said. "Dear Father. You are the acknowledged head of this household. Not one of us here needs a man other than you. You are the King. But when these girls have left here and paid for their mistakes, give them a man to care for them. For it's better to marry than to burn. Let there be a man for each one of them, a man with strong arms and a broad back, a man with beautiful eyes, who will take these girls and hold them close to him . . ."

"Ohhh . . ." Margrethe suddenly gripped the table and half stood up.

"A man who will . . ."

"Oh," Margrethe said. "My water's breaking!" She shuddered up, and the back of her dress was wet.

Mrs. Barker was up and had Margrethe by the arm. "All right. Up to the Lying-in Room, and then I'll call the doctor."

The other girls stayed at the table and waited. They heard

Mrs. Barker talking on the phone. Then they heard a long, low moan unfold from upstairs.

Margrethe slept for hours after giving birth. By the time she awoke, the baby had been taken through the iron gates in the doctor's black car. She was confined to bed rest for nine days by Doctor Rolly and treated like a wounded animal.

On the morning after, the girls were allowed to see her. They filed in and stood around the bed, and they didn't really know how to ask what was on their minds: How much did it hurt? How badly frightened were you? Are you glad it's over? Are you looking forward to going home? Do you miss your baby?

She was sitting up in bed, but her face had a puffed, battered look to it, and her eyes were dark and hollow.

Gretchen took her hand. "It's over now. You're safe. I hope it turns out as well for us as it did for you."

Margrethe turned a little smile. "I guess I will be out of here soon."

"Sure you will."

"Be able to go to parties again. And see friends. And see my little sister."

"Sure."

"But I'm just sad," she said. "I don't know why, but I'm so sad."

"Of course you are," Kate said.

"I never even really saw it," Margrethe said. "And now it's gone, and I don't know where."

Betsy said, "You asked Mrs. Barker?"

"She won't say anything. You may as well ask a stone wall. She won't even tell me what its name will be. It's against my father's instructions."

"It was a girl," Gretchen said. "I heard the doctor say."

Margrethe nodded. "I knew that. I was hoping it wouldn't be a girl. Not that I wanted it to be a boy. But sometimes I hoped it wouldn't be a girl."

Margrethe's father arrived at the end of her convalescence. He came dressed in a long black coat, and after he kissed his daughter on the forehead, he went with Mrs. Barker into her private apartments to talk.

As Margrethe was saying good-bye to the girls, Kate handed her a letter. "Mail it for me," she said. "I trust you."

"How will he answer?"

"I told him to pretend he was my sister," Kate said. "But it doesn't matter. If he knows where I am, he'll come."

Margrethe took Kate's hands in hers. "I hope so."

Then the door to the apartment opened, and Margrethe slipped the letter down the front of her dress. Her father gave her his arm and paid no attention to the other girls.

Margrethe's old clothes didn't fit her yet, so she had to travel in one of the home's gray shifts. She and her father walked, black and gray, out to Mrs. Barker's car, and passed through the gates.

After that, Betsy watched Kate each day when Mrs. Barker came back from the post office. When the matron went into her apartment to sort the mail, Kate's face would glow, and her hands grow slow, and her eyes leave her work and go to the door. Betsy knew that every day she was imagining that Mrs. Barker would come to the door and announce: "Kate. A letter from your sister."

Then, when Mrs. Barker handed out the mail and there was nothing, Kate would shrink and crumble.

The following week, Mrs. Barker didn't collect the mail for several days. She said she was too busy. When the matron did go, she came back with a thick sheaf of letters. Kate stopped work completely. Mrs. Barker would go through each letter before she distributed them, and Kate couldn't move her hands while she waited.

Mrs. Barker came to the door; she had letters for Gretchen and Lissa, and a letter from Kate's mother. Then she said, "Betsy, can you come with me for a moment? There's a letter for you."

Surprised, Betsy stood up. She felt Kate's eyes on her back as she went.

Mrs. Barker took a seat behind a large polished desk and motioned Betsy to sit down as well. She picked up an opened envelope and, holding it so that Betsy could not read the return address, tapped it several times with her fingers.

"What's the name of your clergyman, Betsy?" she asked.

"Is that a letter from Reverend Walters?" Betsy asked.

"Reverend Walters." Mrs. Barker verified the name on the envelope, took out the letter, and checked the signature as well. Then she handed the letter to Betsy.

"Please read it here, Betsy."

From the very first words of the letter, Betsy could hear the anguished, confused voice of the reverend, pleading with her to believe that there was some sense in it all, pleading with her to find some good in what was irrevocably beyond his or her control. He was sure that her mother had loved her very much, because she had asked for her, and missed her, and requested that the reverend look after her. He was sure that her mother had loved her, and he knew that Betsy would be sure as well. The reverend thought that her father didn't realize her mother was about to pass away, because she had been ill so often, and for so long. If he had known, he certainly would have sent for her. Now that there was nothing more to be done, her father had decided that she shouldn't come for the funeral. There might be some talk about her absence, but not nearly so much as there would be if she arrived in her condition. The reverend was certain that her father was thinking of what would be best in the long run for his daughter. He hoped and prayed that Betsy would see things in that light as well.

Betsy read the letter twice, and then looked at Mrs. Barker, square-shouldered behind the large, flat, rectangular desk.

"He should have let me come," she said.

"It's all for the best," Mrs. Barker said.

"I don't care about looking like a balloon," Betsy said. "I should have been there with her. He didn't let me decide."

"You have to accept what's past. He did what he thought was best."

"I know why he didn't want me there. Because he killed her. And I'm the only one who knows it."

"No, Betsy. Your mother was ill. Life and death come for us all."

"He never loved her. And he doesn't love me."

"I'm sure your father loves you very much."

"How would you know?" Betsy said.

"If he didn't, he wouldn't have sent you here."

"I hate it here." Betsy stood up and crumpled the letter in her fist.

Mrs. Barker came around the desk toward her. "Betsy, try to understand him. You need him."

"I don't want to. I want my mother." She pushed away Mrs. Barker's blundering arms and ran out of the room.

The girls all grew larger, ate corn and beans and spinach, knitted and sewed and crocheted. Some other girls came in, only four or five months pregnant. Betsy joined Gretchen in filling them in on how things worked, warning them about Doctor Rolly, ridiculing Mrs. Barker's sayings.

Kate stopped glowing when the mail was brought in. She stopped coming by Betsy's room to talk. Betsy heard her, once in a while, steal out of the house after dark; she imagined her going to the back gate, as though somehow her man had discovered her and would miraculously be waiting for her. But the following morning, Kate would be at the worktable with her head down, speaking very little.

Betsy felt her own child leaping and playing inside her. She was happy that the child seemed happy, and she promised that she would love it always, in spite of her father. She wouldn't do as Margrethe had done. She would hold her child and look in its face.

Gretchen was the first to go into labor. She announced to everyone that the child had dropped and it wouldn't be long now. Two weeks later, she gave birth to a girl who left the home unnamed. After nine days of rest, Gretchen departed alone with a grim smile.

Kate had a long and difficult labor. When Betsy visited her afterward in her darkened room, Kate said, "I didn't want to see it. Maybe I could have if I'd wanted to, but I didn't want to."

"Why not?" Betsy asked. "Why not?"

"What if it had looked like him? Then I never could have forgotten."

"Do you think you can forget it now?" Betsy touched herself where her own child still nested.

"I have to. I just have to forget. That's what everybody says now."

Lissa had a baby boy just a few hours after labor started. Then Mrs. Barker received an urgent telegram from Lissa's father. He'd had a change of heart, he didn't want his blood to be out wandering in the world, he wanted to see his grandson.

For the next nine days, while Lissa rested in bed, the girls had a little baby to play with. They washed him and changed him and held him and sang to him. Betsy sometimes brought him upstairs to where Lissa lay, and watched her give him her breast.

"I'm going to name him after my father," she said.

Betsy looked at the tiny child gazing into Lissa's eyes.

"And I've got such good milk, especially since it's my first baby. That's what the doctor said."

The baby had Lissa's nipple in his mouth, its small hand brushed against the bluish skin.

"Isn't his hair pretty?" she continued. "So fine and blond?"

"Very pretty," Betsy said.

"I just love stroking it," Lissa said.

Betsy painted a smile on her face and left. She told herself it was foolish to be jealous, none of them really wanted to be there. Someday she would be able to love and pet her child too.

Kate and Lissa both left the home, one light and smiling, the other dark and bent. Betsy was the oldest girl remaining, not in age but in months of pregnancy. The other girls watched her, wondered if they could possibly grow that big, wondered how she would do and whether they would do as well. No matter how easy a delivery, no matter how brief the pain, each one hoped that her own would be easier, shorter, less painful.

Betsy was sitting quietly under the elm trees, musing over who had planted the trees, what dreams the people had held for these trees and this house, where they were now, when the first sharp contraction hit. She shuddered, but she shook it off; she had been feeling similar pains on and off for a week or more. When a second one spiked her in the same place some minutes later, she walked inside with chains on her feet. The other girls stared at her. They knew instantly what was happening, and the youngest girl broke into tears when she saw Betsy's face.

"Tell Mrs. Barker," Betsy said. Two girls sprang up to help her up the stairs.

When Doctor Rolly came into the Lying-in Room, Betsy was lying on the bed wearing a pair of white leggings and a sterilized nightgown, with one towel under her and another spread across her abdomen. The doctor was dressed in white with long gauntlet gloves and a surgical cap, and a nurse came in with him, dressed identically. They both raised their masks when they approached her. "So," Doctor Rolly said, "are we ready at last? Let's have that baby!"

With his back to Betsy, he drew back her nightgown and began to probe with his hands on either side of her belly. Then he moved his hands further down and felt around her pelvis. "There's the head all right. Just perfect."

Betsy felt a shock swing through her body, and she clawed at the doctor's sleeve.

"Ho ho ho," the doctor said. "Not as much fun coming out as going in. Ha ha."

Betsy rocked with pain and bit her lips to bloody shreds. She heard the nurse counting out minutes, heard the doctor talking about presentation, heartbeat rates. Then she screamed and spit and twisted the sheets in her hands until it had passed.

She had no idea how long it went on. But when she heard the nurse mention chloroform, she tried to raise up.

"Don't want it." Her tongue felt dry as a cotton rag in her mouth. "Don't."

Then she saw the turtle eyes of Mrs. Barker, also peering between surgical cap and mask. Mrs. Barker was holding Betsy's left leg up and back. The nurse was holding her right leg.

Betsy screamed until all the blood vessels in her eyes seemed to burst, and she saw everything through a red haze.

"Thatsagirl," Doctor Rolly said. "A little harder now."

Then they were talking about swabbing the eyes and clearing out the mouth, and the posterior shoulder.

"Bear down," the doctor said. "Just a little bit more."

She felt the pain swing once more through her body like an enormous pendulum, rip through her and out into the world.

Then she heard it.

She tore through the sheets and towels that seemed to block her off, tore through the red haze and darkness where she heard it calling for her.

"A boy," the doctor said.

Betsy groped forward.

"Let her." It was Mrs. Barker, with a sound like sympathy. "Just let her."

She clutched him in her arms and looked down at him with her bruised face. He looked flushed and red against the white clothes, the white ceiling, and he seemed to turn his tiny wrinkled head away from the bright lights.

"Look at me," Betsy said.

The baby had a fine covering of blond hair, fat hands with five fingers on each, two legs, two feet, ten toes. Between its legs, a tiny penis, smaller than the smallest finger on her hand, limp and moist and rosy.

She looked at his face again. "Look at me," she pleaded.

Then her child opened his eyes, and gazed at her across a long blue distance.

"Blue eyes."

The nurse took the baby back with her long gloved hands.

"You need to rest," she said.

"Blue," Betsy said. "Blue."

They took the baby out of the room, lowered the lights, and closed the door.

· · · · · · ·

"I can't tell you where your baby has been placed," Mrs. Barker said. "It's forbidden."

Betsy had lain in bed three of the prescribed nine days, and milk was shooting into her. The front of her gown was damp, and her breasts felt like two hot weights on her chest. The other girls had told her that her child was already gone, had in fact been taken away soon after birth. But now, with her milk coming in, she had to ask.

"Can't tell you." The matron's face was a closed door.

"Is he all right?"

"He's healthy. But I can't tell you where he is. I'd like to, but I can't."

"One more thing," Betsy said.

"Yes?"

"I want to choose the baby's name."

Mrs. Barker smiled. "Of course. What would you like to name him?"

Not Harold, not Ernest. Not the name of any man she knew. A name of her own choosing. A name that would attach him to her forever. A rock on which to fix her love for the child.

"Peter," she said. "Name him Peter."

14

A View from the Tower   February 1933

Peter was sent as a baby to a woman who was a second cousin to old Ernest Moreberg. Her husband never quite settled into one line of work, and Peter remembered moving frequently as a child. The man would sometimes be gone for several days, then reappear at the dinner table and look at Peter through watery red eyes.

"How's the breadwinner?" he'd ask Peter. "How's the bread-winner?"

"Don't you touch him," the woman warned. "The check from my cousin is all we've got this month."

"You think I'm going to kill the golden goose?" He glared at his wife. Then he turned back to Peter, rubbing the stubble on his weak chin.

"You okay?" he asked.

"Sure," Peter said.

"Bet you are, with somebody sending you money every month." He stretched out his hand to pat him, but Peter stood up and didn't let the hand near him.

The family had a daughter some years younger than Peter, and when she reached school age, the man finally found steady work as a night watchman at the Signal Hill oil field. They moved into one of the few houses in the field left standing after the oil boom, a tidy three-bedroom bungalow that had once had a low picket fence and two orange trees in the front yard. The house was now surrounded by tall, thin derricks poking into the sky out of sheds with corrugated metal roofs, and pumps that looked like giant ants, rhythmically bowing their heads to suck. The earth seemed to constantly reverberate with a low, dull thrum, and the orange trees lost their leaves early and produced inedible fruit.

The man left late every evening with a lantern in his hand and a time clock bumping against his hip. He slept during the days, and the woman sent Peter outside to play in the oil fields. She didn't want him indoors making noise and keeping her husband awake. He ran around with other boys, and played catch, and kick-the-can, and tag along the edges of the large rectangular sumps filled with thick, gooey crude.

Peter told the boys he played with that he was different from them, that his mother lived in a much better place than Signal Hill, and that someday he would live there too. They didn't believe him, so he tried to prove that he could do things they didn't dare. He stood with his body inches from the pistons that pounded up and down on the derrick platforms, and he was the only one who grasped and rode with feet swinging back and forth the long stainless-steel arms that pumped horizontally.

One afternoon near sunset, he stood with Bobby Ewers and Jimmy Smith on a rig floor and looked at the wooden derrick narrowing up to the sky.

"I bet I can climb to the top," he said. "I bet you can see the ocean from there."

"No, you can't. It's too high," Bobby said.

"I bet I can," Peter said.

"My father would whip me if I even tried to climb a derrick," Jimmy said. "He doesn't even want me to play near the sumps."

"Nobody ever whips me, no matter what I do," Peter said proudly.

"Still, it's too high," Bobby reasoned. "And you might not be able to see the ocean, anyway."

"If I say I can do it, I can do it."

"Well, let's see you, then," Bobby said.

"I don't think you should. It's dangerous," Jimmy put in.

"Ha," Peter said. It was clear to him now that he had to climb to the top. Anything else would mean backing down. He looked up. The derrick grew smaller as it rose skyward, until it dwindled to a tiny point high in the air. A series of one-by-six crisscrossed braces climbed up the derrick. There was a ladder, but he could see that toward the top several rungs were missing.

Peter grasped one of the braces and shook it. It was splintery and oil-soaked, and the nails holding it together were rusted.

"I don't think you should," Jimmy repeated.

Peter's hand was streaked with black. He wiped it quickly on Jimmy's shirt. Jimmy jumped back and nearly fell off the rig floor.

"Why'd you do that? Now my father's sure to whip me." Jimmy clutched at his shirt to see the dark stain and looked with hurt eyes at Peter.

"Just because you were so scared of it," Peter said.

"Bastard," Bobby said. "That's what my brother told me. You're a bastard."

"I don't care what you think." Peter turned his back on them and climbed the first ten feet of the tower. He turned and looked down at them triumphantly.

"I'm higher than you are," he shouted.

"I hope you fall," Jimmy said. "I hope you fall and break your neck."

"Just watch me," Peter said.

He began to climb again. The rungs of the ladder were slick and stained, and he had to concentrate with each step to make sure he didn't slip. He felt his jeans and shirt rub against the wood as he pressed close against the ladder, and he knew he would be far filthier than Jimmy was; this seemed to justify smearing oil on Jimmy's shirt.

When he reached the fourth set of braces, he hooked one arm around the side of the ladder and looked down.

The landscape below him whirled. The silver pistons of the pump spun around the tin roof of the shed, and the barren earth around the derrick lost all definition, became a blur of tawny weed and rock. The rectangular sump hole was suddenly a circle, a bottomless pit, a black whirlpool sucking him down.

He held on tighter and squinted. Two white blotches on the rig floor bounced around like pinballs, and a pair of thin voices rose up to him.

"Go higher," one voice said.

"Fall down," the other voice said.

The derrick began to flex, and a breeze grabbed at his shirt.

"Break your neck," he heard Jimmy cry.

He closed his eyes and clutched the ladder.

A roughneck had told him once that you should only look at the horizon, never look down, if you wanted to keep your balance. Just look straight out, and you always get over being scared. Peter waited until the derrick stopped swaying, then he opened his eyes and looked out.

To the east, he saw a forest of derricks, all at the same altitude as he was, all perfectly steady. Each of the derricks rose from a shed with a tin roof, and each sat over a sump of oil, which rested calmly within an earthen dam. The pumps raised and lowered their insectlike heads with monotonous and comforting regularity.

Peter breathed in and out deeply and steadily, and decided not to try looking down again.

He mounted the ladder with care, never thinking of anything except the next slippery rung. The derrick was much higher than it had seemed from below; the ladder went on forever. His arms grew tired, and he stopped once to rest, leaning in against the slight slant.

He couldn't quit before he'd seen the ocean. He had to be able to tell Jimmy and Bobby that he'd seen the beach, seen the long lines of waves cresting and breaking and running white-frothed up the sand, and girls in bathing suits with their shoulders and legs bare and white and soft. Peter only got to the ocean once or twice a year, and then he had to leave early because he was stuck with this family he wasn't part of, and the father always wanted to "beat the rush."

This time, when he reached the top of the derrick, he'd just be able to gaze at the ocean until he decided he was ready to leave. Nobody could tell him what to do up there.

Peter stopped when he came to the missing rungs. He didn't know how far from the ground he was, and he couldn't look down to see. But the platform at the top of the rig was only a dozen feet above him. The other boys were sure to laugh if they saw him turn back so close from the top.

One of the cross braces ran behind the gap left by the fallen rungs. Peter climbed up two steps until he could grab the first rung above the gap. Then he slid a foot out onto the diagonal brace, not looking at all the empty space below him, and slowly put his weight onto it.

His foot slipped on the oily wood, and he hung from the rung by his hands. He caught his weight on his other foot, lowered himself, and hugged the ladder. His heart ran like a train. He waited, cheek against the rig, and felt the wooden joints creak under him.

He reached up again, palms sweaty, and slid out his foot. This time, his foot held. He pushed himself slowly upward, carefully changed his grip to the next rung up, found a spot on the brace for his other foot, pushed up again, and suddenly he was on the last rung of the ladder, up on top of the platform, standing upright, walking around.

He yelled to let everybody know that he was here, on top of the derrick, higher than everybody, and he'd climbed here by himself, without asking permission, without anybody's help.

To the east, he saw the platforms on top of other derricks, all empty of people. He alone was so high, striding along the planks, grasping the wooden railing. He wasn't dizzy at all now, wasn't afraid of anything. But when he looked to the west, toward the setting sun, he couldn't see the ocean. The air was thick with oil fumes, thick with smoke from the boilers running the drills and pumps. Over the hills, he saw only a dirty yellow band of sky, a smudge of oil field air, glowing backlit from the sun, like a curtain dropped between his out-look and the sea.

Peter frowned and waited, but the lowering sun only made the air more opaque, more difficult to see through.

He looked to the north. Once toward San Natoma, toward that better place where he was going to live one day, when his real mother would call him to her side.

He couldn't see anything but dry hills and fields, and more derricks.

The climb down was much easier than the climb up. He was able to lower himself past the missing rungs, sliding his feet along the cross brace. The oil-dark wood took on a reddish hue from the sunset as he descended, still concentrating on each step, still remembering the roughneck's words, not looking down.

Jimmy and Bobby were gone when he reached the rig floor, and he realized with some bitterness that they might not even have stayed to see if he reached the top or not. They hadn't even cared. The only sign that they had been there was a large word, traced out in oil over the planks of the platform.

BASTARD. But if they didn't care about him, he didn't care about them.

Peter wasn't punished for coming home with oil stains on his clothes and a tear in the knee of his pants. The mother just complained to the air about how difficult he was to keep clean and how expensive he was to keep clothed. The father stayed asleep. Peter felt somehow disappointed as he went off to take a bath. He thought that climbing a derrick and smearing Jimmy's shirt with oil were worth more than the same old complaints. He wanted someone to notice what he did, even if it meant they tried to stop him.

The next day at school, Bobby and Jimmy avoided meeting his eyes during class. He cornered them at recess and told them he had climbed to the top and seen the ocean, the waves breaking and women in bathing suits. They hung back from him, silent and mistrustful—so he added that he could see for a hundred hundred miles from the top of the derrick, and had even seen the town where his mother lived.

They didn't believe him, but they were afraid to accuse him of lying. When they remained silent, exchanging glances, Peter asked Jimmy if his father had whipped him.

"No," Jimmy said quietly. "But he said I shouldn't play with you anymore."

"Why not?" Peter demanded.

"Because it's too dangerous."

"My father said the same thing," Bobby said.

"And you believe that? Because of something your dumb old fathers said?"

"My father's smart," Jimmy said.

"No, he's not. He's dumb."

"He's smart. He's smarter than you."

"He's dumb. Dumb, dumb, dumb. A dumbbell."

Jimmy grabbed Peter by the shoulders and began pushing him. Peter pushed back, turned Jimmy around and butted him up against a chain-link fence before letting him go.

"Dumb," Peter said.

"At least I've got a father," Jimmy said.

"Better not to if they're dumb," Peter said. "Go ahead and listen to your dumb old fathers. I don't care."

Peter walked away and left Jimmy and Bobby together. He went to a corner of the schoolyard and stood there looking at the fence post, at his shoes, at anything but the groups of children behind him running around, playing, screaming, laughing.

They were all afraid of things he wasn't afraid of, but it didn't seem to matter.

He wiped his face on his sleeve when the bell sounded.

. . . .

In the spring, two extra photographs of his mother were sent to Peter. He usually received a photo only at Christmas, so he knew that something special had happened.

The first photo showed his mother dressed in black standing next to a coffin, and he was told that his grandfather had passed on to a better life. The second one showed his mother in a pale shade of blue, standing next to a man. She had married.

The second photograph had caused the woman to remark

that at least she wasn't trying to fool anybody, not wearing white, but that spelled the end of this gravy train.

"What do you mean?" the man asked.

"Don't you see she's admitting it all! And she's married a boob who's putting up with it, otherwise she'd be wearing white. She'll call Peter up there as soon as it's decent, and there goes our money every month out the window."

"At least I've got some work now. It's not like twenty-nine, when that's all we had."

"Work! You expect us to live on that?"

Peter looked at the photograph while they argued. He didn't say how much he hoped it was true, how much he wanted his mother to call him to live in San Natoma, or any-place besides Signal Hill with this family that wasn't his own. If she loved him, he thought, she would have called him long ago.

15

The Valley of Heart's Delight   February 1933

Steen Denisen came to the Valley to build.

As a child, he drew pictures of a city, on large scraps of boxes and brown wrapping paper on the floor of his parents' house. He drew glowing little houses spreading this way and that along the arms of a tall mountain, tree-lined streets branching toward a lake blue like the color of his mother's eyes. He populated the streets with green horses, and sun-colored dogs, and men with two heads looking the same direction, and furry purple bears rolling in alleys. Sometimes in his drawings, women in long dresses pointed to the largest house of all, at the head of the mountain, a house with an iron gate and an oak door ten feet high, the only two-story house in the city. That's where he would live.

He sketched floor plans of the houses he would build, with kitchens and dining rooms and servants' quarters and very large playrooms. He made maps of his city, with crooked streets of shops like the streets in his own little town of Sønderborg, and broad avenues like he had seen once in Odense. The largest, most important street was named Steen Avenue. When he drew himself, with a shard of coal from the stove, he was twice as tall as the horses. And he imagined the funny dogs and bears and people who lived in the houses below him would notice him and say, "There's Steen Denisen. The builder of our city!"

When he showed these pictures and plans to grown-ups, they smiled and nodded their heads, but he could tell that none of them really believed in his houses or his city. His father liked to tell friends, "He'll be a good carpenter someday. When he learns to draw a straight line. When he can build a box!"

Once, a man with a beard and steel glasses looked at his drawings and said, "Ah. You'll never build a city like that in Denmark. The only place you'll ever find to build your city is in America."

"Do they have green horses in America?" his father laughed. "Purple bears?"

Steen didn't think the bearded man took him seriously. But he remembered the remark, guarded it for himself, and pondered it.

At sixteen, Steen was an apprentice carpenter. At twenty, he was a framer, constructing the skeletons of houses that other men then finished. And at twenty-seven, having saved his money for years, he emigrated to America, to the golden state of California, the glorious Garden Without Walls of the Santa Clara Valley.

He came to build. He arrived in the spring of 1929.

. . . .

Three years later, Steen was living in the same boarding-house he'd found when he first arrived, still working as a framer. The address of a second cousin working at a cannery had led him to the Danish Lodge in San Jose, and there he found a job with Old Man Moreberg, a contractor who lived in San Natoma. He was glad to have work when so many were walking the streets, but wages were low in the thirties, and Dane or no Dane, Ernest Moreberg wasn't going to pay a worker a nickel more than he had to. So, in 1932, Steen was still living from paycheck to paycheck, still far from his dreams of building a city.

Ernest Moreberg always built the same house, with the same front porch steps, same bay window, same fireplace, same dining room. It rankled Steen to see building sites simply leveled for the same unimaginative building. But he was careful to keep his thoughts to himself. He had heard the old man brag about how he didn't have to pay anybody to scratch lines on paper to build a house.

Steen first saw Betsy out on site. He looked through the vacant frame of the house they were putting up and saw a shiny black car pull up to the curb. The boss put down his hammer and walked to the car.

"Who's that?" Steen asked. The boss was leaning into the car window. "The boss's wife?"

"Wife's dead," Casten said. "That's his daughter."

"Didn't know he had a daughter."

"Something of a cold fish, you understand. Pushing thirty and not married. But maybe it's just her old man keeps her under wraps."

"Maybe." Steen tried to see past old Ernest into the car. He couldn't get a good look at the daughter, but he saw her hand over a lunch pail. "Seems like she knows how to treat a fellow, though."

"She takes care of the boss, all right. And she'll come into a good bit one of these days."

"That so?" Steen watched Ernest straighten up from the car, and he just glimpsed a pale hand and a lock of hair.

"Old Man Moreberg, you know. Tight as a tick."

Steen got himself invited to Ernest's place by talking cards with his partner Anders during lunch within the boss's hearing. He described how he had managed to peg eight and win a game of cribbage even though the other counted first, and he said, "What if we get a few sporting men together on Friday at the boardinghouse for some poker?"

"No need for that," Ernest chipped in. "Come around my place. I've got a little game on with some fellows."

"This Friday?" Steen already knew that a game was on. "Good enough. But don't think you're inviting an easy mark now."

When he walked up the broad steps of the Moreberg house and knocked on the door, the woman who answered barely looked at him. But he recognized her as the daughter in the car, from the sweeping line that her hair pressed against her face.

"My father's in the card room," she said.

"Are you Betsy?" he asked.

"Betsy Moreberg," she said, lifting her head.

"I'm Steen. Steen Denisen." He offered his hand, and she took it for just a moment. He was surprised by the sudden warmth of her skin.

She led him through the hall to the back of the house. Steen noted the oak cabinets built into the walls, and a large Morris chair in the front parlor with an ash stand beside it. But mostly he studied the way the back of Betsy's neck showed when her braid slipped aside.

The card room was old Ernest's one architectural extravagance. He had added on a hexagonal room at the back of the house, then built a hexagonal card table out of redwood inside the room. The table, shaped out of thick planks, with legs four inches square, filled the room and could never be taken from it without being dismantled. It was designed so that there was enough space around its perimeter for one bentwood chair and one card player per side, but there was no room to walk around the player once he was seated. The players had to file into the room in the same order in which they would sit. All this ensured, however, that there would be nobody but card players in the room. There was no place for kibitzers, the kind of person who would look over a man's shoulder and say, "Why didn't you play that card?" or "What are you bidding on?" or "Why did you discard those?"

Steen smiled at the joiner work around the doorway and the precise way the card room was laid out. He recognized the hand.

"So," he said. "You live in an Ernest Moreberg–built house yourself."

"Best houses in the Valley," Ernest said. "Take a seat. My daughter will bring you something to drink."

The players at the table were older men, most of whom he had met at the lodge one time or another. When they found he was from the Schleswig region, that land that had changed hands in so many wars, they asked if he spoke German.

"No," he said. "My father wouldn't allow it in the house."

"There's a good Dane," they said.

Steen played poker well. He kept a straight, sober face during the rounds of betting and sometimes bluffed successfully. But he also took part in the banter between hands, smoked the same small black cigars as the other men, and enjoyed the beer served in heavy round glasses. At the end of the evening, Ernest slapped him on the shoulder and invited him back the following week. After that, he became a fairly regular visitor at the boss's house.

But Steen noticed that the daughter's attitude didn't change at all as he began to frequent the house. She greeted him at the door and then vanished from sight. When he tried to talk to her, his words hit a blank wall.

"Good evening, Betsy."

"Good evening."

"How have you been?"

"Nothing much changes around here."

"The same as ever, then?"

"Same as ever."

And he had to watch her bare neck winking at him while she led him to the card room.

Old Moreberg seemed to grow friendlier to him, and Steen had thought that the way to the daughter's affections was through the father. When he looked at himself—young, Danish, ambitious, carpenter—he couldn't think of anyone else who might be better suited to be Betsy's husband. And he was sure her father would agree. But that didn't seem to matter in the case of this Betsy.

. . . . . .

Women weren't allowed to take a place in the card room on a poker night. Betsy sometimes played cards when the game was cribbage, or whist, or auction. Never poker. Those evenings, she spent in the kitchen with whichever wives were brought by the cardplayers. From there, she still tended the men in the room, filled their glasses with beer or brought them thick white mugs of steaming coffee.

Marilyn Jackson was sitting with Betsy when a voice rose up over the rest, claiming a pot. "There's the man you have to catch," Marilyn said.

"Who's that?" Betsy asked.

"That Steen. That's the one you have to catch. There's a man who's on the ball."

"I'm not interested in catching any man, any way," Betsy said. "And sure not another tobacco-smoking Dane."

"You say that now," Marilyn said. "But you'll see."

Marilyn was married to the town's war hero, Howard Jackson. She had been a loud, bright woman who sneaked out back with the boys at dances and drank out of their flasks and smoked their cigarettes. But as soon as she caught Jax, she began to worry about getting ahead in life, and she tried to talk to her husband about setting goals. Jax didn't listen to her. He still held down the same job at Ida Valley, and Marilyn had to work at Carnegie's Library just to make ends meet. Now she was expert about how marriage was supposed to be, and she organized the Armistice Day celebration, the one day of the year when she was proud of her husband.

"Just take a look at Steen," Marilyn said. "He's a man who's going somewhere. Not like my Howard."

The next time Betsy brought food and drink to the card room, she looked quickly at the men around the table. Her father's eyes were black and pointed as he watched the faces of the other players. Howard Jackson was beginning to sag over his cards, as though he had given up on luck. Steen sat to her father's right, his chest full and his chips high, sure that he could smoke more and spit further than any man in the room.

He noticed her, and he brightened under her eyes, then made a joke to hide his pleasure.

Betsy stopped at the doorway to the kitchen, her hands full of cups and dirty glasses, and dropped her head. She wondered whether somebody was answering the needs of her son, Peter, while she was answering the needs of those six men in the hexagonal room.

Marilyn noticed her trouble and stood up. "What's wrong?" she asked.

"I think he likes me," Betsy said.

. . . .

Betsy walked Steen to the door at the end of the evening, and as he was stepping out, she deftly slipped through the door with him. He found himself alone with her on the dark porch. She looked at him directly, standing erect with her head up. Steen was not sure what to do.

"So," he said.

"What do you think of my father?" Betsy asked.

It was some kind of test. Steen thought quickly about what the right reply might be. His friendship with old Ernest had certainly done him no good. He needed to be approved by the old man, but that wouldn't be enough. So he needed to find some reply that would satisfy whatever the woman wanted, without seeming two-faced.

What did she want to hear? She still had her eyes fixed on him, waiting.

"He's a fair enough boss," Steen said cautiously. "But he's a stiff-necked old cuss. Dead set in his ways."

Steen held his breath. Then he saw Betsy nod slowly, as though she approved.

The front door opened suddenly, and the pair was caught in a flood of light from the hall. Betsy immediately lowered her eyes, and Steen turned embarrassed toward the door.

"Steen." Marilyn Jackson smiled broadly at him. "I'm delighted to find you here. Will you help me walk Howard home?"

Jax stood next to Marilyn, but he seemed to be asleep. Unconsciously he rested one of his big hands on his wife's shoulder, while his head lolled to the right. When Steen took one of his arms, he woke up for a moment.

"What the hell is going on now?"

"Easy there, Jax. We're going to get you home safe and sound."

The big man looked wearily down at Steen, then at Marilyn. He sighed and shrugged his shoulders, and his head drooped slowly forward.

"Thank you, Steen. It won't take long." Marilyn looked knowingly at Betsy as they were leaving, and smiled broadly at her as well. "Good-bye, Betsy. I'll see you again soon."

Betsy nodded and quickly shut the door behind her. Steen and Marilyn walked on either side of Jax, brought him down from the porch one step at a time, and guided him out to the street. When they neared Jax and Marilyn's house, Marilyn peered around her husband's bulk at Steen.

"You just have to be patient with Betsy," she said. "She has to get used to the idea of you." Then she added with a sigh, "She should be grateful she doesn't have to get used to someone like my Howard."

Jax started up again at his name. "Where the devil are we now?"

"Almost home now. Almost home, dear."

. . . .

On Sunday, Betsy squatted beside the rabbit pen out back and coaxed a doe toward her.

"Come on, sweetie," she said. "Hop this way, snookums."

The rabbit looked at her dumbly, and its pink nose quivered. Betsy reached in, grasped it by its ears, and dragged it shuffling toward her.

"There you go," she said in a calming voice once she had it in her hands. She took it over to a flat rock and petted it several times with her left hand. Then she held it down firmly by the spine, took up a thick stick with her right hand, and smashed it on the skull. It still jerked after being hit, so she gave it several more blows until it stopped moving.

She hung the rabbit by slipping its hind legs through two small nooses she left tied, then she took out the skinning knife. The rabbit had been pretty with its soft fur and liquid eyes, but at five months it had to be butchered. Any older, and it was good only for the stew pot. She made two quick cuts around the heels, a third one between the thighs, and a fourth to free the tail. Then she pulled straight down, and the fur peeled off like the casing of a salami and left the rabbit flesh naked and glistening, except for the fuzzy tail still attached.

She stretched the fur over a piece of spring steel that held it taut and open to dry, then took the rabbit down to gut it. The fur would be sold, for a small sum of household money, and the rabbit she would serve hot to her father with carrots and onions for Sunday dinner. She killed a rabbit every Sunday for her father.

She washed the blood off her hands at the outside faucet and went inside to change her clothes. Old Ernest was sitting in the Morris chair, shaking his head and mumbling to himself as she went by.

"Did you say something, Papa?" Betsy asked.

"I'm sending a check off to those people in Southern California," Ernest said. "And I don't see how we can afford it, the way this household lets money slip through its fingers like water."

"Didn't I just use the flour sacks to make new dish towels?" Betsy asked. "Don't I keep rabbits and make clothes, and cook and clean for you? I'm saving you money every month."

"Could have been doing all that, without me supporting somebody who shouldn't be here in the first place." Ernest turned his whole body in the chair to look at her. "And you're not over-grateful for it."

Betsy didn't reply because she wanted him to go ahead and send the check for Peter, and not delay and grumble about it for days, like he did sometimes. He seemed to think that he could keep her under his thumb as long as he was the one supporting Peter. It was best not to say too much around the first of the month, or he could turn unbearable.

"Now if you brought someone into the family who was going to contribute something . . ." her father said.

"What do you mean, Papa?"

"A man like that Steen, now. He knows houses."

Betsy began to shuck her butchering apron. "Don't I have enough on my hands taking care of you? What do I want another man for?"

"I was just thinking," he said.

"You're enough trouble all by yourself," she said. But as she turned her back on him, she saw before her Steen and herself standing side by side. They held hands, and she was happy. At her other side, gazing up at her in perfect devotion, was her blue-eyed son.

. . . .

Several months later, Steen met Marilyn coming out of the library on Oak Street, and she immediately took him by the arm.

"Poor Steen. She's certainly making you wait, isn't she?"

"I'm not sure what you mean, Marilyn."

"Ohhh." Marilyn shook her head and gazed at him. "It's that bad, is it?"

"What's that bad?"

"It isn't her, really. It's old Ernest. She thinks she has to care for him for the rest of his days. She's decided to mar-tyr herself, poor girl, because she was away when her mother fell ill, and she couldn't nurse her. Betsy's blamed herself ever since. But that doesn't mean she doesn't care for you, dear Steen."

"You mean to say . . ."

"I'll put in a word for you, never fear. I can see how upset you are, and I'll tell her so. But don't worry. Whenever she decides that she can't give up her life to her father, you're the one."

"Ernest . . ."

"Ernest is a selfish so-and-so, and don't bother trying to defend him. I'll see what I can do about this other matter, you leave it to me."

She pinched his arm.

"You're the one, Steen."

"Good-bye, Marilyn." He watched her walk away and wondered what exactly he had said, and what she would say he had said.

Steen continued to go to the old man's card games, but Betsy didn't seem to approve of it. If he laughed too loud, or seemed too happy, he felt her frown hovering behind him. There were no more shared, hurried moments on the porch, and she led him back to the card room, back to the room full of men, without a sign that he was especially in her thoughts.

He found that their names had become linked in common talk. For this he blamed Marilyn. Betsy, he knew, must have heard the same talk, and this might be why she had gotten so standoffish. Still, he didn't want to put an end to the talk by putting an end to his visits. He enjoyed having his name paired up with hers. It seemed that if everyone agreed that their marriage was a right and suitable thing, she would have to agree sooner or later.

Steen waited. He worked framing houses, learning everything about what went into a Moreberg-built house, he played cards on the weekends, he lived in his boarding-house in San Jose, and he waited. He was patient. Yet he felt, when he reached the age of thirty, that his opportunities were slipping away from him. He felt himself becoming less eligible, less marriageable, doomed to wait for a match that seemed perfect and yet was out of reach for the present and uncertain in the future.

Perhaps Marilyn was right. Perhaps Betsy would stay devoted to her father and wouldn't think about him or anybody else until he was gone. But what would that mean to him, Steen Denisen, the builder? His future, his plans and ambitions depended on the health of an old man, who, despite his age, still came out on the work site five days a week. Steen began to observe old Ernest with a sickly keen concentration, waiting for the first sign of weakness, the first sign that the old timber was brittle and would soon crumble and fall and make way for the young to push upward.

. . . .

Betsy put the large blue percolator on the gas, then put on a cast-iron pot to boil water for porridge. She knocked on her father's bedroom door once and returned to the kitchen. A pinch of salt for the pot, then she stirred in the rolled oats and cracked wheat that her father enjoyed.

When the coffee was up, she knocked on the bedroom

door again. Old Ernest was usually dressed by the time the coffee was brewed, but sometimes he needed a second knock. Betsy poured herself a mug, topped it with some cream, and stirred the porridge again so that it wouldn't stick to the bottom of the pot. Then she turned off the gas and sat down, and she waited for the sun to reach over the peak of the neighbor's house.

When the sun broke full through the kitchen window, Betsy looked at the wall clock and started up. She walked to the bedroom door and knocked once more. Then she opened the door.

The room smelled green and sick. She heard old Ernest breathing like a furnace in the shadows. There was a long pause between breaths, as though the body was deciding at each moment whether it would continue. Betsy stepped to the bedside and brushed the hair back from her father's forehead.

He opened his eyes. "I'm awake," he said. "I'm awake." He waved his arms and legs as though he were swimming and tangled himself up in the sheets. He tried to get up, but somehow he thrashed around in the same place and then lay back in bed, exhausted.

"Where do you hurt, Papa?"

"Inside. On the inside of my arms."

"You stay in bed." Betsy rushed from the room and called the doctor, then went back to her father's side. He was lying back, and his skin looked purplish against the white sheets.

"Betsy," he said. "You call Steen and ask him to come over. I'll tell him what needs doing today."

"All right," Betsy said.

He dug his elbows down once more, but he couldn't sit up. Betsy put her hand on his shoulder. "Just tell me what you want," she said.

"You'll have to clean me," he said.

"All right."

"I think I've soiled myself. I'd clean myself, but I don't think I can."

"I'll do it."

She brought some sponges and towels and a bucket of

warm water from the bathroom. "Now roll over," she said.

"It's not right," Ernest said. "Damn it, it's not right to have to do this."

"Just roll over, Papa. I'll take care of you." Betsy realized that she would have to nurse her father now. She would feed him and wash him and change his clothes for him. And she realized that everything she should have been able to give to her son had gone to her father. The years had gone by, and her son was growing up far from her side, and now her father would be the baby, still demanding all her care and attention.

. . . .

"I know one man here not sorry the old man's sick abed."

The men looked up from their lunch pails. It was Pedersen, a carpenter in his sixties, speaking in Danish.

Steen raised his head and shoulders and looked Pedersen in the face.

"What's that you say?" he answered in English.

"I say I know one man's not sorry. Not sorry to be put in charge, not sorry to be given the rein over men older than him, who were swinging a hammer before he was born."

Steen put down his lunch box with great deliberation and stood up. He'd been giving directions for a week now, since the old man's heart attack, and the men seemed to have taken it all right. But now here was Pedersen, a man more of Ernest's generation than of his own, who wanted to bring things out in the open.

"You'd better say what you mean." Steen switched to Danish, the language native to most of the men. "You'd better say what you mean, and stop talking roundabout. Talk like a man."

"Yes, I'll talk like a man." Pedersen stood up as well, while the rest of the men watched in silence, not ready to support one side or the other. "I'll say that it isn't right because you've been playing poker over at the house and managed to please a young woman's eye that you're to be given charge over us."

"You might be careful of what you say touching on the boss's daughter," Steen said deliberately. "He's mighty fond of her, and he might not like to hear she's being talked of lightly."

Anders chipped in, "There's not a better daughter in the world than Betsy Moreberg."

All the men on the crew nodded in agreement, and Steen smiled.

"Why, if I thought you were saying something against Betsy, I think I'd make you eat your words, old though you be."

Pedersen sat down unhappily. "I didn't mean to say anything against Betsy," he said.

"Still a carpenter for wages after thirty years in this country, you have no place to talk. You think Ernest Moreberg should have put you in charge?"

"I didn't say that," Pedersen said.

"Before you go complaining about who is given charge over who, why don't you look at whatever face you see when you shave in the morning?" Steen turned to the crew and spoke. "Would anyone rather be working for Pedersen here?"

Nobody spoke, and Steen turned back to Pedersen.

"Would you rather be working under someone other than me?"

Pedersen looked at him, resentful and silent.

"Anything else you want to say about Betsy?"

"I never meant anything about Betsy."

"And it's good you didn't. Jobs aren't so easy to come by these days."

Steen went to the house once or twice a week after that and told Ernest what progress had been made. He found the old man silent and pensive, wrapped in blankets sitting in the Morris chair, answering mostly by nods. One evening, Betsy told him that her father didn't feel well enough to sit up and see anyone. Steen didn't really need to see the old man to ask for directions; he was confident he was doing what was necessary to keep the work moving ahead. So he just asked her to send his respects, and he left.

Betsy was still very reserved around him. But Steen himself didn't think it would be very proper for her to think about other things while her father was ill. And he could wait. The fact that he'd been put in charge was sign enough for him. He could wait out an old man's death when his own prospects promised to be so bright in the aftermath.

. . . .

Old Ernest wheezed in and out of consciousness. When he was awake, Betsy offered him broth and waited for him to say something. But he fell back into a place from which he could not speak, and she left the room again.

She didn't want to be the first one to talk about it all.

She wanted him to say something that would let her bring this time of her life to a close.

She wanted him to ask her for forgiveness. But he only looked at her from a fierce distance and said nothing.

There were other women in the house. Marilyn Jackson, Florence Hogg, Sarah Gordon. They were in the kitchen and in the sickroom, changing towels, bringing water, cooking, making coffee. While Betsy wandered about the house in a long dress, turning down food, looking in on her father, then going to the parlor and sitting beside the empty chair.

Steen came by once, sent his respects through Marilyn. Betsy didn't want to see him. She couldn't think about him yet. The doctor visited in the morning, said he would be back in the afternoon.

"Betsy," Florence called. "He's awake again."

Betsy nodded. Florence stopped her on the way in and squeezed her hand.

"Poor dear," she said. "With no family at all to help you through."

Marilyn stood up from the side of the bed when Betsy came in.

"Can we be alone?" Betsy asked. She felt her father's eyes roll toward her.

"Do you want me to bring anything?" Marilyn asked.

"Just close the door."

Marilyn opened her mouth, shut it, and quietly drew the door closed behind her.

"Papa?"

"Yes." Old Ernest's voice slipped out.

"You're very sick, Papa."

"And?"

Betsy took his hand in hers and looked into his eyes, set deep into his puffy face.

"I'm going to send for Peter," she said.

He tried to look away, but she stood up and leaned over the bed, so that her face was directly before him.

"You kept him away from me for eleven years. Eleven years he's had to live with strangers. And now I'm going to bring him back."

"All for the best," Ernest said. "I did what was for the best."

"Oh, Papa. You're so selfish. It was the best only for you."

"You didn't understand. Still don't understand a thing."

"Listen to me," Betsy said. "I'm going to send for Peter. And I'm going to own this house where I've worked. And I'm going to own your business. And if I want to, I'm going to marry."

A light gleamed in Ernest's eyes. "Steen? Is it him?"

"Maybe."

"Marry him," Ernest said. "Good for the business. He'll keep it up."

"I won't marry him because of the business. No. I will if he's good for me and my son."

"You'll need Steen. For your son. A wild boy."

"No," Betsy said. "He's good. I know it."

Ernest shook his head. "They write me. A wicked boy."

"No, he's not." Betsy spoke furiously. Ernest began to drift away from her, but she rattled his hand to bring him back. "He just needs me, do you hear? He loves me."

Ernest wagged his head slowly. "You think it's going to be easy for you."

"Listen to me. Everything I've done for you, I really did for Peter. Every time I washed your clothes, or cooked your meals, or served you beer at your card games, I was thinking of him. He'll know that. He'll love me. More than you ever have."

"I'm leaving you everything," Ernest said. "Everything."

"It's not enough," Betsy said.

"Everything," he shouted, hoarse and triumphant. "Everything!"

Then his eyes grew wide and wild, and he lifted up from his bed as though drawn by a fishing line through his chest.

"Papa," Betsy screamed.

The door burst open, and women ran in.

"My heart," Ernest gasped.

"Not yet," Betsy pleaded. There were people all around her now. "Not yet."

"My heart," he said.

My heart.

. . . .

The week after the funeral, Steen put on his three-piece suit, a heavy wool suit he had brought with him from Denmark and had kept hanging carefully in a closet for special occasions. He wore a tie, and he polished his round-toed oxford shoes with great care. He brushed his hair—a little thin on top now, but if he brushed it carefully, he could make it cover all of the skin that was beginning to show through. And what did it matter if he was losing some hair, now that he was about to take a position in the community, marry, establish himself? He had no more interest in looking like a young sprout.

Betsy's house had never looked so handsome to Steen. True, it was just the same Moreberg-built house with the bay window and front porch and chimney, yet on this day the house seemed to hold a special charm. The lawn with the orange tree in flower gave out a sweet fragrance, and the petunias that lined the gravel walkway to the front door seemed to have bloomed especially to welcome him. A large vase with tulips was a splash of color in the window, framed gracefully and symmetrically by drawn lace curtains. Everywhere, he saw the touch of a woman's hand, the mark of a well-kept home. The best advertisement, old Ernest had said. And now all these touches were speaking to him, greeting him, drawing him willingly onward.

Steen walked up the broad porch steps and rang the bell. He felt he was coming into his own.

16
· · · · · · ·

Lone Hill March 8, 1933

Shorty knocked at the back door of the little house.

Terra-cotta pots lined the steps and porch, and stood in a row on the railings and windowsills. While Shorty waited, he contemplated the green plants, flowers, herbs that Mrs. Madison kept growing behind the house. There was, in spite of the hodgepodge of plants, a certain order in it all. A certain sense that pansies would look best just in that corner and nowhere else. He could see too that sun-loving plants, the succulents in their dry soil, were out on the edge of the porch, and the flowers that needed to be kept moist were up against the house, protected most of the day by the overhanging eaves.

Shorty smiled. He liked the garden she had made out of her limited space; it was a welcome to him. And restful. None of these plants were going to market.

Mrs. Madison opened the door, wearing an apron, with flour on her hands.

"Come in, Jim. Go wash up and take a seat. Dinner will be ready soon."

Shorty obediently went to the bathroom sink and washed his hands and face thoroughly. It didn't matter that he'd washed before he came, and shaved for the second time that day. She wouldn't be satisfied unless she was sure he had cleaned himself in her clean house before he sat down at her clean table.

He found it easier to do as she wished than to tell her there was no need, in this as in other things. And after a time, he discovered there was a pleasure in the routine of entering, washing while she finished setting the table, and then coming into the kitchen.

He looked over her shoulder at the pots on the stove. "What's cooking?" he asked.

"You'll find out soon enough," she said. "Now go sit down and leave me in peace."

He took his place at the kitchen table. This was also a routine, to be shooed away from the stove. This was also a routine and a pleasure.

Shorty had begun coming over for dinner at Mrs. Madison's house soon after Harold disappeared. He came for the first time to see if she knew anything about where her son might be when he didn't show up for work and his clothes were missing. One glance at her told him that Harold wasn't there, that she didn't know where he was, that she didn't know when he was coming back. But she had cooked a large meal, the kind she was used to preparing, more than enough for two. In case Harold should arrive, there would be enough.

She invited Shorty to stay. So the food wouldn't go to waste. And he had sat down at the kitchen table, in the place Harold used to sit, and hung his hat from the peg where Harold had always hung his.

They both soon realized that neither one had any idea where Harold had gone. So as they talked, their talk turned toward memories of him, scenes or incidents recalled from his youth and childhood. Shorty recalled Harold cutting apricots as a twelve-year-old and finding a slab, a piece of fruit so ripe it felt as though it was completely liquid inside the skin. And being completely unable to resist smashing it into the hair of the girl sitting next to him. Shorty had to break up the apricot fight that followed, but he remembered confessing to the boy that as a twelve-year-old himself he had done the same thing—then telling him that he was on his way to being a man now, and that it would soon be time to leave such things behind.

Mrs. Madison remembered when Harold was seven and brought home a crayon drawing of a horse he'd made at school. He wanted to give it to her as a present. It had looked more like a big dog, but she had carefully avoided saying what she thought it was until he piped up—"It's a horse!" She tacked it onto the wall over the stove, so she could look at it while she cooked, she said. And he ran outside to play, proud and happy with the gift he had made for her.

A week later, Shorty got word that Mrs. Madison wanted to see him. When he came in, she spread a telegram out on the kitchen table for him.

"Look," she said. "It must be from Harold."

Shorty looked at the wire from San Francisco and saw that Mrs. Madison had received a money order for one hundred dollars.

"Couldn't it be from your husband?"

Mrs. Madison laughed bitterly. "After all these years?"

"But where could Harold have gotten that kind of money?"

"I don't know. I don't care. Doesn't he know that I don't care at all about money? I just want him to come home."

She looked at Shorty with great concentration and said, "Go to San Francisco. Find him for me."

Shorty immediately thought of the work of the ranch. Pruning time, slack time. He could take a few days off.

"All right," he said.

He spent a week in the gray city in November, up and down the streets near the waterfront, in and out of the boardinghouses of Finn Alley and the Tenderloin. The description he gave of Harold seemed to fit every young man who had just blown into town. He saw some shape-ups on the docks, where able-bodied men clamored around a boss for a day's work unloading ships, and only those who kicked back part of their wages were taken on. He looked for Harold's face among the shouting mill of men, but everyone looked the same. It depressed him to think of Harold somewhere in that brawling crowd, somewhere in the city. And he left finally, hoping that the boy would come back on his own.

He went over to see Mrs. Madison when he was back, and they talked and ate together. Shorty asked for seconds, and then took a big helping of the peach brown Betty and said her coffee tasted better than the gut rust they served over at the house where the full-time-men lived. And when it was time to leave, she had asked him to come again. It seemed like he needed some home cooking.

"I'd like that," Shorty said.

"Can I ask you something?" she said. "I feel so funny calling you Shorty. Can you tell me your name?"

"Well," he said, "almost everybody 'round here calls me Shorty, and it doesn't bother me. But if you want to know, my given name is Jim. James, but they used to call me Jim."

"Jim," she said. "My name is Karin."

"All right. Karin."

"And Jim."

The next they heard from Harold was a picture postcard from Hawaii. He said he'd found work as a seaman, but he'd be back some day. Shorty came over, and they talked about it, and there was nothing they could do. Mrs. Madison sent a letter to her son care of a union hall in Honolulu. But the next she heard, months later, was a short note from Manila. Then a card from Kowloon. Then, finally, long silence.

The dinners with Shorty became a habit, a custom for them both. Shorty came over once a week, except during harvest when he worked eighteen-hour days. In the beginning, they talked mostly of Harold. They shied away from speculating where he might be, and instead shared their memories of him. With time, they talked more of their daily lives, the account of whom they had seen and spoken with, what had happened in the market or the orchard or the big house, what they were going to do tomorrow. But always, tying them together in some deep, shadowy way, was the knowledge of the missing son, the lost apprentice of the orchard, which left a hole in both their lives and made them both feel they had failed in some way.

Shorty was the sole supervisor of Ida Valley now, in 1933. But he found little pleasure in his advancement, when the orchard itself was sliding downhill. Prune prices were down, apricots were no better. Prices had begun to slide in 1930 and had slipped a little more each year since. Shorty often held that the only ones handling fruit who had any humanity to them were the producers and the consumers.

The reputation for Ida Valley fruit that he'd spent his life building didn't mean anything anymore. Shorty understood bad years; every farmer did. There had been some bad years after the war, when too many trees had been planted and there was no longer an army to feed. But the Depression was something new to him. It didn't make as much of a difference anymore that a man worked hard and did his best and produced a beautiful grade of fruit. A four-pound box of Santa Clara prunes went for nineteen cents in the city, and even Ida Valley was not going to get much of an offer per ton.

The ranch didn't keep twenty-five full-time men anymore. There was no money to pay them. Wages were cut, and some of the best men, some of the youngest men, were gone. Searching for something better, searching for some other way to thrive. In the past, Shorty could have said that nothing was better than staying on the land, working through the lean years. He couldn't find it in himself to say that now.

The men who stayed behind were the older ones, or men who were hanging on because they didn't see anything better. Like Jax. And Shorty couldn't care for the orchards like he wanted to. New tractors and new machines helped some, but not enough. He had lost a part of this year's crop, just because he didn't have enough men to set smudge pots in all the sections before a killing February frost. Most of his workers were good, but a man of fifty just doesn't move as fast as a man of twenty, and you can't ask it of him. It was during times like that frost that he thought especially about the young man who had disappeared, the tall young working man who had grown up on the ranch, grown up among the fruit trees and the tasks of the harvest, and then was lost.

Shorty, like everybody, had heard President Roosevelt remind Americans that theirs was a rich country. That they still had the land, the mines and factories and farms. The only thing to fear was fear itself. But the new president hadn't quite swept away the fears and doubts Shorty had begun to have. Prices were going to be low again this year by all accounts, and he couldn't see the end of it.

The Robertses had been leasing out land for some years, to cut down on the number of employees they had to keep. Now even they said they were considering selling off part of the ranch to pay debts. It was too big, and it just didn't pay anymore to keep all the land. Shorty understood that. He helped keep the books, and he could read a column of figures as well as the next man. But even so, cutting off a part of the ranch seemed to him like cutting off a part of his body.

And he was afraid that once Old Man Roberts died and it was passed on to his children, Ida Valley would fall apart little by little, sold off piecemeal to anybody with money. Selling a section seemed like the first step down a road with no returning.

Shorty held off telling Mrs. Madison—Karin—about how deep the troubles were. But he had begun thinking he had to. If the ranch was split up, there was no telling what would happen to the little house, whose occupant no longer had a son working on the ranch.

· · · · · · ·

Karin Madison served Shorty coffee and then sat down heavily.

"I'm tired," she said.

"Did they keep you busy up there?" Shorty asked.

"I was on my feet all day long," she said. "Mr. and Mrs. Roberts still have a kind word for me, but Brandon, who I saw grow up, takes me for granted now. And both he and his wife ignore their children. Olivia is after me to help her with sewing things, and little Albin mopes around because nobody pays any attention to him."

"That's a shame."

"And Brandon and Eugenia breeze in and out, as though they haven't a care in the world."

"Brandon doesn't care for fruit growing, that's sure."

"Doesn't care for anything but himself, if you ask me."

"So much has changed." Shorty said this as though musing over his coffee, but he watched Karin carefully. He wanted to see how far he could go on this line to bring up the subject of the sale of land and what it might imply.

"Since you and I were young?"

"Oh, when we were young, they were still changing over from wheat fields to orchards. And I was taught that planting trees was doing God's work, and I thought I'd found the best place in the Santa Clara for a man to work. Ida Valley seemed like it was going to get bigger and better forever. But now, the Robertses don't want to invest in the ranch anymore."

"Are things so bad?" Karin asked.

"This year, for instance, we're sending some of our fruit to a dehydrator instead of out on the dry yard. Ten years ago, I guarantee you that Ida Valley would have had its own dehydrator built, the best and most modern in the county, and taken in fruit from other farms. Instead, we're sending out our fruit to somebody else's dehydrator."

"They don't want to spend money on the ranch," Karin said. "But they're trying to live the same as ever."

"There you go," Shorty said in affirmation. He was glad that she had noticed, though he wasn't surprised. He had a high opinion of her intelligence, especially in practical matters. It would make telling her what followed easier if it wasn't like he was bringing up something completely new. "And I think maybe things are going to change for the worse before they change for the better."

"That doesn't sound like you, Jim." Karin looked at him now, paying attention.

"Well, I heard something that I never expected to hear at Ida Valley. They want to sell part of the ranch."

"Sell part of the ranch?" Karin couldn't believe it. In spite of the many changes, most of them for the worse, that had happened over the years, the ranch itself had always seemed fixed and eternal.

"Just like I'm telling you," Shorty said. "First they sell one piece, and then who knows?"

"You really think the ranch might break up?"

"Brandon doesn't care for it. And Albin sure isn't being brought up for it. Mr. Roberts has known us both for a long time, and he knows what he owes us. But what's going to happen when he passes away?"

Karin understood now what Shorty was driving at. She thought about the little house, which she'd taken for her own and lived in without question. If Harold had stayed, she would have had a resource, someone who could love and sustain her, apart from her work for the Robertses. Nobody could have taken her for granted if he had stayed. Now, her place and her house could be swept away by bigger changes that she had no power over.

She stretched her hand across the table toward Shorty.

"One thing isn't going to change," she said. "You're still going to enjoy telling me about your day, and telling me what you think of things. And I'm still going to enjoy being with you. That isn't going to change. Is it?"

She asked the question in such a way that allowed only one answer, and Shorty took her hand and gave it.

"Of course not," he said.

She gave his hand a little squeeze, then let it go and looked around her kitchen. It had seemed so stable.

"Jim," she said, "what section of the ranch are they thinking of selling?"

"The section I didn't get to with the smudge pots last winter, over by the San Natoma–Los Gatos Road. It's a damned pretty section, Lone Hill."

17

Gambit   April 1933

Betsy hadn't touched a man for thirteen years. Not since
Harold had disappeared in the fall and left her alone with
her father. Old Ernest had watched her then, made sure he
knew where she was in the evening, and with whom. But it
hadn't really been necessary. Since Harold had abandoned
her, she hadn't wanted to let another man run his hands
over her, kiss her neck, nurse at her breast.

Yet sometimes, at night in the dark, she had run her own
hands over herself. She massaged the sides of her body
through her nightgown, rubbing slowly up and down, and
after a time reaching down below her waist, around her
hips, along the outside of her thighs. She ran her hands
nearly the whole length of her body, felt the warmth of her
fingers digging into her, understood her legs gradually opening.

Then she reached down as far as the hem of her gown, ashamed, frightened, excited, and worked it up over her body, feeling along the inside of her legs and thighs as the hem inched upward. She felt herself naked under her hands when the gown slipped under the small of her back, and she kneaded her belly and the inside of her thighs.

Under the thick down comforter, under the cover of night and darkness and with her eyes closed, she touched herself with a moistened finger. First feeling her tuft of tangled hair. Then, peeping out, the soft, delicate head of her sex, soft and yet firm.

She didn't bury her finger in herself for a long time, not until she was ready to cry out and was tearing at her breast with her other hand. But when she did, with her eyes closed and her head turned to one side, she didn't think about Harold, the one man she had known. She thought about Peter, little Peter emerging naked and hairless from her body, and it was as though he was back with her in the savage moment of his birth, forcing her wider apart until she had to scream.

. . . .

The day after her father's funeral, Betsy began to go through his papers. She collected gray and straw-colored file folders from his office in town, and from the closet and locked secretary at home, and she spread them out on the oak dining room table. A lawyer and an accountant would come in tomorrow, but she wanted to have a look at everything once before they came.

Betsy wanted to be sure that she was still the legal parent of Peter. She had never to her knowledge given up that right, but she wanted a lawyer to make certain. She also wanted to make sure that the family with whom Peter had been staying would give him up with no problems. Betsy thought of them as grasping people who had made a profit on her unhappiness, and she thought she might have to buy them off. Finally, she wanted to own Moreberg Construction Company free and clear, and to understand just what it meant to own a company and have employees.

In one folder, she found Peter's birth certificate. Seven

pounds, two ounces. Boy. Blue eyes. Blue eyes, she remembered. The space for "Name of Father" was marked "Unknown."

In the same folder she found a sheaf of correspondence. The first piece she looked at was a wire from San Francisco to herself for one hundred dollars.

The date was a week after Harold had left. Betsy looked through the other letters and wires, and she began to piece together her father's actions. First he tried to send the hundred dollars back; there was a copy of an angry letter to Western Union, saying that he wanted no money from a scoundrel. Western Union replied that it was impossible to return the money, as it had been sent without a return address. Ernest then wrote them saying they could keep the money, because he wanted nothing to do with it. Western Union didn't reply.

A week later, Ernest wrote them again, saying that he had tried to pick up the hundred dollars but had been turned away at the window. Western Union replied that at this point it was impossible to trace the money. Ernest wrote angrily that one stack of money was as good as another, and that the hundred dollars belonged to him and his family. He wanted it now, and he'd be satisfied for it if he had to have the law on them.

There the correspondence from the fall of 1922 ended. Betsy wondered what Harold had meant by trying to send her money. Was he trying to allow her to join him? Was he trying to ease his conscience? Either way, it was too far in the past to make much difference. All he had done was make her tightfisted father struggle between his desire for money and his sense of honor.

"My stupid father," she said. "My poor stupid father."

After she saw the lawyer, she would send for Steen. Leave her poor father in the past, leave all the stupid things he had done to her and her son under cold, unvisited earth.

. . . .

Steen knocked on the door. He smiled out at the street as he waited, dressed in his only good wool suit, freshly shaved around his mustache, hair carefully combed over his bald spot. He had thought about bringing flowers or a box of chocolates, but he saved himself the expense by telling himself it was too soon after the funeral to bring such signs of joy into the house.

Betsy greeted him in a plain gray dress. He started toward the parlor, where he thought they would sit and talk. But instead she led him to the dining room table, piled high with neat stacks of file folders. He took the seat offered him, then looked up at the sharp angles that had grown over her face.

"Coffee?" she said.

He nodded, and she disappeared. He straightened his tie and looked at all the paperwork that crouched before him.

She came back in with coffee and cream on a wooden tray and set it down in front of him. "Are we on schedule with the Meadows house?" she asked.

After a pause, Steen said, "Anders is raising the roof today."

"And we've got two more lined up after this?"

"Contract jobs." Steen was completely baffled. He hadn't thought he was coming over to talk business. He suddenly felt foolish and overdressed, as though he had misunderstood everything.

"A contract job," he said, "is where someone else owns the land, and we're just putting up the house for them."

Betsy frowned. "I know what a contract job is."

"Of course you do. You're your father's daughter."

"Sorry. I didn't mean to snap. Steen, you've been a great help."

"And I'd like to do more."

"And I want you to."

Steen leaned forward in his chair.

"I want you to keep managing things. My father thought you would be best for the business. And I feel I can trust you."

Steen settled back, and the chair sighed under him in disappointment.

"Pay you more, of course."

"Of course."

"Can you think of any business we could get, or land we might buy, after we finish what's lined up?"

"I'll keep my eyes open." Steen stood up, adjusted his coat, which now felt too tight. "Best change to coveralls and get back on site."

"Wait, Steen." Betsy was looking up at him. "I want you to know about something. Everyone will know soon, but I want you to know now."

Steen remained standing.

"I have a son," Betsy said. "Named Peter. He's almost twelve years old now, and I want him to come live here with me in San Natoma."

Steen's body grew tense and hard. He felt, suddenly and without reason, that this boy was coming to usurp the place he had wanted for himself.

"Who was the father?"

"I knew you'd ask that," Betsy said.

For a moment, wildly, Steen thought that the father had been old Ernest.

"A boy who has been gone a long time," Betsy said, "and won't be coming back."

"Why are you telling me?" Steen asked. Betsy's eyes were like hands, both pulling him nearer and pushing him away.

"I want him to come and be a part of a family. I think that's what's best for him. And it's what I want too."

Steen had felt foolish once today. But now he thought he understood the terms of the deal. He would accept this child of hers, and she would accept him.

At the door, Betsy gave him her hand. "Think about it," she said. "And come back and see me."

Steen went back down the gravel walkway lined with petunias, passed by the single orange tree in flower, and he knew what his decision was going to be. Control of the company was within his grasp: old Ernest's place, marriage, standing. They would work things out about this Peter. Right now, he just wanted to close his hand into a fist and squeeze.

. . . .

Steen said he didn't want to go away on a honeymoon. Didn't want to go anywhere but into this house and into the big bedroom with the private bath. He said that after so long in a boardinghouse, living in his own home would be adventure enough.

It grated on Betsy to hear him call it his own home—he who hadn't had the cleaning and upkeep of it for a dozen years. But she had consented. It was a small enough sacrifice to make at the beginning of things.

A larger sacrifice was waiting to send for Peter. She wanted to send for him right after the wedding, but Steen thought that it would be better if they waited a while and got settled. It might be easier for Peter if he joined a stable household, not a pair of newlyweds. Again, Betsy consented. She thought that the time they spent alone together would be like a gift she could give Steen, before she asked him to accept Peter.

When they came home after the wedding party, after the cake and the toasts and the dancing, Steen had walked around the house once, smiling. Then he led her into the bedroom and began to take off his shoes.

"These new shoes hurt my feet," he said.

She watched him take off his coat and vest and hang them up. Loosen his tie, free the knot. Take off his shirt with his back to her, sitting on the edge of the bed. There was a dark ridge of hair starting at his spine and spreading in a curve over his shoulder blades, cut by the white halters of his undershirt.

It was clear that she was expected to do the same as him. But she only watched his bones and muscle move under the thick mat of black hair as he unbuckled his belt and took off his braces.

Steen turned to look at her, his pants unbuttoned but still up around his waist.

"I'm going to turn off the light," she said.

"All right."

In the darkened room, she heard Steen finish undressing himself and slip into bed. With her back to him, she undid her pretty dress and hung it in the closet. She unhooked her stockings and rolled them down her legs carefully, to avoid runs. She took off her garter belt. Then she pulled her slip quickly over her head, unhooked her brassiere, and put on the new nightgown she had chosen, of the same light-blue color as her wedding dress. Only after the night-gown had fallen safely down to her knees did she take off the rest.

She felt Steen watching her at each point of her undress-ing.

When she turned back toward the bed, she could make out his square, dark bulk under the covers, tense and un-quiet. She got into bed beside him and pulled the covers up to her chin.

He rolled over and immediately put his hand under her gown, lifting it up, his hand reaching far up along her naked side, up to her breast.

"Take it off," he said.

She did as he told her, crossing her hands and lifting the nightgown up over her head and leaving it there strewn above the pillow like windblown fallen blossoms.

He reminded her of her father. But she was astonished sud-denly at how much she wanted him.

She put one arm around his back and felt the ridge of hair along his shoulders. He was hairy everywhere, on his chest, on his back, along his arms and legs. She grabbed a handful of him and pulled him against her.

. . . .

Two months after the wedding, Betsy still wasn't pregnant, and Steen didn't like it. He thought she should be by now. Then she would begin to spend time at home and let him run the business.

Instead, he had to stand by her side while she sat at her father's old secretary and wrote checks. Checks for lum-ber, shingles, and nails. Checks for hammers and saws. She wrote the checks for everything involved with More-berg Construction; he couldn't buy a thing without going through her. She cashed all the checks from the clients, too, and it galled him. He was the one doing the work, after all.

On a Friday noon hour, Steen came in through the back door to pick up the paychecks for the men. He found her with the secretary open, looking through one of the old file folders.

"Hello, my dear." He bent over and kissed her on the cheek while she smiled faintly. He didn't want to come out and ask her for the paychecks; she knew what he had come home for, and he could wait for her to deliver them to him, without having to actually ask for them.

But she turned to him as though she were waiting too. The checks stood in a pile, he could see, filled out but unsigned, and she looked at him and waited.

Finally she spoke. "Steen. When are we going to send for Peter?"

Steen acted surprised. "Why, aren't we happy as we are?"

"Of course we are," Betsy said.

"Then is there any hurry? Peter's probably happy growing up in Southern California, or at least accustomed to it. I don't see why we have to upset things now."

"Steen, we said that when we got settled, we would send for him. I feel settled, and I feel happy. Don't you?"

"Well . . ." Steen began.

"And I've been waiting for you to say, now we are a couple, now we are happy, now we can send for Peter."

"I don't say we're not happy," Steen said.

"Are you sure?" Betsy looked at him. "Is there something that's bothering you that you're not telling me about?"

"No," Steen said. "Everything's fine."

"Good," Betsy said.

"I just don't want to rush."

"Steen, I don't want to force you into anything."

"You're not forcing me," Steen said.

"But since we're happy, there's no reason to wait. Is there?"

Steen felt trapped. He couldn't really stop her from doing what she wanted to do. And he couldn't make it seem wrong for her to do it, because everything he said she managed to stand on its head.

The tower of unsigned checks stood at Betsy's right hand. He couldn't leave without them, and she wouldn't sign them until things were decided.

"All right," Steen said. "You send for Peter, and we'll welcome him in."

"And I want charge of the boy when he comes. I want to be in charge of raising him."

Steen gave in. "Whatever you think is best, dear."

She stood up and held him and kissed him, happy-seeming now. Steen wanted to take her, take her in the bedroom, even though it was the middle of the day. He felt he was a man who had made a compromise, and that Betsy respected him less because of it. He wanted to get her with child, a child of his own. Then she would have to treat him like the head of the household, the same way she had treated her father.

18

. . . .

The Forge   June 1933

The blacksmith scraped a few clinkers and some ash into the ash pit and added some raw coal to the fire from a half barrel to his left. Then he bent down and turned the crank on the blower.

Peter leaned nearer as the air rushed up under the coal with a hollow moan. The forge suddenly flared bright orange-red in the midst of the dark building, cast a pure, fiery light on all the soot-blackened timbers of the shop. Large angular shadows played on the peaked ceiling. Each chunk of coal glowed with an angry heat, burning and yet not consumed, burning from a flame buried somewhere within. Peter felt his own face turn flushed and red as he watched, too near the scorching heat, yet too delighted with the fire to move further away.

A shot of tobacco juice rang into a coal oil tin, and Peter raised his head. The smith looked at him disapprovingly. Peter sat up straight again and edged back from the forge.

The smith picked up a great circle of flat stock, a rim for a wagon wheel, and laid it on the forge with two long-handled tongs. The circle was more than three feet across, yet he handled it easily with his large, ash-streaked hands and his thick forearms below the rolled-up sleeves of his shirt. When the metal of the rim began to take on the same glowing shade as the fire, he grasped it with both tongs and lifted it into the air. And in the flaming light and shadow of the vast, blackened shed, the smith seemed like a giant lifting a great ring of fire, a titan who had mastery over heat and metal and could shape it at his will. And this giant, this titan, had accepted Peter into his place, welcomed him, protected him.

The blacksmith's shop was Peter's fort, his dark cave. He found the shop during his first days in San Natoma, when he needed someplace to go. Here he could sit in the semi-darkness and not be bothered by anyone, not have to talk to anyone. His mother couldn't ask him how he was feeling, and his father, who wasn't his father at all, wouldn't be observing him to make sure he gave the right answer. He could sit, and watch the smith work silently, and gaze at the changing spectacle of the coals burning on the forge.

Peter had been sent north on the *Coast Daylight* in May, a month before he finished the sixth grade. His mother told him that she thought it would be good if he spent a little time in school in San Natoma before summer started. Maybe he could make some new friends to play with, and so he wouldn't miss Signal Hill so much.

Every day at dinner, with Steen looking on, she asked him how school was. He usually answered that school had been all right.

"What did you learn today?" she asked. "Did you study any math?"

"No."

"Did you read any?"

"A little."

"What did you read?"

Peter didn't answer right away, and Steen prompted him. "Your mother asked you a question," he said.

"Let him answer, Steen," his mother said.

"What did you read, son?" Steen asked.

"Steen, just be patient."

"All right." Steen leaned back in his chair. "I'll be patient." "What did you read, Peter?"

Peter wished Steen would disappear. "We read about the Gold Rush."

"That's interesting," Betsy said. "Is history your favorite subject?"

Peter shrugged. "Not really."

"You know, if you want to have a friend over to play sometime, that would be fine," Betsy said.

"Okay."

After dinner, Peter was left alone to do homework; his mother helped Steen with his citizenship books.

The first week of school, Peter wandered around the playground by himself, running his hand along the fence, studying the trees. Everyone had long since decided who to play with, who took which position, whose name was called when choosing sides. And Peter wandered alone, proudly unhappy.

In the second week, he walked by a group of boys who looked at him and snickered. Peter stopped, and an eight-year-old boy with a round head and scrawny arms was pushed out of the group toward him.

Peter looked from the boy to the group. The group watched the two of them, smiling and expectant.

"Well," Peter said.

"Are you . . ." the boy began to speak, then stopped. He looked back at the group.

"Go on," someone insisted.

"Are you a . . . a bastard?" the boy pronounced the word and then ran immediately back to the safety of the group.

Peter chased him into the pack of boys and tried to grab him, but the others shielded him.

Peter looked around. He was surrounded by grinning faces.

"Who?" he asked. "Who told him to say that?"

Another sixth grader, a boy his size, spoke up. "Hey, do you know why Mary Ellen flunked out of home economics?"

"Why?" someone else asked.

"Because she couldn't *mend straight!*"

Everyone in the group laughed, and Peter laughed too. He had heard the joke before, but that was all right. It was a joke on someone else, someone outside the group, and so he could laugh as part of the group.

The boy who told the joke laughed harder than anyone. He wiped his mouth on his sleeve. "Here's a new one," he said.

Peter looked at him suspiciously.

"What did Betsy have to do when she sewed two pieces of cloth together?"

"What? What?" the boys shouted.

"She had to *baste hard*. She hadda *bast-hard!*"

The group delighted all around Peter, dancing and grinning, looking at him in their midst. The boy who told the joke was doubled over with laughter, snorting and wiping his nose and mouth.

Peter tackled him.

Immediately a circle formed around the two of them, and everyone shouted.

"Fight! Fight!"

Peter and the boy bounced up from the ground and flew at each other. Peter drew the boy's head under his right arm in a headlock, but the boy also took Peter in the same hold, and the two struggled around stooped over, each trying to force the other to walk his way, or else fall to the ground.

A whistle blew.

The boy tried to free himself, but Peter held on with his right arm and punched the boy's nose with a left uppercut. Blood fell in round drops on the asphalt.

The whistle blew again, and the boy slipped out of Peter's grip and rejoined the circle.

"You all are witnesses, he hit me first."

Peter looked around him at the eager, excited faces, waiting now for his punishment.

He rushed them, cut left and right, trying to catch one of them. They fell out of his way like stalks of wheat.

The whistle blew a third time, and someone much larger and stronger caught him from behind and hugged him to his body.

Peter went limp.

. . . .

When boys came before Principal Brent, he usually posed one or two brief questions, and then waited. After a short time, faced with the square-jawed, impassive man behind the large desk, the boy in question inevitably began to squirm, elaborated his story, and ended by telling everything.

The Keller boy was like that. He had come in, embarrassed by the clownish wads of cotton in his nose, and started off saying only that the other boy had hit him first. After some questions and some silence, he finally told Mr. Brent what he had said to provoke the Moreberg boy. At first he'd been almost proud of his cleverness, but Mr. Brent didn't let him go until he said he was ashamed of himself.

"Now go outside and apologize to him, and tell him to come in," he ordered. "And I hope I don't have to see you in here again before the end of the school year."

"Yes, Mr. Brent."

The boy with the white cotton in his nose disappeared quickly out the door.

Mr. Brent felt that discipline was absolutely essential for the school to work. The Moreberg boy had been provoked, no doubt. But the Depression was on. This was no time to be running wild. Everyone had to work, and work together.

The door swung open, and Peter walked into the office with his mouth in a line and stood before the desk.

Mr. Brent spoke first. "Hello, Peter."

"Hello, Mr. Brent," Peter said.

Mr. Brent waited, but Peter added nothing more.

"You've only been here a week, and you've already had a fight," Mr. Brent said.

"Yes," Peter said.

Mr. Brent paused, but the boy refused to say anything. "Do you think that is a good way to begin?"

Peter shrugged. "I don't know."

"And what was the fight about?"

"I don't like him."

"Why don't you like him?"

"Because . . ."

The boy searched for words, looking up with his mouth open, and Mr. Brent thought he was going to speak. But the boy's eyes fell level again with his own.

"Because I just don't like him."

"And that seems to you to be a reason to fight."

"He doesn't like me either."

"How do you know?"

"Because he doesn't."

"Do you even know his name?"

"No. But I know he doesn't like me."

"And how do you think a school can function if students who don't know each other decide they don't like each other and start fights? How do you think teaching and learning can go on if . . ." Mr. Brent stopped. He was speaking too much, and this was about a boy's actions, not about his idea of a well-run school.

He resumed his expressionless gaze. "Do you think this is what your mother expects of you? To be in to see me after only a week?"

"I don't know."

The principal heard something in this reply. A hint of some feeling, a hint of what the problem was. Some trouble between the boy and his mother, some trouble at home. It made sense.

But no matter what the trouble at home, he couldn't allow it to disrupt his school.

"We'll find out what your mother expects," he said. He took a thick fountain pen from his pocket and wrote a short note to the mother, describing what had happened and asking her to contact him. Then he blotted it, sealed it in an envelope, and wrote "Mrs. Moreberg" on the outside.

"After she's read this note, we'll all talk again." He handed the envelope to Peter, and the bell rang.

"Go right to class," he said.

The boy left the office, neither slowly nor in haste. Mr. Brent frowned at the firm click of the closing door.

. . . .

The wooden wagon wheel lay on its side on a grating suspended above a bath of water.

The blacksmith placed the fiery ring of iron around the wooden rim, maneuvering it with two tongs. The metal had expanded enough to fit easily. He hammer-tapped it in two places, then spun the wheel around to be sure the metal was centered.

Peter inspected the rim as well. It seemed fine to him, but the smith frowned, gave it another light tap, and spun it around once more before he was satisfied.

He pulled a long, polished lever. The grating with the wheel on it was lowered into the water all at once. The water exploded into steam and a great reddish vapor cloud burst into the air as the metal rim cooled instantly and clenched down on the wooden wheel.

The smith threw the lever in the opposite direction, and the wheel rose out of the bath, water spilling through the holes of the grating. He lifted the wheel to the ground, took a few nails from a pocket of his leather apron, and placed them in his mouth.

"Can I hold the wheel, Bert?" Peter asked.

The smith nodded gravely. He placed flathead nails into the pre-made holes in the metal rim and drove them in while Peter rotated the wheel. When he'd driven the last one, he spoke.

"Done," he said.

Peter felt the rim. Cool, dull iron now, a part of the wheel, ready to serve on a wagon over the lanes of San Natoma. Proof of Bert's mastery over fire and metal.

The smith placed a blackened metal coffeepot in the center of the forge and gave the blower one crank. The coals turned red around the battered old pot. After a minute, he plucked the pot from the fire with a long pair of tongs and delicately poured a stream of steaming black coffee into a stained mug.

Peter watched the smith drink his coffee. He was aware again of the note in his pocket, the letter from the principal, that he was to deliver to his mother. But the note was addressed to Mrs. Moreberg, and there was no such person. Miss Moreberg. Mrs. Denisen. But not Mrs. Moreberg.

Since the note was addressed to Mrs. Moreberg, the best thing was just to throw it away. If he gave it to his mother, she might show it to Steen, and he didn't want that. If his mother had married somebody like Bert, it might be different.

"Bert," he said, "I want to be a blacksmith when I grow up."

The smith smiled and sipped his coffee.

"Bert?" Peter asked.

The smith turned his large head toward him.

"Am I a bastard?"

He regarded the boy, some twelve years old, in a new place faced with strange insults and indignities. Not unlike he himself when he emigrated to the United States.

He put one of his big hands on the boy's shoulder.

"You're a good boy," he said. "You just work hard to stay good."

He reached into a pocket of his apron and took out a narrow, flat-sided horseshoe nail.

"Give me your hand," he said.

Peter put his hand in Bert's hand, and the smith felt his fourth finger. Then he took the horseshoe nail in a small pair of tongs and laid it over the forge. In a short time, the nail heated up red.

He took the nail from the forge and quenched just the head of it in water, so that the head was dull and the rest bright orange-red. Then he laid it across the sharp, narrow nose of a small anvil and hammered lightly on the dull quenched end. The nail quickly shaped itself into a ring.

The smith held the ring up by his tongs, eyed the roundness and diameter, and then plunged it into the water. He held it out to Peter, who slipped it on his right-hand finger.

"It fits perfect," he said.

The smith nodded.

"You go outside now, and go home. And work hard. Remember."

"Thanks, Bert." Peter twisted the ring around his finger, but he didn't go outside immediately. He waited until the smith had his back turned, and then he slipped the letter out of his pocket and threw it onto the brightest part of the forge. It caught fire quickly, flamed briefly.

Peter ran outside. It was the right thing to do with a note like that. Nobody was going to do anything to him anyway.

. . . .

The smith dragged the good coals together with a poker and reformed his fire. There were still a few tasks he could do before his wife would have dinner on the table. And with four children, he couldn't afford to let the end of the day slip away from him.

But he wanted to send the boy outside. He'd have to learn sooner or later that there were things that a blacksmith shop couldn't protect him from. Many things. Everything.

As for wanting to become a blacksmith, Bert had heard that at least once from every boy who came and watched by his forge. But he knew that nothing of the sort would happen. There were automobiles with pneumatic tires now, and tractors on all the farms. How many more wagons would need mending? He would always have work, building iron gates and balustrades for the big houses in the Valley. Decorative ironwork, rather than the repair of farm implements. But he saw clearly that when he closed his shop, when age took him away from the forge in ten or fifteen or twenty years, there would be no more blacksmiths in San Natoma.

. . . .

The following week, while Betsy was drying dishes, the phone rang. She walked to the secretary and picked up the receiver.

"Hello, Mrs. Moreberg?" A man's voice spoke with a certain authority of tone that she almost recognized.

"Mrs. Denisen, please."

"Ah, yes, Mrs. Denisen, excuse me." The rustling of papers on a desk at the other end of the line. "This is the principal of the school, Mr. Brent."

The first principal whom Betsy thought of was the principal at the high school. The one who had encouraged her to become a math teacher. How could he be calling her now? What could he tell her to make of her life now?

The voice continued. "I am speaking with the mother of Peter Moreberg?"

"Yes," Betsy said. "Of course." She wasn't yet used to being the mother, having a child at school. Any principal who called her now would be the head of Peter's school.

"Peter has been very disruptive at school. I sent a letter home with him last week, asking you to call me."

The voice left this statement hanging, waited for her to provide him with the continuation. Somebody had done something irresponsible; who it was had to be determined.

"I'm sorry, Mr. Brent," Betsy said.

"Yes?" the voice said after a slight pause.

"I've just been so busy." Betsy found herself clutching the teacup. "I meant to call you, but I just didn't find the time."

"Ah." The voice took on a disapproving tone. "Well. Peter has had several fights since he has been here. He doesn't mix with the other students, and he is either unwilling or unable to make friends. Not all of the fights have been without provocation. But I think we should have a conference about it. Has he talked to you about his problems?"

Betsy took a deep breath. "Yes, Mr. Brent. He's told me about the problems he's had. And I think. For right now. That it's best if we work on his problems here at home, just the two of us."

She felt the rigid man at the other end of the line hesitate; if he insisted, she would confess that she had lied. But he said, "Perhaps you know best. We won't have Peter with us for very long, after all. But children his age are making an important transition, and small difficulties can very quickly become large ones."

"Thank you, Mr. Brent. I'll keep that in mind."

The principal hesitated still, and Betsy felt he was unsatisfied with the results of the conversation and reluctant to have it come to an end.

"It was nice of you to call," she said.

"It's part of my job," he said. "So I'll leave the matter in your hands?"

Still trying to extract some promise of action on her part, action in line with his way of thinking.

"Rest assured," Betsy said. "Good-bye, Mr. Brent."

"Uh, good-bye."

She pressed down on the telephone with one finger, to close off the principal's voice, and she held the receiver to herself in the quiet house. She rocked it back and forth, as though it were the baby she had barely known, as though it were the son she had imagined would come back to her. She'd wanted a boy who would stay by her side and make her happy, a friend who would listen to her troubles and pains and make her feel as though she had done the best she could. She wanted a child who would forgive her and love her completely. A compensation for the years she had spent serving her father.

Then she put the receiver away from her, placed it on the phone as though it were the lie she had told, walked back to her dishes. She decided to talk to Peter, as she told Mr. Brent she would. If her son wouldn't talk with her, it might be time to let Steen be the father he now claimed he wanted to be.

. . . .

When Peter came home, he found his mother prowling on the front porch. He was about to go around to the back door, but she spotted him first and waved him up to her.

Betsy sat on one side of the porch, and Peter sat on the other side. He waited for her to say something. He didn't have to volunteer anything, and it made him feel good if she asked him something. Then he could decide whether or not to answer.

"Was school good today?" she asked.

"It was all right," he said.

"Do you like anybody at school? Are you making any friends there?"

Peter cocked his head to one side. He couldn't tell her about the skirmishes he was fighting all the time. Then she would want to know all about it, and that would bring up the note he'd burned up. But he couldn't tell her he was making friends, because then she would turn happy and want to meet them. He didn't want her to be happy. Not yet. Not while Steen was still around.

"I haven't made any real friends," he said. "Not really."

"Do you like the other children at all? Or do you have problems with them?" His mother was looking at him brightly.

"No," he said. "No problems."

"You know what I liked best about this time of year when I was your age?"

Peter stared at his mother. She was talking funny and fast.

"It wasn't that school was almost over. I loved being in school. I loved doing math problems. And my teachers were always proud of me. No, what I loved was just looking forward to spending time out-of-doors. I was inside all the time during the school year, morning and night. But in June I could look forward to walking in the hills and finding poppy fields, and hearing the bees buzzing in and out of every blossom. And I thought about how much fun it would be to become a bee, and spend all my time rolling in flowers."

"Why couldn't you go outside?" Peter didn't understand.

"Oh, it had to do with your grandfather," she said. "And then, later in the summer, I could look forward to the fruit harvest."

Suddenly she stood up and wrapped him up in her arms. "Peter, I love you so much I could just eat you up sometimes. You know that, don't you? I love you no matter what."

Peter let her hug him, then freed himself. "Okay, Mama," he said. He slipped into the house, dropped off his books, and went out the back door.

. . . .

Steen paced slowly through the trees, counting aloud in a low, monotonous voice. He walked with his head down and his eyes on the unturned earth just in front of him and deliberately set one foot three feet in front of the other. It was an old habit with him, something he had seen the master builder do during his apprenticeship in Denmark. Later, a surveyor would come to measure the land precisely, and set sticks and string. But always, before he planned and built, Steen wanted to walk the land step by step, from one property line to the other. It gave him a grasp of the land, later realized when he sank a foundation, built the frame, shingled the roof, and hung the front door.

". . . fifty-four, fifty-five, fifty-six . . ."

Anders walked with him. He didn't pace, but rather strolled with his hands in his pockets and observed the fruit trees that Steen passed by every six or seven paces. The trees hadn't been pruned for two or three years and were beginning to lose their shape. Stray branches, thin and unsupported, snaked toward the ground, or waved above the crown of the tree, and distorted the perfect wineglass form of a well-pruned tree. The branches were in leaf, but the fruit were few and poor, the stunted survivors of the February freeze.

". . . sixty-eight, sixty-nine, seventy . . ."

Anders could see why the Robertses were interested in selling this piece of land. It wouldn't be worth harvesting this year, and they wouldn't want to spend the money to bring it back into shape next year, not with prune prices rock bottom. He thought to mention this to Steen; it should be a factor in whatever price they negotiated for the land. But he didn't want to interrupt Steen's count. His friend regarded the ground single-mindedly as he paced, seemed to notice nothing more than the shape of the earth and the length of his stride.

The hill sloped more steeply as they turned down toward the San Natoma–Los Gatos Road. Steen finally stopped at the edge of the drainage ditch along the edge of the road and turned back to look at the property.

"One hundred and seven wide," he smiled.

"There's enough for a few houses," Anders said. "More than a dozen if you have the hill bulldozed."

"I'd rather not flatten the hill," Steen said. "Rather lay the houses around the hill, with a road that curved up. Put the largest house on the crest of the hill, with a view."

"You'd make less money, then. Less houses, less money. More headaches, building on the side of a hill."

"True enough. But we could build a beautiful house up there, just where the crest dips a bit."

"And who is to buy a big, beautiful house? If the Robertses themselves are selling off pieces of land?"

Steen frowned and fell silent. There was some truth in what Anders said. The houses they were able to build and sell in San Jose were still the most basic Ernest Moreberg houses, with a front porch and bay window, on a forty-by-sixty lot. But he wanted to build something beautiful, on top of a hill, that people could look up to.

"Either way," Anders said, "this would be the biggest piece of building we've done. Are you going to make an offer on it?"

"I don't know," Steen said. "Depends on the bank."

"Look at the trees, look at the fruit. They aren't taking care of this section anymore. They'll let it go cheap."

"Still depends on the bank. We can't buy it outright, or we wouldn't have enough money left to build. We'll see what price we can get, and see how much the bank is ready to put up, and then we'll make a decision."

"You shouldn't let this parcel get away."

"I know," Steen said. "I know."

He had made it all sound easy and evident to Anders. Planning the houses, negotiating the price, arranging a loan, making a decision. But he didn't admit that it really wasn't his decision to make. All the big decisions in the business had to be made by Betsy. And she didn't want to build on Lone Hill.

She wouldn't say exactly why she was opposed. Only that it didn't seem like a good place to build houses. That it would hurt her to see the fruit trees uprooted. Or other reasons that didn't make any sense. He had tried to explain to her what an ideal location it was, now that the Interurban had shut down and most people got around by automobile. That the land wasn't best used as fruit orchard, the way things were going. And that if they didn't build there, somebody else would.

To all of these reasons, she presented a blank wall of opposition.

That was not the kind of thing he could talk about with Anders. To the other men on the job, he was the one in charge, and he didn't want to change that. Better to be able to blame the bank if the deal fell through, and not a wife he couldn't control.

As they walked back to the truck, Anders asked, "Have you had any luck straightening out young Peter?"

"He hasn't had a proper raising," Steen said.

"Heard he gave Wheeler's kid a shiner last week."

Steen nodded. He didn't know Peter had been fighting at school, but it didn't surprise him. Betsy wouldn't let him say two words to Peter, but sooner or later he thought he'd have to take the boy in hand. He was content to let her struggle with him for the time being. She might learn that he was right about a few things. Including the decision to put houses on Lone Hill.

. . . .

Peter stood outside the chain-link fence and watched the game.

The boys hit and ran and caught and threw, and then loped easily into the dugout or out to the field. It wasn't organized baseball; there were no umpires, and the boys wore jeans and T-shirts, not uniforms, although many of them sported caps from the Seals or the Oaks of the Pacific Coast League. Most of them were older than Peter, but he recognized the right fielder from the playground at school, and he thought of his own glove at home, the one his mother had sent him when he was playing catch among the oil rigs down in Southern California.

Yet something kept him from running home for the glove, coming back, presenting himself eagerly and asking if he could play. If one of them came to him and asked him to play, he would have been very happy. But he didn't want to ask. It didn't really mean anything to him if they wanted him to join them or not. They could play, they could go ahead and play, and he was perfectly content to be where he was, watching from the other side of the fence. If they thought they needed him, that was fine, but he didn't need them at all.

A left-hander was up, and they motioned the boy he recognized far back in the outfield. On the second pitch, the batter hit a fly ball to right, and the boy first ran in toward home plate. Then he reversed his field and ran out again. The players on his team shouted at him. The boy circled, and as the batter was rounding first base, he stuck his glove into the air. The ball hit his glove and fell to the ground in front of him. He picked up the ball and threw wildly to the second baseman, who had come out toward him. By the time the ball was recovered, the batter was at third, and the players in the dugout were hooting and shouting.

"Triple, triple," they laughed.

The right fielder went back to his position with his head down. Peter smiled disdainfully.

"I would have had that one," he said to himself.

He rattled the chain-link fence once with his hand. Nobody noticed him. So he turned and wandered off toward home through the orchards.

The fruit trees were in leaf. Peter walked over the turned earth in the cool green shade and looked at the fruit hanging heavy and making the branches droop. He picked up a dirt clod and weighed it in his hand. Then he wound up like a pitcher and hurled it against a tree trunk.

It smacked against the trunk and burst apart.

"Hey!" a man's voice shouted.

Peter ducked between trees and found a short man in overalls placing a white brace under one of the heavy tree branches. A young Japanese man, a little less than twenty, stood next to him with a mallet. Nearby, a small tractor and trailer were loaded with whitewashed boards.

"Too much energy?" the man asked. "Why don't you give us a hand?"

The short man took the mallet from his helper and whacked at the lower end of the brace. The tree shuddered as the brace scraped along the dirt, then grew still.

The man handed the mallet to Peter and told him to hop

on the trailer, and they rode forward to the next tree. Peter helped the young Japanese man carry and place the braces around all the fruit-bearing branches, while the short man whacked them into place. Then they moved down the row, tending to each tree in turn. The short man began to let Peter use the mallet, instructing him to hit the brace at the bottom so that it would scrape along the dirt and not harm the tree bark.

After a time, the man asked Peter if he didn't have to be getting home.

"Not really," Peter said.

"Better head on home anyway. Your mother might get worried, and we're working on 'til sundown. What's your name?"

"Peter."

"I'm Shorty Farrell. The supervisor. And this is Kenji Yamamoto—who's working for some wages, since his father don't pay him anything."

Kenji smiled. "I have to be able to take a girl to the movies."

"Hi," Peter said. He had known some Japanese boys at school down in Signal Hill. He hadn't known them well, but he liked them. They had never called him names.

"Tell you what," Shorty said. "You come back in a month or so and you can pick prunes for me. Okay?"

"Sure thing."

Peter stood there and watched Kenji take another board off the pile.

"See you," he said.

"You bet," Kenji said, and winked at him.

. . . .

When he came through the kitchen door, he found his mother and Steen sitting together at the table. They both looked at him, as though they had been waiting for him.

"Peter," his mother said. "Where have you been?"

"Around," Peter said. "Is dinner ready?"

"Dinner's over," Steen said. "And there'll be no dinner for you until we've had a little talk. Come along with me."

Peter looked at his mother, who nodded. He followed Steen cautiously; he had never talked with his stepfather alone before, and he didn't like the idea that he was supposed to listen to what he had to say.

Steen led him into his bedroom, shut the door, and sat down on a chair while Peter sat on the bed.

"So," Steen said, "you've been in trouble at school."

"No, I haven't," Peter said.

"No? You didn't have a fight on the schoolyard? You didn't go see the principal?" At Peter's surprised expression, Steen added, "You see, I know more than you think. I know what you do even when I'm not around."

"All right," Peter said sullenly. "I had a fight at school."

"Tell me what it was about."

"If you know everything already," Peter said, "why do I have to tell you?"

"Don't get smart with me, young man. I know. But I want to hear it from your mouth."

"I got into a fight with a kid who called me a name."

"What did he call you?"

Peter mumbled a reply.

"What? Speak up."

"A bastard. A bastard."

"A bastard?" Steen felt the word directed at him. Not just at Peter, but at Betsy and at himself. At his house, and the place he wanted for himself. "And you hit him?"

"Yes," Peter said. "And I would again, too."

"Well, good. I'm proud of you. If anybody ever calls you that again, I want you to fight him again. And you don't have to be afraid to tell me about it afterward, either."

Steen smiled and clapped him on the shoulder, but Peter started back from the touch of his hand. Maybe Steen wanted to be his friend now, wanted to be on his side against everyone else. But he didn't need anyone to be on his side, he was all right by himself. And he didn't want Steen to be his friend. There was nobody he wanted less to be his friend.

"Don't worry," Steen continued. "I'm not going to punish you. Is that why you didn't bring the note home? Because you were afraid of me?"

"I'm not afraid of you. I didn't bring the note home because it was addressed to Mrs. Moreberg."

Steen stopped smiling. "Yes? And so?"

Peter took a deep breath. "There is no Mrs. Moreberg. There's only Mrs. Denisen. But I don't care."

"You don't care?"

"I'd rather be a bastard than have you as a father."

Steen raised his hand. "Say that again."

"I like being a bastard. I'd rather be a bastard than have you as a father."

. . . .

Betsy listened to the pitch of the voices at the door of her mother's old room. She moved Peter in here to brighten the sad room, replace some of the memories of her thin mother wasting away in the darkness with the presence of her young, growing son. The voices sounded reasonable and gentle at first. And Steen laughed once, and Betsy thought she had done the right thing when she'd asked him to help her with Peter.

Then she heard the voices suddenly rise, high and awful. The crack of a large open hand on flesh burst out at her through the door. The blow fell again, and Betsy remembered herself in front of her own father, head bowed, waiting for punishment. Again a blow. Again.

—*Again,* she seemed to hear her dead father say, terrible and miserable.—*Again.*

The door opened. Steen came out and closed it behind him, didn't allow her to see in.

"Peter's to have no supper tonight," he said. He looked at her face.

"I'm sorry," he said.

. . . . . .

Steen waited in bed while Betsy finished undressing and slipped into her nightgown. He didn't know why his wife wanted to put on a nightgown every night, when she would have to take it off afterward. He thought it somewhat foolish, a waste of time. But he accepted it of her, didn't try to break her of the habit. It was a small enough piece of whimsy.

She got into bed and lay with her back toward him. She did this from time to time. He was always able to lie close up against her and caress her side and flank, and then run his hand under her hem. Eventually she would roll over and he would work her garment up until she took it off.

But on this night, when he reached down to her legs, he felt her hand take his quite firmly and remove it.

He reached down again, and again her hand took his by the wrist and moved it away from her body.

"No," her voice came muffled from her head turned away from him.

"What's wrong?" he asked.

"I just want to sleep in my bed," she said.

"But ..."

"Can't I just sleep in my bed?"

"Of course ..."

"All right, then."

Steen rolled back to his side of the bed and lay, tense and unmoving. He felt her beside him, also tense, waiting.

After a time of silence, Betsy spoke.

"Good night, Steen."

"Good night. My dear."

The covers rustled as she settled into a sleeping position. He lay on his back and stared at the ceiling.

As he fell into sleep, he dreamed of Betsy's body melting into his own. The flesh of his hand, thick and flat, landing on the skin of Peter's legs and sinking in. Across his chest and down his arms, there grew green horses and purple bears, and dogs the color of the sun began to swarm.

19

Poker   June 10, 1933

People love to read about themselves.

Bill Finney knew this when he bought the *San Natoma Star*. People love to read about themselves and their neighbors, and they're willing to spend a nickel to do so. Local news was his specialty. Printing what the people of San Natoma wanted to read. And so he or one of his staff of three wrote up every local softball game, every meeting of the Foothill Club or the Modern Priscillas or the Oddfellows, every engagement, wedding, birth, or death, every little incident that showed the wit or sentiment or kindly humanity of a San Natoma resident. The boy's lost dog returned. The fiftieth wedding anniversary. The parents sending their son or daughter off to Cal or Stanford.

When it was a young child's birthday party, Bill Finney always sent a photographer with instructions to get as many kids in the photo as possible, with their faces in clear view and their names (correctly spelled!) in order. For each boy or girl, that was one paper sold, maybe two if there were grandparents in Bloomington who liked to receive clippings concerning their nearest and dearest.

Local news. But never bad news, never scandal or meanness. That kind of reporting might sell a few more papers over the short term, but in the long run it did the paper more good to be seen as a good neighbor than as a petty gossip. If people thought that appearing in the news could mean embarrassment, the paper would find doors closed to it that were once open and welcoming. So the rough edges were smoothed in the *San Natoma Star*. All stories were shaped and guided by Bill Finney's sense of what people wanted to read about themselves and their neighbors, what would make them feel happy with themselves and their town, and what they would be willing to spend a nickel on.

Bill had been a regular at old Ernest Moreberg's card games. After the old man's death, he began to hold Saturday afternoon games at his own house. He invited only men of some standing in the community. Not the very wealthy, like the Robertses, who seemed above petty concerns, but men like himself, small-business owners who dealt with the public on a daily basis. These were the men who could tell him something important about what was happening and why. The drugstore owner knew far more about San Natoma than the owners of Ida Valley Ranch did.

He had never yet invited Steen to one of his games, though he had played with him over at Moreberg's. The long obituary he wrote for Moreberg had praised him as a builder, an honest businessman, an immigrant who had made good. He even mentioned toward the end that the day-to-day management of Moreberg's construction business had been taken over by Mr. Steen Denisen, another immigrant. And yet, something didn't smell right in the too quick courtship, engagement, and marriage of Steen and Betsy, although he had his staffer write it up with the same flowery prose he used for all marriages. He didn't want to accept

Steen into his circle until he'd had a little time to prove himself.

The appearance of Peter showed he'd been wise to be prudent. It was a bit of a scandal, and he felt he had to report it, but he also wanted to put the best face on it he could. So he buried it on page seven, and merely described the reunion of Mrs. Betsy Denisen with her long-absent son. Peter would begin attending school in the area, and both mother and son were wished well in the life they would be able to share.

Things had been more or less quiet on Oak Street since then, though Peter was said to be a hard case to discipline. But if Bill Finney had decided now to invite Steen over for cards, it was because he'd heard from Albert Jackson that Steen was ready to put in a bid on Lone Hill. That was news, real news, that he had to find out more about. It could be the biggest number of new houses to come into San Natoma all at once since the town began.

Finney knew he could count on Albert to arrive on time, before the others, and he wasn't disappointed. The young banker knocked on the door at two o'clock sharp, dressed in a coat and tie; always dressed well, always retaining his banker's habits of politeness and punctuality. Finney let him in and served him a glass of lemonade—Albert drank very little, and never before a poker game—and sat down with him at the card table.

"So how's business at the Bank of *America*?" Finney emphasized the last word because the bank had changed its name from the Bank of Italy only a few years earlier. The little Italian bank from North Beach had outgrown the Italian neighborhoods both in San Francisco and in San Jose, and it had outgrown its original name as well.

"Still making loans. That's the business of the bank. And Mr. Giannini just bought six million dollars' worth of bonds for the bridge across the Golden Gate. *He's* not afraid to invest in the future."

"Speaking of investing in the future, I invited a customer of yours to play some poker this afternoon. Steen Denisen."

Albert leaned back. "The bank is interested in his project," he said slowly. "It could pay. But the plans have to be shaped with regard to certain economic realities."

Finney smiled to himself. Whenever Albert began speaking of what "the bank" thought, or what "the bank" felt, he took on a reserved, judgmental air. As though he, as a human being, were no longer involved.

"There's a risk involved, then."

"There's always a risk in construction on spec. If the bank is to risk its money, which really belongs to its depositors, it wants a project that will pay, and a creditor who is willing to take a risk himself."

Someone rapped on the door, and Finney rose to answer it.

"Of course," Albert continued, "Steen hasn't actually made a final decision to go ahead."

Hogg, the drugstore owner, and Gordon, the real estate agent, were at the door. Finney ushered them in and got them drinks. Hogg sat at the table and began to shuffle the cards absentmindedly.

"We've just been talking about Steen Denisen's plans to put some houses on Lone Hill," Finney said. "Some risk involved, Albert thinks."

"Denisen is selling the houses he builds in San Jose," Gordon said. "But he's just building the same old dependable one-story house. I don't know what he's got in mind for Lone Hill."

Finney looked at Albert; the banker pursed his lips and didn't comment.

"It's a good location," Hogg said. "Cars are bringing everything closer together now. Why, you could drive from there to my store in less time than it would take to hitch a wagon."

"But Steen's never done anything this big," Finney said. "Do you think he can pull it off?"

Once again, Finney tried to read Albert's face. But the banker was giving no clues for now.

There was a polite knock on the door. Finney came back into the room with Steen, who saw that everyone was smiling at him. He smiled back somewhat cautiously, for though he knew them all, he was not a close friend to any man in the room.

"Speak of the devil," Hogg piped up.

"You were speaking of me?" Steen asked.

"We were waiting for you so we could begin," Finney said. "Let's play cards."

"Didn't you invite a sixth?" Gordon asked.

"I invited Shorty over from Ida Valley," Finney said. "But he called to say he might have too much work today. Come on, sit down and ante up."

. . . .

Finney looked at his cards, and looked at the bet Albert had on the table. He folded his hand.

"I'm out," he said.

He took up his pipe, tamped down the tobacco, lit it, and leaned back in his chair.

Gordon threw in his hand. Hogg was already out. But when the bet came to Denisen, the Dane frowned slowly.

"I'll raise you two blue chips," he said.

Finney smiled. It was the last hand of the day. This could be interesting.

The air was yellow and hazy in the card room from Finney's pipe, Steen's small black cigars, and Gordon's cigarettes. The game had gone on for three hours with the normal ebb and flow of luck. The circulation of chips from one side of the table to another went on smoothly and ceaselessly, punctuated every now and then by the coincidence of strong hands, and one player raking in a big pot. None of the players had had particularly bad luck, and none had had a string of extraordinarily good hands. And yet all noticed that the pile of chips next to young Denisen was higher than anybody else's by a good margin.

The four other players had tried to read how Steen played the game. They had all played together enough to have learned each other's habits, but the new player had baffled them. When he bet reluctantly, seemingly only to keep the other one honest, he turned out to have the winning hand. When he bet heavily, he might have something in the hole, or he might not. And yet his shows of satisfaction when he took in a pot never revealed whether he had bluffed successfully or whether he really had the card to fill the inside straight he had showing. A new player could get skinned when he came into a game that had been running for some time. But in this case, the new player had skinned them.

On this hand, Albert had a pair of jacks showing, along with a deuce. Steen had a queen and two sevens. Albert had drawn the two jacks in the first two rounds, and had bet up the pot, forcing everyone to spend heavily to see another card. Steen had done so calmly, without showing too much hesitation or too much eagerness. His lone queen on top of his hole card smiled, suggesting that her double lay just underneath her.

Albert grimaced when he saw Steen draw the second seven. He wasn't convinced that Steen had a queen hidden away. But now, even were he to pair up his deuce, or the five he had in the hole, he wouldn't have a winning hand guaranteed. Albert liked things to be as sure as possible, and now the only way he could be sure was to draw a third jack on the last card. He bet up again, and managed to drive out Finney and Gordon. But Steen, with his little queen sitting serenely at the head of his cards, had not only called him but raised him.

"I'll call your raise," Albert said. He hoped that Gordon would just deal him a third jack, to make things easy. If he quit now, he would end the day slightly ahead. If he won the last pot, he would end a fair amount ahead, enough to brag a bit. But if he continued to bet, he could end the day losers. And he hated to end the day losers.

"Last card." Gordon tipped the deck with the edge of his thumbnail and prepared to deal.

Steen smiled and said nothing. There was less banter at this game than at other games he had played in, and he adapted himself to the circumstances. He gave no tells, in speech or manner, and his passing smiles or frowns could mean that he had a good hand, and was concerned that others were going to drop out, or that he had a bad hand, and was concerned that others were going to stay in.

In this case, he had a ten in the hole. He was bluffing. Yet he had bet from the beginning as though he had a pair of queens, and no other queens had shown up in anyone else's hand to make the claim less believable. The pair of sevens had helped, in that with his presumed queens he had a nearly unbeatable hand. But he would have to make Albert fold. That was the game. To make another player believe what you wanted him to believe, and act as you wanted him to act.

Gordon slowly slid a card along the felt to Albert, and flipped it over.

"Five," Gordon said.

"Five." Albert looked unhappily at the card. That gave him two pair, but was not good at all against Steen's queens and sevens.

Gordon dealt Steen's last card in the same way, inched it along the felt and turned it face up at the last moment.

"Jack," the dealer said.

"My jack!" Albert said.

"My jack," Steen replied.

"Pair of jacks still bets," Finney said.

"If you hadn't dropped out, Bill, I would have gotten that jack," Albert said.

"If wishes were horses, beggars would ride," Finney said. "You two high rollers made it too expensive for me."

"Are you going to bet?" Gordon asked.

Albert twisted his mouth. "I'll check," he said.

Everyone looked at Steen, who raised his eyebrows once. "I'll bet five."

"Five?" Finney asked.

Steen pushed out five blue chips. "That's the limit, isn't it?"

Albert looked at his hole card once again, as though it might have changed into the fourth jack. Then he looked at his piles of chips, neat stacks of white and red and blue, just a bit more than he had started the day with. Then he looked at the offending jack at the end of Steen's line of cards.

He shrugged his shoulders. "I'll fold," he said.

Steen smiled, gathered in the last pot, and quietly mixed his cards into the deck. The others watched him.

"Well," Finney said. "Did you have a queen?"

"Might have had a queen. Might have had a third seven, too. But nobody wanted to pay to find out."

"That's right," Gordon said. "Nobody wanted to pay to find out. So I guess we'll never know."

"You'll just have to wait until next time," Steen said.

"You don't mind taking a risk, do you?" Albert said.

"No," Steen said. "I don't mind taking a risk."

"I like to have a sure thing when I can get it," Albert said. "But you don't mind taking a risk."

"Not a bad quality in a man," Gordon said. "Especially one building houses these days."

Everybody shook hands before they left. Albert Jackson looked forward to his meeting with Steen the following week. Gordon thought about selling new houses in the Blossom Belt, and Hogg thought about serving new customers. Bill Finney was convinced he knew who the new owner of Lone Hill would be.

Steen was certain he had everything in the palm of his hand. If he could somehow get Betsy to understand how things had to be.

20
. . . .

House Fire   June 10, 1933

"You can't be only halfway married, you know."

Marilyn Jackson looked at Betsy across the kitchen table and sipped her coffee. She wanted to help.

"I mean you can't be married to someone and not let him be a father to your child. A boy needs discipline."

"But Peter's only getting worse."

"If Steen's in his proper place, it will turn out all right in the end. Is Peter's last name going to be changed?"

"I thought I'd wait a year and see how he felt."

"That's just the kind of thing you shouldn't leave up to a child. How can Steen feel like he's really head of the household if Peter keeps his grandfather's name?"

"It just seems so soon," Betsy said.

"The sooner the better," Marilyn declared. "After all that Steen did in marrying you."

"Do you think I didn't do anything in marrying him?"

"Look at all you did for your father," Marilyn said. "Isn't it right to do as much or more for a husband?"

Betsy didn't answer.

"Let Steen be the father. Never contradict him in front of Peter. It's best for the family that way."

She looked at her watch.

"I have to go home and start dinner," she said.

"I'll see you to the door," Betsy said, pushing back her chair.

On the porch, Marilyn took both Betsy's hands in hers.

"Believe me, things will be better if you keep doing as I say," she said.

"Thank you," Betsy said.

"I only want you to be happy." Marilyn squeezed her hands and turned to walk home.

When Peter came home from school, Betsy called him into the bathroom. She took Mercurochrome from the medicine cabinet while Peter stood sullenly with his books still in his hands.

"Turn around, Peter," she urged. "Take down your pants."

He let his books thud to the floor and land in a heap. Then he slowly turned his back to Betsy and lowered his pants.

Red welts lay across the backs of his thighs, still raised and swollen. The skin was broken across three of them. Betsy brushed the candy-apple-red antiseptic over the wounds and bit her lip as her son flinched at the sting.

"You have to learn not to provoke him, Peter."

"Why doesn't he learn not to provoke me?"

"Because he's the father. You can't make him mad."

"He's not my father," Peter said.

"He's the head of the family, and the breadwinner." Betsy waved her hands over his legs to dry the Mercurochrome. "Steen works very hard, Peter, and in part he's working for you. You should see him out on site, sweating, hammering, lifting the frame of a new house into place. And not only that, but also making sure everyone else is doing their job, too. And meeting with the banks and the new owners. He works all the time, and he's a good provider."

"I don't care if he's a good provider or not," Peter said.

"You only say that because you're too young to know any better."

"Nobody ever beat me down in Signal Hill," Peter said. "And I always got enough to eat down there too."

Betsy wanted to promise him that nobody would ever beat him again. She had stopped letting Steen touch her in bed because of the awful memory of her father hitting her when she was pregnant.

But she didn't want to turn on her husband in front of Peter. "You have to learn to control yourself, so that you don't make him mad," she finally said. "You have to learn that he's the father."

Peter yanked up his pants over the drying red patches and turned on Betsy. "I don't care how hard he works, or how many houses he builds. He's not my father, and he never will be. I wish he would just go back to Denmark where he came from."

"Peter, you shouldn't say that."

"Or else I wish I was back in Signal Hill. Everybody was nice to me all the time down there. Nobody ever hit me or called me names, or sent me to bed without my supper. Everything was better down there."

He walked to the back door. Betsy chased after him and grabbed him by the arm. "Peter, don't leave."

Peter pulled free. "You don't love me," he said.

He ran outside. The door flapped open behind him.

．．．．．．

Peter was still missing in the evening.

Steen and Betsy ate supper alone and then drove to citizenship class together. Steen refused to let her hold up supper, or do anything that would give the wrong sign to Peter. They shouldn't show that they were going to let his childish running away affect them in the least. The boy was behaving badly, and he wasn't to be entreated back. If anything, he should be punished again for frightening Betsy by staying away.

"Leave the back door open," he said. "He'll come home when he's hungry enough, no doubt. And then we'll see what's to be done. I believe we'll find him sleeping in his bed when we come back."

Betsy followed Steen out to the Jordan. As they pulled out of the driveway and turned down the street, she gave a backward glance at the little house, still hoping for a sight that would reassure, her son on the porch of her house, waving good-bye, smiling, letting her know he would be happy when she returned.

Steen noted her glance.

"You're worrying too much," he said. "He'll be there when we come back."

Betsy turned her head forward. The porch had been empty, dark and cheerless.

. . . .

The blacksmith shop at night was vast and filled with shadows, dark on the wide cement floor and darker still in the corners and up among the rafters. A single shaft of moonlight fell on the cold forge and anvil, a dull luster coming from the smooth, hard metal.

Peter dropped in from the back window and landed lightly on his feet.

He walked forward in the half-light and stopped when he stepped on something hard.

He knelt down. It was a large iron gate, half finished, laid out on the floor. Peter traced the graceful, curving metal with his fingers, felt the joints where the thin decorative twisted iron joined the main frame of the gate. Under the metal, he could make out the rough chalk lines Bert had marked on the shop floor. That was how the blacksmith did it; he drew the shape of the gate onto the floor, and then bent the metal to match what he had drawn.

The edge of the gate lay in darkness. When Peter reached the end of the gate, he heard a sudden scurrying of tiny feet.

A frightened mouse scuttled across the cement floor. In that moment, a sudden explosion of wings from the rafters and a screech.

A night bird dropped sharply through the moonlight, long

gray feathers and a sudden flash of its bone-white face. The wings folded around the mouse as in a mother's embrace, and there came a short, high-pitched scream.

The scream died, and with a muffled beat of wings the bird ascended again to the rafters, invisible in the darkness.

Peter peered up toward where he thought the owl had alighted, but he could see nothing. He looked all around into the blackness above him; it could all be crowded by sudden killers ready to descend upon him, like his stepfather's meaty hand.

Quickly, he stepped toward the forge and grasped what he had come for: the can of coal oil Bert kept to light his forge in the morning. He poured some shakily into a milk bottle he had stolen off a front porch; a little spilled onto the cuff of his pants, but he ignored it. Then he took a handful of matches from the tin dispenser and shoved them into his shirt pocket.

He looked up again and heard the sound of a long, slow *hoo.*

He backed toward the window, glancing into the black corners all around him. Then he placed the milk bottle on the sill and hoisted himself carefully up. Before he shut the window behind him, he heard the rustle of feathers and the crunch of tiny bones.

He had walked the route through the orchards during the day and he thought he knew the way. But the orchard had a fearsome aspect at night. The trees in leaf cast thick ragged clumps of shadow, left only a narrow, crooked line of moonlight between them. He kept to the light and walked warily, trying to see into the shadows that surrounded him.

The smell of fruit hung in the air and made Peter nauseous. He had stuffed himself with unripe prunes and apricots during the day, and in the afternoon he had gotten sick and thrown up everything. He didn't feel hungry now; he felt thin and faint, as though his stomach had shrunk within him.

At San Natoma–Los Gatos Road, he hid in a ditch to let some car headlights pass him by. While he crouched there, cars were coming from the opposite direction. The dog continued to bark, and he heard the rattle of its chain.

The cars sped by, one, two. He looked up again, and the road was clear except for the taillights winking red in the distance. The dog barked again, and Peter clutched his milk bottle full of fuel close to his body and stole across the street.

The orchards he passed through then were like a deep, silent river he had to cross. The shadows lapped up against him, threatened to swallow him up. But he felt with every step he was proving something. He felt he was growing bigger and stronger.

The structure loomed up at a crossroads, in the center of a lot newly cut into the fruit trees. It looked larger now than it had in the daylight, a gigantic insect with a thousand thin legs squatting in a corner of the orchard. The moonlight cast fantastic patterns onto the bare earth, skeletal bars of black separated by silvery-white squares and rhomboids.

It was only as Peter stepped closer that the structure took on the more familiar aspect of a house frame, nearly completed, nearly ready to be roofed and sheathed with clapboard.

His stepfather was such a hard worker, such a good provider. Peter stepped in through the hole where the front door would go and looked overhead to the roofless sky.

He walked through the rooms of the house, skipping from two-by-six to two-by-six, and he recognized that the layout of the house was the same as the house on Oak Street, the same porch, the same front room and bay window, the same dining room and kitchen and bedrooms. He began to dance and laugh in the house's empty skeleton, swinging the milk bottle around at the end of an outflung arm.

He sat down in the front room and dangled his legs between the open stringers. Just where his stepfather sat in the Morris chair and smoked a pipe and watched him.

He closed his eyes.

The house appeared, complete and familiar and comfortable. Steen had disappeared. Gone were the narrowed, distrustful eyes, the lips pursed around a pipe stem, the hairy, beefy arms crossed over his lap.

Peter himself sat in the chair, light and happy and in control.

able. Steen had disappeared. Gone were the narrowed, distrustful eyes, the lips pursed around a pipe stem, the hairy, beefy arms crossed over his lap.

Peter himself sat in the chair, light and happy and in control.

His mother came to him, stood by his side, stroked his hair. *What do you want, Peter?* she asked.

She curled his hair around her finger and tugged it.

What do you want, Peter?

Peter opened his eyes. The black shadows fell like jail bars across him.

He stood and walked through the doorway to where his bedroom would be. Here Steen had beaten him.

He poured coal oil carefully over the stringers all through the room, and then jumped through the wall down to the ground. Nobody could lock him in a room in this house.

He lit a match against a rusty can and watched it burn brightly between his cupped hands, fascinated by the small, sharp flame. Then he touched it to one of the floor timbers.

The fire twinkled down the length of the timber, bluish at first, then growing yellow as the wood caught. He lit another timber in his bedroom, and then another. Soon there was a merry little blaze in a neat rectangle, blackening the wood beneath it and beginning to lick at the upright boards in the walls and doorways.

Peter watched in savage delight as the fire spread. It wouldn't stop now until the house was destroyed. When he turned back into the orchards, a path through the darkness seemed to open before him. He ran toward home, where his mother would be waiting.

21

. . . .

Coal Oil   June 10, 1933

The gravel crunched under the tires as the Jordan pulled
into the driveway.

Steen turned off the ignition, and the engine sighed to a
halt and burbled slightly as it cooled.

Betsy looked at him. They both hesitated in the car beside
the dark, silent house and listened to the engine.

"Probably," Steen finally said, "he's in bed asleep. It's late
enough."

Betsy had wanted to rush home right after class. But Steen
ignored her, and they stayed longer than usual afterward.
Smoking, coffee, conversation with the other immigrants.
Everyone wanted to practice their English with her, and so
she talked about the weather and the crops and wished everybody luck on their exam.

"You are a lucky man to have such a helper, Steen," said Mr. Fontanella, grinning like a gnome. "I think you be a citizen soon."

"*Will* be," Betsy corrected automatically.

"Ah, the future, the future tense. I never learn the future." The elderly man tapped himself on the head.

They were among the last to leave.

Now Steen stepped heavily on the gravel and walked around the car to open Betsy's door. She got out and waited for him to lock the car, and they walked to the house side by side. She wanted to run to the door, but she felt him beside her, forbidding her to get ahead of him or show any signs that she was more anxious than he was.

He unlocked the front door and folded her arm in his. They walked together to Peter's room, slowly, ever so slowly. Then he let her open the door.

Peter lay on the bed, fully clothed, fast asleep.

Betsy went to the bedside and looked at her son. She knelt beside him and stroked his hair, and the boy stirred and smiled, as though in a happy dream.

"You see," Steen said from the doorway. "Things will work out."

Betsy lifted her head and knit her eyebrows. She sniffed the air.

"I smell . . ."

Steen entered the room and sniffed as well.

"Is it gas?" he asked.

The doorbell rang, and a fist pounded on the door, loud and urgent. Steen went swiftly to the door and opened it to Murphy, the town constable, dressed in only jeans and undershirt.

"Steen, the house you were building caught fire, and I don't think we'll be saving it."

Steen looked back at Betsy, who stood in the corridor outside Peter's room. She glanced guiltily in at the sleeping boy and then back at Steen.

"How did it start?" Steen asked.

"Who knows? Act of God."

"Let's go, the car's warm."

On his way out the door, Steen turned and gave Betsy a look of awful intelligence.

One timber, charred and broken, still pointed skyward. The rest had fallen inward and burned. The house looked like the remains of a boy's campfire on a huge scale, an ugly tract of black earth and whitish ash cut into the surrounding trees. The shape of the roof was still vaguely visible where it had fallen into the center of the foundation, two timbers nailed together at a precise angle lay smoldering together on their side. Everything else was gone.

Faint wisps of steam and smoke escaped in places from the heap of blackened wood, and a yellow-coated fireman still picked his way through the wreckage and directed another to turn the hose at the remaining hot spots. But the fire had mostly burned itself out before the Model-T fire truck had arrived. Yesterday there had been a house rising from a foundation, ready to support a roof, to give shelter. Now there was a dark, useless ruin.

"We have insurance, don't we?"

Steen walked slowly around the circumference of the house and didn't answer. Anders stayed at his heels, walking with him, knowing enough not to press Steen for an answer. He would speak when he was ready, when he'd walked all the way around the house and had seen the damage and weighed everything in his mind.

Steen paused when he came to where the front door had been. The steps leading to the porch were crumpled in as though a giant hammer had smashed them to the ground. Then he continued to a place a little apart from the house, away from the trucks and hoses and men, and looked at it all from a distance.

"Yes, we have insurance, all right."

"That's a blessing," Anders said.

He looked at his friend's face, pale as a half-moon from the bullet lamps of the firemen.

"Don't you think . . ." Steen's voice came quiet through the night. "Don't you think this fire could free up some money for us?"

"Yes," Anders said slowly. "It might."

"For something more important. That's what I'm thinking."

"Lone Hill."

"Yes. Lone Hill." Steen looked down at the men still over-turning wood and pumping water over the dead foundation.

. . . .

The front door crashed open, and Betsy sprang to her feet.

She'd been sitting up, waiting for Steen like a condemned prisoner waits for the hangman. She had paced in the front room, gone to the porch to look for headlights, made tea in the kitchen, sat again in the front room, and then looked again for headlights through the curtains. From time to time, she had looked in at Peter. He still lay sound asleep, with a sweet smile on his face and a telltale odor of fuel rising from his clothes.

She rushed to the hallway at the sound of the door and met Steen. His face was terrible, a blunt instrument when he looked at her.

"It's gone," he said.

"Do they know that the fire was set?"

"They will. Unless your darling son is smarter than he looks."

"You can't be sure it was him."

"I'm sure. And you are too. And he'll confess it this night. Wasn't I right when I said he was better off staying in Southern California?"

"But Steen . . ."

"Wasn't I? At least he didn't commit any crimes down there."

"But *I* wasn't better off, Steen. I wanted him here, with me."

Steen barked, "Now he'll be someplace worse than Signal Hill. When the truth comes out."

Betsy stood deadly still. "How are they going to know?"

Steen smiled. "Do you want me to lie?"

"You can't let them take Peter away." Betsy grasped his arm.

"The only man who might hold something against me is old Pedersen, since I let him go last month. Do you want me to tell them it might be him?"

"I don't know. But you can't let them take Peter away from me."

"You do want me to lie, then." Steen took Betsy's silence for confirmation. He spoke low and earnestly. "And what have you been doing for me? Putting obstacles in my way. Stopping my plans. Everything you could do to frustrate me."

He walked past her as though she were made of straw.

"I'm going to see what the boy himself has to say," he said. "I'll do what I can. See that you do the same."

She watched helplessly as he entered Peter's room and closed the door behind him.

. . . .

Peter woke up with Steen's hand on his shoulder, shaking him.

He sat up, and Steen leaned back.

"You've had quite an adventure today." Steen watched him with small eyes. "Do you want to tell me about it?"

Peter looked around. "Where's my mother?"

"Outside. You'll see her soon enough. But first I want you to talk to me. What did you do all day long? Besides scaring your mother to death."

"Nothing."

"Nothing? Remember, I see what you do even when I'm not around. What did you do tonight?"

Peter didn't answer.

"You don't know anything about a fire, do you?"

"A fire?" Peter's voice sounded false, even to himself.

Steen grabbed the boy's shoulders and shook him roughly. "Yes, a fire. At a house I was building with my own hands, to put bread on the table for you and your mother. Do you know anything about a fire?"

"No, I don't know anything about a fire. What fire?"

Steen shook him once more, then threw him back onto the bed. "Take off your pants," he ordered.

"What?"

"Don't ask questions, just take off your pants."

"Don't want to."

"It's not a question of whether you want to, it's a question of doing as I say. Take off your pants."

"No."

Steen cuffed him on the side of the head. Peter suddenly plunged at Steen, windmilling his two fists. Steen ignored the small stinging blows, stood and pushed Peter down onto the bed. Then he grasped the boy by his kicking legs and hauled up on the cuffs of the pants.

Peter struggled and squirmed, but suddenly felt his pants slipping down around his slender hips. He grabbed at them too late. Steen held them up in his fist, and Peter huddled in a corner of the bed, suddenly ashamed at his naked legs, scrawny and hairless and white.

Steen threw a pants leg into Peter's face.

"Smell," he said. "And tell me where you were tonight."

Peter smelled the coal oil and looked up at Steen's unblinking gaze.

. . . . . .

Steen handed Betsy the pair of pants.

"Wash these," he said. "You can go in and see him, but wash these tonight. And I think things will finally be straightened out."

She nodded her agreement. Just as he expected her to. She had agreed to everything in exchange for Peter, and she felt just as powerless before Steen as she ever had before her father. She realized that he had finally gotten what he really wanted; he had finally taken her father's place.

But just then he turned away, and she rushed in to see her son.

22

. . . .

Shorty's Dream   October 1933

At the end of the harvest that year, Shorty took Karin Madison downtown for dinner. He hadn't seen her for some time, but he was sure that she knew the same things he did: The harvest had been good, but the prices had been bad. Lone Hill was to be sold, and more full-time men were going to be let go. Ida Valley would not thrive under his care; it would grow smaller with every passing year.

Usually when Shorty was in San Jose, he just grabbed a bite to eat at the Coffee Pot, or Chilrudd's Creamery. But tonight he'd actually called for a spot at Chez Gilbert and told Karin that he wanted to take her someplace special. The end of the harvest had been no great cause for celebration. But he was accustomed to going someplace nice when the fruit was in and packed and shipped, and he wanted to be there with Karin, wanted to talk with her.

He missed talking with her. Funny it seemed, but he missed talking with her more than anything else about her, more than her cooking or the little fuss she made over him when he came or the game of cribbage they sometimes shared. Something about the way she listened to him when he spoke, the way she looked at him and added a word here and there, made everything he said more meaningful. His thoughts and feelings seemed to straighten out and make perfect sense when he told them to her. And his thoughts now, at the end of this harvest, were as confused as he could remember.

He picked her up in his Chevrolet, which he'd found time to wash and polish. And he complimented her on her dress, which pleased her. In fact, she wore the same dark crushed-velvet jacket and skirt she always wore when she went someplace fancy, and he'd seen it before. But she wore it so seldom that it still looked new, and he was always surprised and impressed by it. She looked the height of fashion, he said.

The walls of the restaurant were hung with heavy purple curtains, and the chairs had plush seats of the same color. All the tables glowed softly with candlelight and glassware and stiff white tablecloths. Gilbert himself greeted them at the door, and a waiter wearing a white shirt and a red bow tie took Karin's coat and handed them both menus. Karin thought aloud that she had never seen such an elegant place.

They each ordered the pressed duck at the waiter's suggestion. The duck came fresh from hunters in the south bay, he said. And while they ate, Shorty talked about the changing times and what it was going to mean for Ida Valley. Lone Hill, he thought, was just the beginning. The ranch was going to be sold off piece by piece until, five or ten years down the line, there wouldn't be much left. The times wouldn't support a big, integrated operation where everything from growing to drying to packing to shipping took place, and young Roberts wasn't going to stay on the ranch like his parents had. It was all going to disappear.

He was talking about Ida Valley, but Karin realized that he was really talking about himself, and herself. Their lives were tangled up with the life of the ranch. He couldn't talk directly about them until he had finished with Ida Valley; but she thought that if she were patient and encouraging, he finally would.

They ordered coffee and dessert, puff pastries filled with cream. Shorty lifted the pastry off his plate and looked at it quizzically.

"It's so light," he said.

"It's delicate," Karin said.

"In two bites, it will be gone. I think I like your pies better."

"And the coffee?"

Shorty lifted the white porcelain cup and sipped critically.

"Good," he pronounced. "But not as good as yours."

Karin smiled. "So, Jim," she said. "If Ida Valley is so bad off, what are you going to do?"

"I'm not worried about myself," Shorty said. "I've got enough money socked away to last me out."

"But you're not a man who can sit idle, Jim. You need to have something to work on, or you won't be happy."

"That's true. I guess I never put it into words like that before, but that's true."

"What will you do if they just don't need a supervisor at Ida Valley?"

"And they won't," Shorty said. "Somewhere down the line."

"What do you think you'd be happy doing?"

"I only know how to do one thing, and that's grow fruit."

"So how can you do that?" Karin pursed her lips in thought. "Are the other big ranches in the Valley in the same spot as Ida Valley?"

"The same or worse," Shorty said.

"You wouldn't like working under somebody else anyway, would you?"

"I don't suppose I would. Not after working my way up to foreman, and then being supervisor, I wouldn't want to go back to being what I was. A man likes to feel like he's moving forward, doing something for himself, even in the Depression."

"So what do you think you'll do?"

Shorty pondered over his coffee. "I'm not sure," he finally said.

Karin had helped him come to this point, and now she wanted him to advance a little bit on his own. But it seemed he still needed more encouragement.

"How much did they sell Lone Hill for?" she asked.

"Dirt cheap. Dirt cheap. Denisen made a good deal for himself, carrying off that piece of orchard. Nobody else was about to make an offer. All the land around here is dirt cheap these days."

"Really?"

"Prices couldn't get much lower." Shorty suddenly looked up. "Maybe what I should do is just buy a little place for myself."

"That sounds like a good idea."

"Not anything big, nothing I couldn't handle myself with one other man, five or ten acres in prunes or 'cots . . ."

"A house . . ."

"Sure, a house and a barn. Big enough to live on and keep working. Even if I don't make much, I'll be able to grow it and get it to market. People will eat it. It will be doing some good."

"That sounds wonderful. You'll be happy."

"Sure."

"You'll find some satisfaction in what you're doing. You won't have to be working under anyone else."

"No. I'll be the supervisor, and I'll also be the man in the house signing the contracts."

"You're all set."

"That's just such a fine idea. I think it will be perfect." Shorty picked up his piece of pastry and bit off half. Some of the cream spilled over onto the corner of his mouth, and Karin reached across the table with her napkin and touched his face up gently.

"Now you're happy," she said.

"Well, it just seems to answer so many questions." Shorty swallowed some coffee. "I won't have to worry about what the Roberts children are going to do once the old man goes. I'll be able to make my own decisions, I'll be independent."

"Yes, you will. Free and independent."

Shorty stuffed the other half of the pastry in his mouth and washed it down with more coffee. Then he noticed how quiet Karin had become. Her replies only echoing his own. Her face no longer sharing his happiness, but grave and distant.

"I started off saying," he began, "that I wasn't so worried about myself."

"Yes?" Not discouraging, but neutral.

"Well, I kind of wanted to say that I was a little worried about you."

"Oh, you don't have to worry about me. There's always a place for a woman who isn't too proud to work." She looked down at her hands, blunt and red, and then looked back up at Shorty. "Hands that can cook and clean and sew will never be idle. I can take care of children, or take care of an older lady, or nurse a man back on his feet. You don't have to worry about me."

"Well, I was kind of thinking now. If I get this little place . . ."

"With a house."

"Sure, with a house. And I'd sure hate to not be seeing you. And if we weren't both living at Ida Valley."

"Jim. You know I'm still married." She decided that if she didn't say the word first, it would never be said.

Shorty looked at her in silence for a full minute. All the contentment he'd felt in the prospect of his ten acres, his fruit trees, his barn, left him suddenly. He wasn't free, wasn't independent at all. He had placed his happiness in her keeping. He didn't know exactly how it had happened, gradually over the past ten years, but he had given all his happiness into her hands.

"I know you're still married, legally," he said. "But you can do something about that, can't you?"

"Do you want me to?"

Shorty hesitated.

"Yes. I want you to get unmarried."

"Why?"

"Why?" Shorty looked at her in confusion. "Because . . . so that I can marry you."

Silence.

"I want to marry you." Shorty suddenly felt panicked. "I want to marry you. I love you. I mean, you want to, don't you? Don't you? Say you'll marry me, Karin."

She took his hand and squeezed it. "It's all right, Jim. It's all right. You buy your land, and I'll marry you."

Shorty looked down and shook his head. "I don't think I ever felt this way before."

"We'll be fine, Jim. We just have to get used to it. It's a big change for both of us."

23

. . . .

New Deal   October 1933

Millie Austen had a job because she was a cheerful, pleasant girl.

That's how her teachers described her in their letters of recommendation: a cheerful, pleasant girl with a good head for numbers. The letters, and her blue dress, and the dimples on her cheeks when she smiled won her a spot behind the teller window at the Bank of America. They wanted tellers, the manager said, who would be friendly to customers and make them feel at home.

"I try to have a smile for everyone," she said.

"That's perfect," the manager said. "Act just that way, and you'll do fine."

It had been a long day when the man came in, just before closing time on a Friday, and her feet were biting her. She wanted nothing more than to turn the key in the brass lock of her teller drawer and go home to the familiar sounds and smells of her mother cooking in the kitchen, give her paycheck to her father, be praised and petted, and take off her shoes. Maybe she would run a hot bath and just sit in the tub for a while before dinner. But when the man approached her window, she did her best to have a smile for him.

She had seen some men like this one before in the bank, but not many. A tall farming man, clothes stained with old sweat and fresh dirt. A face burned and wrinkled by the sun. The people who had worked at the bank a long time, since back when it was still called the Bank of Italy, told her that in the beginning, most of the customers had been farmers or country folk. She'd even heard the men in the bank refer to customers like this one as shitheels. Nowadays it was mostly clerks or cannery workers, or, down at the commercial window, people in business.

The bankbook was grimy and curved from his hip pocket, but Millie kept her smile on. There was something familiar about this man, though she couldn't quite place him. It seemed she had seen him before, but she didn't remember him ever coming to the bank before.

"I haven't used it for a long time," the man said. "I wanted to see if I had any money left in the account."

The last entry was years ago. Millie looked up and saw the minute hand of the clock click over to the twelve. But she took the book back to the files, found his account card, and began to carefully fill in by hand the interest earned and the quarterly balance in neat columns, initialing each entry with an "M.A." in script.

"You have a balance of fifteen dollars and thirty-six cents."

"Fifteen thirty-six." The man looked at her with thin lips. "You're mighty chipper. Are you always so happy?"

"I always try to be, sir."

"Must come from handling money all day. Is Albert in?"

"The manager?"

"Yeah. The *manager*."

"I think he's still in his office. But it's after closing time."

"That doesn't matter. Just tell him I'm here."

"All right, Mister . . ." Millie looked down at the bankbook.

"Just tell him that Jax is here to see him. Howard Jackson."

Albert didn't know why his brother had come to the bank. He used to come in only when he wanted to cash a check and do some tomcatting around San Jose, used to blow into the bank big, bright, and loud, and blow out again with a smile on his face and money in his pocket, heading for the nearest speak. Every once in a while, he asked Albert to go with him. When Albert refused, talking Jennifer and the kids, Howie would snort.

"You take life too seriously, Al."

He hadn't seen him as much since Marilyn caught him. He imagined his brother handed over his check to her every month, especially since the kids had come. But when Howie did come in, he didn't seem to have changed so much. Still loud and genially disrespectful of the bank and the people who worked there. It caused Albert embarrassment sometimes. But still, he liked Howie to come in, if only to break the routine, and when he hadn't seen him for some time, he found that he missed him.

Howie looked different this time. Came in quiet, sat in the chair on the other side of the desk, folded his hands in his lap.

"How are you doing, Al?" he'd said.

"Things are good," Albert said.

"That's good."

He waited for Howie to say why he was there. When he didn't, Albert finally said, "Do you know what my plan is now?"

"No. What's your plan now?"

Albert had decided to find a place up in headquarters in San Francisco. His old boss, the one who'd been branch manager before him, was up there now, and said that San Francisco was where they were really making decisions about banking in this state. He'd had a good record as a branch manager, given the customers good service, and made good loans, and now he felt he'd gone as far as he could here. His old boss was Italian and said he'd look out for him if he wanted to come. Albert loved San Jose and all, but a man likes to keep moving ahead in the world. And the place to move ahead was in San Francisco.

Howard nodded to all this, approved. Albert offered him a cigar from the humidor on his desk, took one himself, and leaned back in his green-leather chair.

"What does Jennifer think about leaving the Santa Clara?" Howard asked.

"She'll go along. She's not short on ambition herself, that girl."

"Well. You've certainly done well for yourself, Al."

"That's because I've always had a plan. You don't go anywhere without a plan."

"You've certainly made it pay."

Albert bit off the end of his cigar and lit it.

"So I've been shooting my mouth off here. What's with you?"

Howard rolled his cigar unlit from one hand to another. "Not so hot, Al. You heard that they sold off a piece of the ranch?"

"Lone Hill?"

"Yeah. To some squarehead who's putting up houses."

"I heard about it," Albert said cautiously.

"Well, they decided they've got too many full-time men at the ranch now. So they're giving some of us the boot."

Albert looked at his brother closely. "You have any savings, Howie?"

"None to speak of. We're going to need some help, Al."

"But Marilyn's still working at the library."

"That job pays dirt."

"At least you've got some money coming in. You have to look at the bright side. Here, I'll tell you what to do."

Albert placed a long yellow legal pad on the desk between him and Howard and drew straight vertical lines down it with a ruler. He wrote "Expenses" neatly at the top of one column and "Income" at the top of another. Along the side, he wrote "M.'s salary" and then stopped.

"So you've got no interest income on any kind of savings?"

Howard shook his head silently.

Albert paused, then skipped down several lines and wrote "Rent" in red ink.

This was something he had done many times for other men, men who had trouble making a loan payment on a house after a fourth child was born, or older men who found that money slipped through their fingers every month and were wondering what they would do for their retirement. Or for women who told him they found it hard to keep their family decently clothed and fed. They came to him because he was the banker, he knew something about the mysterious ebb and flow of money, he could tell them what to do. And he always laid it out in straight lines and columns for them, precise numbers in ink, with a total at the bottom. They would watch silently during this process, attentive, as though he were a Gypsy casting their future in cards. When the total came out red, he encouraged them, asked where in the expense column they might spend a little bit less. When the total came out black, he praised them, asked what their long-term goals were.

The process worked. He had seen it work. If a family could make a budget and stick to it, he knew they would be better off in a year and in five years than they would be without it. It all depended on them. He could show them what they had to do, he told them, but it was up to them to carry it out.

"You don't know what your expenses are for food, clothing, that kind of thing are, do you?"

"No."

Albert pushed the yellow pad across the desk toward his brother. "You take this home and show it to Marilyn. Work on it with her, or better yet, come in with her and we'll work it out together. Think about what you need money for, where you're spending it, and what you can cut back on. Then we'll total up the numbers, and see how I can help out."

Howard looked at him, then looked down at the lines on the paper.

"Do you have any ideas about finding work, Howie?"

"Haven't had time to think about it yet."

"Make a plan, follow through on it. You'll find something."

Howard made no move to take up the budget. "Did I ever tell you why, when I came back from France, I didn't go to school? Why I just took a dirt job out in the orchards?"

"No, Howie. You never did."

"I remember taking over a patch of land from the Germans. One that had been swapped back and forth a few times during the war. And when we dug in again, I stuck my spade in the earth and came away with teeth rattling in the dirt. You couldn't move any soil without moving the bones of soldiers who had been sown there years before."

Howard spoke tiredly. "When I came back, I just wanted to find a patch of earth and make something grow there."

"That was a long time ago, now." Albert ripped the budget carefully from the legal pad. Then he stood up, took out his wallet, and laid a twenty-dollar bill on top of it.

"In case you need something to tide you over," he said. "Come back and see me in a day or two."

Howard picked up the money and the budget, folded them carefully together, and placed them in his shirt pocket. Then he placed the cigar in his pocket as well.

"Want another smoke, Howie?" Albert took the top off the humidor.

"No, thanks," Howard said. "I'm quitting smoking after today. It won't fit into my budget."

"That piece of paper will help, Howie. I know it will. I've seen it work a hundred times."

"Sure." Howard stood at the door on his way out. "I bet you have."

After the door closed, Albert decided that he should talk to Jennifer tonight about moving to San Francisco. That was where the future was. Albert felt himself rising effortlessly through the ranks to the upper stories of the tall building on California Street, surrounded by good men who thought and acted as he did, making the right decisions about banking in this state.

. . . .

Outside the bank, Jax took the cigar from his pocket and ran it slowly under his nose, inhaling deeply. It smelled rich and fresh and golden, fine tobacco hand-rolled in Cuba. He bit off the end of the cigar and spit it into the gutter, and placed the cigar carefully between his lips. He struck a match along his denim pants, lit the cigar, and began walking.

When he reached the Goosetown Saloon, he found Giancarlo loading a fruit packing box onto the bed of a pickup truck. The scar-faced bartender broke into a smile, put down the box, and wiped his forehead with a bright red handkerchief from his hip pocket.

"Jax," he said. "Long time no see."

"Not since the harvest started." Jax took a long pull on the cigar. "What's up?"

"I'm shutting down. Moving."

"Moving?"

"To a place downtown. Getting ready to go legitimate."

"You don't say."

"Come on in. I've still got a jug of red in the back for old friends."

Jax followed him through the two doors into the saloon. All the tables and chairs were gone, and their heels echoed as they crossed to the bar. Giancarlo pulled the cork from an unmarked jug and poured two glasses as Jax put his foot on the rail. He puffed on his cigar and watched the smoke disappear among the uncovered rafters. The cigar was growing short now.

They clinked glasses, and Jax drank some of the rough red wine. "The place sure seems empty," he said.

"Has been for a while."

"That why you're moving?"

"Times are changing, and you got to change with them. Prohibition's dead. I smelled it when they made three-point-two beer legal. There's no place for a joint like this anymore."

"Maybe not."

"So I decided to open the first legal bar downtown. You got to plan ahead, you know."

"Right."

"You want some more? Then I have to get back to moving."

"Sure."

Giancarlo filled Jax's glass again, then walked to the pile of boxes and picked up the top one. A faint clinking came from the box.

"Shot glasses," Giancarlo said.

Jax watched him carry the box across the empty floor and back through the door, and a sliver of sunlight fell for a moment into the room. He felt that in a moment, he would join in and help carry the boxes of glasses and bottles and tablecloths out into the sun, onto the back of the truck, into downtown. But for right now, all he cared about was savoring the very last puff.

24

. . . .

Steen's Dream   October 1933

One minute per tree.

The yellow Caterpillar bulldozer lowered its blade and rumbled forward. The blade cut into the ground just short of the trunk of the prune tree, and the roots split and cracked. The tree shuddered as the bulldozer paused, downshifted, and pushed ahead. For a moment, both tree and machine seemed to lift into the air, blade against trunk, joining and rising together to the quickening hammer of the diesel engine. Then the tree bowed slowly backward. The roots that still remained cracked one by one, and the tree, green and dying, bent back before the clanking treads of the bulldozer.

Steen looked up from his watch in satisfaction. At one minute per tree, Lone Hill could be cleared by day's end. The bulldozer scraped the bare-branched tree to one side and continued forward to the next.

"Quite a sight, eh?"

Steen clapped Peter on the shoulder. The boy looked up at his stepfather in resentment, but Steen didn't notice.

"Let's take a walk around the land," he said.

From the road to the cut, from the fence to the creekbed, the land was Steen's to build on. Not yet the houses of his dreams, not yet the houses on winding, tree-lined lanes nestling into the shape of the land. The bank had wanted the hill leveled to fit more houses on the parcel. And he gave in finally; he convinced himself that this was a step along the road, this was an opportunity he had waited for. The drawings he had made as a child in Denmark, the beautiful house on the hill—that would come in time. For now, he would build the houses the bank wanted, build them well, sell them well, and look for the next opportunity. Other ranches, without a doubt, would want to turn a piece of land into ready cash.

A biplane flew low over Lone Hill and traced a slow figure eight. The pilot, dressed in white, leaned over the side of the plane. He waved to the tiny men below him, then continued to fly north.

Steen watched Peter's gaze follow the plane. "Going to Moffett Field," he said. "The air base is a good thing. It's bringing in jobs. New kinds of people. And maybe somebody to buy these houses."

Peter nodded and continued to watch the plane grow smaller in the distance.

Steen judged that Peter had improved since the fire. Maybe too silent, maybe sullen. But obedient, that was the main thing. And now that Betsy was going to have a baby, he didn't worry so much about her paying more attention to her son than she did to him. The boy didn't know it yet, but soon he'd be learning a lot more about how this world really worked.

The bulldozer roared, and the next tree bent down before it. "Next summer," Steen said, "if we're still building here, I want you to come help out on site. Learn something about wood and hammer and nails. I wasn't much older than you are now when I went out as an apprentice. And you'll learn something more than you would by stooping for prunes on the ground. What do you think of that?"

"Okay," Peter said.

"Your grandfather was a carpenter, you've got the blood in you. You'll like it, you'll see." Steen clapped Peter on the shoulder again.

"Come on, let's go make sure we're getting our money's worth from this bulldozer."

Peter lagged behind Steen and looked from the back of the square-shouldered man to the small dot flying above the northern horizon.

He twisted the tarnished horseshoe-nail ring on his hand. Another tree sighed and fell.

THE SAN NATOMA STAR
OCTOBER 20, 1933

FROM THE ASHES
Bill Finney

Three months ago, Steen Denisen could only watch as a house he was building burned to the ground. Yesterday, he watched as work began on the largest tract of new homes ever to be built in San Natoma, located on the Lone Hill section of land along San Natoma–Los Gatos Road.

Under a bright October sky that seemed to promise success, a bulldozer began to prepare the land for fifteen new houses. The grading will take several weeks, and construction is slated to begin in late November. The first of the homes should be ready for occupancy by the spring of next year.

Mr. Denisen expressed confidence in the local economy as the work began. "A well-built house will always find a buyer," he said. "The Santa Clara Valley will continue to grow, in spite of current hard times, and the people who come will need a place to live." With the advent of the automobile, he pointed out, a man can live in our lovely town and still work in San Jose. The opening of the naval air station at Moffett Field seemed to him to confirm his prognostication on local growth.

Lone Hill is Mr. Denisen's first major project since he took the reins of the late Ernest Moreberg's well-respected construction company. He is married to Mr. Moreberg's daughter, Betsy. The project seems to give fair promise that he will continue in Mr. Moreberg's tradition of building solid homes for the working families of our community, and that this company will be a source of pride to San Natoma for many years to come.

Also assisting at the scene was young Peter Denisen, Steen Denisen's stepson. The lad watched in fascination as the heavy machines moved earth to make way for the coming houses, and he expressed interest in helping his adoptive father on site next summer. Perhaps the Moreberg company will someday go into its third generation of ownership.

We at the *Star* wish Mr. Denisen, his family, and his employees great happiness and success in the coming years.

three : The Blossom Festival

25

The Year of the Rooster   1929

Even after many years had passed, Fumiko would remember the feel of her father's hand while they waited on the corner of South First to cross the street and enter the Bank of America. Her father had a long scar across his palm, a hard, raised string that was a little bit whiter than the rest of his skin, and Fumiko liked to run her thumb across it when her hand was in his.

"Where did it come from?" she'd asked her father.

"Oh, maybe I got it killing a dragon," he always answered.

After a streetcar passed, he gripped her hand more tightly and they plunged out into the street. Everything was bigger here than in Nihonmachi. The street was wide and sunny and busy with carriages and shiny automobiles, and the buildings were three stories tall, built of brick and stone. In Japan town,

233

the streets were narrow and rutted, and everything was crowded into low wooden buildings.

They went into the brown bank building and stood quietly in line. The inside of the bank was cool, with high curtained windows and a black slate floor. Everyone spoke in whispers there, as though everyone had a secret.

The teller looked through a brass cage at her father. He held up his hand and pointed to the scar. They couldn't tell his face from other Japanese, but they could recognize his hand.

"Akiro Yamamoto," he said.

The teller shook her head; she still wasn't certain.

He lifted Fumiko up and sat her on the cool white marble counter.

"Tell them who I am," he said in Japanese.

"I'm Fumiko Monica Yamamoto, and this is my father, Akiro Yamamoto," she said in a loud voice.

Then the teller smiled, and her father did what he wanted to do. On the way out of the bank, he took Fumiko's hand again. "The *hakujin* like you, Fumi-chan. You are my good luck."

. . . .

Fumiko's mother always woke up before everyone else on workdays, to make food for her father and her two older brothers. For lunch she packed rice balls sprinkled with scs ame seeds and salt with a red pickled plum inside. She also gave them mason jars full of green tea, so they could stand up to the hot sun. She woke up Fumiko to help her with the rice balls while her brothers still slept.

"I don't want to make rice balls," Fumiko said. "I want to go out under the trees with Kenji and Yoshi."

"Then who will help me?" her mother asked. "Don't be stubborn. A stubborn sapling does not grow straight. And don't spill rice on the floor."

Fumiko knew that her mother used to work in the fields. She told Fumiko that when Kenji was born, she had to carry him out with her in a tomato box, and set him down with some cheesecloth shading his face, and help her father with the strawberry plants. But now, she spent all her time bent over at home, caring for the chickens, or cooking in the kitchen, or taking in laundry for other men.

Fumiko thought about her mother staying in the fields; if she had stayed, she would have grown gigantic, taller than the tallest apricot trees. She would have been able to look down on the foreman himself and tell him what to do. It made Fumiko mad that her mother had to work bending over at home, and even more mad that she had to stay with her. Her mother never allowed her to go beyond the smelly chicken coops.

In the winter, her father had turned new earth and planted saplings from the nursery. "Someday," he said, "we'll plant saplings in our own land, not just land we lease." Fumiko wanted to see the saplings. She wanted to see if they were growing straight or if they were stubborn. Or, maybe, if they could be stubborn and grow straight as well. So she slipped quietly out of the house one morning, while her mother was busy with ironing. The orchards began just beyond the back fence. None of the trees had any leaves. Their branches were bare arms stretching out from the trunk. Wintertime, winter pruning.

Fumiko knew that the new trees would be furthest from the house, but she didn't know exactly where. Still, it seemed like going away from the road was the best idea.

The sky was cool and gray, and the dirt between the tree rows was bare and uneven from the last plowing. No mustard flower yet, no bright yellow. Everything was brown and black and gray. Fumiko had to hop from one dirt clod to another. The trees seemed far apart. Many hops to get from one tree to another.

She had never been this far out into the orchards. Nobody had ever thought to carry her out in a tomato box. At the edge of the old orchard, Fumiko discovered rows of young apricot trees, each tied to a light wooden frame with string. Between the rows of trees, low, leafy strawberry plants had been placed. Fumiko measured herself against one of the young trees. Even though it had been planted that year, it was already bigger than she was.

A breeze ghosted in from the north, and Fumiko suddenly felt cold. Did trees feel cold in the wintertime, with no clothes on? She spread her arms out like a tree, but she was still cold. After a moment, she brought her arms back in to her sides and crouched down into a little ball. She didn't want to go back to the house, even though she was cold.

She laid her cheek against a mound of dirt. It was cool and moist, like the sky.

Then she heard a voice. A big voice, deep. It came from high above her, from higher up than the biggest sapling.

The voice was American. "Well, look what's in my orchards now."

Fumiko got up on her knees. It was Foreman Farrell, with his pointy chin and tufts of hair growing out of the side of his head, smiling down at her from the sky. "What are you doing out here all by yourself?" he asked.

"Growing," she said.

"Why, can't you grow at home?"

"Not enough," Fumiko said.

"No? Well, come along with me and we'll let your father decide if you're growing enough." He bent down and lifted her up, and suddenly Fumiko was riding higher than the saplings, perched on top of the foreman's shoulders.

Foreman Farrell had a shiny bald spot, and Fumiko rubbed it. The foreman laughed.

"You're tickling me," he said.

Then she saw her father squatting beside a new strawberry plant and carefully patting the soil around it. Kenji and Yoshi were digging new holes further up the line, and a flat of new plants from the nursery lay near by.

"Hey, Yamamoto," the foreman shouted. Her father stood up and bowed. Fumiko saw his eyes on her, crinkled with amusement.

"Ho, Fumi-chan," he said.

"Look what I found out in the fields," the foreman said. "You can grow anything in this soil, that's sure."

She was lifted high in the air, then set down gently beside her brothers. They looked at her impatiently.

"What are you doing out here?" Kenji asked her. "Does Mama know?"

"No," Fumiko said. "I just wanted to come and work out here."

"Stupid," Yoshi said. "Girls don't work out here."

"Why not? Mama used to."

"Mama's going to be mad at you. She's going to use the *okyu* on you."

The *okyu* was a way to punish children by applying a hot punk to bare skin. "She will not," Fumiko said.

"Yes, she will. *Pssssst!*" Kenji knew that their parents had never used *okyu*, but some of his friends' parents did, and he liked to scare his little sister.

"Kenji," Mr. Yamamoto called in Japanese. "Leave little sister alone and come help me understand what Mr. Farrell is saying."

"Like I say, I don't care if you intercrop with berries." Fumiko watched the foreman as he spoke. He seemed like a nice man, with a hawk nose and kind eyes. But now she could tell that he was saying something bad for her father.

"You want to climb the agricultural ladder, more power to you. The Robertses don't care, as long as their saplings are okay. I'm just telling you to keep it quiet."

Mr. Yamamoto looked to Kenji for a translation, so that he could be sure he had understood. His face grew grave. Fumiko suddenly felt frightened, and she ran to her father and grabbed his pants leg.

"I understand," she heard her father say. "I keep it quiet, but I keep growing, okay?"

When the foreman walked away, her father looked at her. "Fumiko, you've been naughty," he said.

"I wanted to come help you," she said.

"Well, maybe you have. You're my good luck. But now I have to take you back to your mother, or she will be worried."

He lifted her up, and again Fumiko got to ride higher than the saplings. He turned toward Kenji and Yoshi.

"You two keep digging while I take Fumiko back," Mr. Yamamoto said. Her brothers looked at her jealously. Fumiko waved at them. Then they set off toward the house.

While they passed under the bare trees, Fumiko asked her father, "Are you in trouble because you spend too much time in the field?"

"Something like that."

"Because he doesn't want you to be big."

"Ho. It's all right to be a little bit big, but not too big." She felt her father smiling. "But we'll get big enough. Big enough to buy our own land."

"I want to be big, too," Fumiko said.

"Good," her father said. Then they both saw Mrs. Yamamoto running toward them, talking about bad daughters who wouldn't stay home.

The next time her mother invited Mrs. Hayashi and Mrs. Kikuchi over for tea, Fumiko was ordered to stay still and quiet.
Whenever her mother spoke to her, she said, "Yes, *Otoh-
san*" or "No, *Otoh-san*." The other two women seemed impressed, and Mrs. Hayashi said, "What a pretty girl. And so
well behaved, too."

"Don't be fooled by her," her mother said. "She is too head-
strong to know how to mind her mother and do all her chores.
She tells me she doesn't want to be in the kitchen with me. She
would rather be outside like a wild beast."

Fumiko pretended not to hear.

"Such a shame," Mrs. Kikuchi said. "She seems quite polite
today."

"She comes back with dirt on her clothes if I don't watch
her," her mother said. "She was born in the Year of the Rooster. I think she has more of the rooster than of the hen."

"Very hard for such a girl," Mrs. Hayashi said. "Sometimes
hard to find a husband."

"She doesn't know yet that she needs to find a husband. And
yet, she thinks she doesn't have to learn. Anything!"

"Ohhh. Too bad," the other two women said.

"My husband is too indulgent," her mother confided.

When Fumiko started school, she saw that all the boys and girls
were bigger than her. The second and third graders, who
shared the playground with them during recess, were bigger
than anyone in her first-grade class. And some of the girls in
third grade were bigger than any of the boys. That was exciting.

The teacher had them memorize the days of the week and the
months of the year. One day, they all recited their own birth
date. Fumiko stood up beside her desk and put her hands behind her back.

"I was born on January seventeen. Nineteen. Twenty-two."

"Seven*teenth*," the teacher corrected.

"Seventeenth," Fumiko said.

All the children in her class were born in 1922 or 1923. When
everyone was finished, she raised her hand.

"What year were the third graders born in?" she asked.

The teacher smiled at her. "That's a very good question, Fumiko. They are older than you because they were born in an earlier year. 1920 or 1921."

Fumiko raised her hand again. "My mother says I was born in the Year of the Rooster."

Several of the boys snickered, but the teacher looked at them. "That's very interesting, Fumiko," she said.

Fumiko had already figured out that when the teacher said something was very interesting, it meant that she didn't want to say anything about it.

A couple of boys called her a rooster on the playground afterward, but she ignored them. She was thinking about the connection between number years and animal years. The animal years were more important, because they were the years her family celebrated. They always changed a little bit later than the number years. But the number years seemed to matter more for getting to third or fourth grade.

. . . .

Fumiko started Japanese school when she started grade school. At three o'clock, when everyone else ran outside free to play, she had to walk with Kenji and Yoshi down the hill to the hall where Nihon Gakko was held. Kenji accused her of always walking like a snail. "We're not crazy about it either," he said. "But you have to go. You're Japanese."

In school, she learned that the islands of Japan were Hokkaido, Shikoku, Kyushu, and Honshu, that the tallest mountain was Fujiyama, and that the emperor lived in Kyoto and was descended from the gods. But most of the time was spent in learning to read and write the Japanese language. She struggled to draw simplified versions of the basic Japanese characters, and she recited in a chorus with the rest of the class the day's lesson. The teacher always checked posture during recitals.

At precisely five-thirty, the students stood up beside their chairs and bowed to the teacher. When she returned their bow, they could all file out of the room except those who had to clean up the blackboard and sweep the floor.

Fumiko found out that she was one of the few children who

had to go to three schools: grade school, Japanese school, and Sunday school. Most of her friends at Japanese school were Buddhist. She wasn't sure exactly what that was, but it meant that they didn't have to go to Sunday school. And at church, there were only two other Japanese families who had children.

This didn't seem fair to Fumiko. She told her mother and father that she should only have to go to two schools, because everyone else did. And she asked if they would let her choose which school to stop.

Her father laughed. "Maybe you're right, Fumiko. You're so smart now, if we keep sending you to so many schools, you will be *too* smart."

"Don't say such things," her mother said. "You are too easy on her."

She turned to Fumiko.

"You must go to all three schools. You have Japanese blood, you must learn Japanese. And you must go to Sunday school, to be a good Christian. And grade school, to learn to read and write English. Do you think any of these is unimportant?"

Fumiko hadn't thought about it that way. All she had done was think about the number of schools she had to attend, and how unfair it was. She looked to her father.

"Your mother is right, Fumiko. You should go to school and grow wiser, so that someday you may help your husband as you help me."

"But I help you now," Fumiko pointed out. "You said so."

This was perfect logic. But her father smiled.

"You will help your husband in a different way," he said.

. . . .

One day, Fumiko's father dressed in a suit and tie and told her to put on her prettiest dress. Kenji also dressed in the coat he usually wore only to Sunday school, and both he and her father slicked back their hair with sweet-smelling camellia oil.

They went to the Bank of America, but they didn't stand in line to see a teller. Instead, they walked into an office in the back. The office was dark and smelled like cigar smoke, and her father shook hands American style with the banker, then sat down across the desk from him. Fumiko sat in his lap, and Kenji stood beside him to translate.

"The bank wants to loan you money," Mr. Jackson said. "But you can't own land in your own name. You're not a citizen."

Mr. Yamamoto spoke in Japanese, and then Kenji said, "He wants to become a citizen. But he can't."

"That's right. He can't. The only way he can purchase land is to buy it in his children's name. But none of their births were recorded. I checked."

Kenji translated his father's reply. "'My children are all born in this country,' he says."

"Did Doctor Haft give you birth certificates?"

Mr. Yamamoto and Kenji looked at each other, and Fumiko leaned back into her father's chest.

"Haft was a drunk," the banker said. "He didn't keep any paperwork."

Mr. Yamamoto frowned and spoke directly to Mr. Jackson. "Dr. Haft was no good," he said. "But nobody else would take Japanese."

"You'll have to go to court. Get testimony from people who know your family. Shorty Farrell, the foreman where you've been tenants, for instance. Then come back and we'll buy some land for you in Kenji's name."

Mr. Yamamoto listened carefully to Kenji's translation, to be sure he had understood the banker correctly. Then he said to Kenji, "Tell him I want to plant pear trees. The land I want there is moist, good for pear. Tell him I don't want to grow just truck crops. I want to plant pear."

Kenji told him. The banker nodded. "We have a saying. 'A man who plants pear trees, plants them for his grandchildren.'"

Kenji translated, and Mr. Yamamoto smiled. "Then Kenji's children will enjoy the land."

Fumiko looked jealously at Kenji's proud expression.

That night, Fumiko helped her mother dry the dishes. She had to stand on a little stepladder to the right of the sink, because otherwise her head would hardly come above the counter. Her mother handed her the lacquered rice bowls and chopsticks, and the plain hardware-store plates and silverware, and Fumiko dried them and stacked them. Her mother didn't give her the tea things to dry; she said that Fumiko was too clumsy to be trusted with fragile things.

"We have to make sure Kenji becomes an American," her father was saying. He was sitting at the kitchen table with Kenji and Yoshi.

Fumiko thought that if *she* were American, she wouldn't have to stand on a stepladder, and she would be big enough to dry anything.

"A lawyer costs money, *neh*?" her mother asked.

"Kenji must be a citizen so that we can buy the land."

"It's right that Kenji should have the land in his name," Mrs. Yamamoto said. "He is obedient and works hard, and he is the firstborn."

Fumiko looked over her shoulder at Kenji. He was swelling up like a balloon, even though he didn't speak.

"Mr. Carson doesn't cheat the Japanese," her father said. "And Mr. Farrell, who has known us for so long, will tell the judge that Kenji was born in this country."

He smiled at Kenji.

"Kenji will be honored to have the land in his name."

Suddenly, Fumiko got down off the ladder and grabbed her father's hand.

"Papa," she said. "I want to be American too. It's no fair that only Kenji gets to be American."

Kenji looked at her. "Nobody's going to buy land in your name."

But she kept hold of her father's hand, and he laughed and took her onto his lap.

"Of course, Fumi-chan. The lawyer will talk to the judge about Yoshi and you at the same time. I want all my children to be citizens here."

Fumiko put her arms around her father's neck. Her mother shook her head.

. . . .

On the court day, Fumiko stood in a line with her two brothers and was inspected by her mother. Mrs. Yamamoto made certain that their clothes were spotless and well pressed, that their hair was in place and their shoes were tied, and that they had scrubbed their hands and faces and cleaned behind their ears. "If you are dirty," she said, "they won't want you to be Americans."

She looked at all three of them and frowned.

"No matter what, don't say a word unless you are asked. Be quiet and respectful. The *hakujin* want only Japanese who are quiet and polite. Act like they think Japanese are, and they will surely let you be Americans."

Fumiko decided to be so quiet and still that if her mother wanted to scold someone, she would have to scold Yoshi. She never scolded Kenji no matter what he did.

Outside the courtroom, Mr. Carson told them to just file in and sit behind the railing in the front row. Then the judge would come in and they would stand up. Then they'd sit down again. Then he would ask them some questions. Then it would be over.

"There should be no problem," the young lawyer said. "I know this judge, and he's helped you people before."

The large oak doors swung open, and they filed in past a man in uniform. Mr. Yamamoto first, then Mrs. Yamamoto, then the three children behind them. Fumiko, last in line, looked all around as she followed. This truly seemed to be a hall built for giants. The ceiling was unreachably high, shining with glass and metal lights. The floor gleamed with polished wooden planks wider than both her feet. When they took chairs behind a heavy wooden railing, Fumiko gazed up at the tall desk in front of them. It stood eight feet tall, with mysterious plaques and seals on the wall behind it and large flags hanging from eagle poles on either side.

Mr. Carson came in and sat beside them, and Fumiko followed his eyes to the man standing next to the American flag. He was a huge man, with a thick head that seemed to grow straight out of the blue collar of his uniform, and he wore a silver badge and a gleaming leather holster.

"All rise," he said.

Fumiko stood up when she saw everyone else stand up. But the man who scrambled out from behind the bailiff was a short man, not a giant, shorter even than her father, littler than all the other Americans in the room. His head poked out of his black robes like a bird's head; he had no hair, and his nose was too big for his face.

The little man climbed up to the desk and banged the gavel. Everyone sat down.

They waited through other cases until their number came up on the docket. Fumiko swung her heels and tried to make sense out of the tiny head perched above the massive desk looking down on them. Then Mr. Carson stood before the judge and talked about her mother and father, how they had come to America and married and had her brothers and her. He talked about the doctor who hadn't done his job. The judge nodded.

Shorty Farrell was sworn in, and he nodded at Fumiko's father as he began to testify. "Sure, I've known all those kids since they were born."

"You couldn't be mistaken about their identity?" the judge asked. "They don't look like any other Japs or Celestials to you?"

"I know 'em, Your Honor."

Shorty stepped down. The judge said, "Can we have the oldest boy on the stand?"

Mr. Carson gestured to Kenji. He stood and marched to the front of the courtroom, proud and erect. When he sat down, he held himself just as he'd been taught in Japanese school, with his shoulders back and his eyes looking directly forward.

Fumiko looked at her mother. She was glowing.

The judge asked Kenji where he was born.

"San Jose, sir."

"Say 'Your Honor,'" Mr. Carson said.

Kenji's face didn't change expression. "San Jose, Your Honor."

"Have you ever been to Japan?"

"No, Your Honor."

"Would you like to go?"

Kenji hesitated. "I would like to go to visit my grandparents."

"A good answer," the judge said.

Kenji moved his eyes toward his parents for their approval. Fumiko stuck her tongue out at him.

The judge asked him a few questions about how many states there were in the Union and who was the governor of California, and he asked him to recite the Pledge of Allegiance. Kenji responded flawlessly.

"All right," the judge said. "Can you point out your brother and sister for the court?"

"That is my brother, Yoshiki," Kenji said.

After a moment, the judge said, "And your sister?"

"Your sister, Kenji." Mr. Carson pointed to Fumiko.

"No prompting," the judge warned.

"That is my sister," Kenji said grudgingly.

"Let's have the girl on the stand," the judge said.

Fumiko stood up. She was glad that Kenji wasn't the only one who got to show off. She walked toward the enormous desk and ignored Kenji going back to his seat.

Mr. Carson seated her behind the railings to the left of the judge. The room was filled with alien faces staring at her. She looked to her father for encouragement, but she noticed that his face was worried.

"Just answer the judge's questions as best you can," Mr. Carson said.

"All right." Fumiko suddenly felt a little afraid.

"Where do you live?" the judge asked.

"In San Natoma, Your Honor."

"Have you always lived there?"

"No. We lived in Nihonmachi before."

The judge pursed his lips. "Nihonmachi?" he repeated. "Where is that?"

"Japan town," Mr. Carson said. "In San Jose."

"Hmmm." The judge turned back to Fumiko. "Who is president now?"

Fumiko had learned that in grade school. "Calvin Coolidge."

"And who is emperor of Japan?"

"The emperor of Japan is Emperor Hirohito," she said without hesitation. Both the judge and Mr. Carson frowned, so she added, "He lives in Kyoto and he's descended from the gods, Your Honor."

"Are you Japanese or American?" the judge asked.

"I'm Japanese," she said. "But I want to be American, too. Can I be both, Your Honor?"

"Don't ask the judge questions," Mr. Carson said. He looked as worried as her father.

"Is there a park in downtown San Jose?" the judge asked.

Fumiko wasn't sure. She looked at Mr. Carson for a clue. "Yes," she guessed.

"Do you know the name of the park?"

Fumiko shook her head. "I don't know, Your Honor."

"Is there a river that runs through San Jose?"

Fumiko looked at her parents and looked at Mr. Carson. Nobody was smiling, and the courtroom was very quiet. "I don't know, Your Honor."

"Your Honor," Mr. Carson said. "The Japanese don't go to St. James Park. You never see them there. And the Guadalupe River is a long ways from Japan town. This girl has probably never seen either one."

"She must know something about San Jose if she's really lived her whole life here."

"I know something," Fumiko said suddenly. The judge and Mr. Carson turned to her. She knew she was disobeying her mother, but she kept on talking.

"I know where the Bank of America is. It's on South First Street, and it has big windows and a black floor. And the people there work in cages."

"She's right, Your Honor," Mr. Carson said.

"What color is the bank painted?" the judge asked.

"Brown," Fumiko said.

"All right. Let's hear you say your Pledge of Allegiance."

Fumiko recited it with a little help. The judge told her to step down, and she ran back to her parents. Her father didn't say anything, but he smiled, and even her mother looked satisfied. Fumiko reached for her father's hand and felt the scar crossing his palm, hard and white.

"Can we have the mother under oath concerning the birth dates of the three?" the judge asked.

Fumiko watched her mother look at her father. "Why do they want me and not you?" she asked him in Japanese.

"Best to ask no questions," he replied.

She stood up slowly and walked in front of the tall desk and put her hand on the Bible. Then she sat down in the big chair beside the judge.

"Please state the complete names and birth dates of your three children," Mr. Carson said.

"The names and when they were born?" she asked.

"Just to make it official."

Mrs. Yamamoto thought carefully for a moment. Then she

said very slowly, so that she wouldn't make mistakes, "Kenji Augustine Yamamoto, July fifth, the Year of the Tiger. Yoshiki Thomas Yamamoto, October tenth, the Year of the Snake. Fumiko Monica Yamamoto, January seventeenth, the Year of the Rooster."

The judge sighed, and there were a few titters from the courtroom. "Can we have a translation of that, Mr. Carson?"

"As you know, the Japanese use the same lunar years as the Chinese..."

"I know all that," the judge said. "Just give me the years in words a white man can understand."

Mr. Carson took a small notebook from his coat pocket. "This is 1929, so we're in the Year of the Snake right now." There was more laughter in the court. "The Year of the Tiger would have been 1914. The Year of the Snake would have been 1917. And the Year of the Rooster would have been 1921."

As soon as Mr. Carson spoke, Fumiko clapped a hand over her mouth. She knew that Mr. Carson had made a mistake. She was born so late in the Year of the Rooster that the number year had already changed.

She wanted to tell him. But she also realized that she was suddenly going to be a year older. In the fall, she would be a third grader. A big third grader.

She looked at her father. He probably hadn't understood enough to catch the mistake. Kenji's face was puzzled, but he hadn't quite figured it out enough to say anything.

"Do you agree with those dates, Mrs. Yamamoto?" the judge asked.

She looked at her husband, who nodded very slightly. It was best to ask no questions.

"Yes, I do," she said.

"All right, then. We'll have some papers drawn up, and your children will enjoy all the rights and privileges of native-born U.S. citizens."

Fumiko's father stood up. For a moment, Fumiko thought he was going to point out the error in the date, and throw her back a year. But instead, he bowed to the judge, a very precise and formal bow from the waist.

The judged nodded in return.

Mr. Yamamoto bought land for a pear orchard in Kenji's name, and the family moved in the summer. They again intercropped the young trees with strawberries, and Mr. Yamamoto let Fumiko spend time in the field with him and Yoshi and Kenji. He said that when her little hands patted the ground around the plant, the fruit would be sweet and juicy, and bring a good price. She was his good luck.

In the fall, she went to a new school. When they had been tenants, they had lived closer to Los Gatos, but their new land was close to the center of San Natoma, so she was transferred there. And she began the third grade because of the year on her new birth certificate. But she discovered that, instead of being big, she was the smallest one in the class. All the boys were bigger than her, and all the girls were bigger than her too.

She was the only one at this new school who had to go to Japanese school. It was hard to make friends, because she had to run to catch a bus right after school let out.

But Fumiko tried to be friendly. And she chose especially Olivia Roberts to be friendly to. Olivia's family owned the Ida Valley Ranch, where they had been tenants, and Fumiko had only seen her from a distance before. The other girls seemed a little standoffish toward Olivia, because she was tall and slender and graceful and came from such a large ranch. But Fumiko admired Olivia, a girl as big as her dreams for herself.

Olivia accepted Fumiko's attention, and they became friends.

26

The Fairy King   January 1939

When Miss Johnson tapped her walking stick on the hardwood floor, Olivia Roberts made a *revérence*. The rest of the girls followed Olivia's example. They swept their right feet back, spread their arms out gracefully to each side, and bowed their heads forward.

Miss Johnson looked over the class with her chin high. "Arms open gently, like the wings of a swan, not stiff like a scarecrow. Miss Fogle," she called out to a young girl in the last row, "look at Miss Roberts."

The girl looked up, then loosened her arms a bit. Miss Johnson tapped the floor with her cane again, and the students swept out of their bow.

"Miss Roberts?" she said. Olivia was the oldest girl, and she had been with Miss Johnson the longest. She turned to face the class while her teacher walked slowly to the piano, helping her right side along with the cane. Miss Johnson leaned there, met Olivia's eye, and held up a finger to the piano player.

"Now," she said. "First position."

The piano player struck a note. Olivia put her heels together, toes out, and in a shuffling wave back from the first row, all the young girls followed her lead.

"Very good," Miss Johnson said. "Now, second position."

The girls shifted their feet out. The students in the first row, the older ones, made the moves without much awkwardness. Those in the back never remembered how to move from one week to the next.

"Gracefully, gracefully," Miss Johnson said. "This is the time in a young lady's life when she acquires habits that will last a lifetime."

She looked at Olivia, then signaled the piano player.

"Third position," she said.

Toward the end of class, some fathers drifted in from the bar at the Lindstrom Hotel and sat against the wall. They were tolerated as long as they sat in silence and just watched. The hotel let the meeting hall at a bargain rate in part because of the liquor these men drank while they waited for their daughters, on a weeknight when business would otherwise be slow. Now they sat with beaming red faces—carpenters and mechanics and the owners of small orchards—and they watched the girls repeat the steps in time with the music.

Miss Johnson again walked slowly to the center of the polished wooden floor and tapped once with her cane. The children all bowed to her once more. She looked carefully at the Fogle girl, and then tapped again and nodded her head.

"I'll see you all next Tuesday," she said.

The girls broke into talk and laughter in the previously quiet hall. They ran for their coats, lying in piles on the chairs that lined the room, found their friends, looked for fathers or mothers, practiced one last time at the barre the plié they'd learned that evening. More parents filtered in from the crisp evening outside the room, loosening their collars and taking off their hats. A Mr. Chapman came up to Miss Johnson, holding his daughter by the hand.

"Rebecca certainly does enjoy your lessons, Miss Johnson,"

he said. "And she seems so much the better for them. Afterward, she's so much better behaved and all."

The girl looked up at her father speaking eagerly to her tall, elegant dance teacher. Miss Johnson favored her with a glance, and then spoke to the father.

"I'm very pleased to have her in my class, Mister Chapman. Here, I assure you, she has never been anything but very willing and cooperative."

Mr. Chapman went off smiling proudly with his daughter.

Miss Johnson found Olivia Roberts with her eye. The tall girl came instantly to her.

"Thank you once again for leading the exercises, Olivia."

"Oh, it was a pleasure, Miss Johnson."

"Tell me, my dear. Would you care to come to my house for a cup of tea this evening?"

"Yes indeed, very much."

"Good. There's nobody coming for you, nobody you have to tell?"

"Oh, no, Miss Johnson. My parents let me walk home by myself."

"All right, then. Stay here until everyone has gone, and then we'll go to my house together. Could you bring me my coat and scarf?"

"Of course."

Olivia retrieved the clothes and sneaked the smooth, light scarf between her thumb and forefinger several times. Rich Italian silk, the color of clouds and blue sky.

Miss Johnson took the scarf, and it seemed to glide around her neck.

. . . .

Olivia Roberts danced in the Blossom Festival in 1930. In that year, her first of taking lessons from Miss Johnson, she had played a string bean in the pageant. She wore a dress with green leaves sewn on, a stuffed hat that looked like the top of a string bean, and elf shoes with curled toes. Mrs. Madison showed Olivia how to cut and sew the leaves, but then she'd done the work herself. She was sure that her string bean costume had looked the best of all the other string beans. But still, she remembered how envious she was of the older girls who got to wear lacy dresses, who came down the hill into the festival glen singing, "The sun is a-shining to welcome the day / Hi, ho, come to the fair."

Olivia took lessons every year with Miss Johnson, even in '34 and '35 when there was no Blossom Festival because fruit prices were so low. And every year, she moved closer to the front of the class. She saw that there were fewer girls in her group as she grew older. They found other interests, or their parents decided to skimp on the cost of lessons, or they just didn't love to dance as much as Olivia did. And so she thought, each year, she was closer to being one of the two or three girls whom Miss Johnson would choose to dance the leads in the Blossom Festival Program.

At the beginning of the school year, when Miss Johnson began to choose her to lead the exercises in front of the class, Olivia felt she was almost there. But she'd noticed over the years that the girls who were chosen to be the lead were invited to Miss Johnson's house at some time or other, before they were officially given the part. She had been waiting for this invitation.

Now she had it.

A small brown dog with large pointed ears greeted them at the door and danced around Miss Johnson's feet as they walked in. Miss Johnson picked the dog up and looked into its moist eyes. "Have you been a good boy?" She turned to Olivia. "This is Cupid."

"Hello, Cupid," Olivia said.

Miss Johnson put the dog down and asked Olivia to sit in the parlor while she made tea.

"Can I help you in some way, Miss Johnson?"

"That's quite all right. I'll be right back." She left for the kitchen, beating a light rhythm with her cane while Cupid gave out short, high-pitched barks.

As soon as Olivia was alone, she began to look at the photos and newspaper clippings that hung in frames around the walls. There was a full head shot of Miss Johnson, with her hair bobbed, and her lashes long and dark, and her mouth full and shaped like a bow. It must have been a publicity photo, because her name was printed across the bottom. Next, a candid photo of Miss Johnson smiling between a man and a woman. The man wore a tuxedo, and Miss Johnson and the woman wore long dresses, the kind that dipped down in front. Olivia looked at the photo and touched a finger to her own left shoulder. She traced a line down at an angle over the top of her breasts, to a point right above her heart, and then back up to her right shoulder. Miss Johnson looked very beautiful in the photo, and although Olivia couldn't be sure, she thought that the other two people in the photo must be Ted Shawn and Ruth St. Denis, the famous dancers who had schools in all the big cities.

Finally, there it was, just as she had heard from an older girl who had been here before. A yellowed clip from the Entertainment page of the *New York Daily News*, 1924, with a review of the Denishawn production *The Vision of the Aissouah*. Halfway down the column was Miss Johnson's name. "One of the features of the show was the little dance with silk scarves performed by Dorothea Hampstead Johnson."

There was a sound of china from the kitchen, and Olivia quickly sat down on one of the red fanback chairs. Miss Johnson placed a tray slowly down on the low table and sat in the other fanback chair. Cupid jumped up on her lap and sat there, watching Olivia through his bottomless eyes.

"Now to let it steep a little while longer," she said.

Olivia admired the delicate porcelain cups, the matching sugar bowl ringed with a flower garland pattern.

"I'm glad you could come this evening," Miss Johnson said, "because I wanted to show you the costume designs for the Spring Pageant."

"You've thought of the theme?" Olivia asked. Nobody knew yet what the dance was going to be; Olivia would be the first.

"We're going to present an Enchanted Wedding. Look." She drew a large sketch pad from the table and opened it to the first page. "This is the costume for the sprites. Here we'll have some dancing sweet williams, dragonflies, lady slippers. That's for the younger dancers."

Miss Johnson turned the pages one by one, revealing a garden of nymphs, fairies, and flowers. Olivia saw the colors dancing under the arch in the Festival Glen, the orchestra from the high school, the five thousand spectators in a ring facing the stage, the fruit trees in blossom on all sides. And as the pages turned, past the group roles for the ten- and twelve-year-olds, she saw herself on stage in a costume different from all the rest, a role all her own, dancing a solo.

"Now here is Silverheels," Miss Johnson said. "She's the fairy princess who is to be married."

Silverheels was sketched in a short Greek-style chiton, with her hair braided around her head. She looked as beautiful as a goddess in a book. But Olivia noticed that the watercolored hair was blond, while her own hair was dark.

Miss Johnson turned the page. "Titania, Queen of the Fairies."

Another beautiful Greek figure, with a longer tunic and a diadem. Olivia looked at Miss Johnson and waited. Cupid was breathing very fast, and his small ribbed sides heaved in and out.

Another page turned. "Now, Oberon."

Oberon was a king, the King of the Fairies, with a flowing cape and a crown and a golden sword at his side.

Miss Johnson smiled. "I've chosen you to dance Oberon."

Olivia felt the delight freeze onto her face like a mask. She smiled while Miss Johnson continued to talk. "I thought about you for Titania, but you're so much taller than the other girls, that I finally decided that Oberon was right for you."

"Thank you, Miss Johnson. I'm sure it's a wonderful part, and I hope I do well in it."

"I'm certain you will. You've been one of my most dedicated dancers over the years."

"Will I have a solo?"

"There'll be a short pas de deux with Titania. I wanted to give you a good role, because this may be your last Blossom Festival."

"My last Blossom Festival? Why?"

"Well, Olivia," Miss Johnson said. "You're the oldest girl dancing with me now. It will be time to let others have their turn in the sun."

"But Miss Johnson, where will I dance? How will I keep learning if I don't stay with you?"

Miss Johnson raised one eyebrow. "But you haven't learned so much with me in the last couple of years. You've just repeated the same classes you've had since the beginning."

"I thought I'd improved," Olivia said.

"You've improved, Olivia. But to really learn, you would have to go to San Francisco, or New York. You're happy, aren't you, to be dancing Oberon?"

There was only one reply Olivia could make. "Yes, of course. I'm sure it will be wonderful."

"And I'm sure you'll make a wonderful King of the Fairies. Now." She picked up the teapot and poured a thin, elegant stream into Olivia's cup.

Olivia picked up the cup and held it close to her face, breathing in the aroma. It smelled of amber teardrops, it smelled of fallen leaves and puddles in the road.

"What kind of tea is it?" she asked.

Miss Johnson smiled distantly. "Earl Grey," she said. Cupid licked his nose with a red tongue.

. . . .

The following day at school, Olivia told her friend Fumiko to be sure to wait and walk home with her. She had some exciting news to tell, but she didn't want to say anything on the schoolyard, where there was always somebody listening in.

The girls walked toward home under the bare, sleeping trees of the Ida Valley Ranch, and Olivia told Fumiko that Miss Johnson thought she should go to San Francisco or New York to study dance.

"She invited me to her house for tea after the lesson," Olivia said. "And she showed me all the drawings for the Blossom Festival costumes. I was the first one to see."

"What's it going to be this year?" Fumiko asked.

Olivia looked down the long rows of trees over the brown, broken soil. Not even a bird disturbed the stillness. "Promise not to tell anyone?" she asked.

"Of course."

"It's going to be about the enchanted fairies. And I'm going to be Oberon, the Fairy King."

"You're going to be *king*? What are you going to wear?"

"It will look Greek. With a long white robe. And I'll get to wear a crown and a sword."

"And did she really say that you should go to San Francisco or New York?"

"She said that she couldn't teach me much more here in San Natoma. That if I really wanted to learn more, to be a real dancer, I would have to go to the big city. And she thought that New York or San Francisco were the best."

"And you're going to go?"

"I have to," Olivia said.

They reached the paved road at the edge of the orchard, and Olivia took Fumiko's hand. "Can you come visit for a while?"

Fumiko shook her head. "Japanese school. And then I have to take care of my baby brother."

"I know." Olivia didn't let go of her hand. "I wish you were dancing with me."

"I do too," Fumiko said. "I wish my father had let me take lessons."

"You're so graceful. You could have been queen."

Fumiko squeezed Olivia's hand. "But I'll come and see you dance, even if I have to sneak away from church to do it. And I'll come and see you in the big city."

"If I were really the Fairy King, I would just twirl around, and abra-ca-dabra! Everything would be perfect."

"We could be in San Francisco."

"We could be dancing on stage."

"We'd never have to go to school again."

The girls laughed together at themselves under the quiet branches.

"See you tomorrow in homeroom," Olivia said.

They released each other's hands and walked in opposite directions. After a minute, Olivia turned to look after Fumiko, and she saw that her friend had turned also, mirrorlike, to look after her.

Olivia cupped her hands around her mouth and called, "Abra-ca-dabra!"

Fumiko answered, "Abra-ca-dabra!"

"Abra-ca-dabra!"

Cherry Rain   1938

Peter first worked carpenter for Steen in 1934, the summer after the fire, when houses were still going up on Lone Hill; he last worked for him in 1938, a bad year for cherries. During Peter's first summer on site, he worked for Steen coldly and furiously, determined to do everything as well as it could possibly be done, determined that his stepfather would never be able to criticize him. And Steen read the young man's mind. He gave him only the shit jobs, bucking kegs of nails and picking up garbage, and he made sure Peter barely got a chance to handle a hammer. He would see if Peter would break under the grinding monotony of work, and he would enjoy his stepson's angry mask.

At lunch the carpenters sat in a circle and chewed tobacco, talking and spitting. Big, square-built men mostly, with blue eyes lost in flat red faces. And Steen was like a king among them, laughing louder, spitting farther, and speaking about Peter as though he weren't there.

"Petey here, he wants to be home with his mother."

"No, I don't," Peter said.

"Sure," Steen said, still talking to the other men. "He'd rather be home under his mother's apron."

"I would not."

"Sure," as if he hadn't heard him speak. "He's got a lot to learn before he's a man, but he don't want to stay out here and learn it. Dag, what do you think?"

Dag was a Dane who had never learned much English and could be depended on to repeat the same phrase over and over again. He wagged his white head toward Peter. "Maybe he will be a good carpenter one day. Time will tell."

Steen looked at Peter with merry eyes, as though to ask him if he were going to stay or go. Peter wanted to quit, run off for home or for the hills, tell his mother that Steen was a monster. He wanted to play baseball or pick prunes or even be back in school, anything but be thirteen years old and stuck for the summer working for his stepfather. But if he went, it would be because he wasn't good enough, wasn't tough enough.

"Time will tell," Steen said, delighted. "He wants to go home, even though he's staying for now. But time will tell."

Peter looked down at his feet and said nothing, though he felt his ears burning.

· · · · · · · ·

At the end of the first long summer month, Peter stood around on a Friday while the other carpenters received their paychecks. He watched them come forward one by one as Steen called their names, watched them take the check, look at the amount, and place it carefully in their billfolds. One old carpenter named Lasse creased his check carefully twice and then put it into the short metal cigar case he kept in his shirt pocket. Peter waited for Steen to call him over, recognize that he had been out on site six days a week just like everyone else on the crew, and pay him some wages. But he felt his stepfather ignoring him, looking past him and then slapping shut the leather portfolio he carried on paydays.

Peter didn't want to ask to be paid; he didn't want to ask

Steen for anything. But he knew that most of the boys and girls his age were picking prunes or cutting apricots, earning a dollar a day or more. He thought he must at least be earning that. When they were in the Jordan together, driving home from Lone Hill, he asked what his wages were going to be.

Steen looked him over. He had been expecting the question and had only wondered only how long it would take the boy to pipe up.

"Do you know how much I was paid as an apprentice in Denmark?" he asked.

"No," Peter said.

"Of course you don't." Steen turned his eyes back to the road and continued to drive.

Peter stayed quiet for a couple of blocks. Then he said resentfully, "Other kids are earning money for school clothes picking fruit."

"Oh, picking fruit," Steen said. "Picking fruit, you don't learn anything. Out on site, you learn to be a carpenter."

He waited a bit, then spoke judiciously. "School clothes, though. Tell you what." He looked over and gave Peter a big wink. "You'll have to depend on me to pay you what's fair. But don't worry. I'll do right by you."

. . . .

Peter worked out on site through the beginning of September, when all the harvests were in and school was to start. Then he went with his mother and stepfather into San Jose, and they bought white socks and underwear and stiff plaid shirts and a new pair of overalls. At Woolworth's they bought pencils, an eraser, and notebooks in four colors. Afterward, they sat at a round table at Chilrudd's Creamery and sipped malts, while stacks of crisp brown paper packages tied with string sat hunched on a fourth chair.

Steen pointed at the packages. "Good wages. When I was apprentice in Denmark, I barely made enough to keep clothes on my back. And *I* couldn't go back to school, either, after I started."

"What did you do?" Peter asked.

"I worked," he said. "Worked until I could come to this country, and then I worked some more."

He pulled his billfold out of his pocket, drew out a five-dollar bill, and laid it in front of Peter.

"You worked too, this summer. But I'm going to keep what you earned for you. You'll need it more when you're older than you do now."

Betsy opened her mouth once, about to say something, then shut it again. Steen looked at her, then at Peter, waiting for him to complain to his mother, daring him to.

Peter saw that if he complained, it meant he wasn't as much of a man as Steen had been. He took the bill, and creased it twice, and placed it in his shirt pocket, and he didn't say a word.

. . . .

Peter's half sister Peggie was still less than a year old that fall, and he sometimes overheard loud talk between Steen and his mother about having another baby soon. Peter thought that Steen badly wanted a son of his own. A stepson wasn't good enough. But the following year, his mother had another daughter, Jenny. After that, she didn't have any more.

Steen kept taking Peter on every summer, and he began to look forward to having him on crew. He was getting used to the idea that Peter would be the only boy in the family, and he gave him better jobs to do, jobs that would actually teach him something about building houses. He didn't start paying him, though. Times were bad in the Valley, so bad that the Blossom Festival was canceled in '34 and '35, and Steen always found reasons that Peter didn't really need wages. And Peter didn't complain.

When Peter was fifteen, Steen put him under Anders to learn roofing. Anders was a master roofer. Peter had seen him obtain the length of the rafter with just his burnished-steel carpenter's square and a wide, flat pencil, measuring it out in inches and then stepping it off twelve times on the two-by-four. Then Anders would mark out the bird's mouth where the rafters joined the walls, make the tail cut at the end of the rafter, measure the purlin studding and collar beams. And at the end of his measuring and sawing, the pieces of wood kissed together, joined so perfectly that they seemed to have grown touching and weren't the product of a man's labor.

"Measure twice, cut once," Anders told Peter at least once a day. He had a low, flat voice, almost a monotone. Peter didn't want to like him. Anders was close to Steen, came by the house many times for pinochle on a Saturday afternoon, drinking beer and smoking short black cigars, eating the herring and smoked ham and pumpernickel that Betsy brought into the card room. But out on site, Peter leaned in to listen to him, and he found that the closer he stayed to him, the more he learned and grew.

Once, Peter was up on roof jacks and planks with Anders, nailing shake. Anders was explaining that shake had to be laid half an inch apart, because it expanded in the sun more than shingle, which could be laid a quarter inch apart. Steen, down on the ground, spotted them talking and called up to Anders.

"Anders," he shouted, "how many shakes has the boy split today?"

"Not many," Anders called back. "He's not so bad with the hatchet."

Steen laughed and turned away.

"He's always pushing at me," Peter said to Anders. "Push, push, push."

"He pushes himself more," Anders said. "And everyone. Because he wants the best for all of us."

"He only wants the best for himself. And his company."

"And isn't that what keeps you and your sisters eating? And me roofing through the Depression?"

"I don't care," Peter said.

"Someday," Anders said, "you will."

"Maybe," Peter said. "At least I'm up here with you, and not down there with him."

They both looked at the carpenters below them, moving heavily. Anders smiled. "You see a little bit more from up here, don't you?"

. . . .

In June of '38, the company was working on a roadside café and motel for Paolo Pirelli, putting it up alongside his Associated Gas Station. Paolo said he'd seen enough tired and hungry people stop for gas that he'd decided it could pay, and the bank agreed. Steen's bid for the work had been low, but the bank insisted on penalties in the contract if the work wasn't done on time.

The café had a hip roof with fancy cornices sweeping out from all four sides, and Anders and Peter were working on opposite sides of the building, laying down the long parallel planks of roof deck. When they felt the wind come up soft and moist from the south, they found each other with their eyes across the empty space marked out by the angled rafters.

"Feels strange," Peter said. "A funny wind."

"Could be a cherry rain coming," Anders said.

Peter looked to the south and saw some tall black clouds, still distant, marching toward them. "Bad for the crops if it comes," he said. "Cherries are ready to be picked."

"Bad for us, too," Anders said. "But for now we got to keep working."

They were both working up toward the roof ridge, building toward each other, and Anders had told Peter that they needed to finish sheathing the roof that day, since the work was running a little behind schedule. But after noon, half the sky was covered over, and the soft, warm air began to feel thick and heavy.

Steen came by once, wearing a suit and tie, on his way to talk with the banker in San Jose, and he brought Paolo Pirelli over from the gas station to show him how the work was coming along.

Paolo wiped his hands on a red shop rag, and they watched Anders and Peter against the gloomy sky. Then Peter heard Paolo's voice float up, asking his stepfather if the building would be finished by the date in the contract.

"Of course," Steen said. "You have my word on it."

Peter glanced over at Anders to see if he had heard, but Anders was already placing a nail and driving it in clean. Steen looked up at them once more.

"Keep going," he said. Then he ducked into the black Ford pickup and headed into town.

They were both three-quarters of the way to the ridge when the rain first hit. A cherry rain falls in fat, full drops, round and heavy, splashing straight down out of the clouds, crashing between leaves to split the fruit's skin or bring it to the ground. The rain will last a couple of days at most, sometimes only one day—just long enough to ruin the fullest and ripest.

Peter had kept up with Anders until the rain came, driving in nails the way Anders had shown him, with the nail held in the left hand palm up, and the head of the hammer like the end of a long lever that began at the elbow. But when the first drops began to fall, Peter saw Anders speed up. Each of his movements, sweeping a nail from his pouch, placing it, driving it, and shifting crablike to the next rafter, became a little more precise, a little more efficient.

"Sooner we finish," he called, "sooner we knock off."

Peter knew then that he wasn't planning on being chased off the roof by the rain.

The wood of the roof decking changed color gradually beneath their feet. At first the drops hit individually, created a pattern of sleek, hard fish scales layered over the light blond of pine. Then the tumbling water darkened the wood into a single slick orange glaze, running with rippling liquid sheets.

Peter picked up the pace of his own work as well, but he couldn't go as fast as Anders. The cotton shirt under his overalls was soaked, and water ran in two streams down his cheeks around the brim of his ball cap. On the other side of the roof, Anders seemed to move effortlessly on the wet, sloped surface, quick as a sprite in his soft-soled shoes, never pausing for balance or traction.

"When I'm through with my side," he said to Peter, "I'll come over and help you finish up."

The sky was black and close overhead, and Peter felt like the tall clouds were looking right over his shoulder, spilling another bucket of rain just when it would make him drop a nail. Whenever he looked across the rafters at Anders, he saw him smile and lick the little water drops that formed on the end of his bristly mustache.

Anders had one more plank to lay to reach the roof ridge when the black pickup pulled back in. Peter didn't see Steen get out of the truck; he imagined him sitting there, peering at them through the fogged-up windows, telling them to keep going, keep pushing. Anders waved toward the truck with his hammer and pointed to the ridge.

Then Peter felt the cherry rain fold them both inside of itself, surround them like a thick gray blanket. He couldn't see the clouds anymore; they were right down on top of him, and he felt cut off from everything except the site, cut off from everything except his hammer and the roof, Anders opposite the ridge, and the black truck with the windows like sheets of beaten metal.

Anders began to work a little faster still after he waved at Steen, and Peter did as well. He didn't want to hear Steen twit him too much about needing help to finish his half of the work.

Then, while Anders and he both moved sideways, the rain seemed to give a little tug, just the tiniest of pulls on the sheet of water under Anders's feet. Peter saw him suddenly collapse flat onto the roof as his right foot shot out from under him. His left knee hit and skidded down, and he reached toward Peter with his hand, then tried to grab hold of the ridge beam he had almost nailed home.

Peter lunged uselessly across the five feet of bare rafters between them while Anders slid down the roof like a chip of wood down a fast-moving stream, twisting and clawing for something to hold on to. But his own handiwork on the roof deck was too smooth, the planks so perfectly mated that he might as well have been trying to get a grip on a block of ice.

Peter watched him fly straight out when he passed over the sweet angle of the cornice he had framed up.

The door of the Ford winged open, and Steen ran toward Anders. Peter skinned down the ladder. The other carpenters had already circled the fallen man, and Steen was kneeling beside him, holding his broad-brimmed hat a foot over his friend's face to keep the rain off.

"Anders," he said, "can you speak?"

Anders moaned but didn't open his eyes. Paolo Pirelli came into the circle and looked down.

"Madonna!" He crossed himself.

"We'll take him to the hospital," Steen said. He slipped his wide hands like spades under Anders's shoulders. Another carpenter supported the lower back, and a third took the legs. They lifted him up slowly. His head sighed to the left.

"It's too wet to work, maybe," Paolo said. "Maybe he shouldn't have been working on the roof in the rain."

"It's not too wet," Steen said.

Peter felt that Steen was talking to him, even though he wasn't looking at him.

"It wasn't too wet to be working," he repeated. "Come on, easy now."

They walked slowly toward the truck with Anders, leaving Paolo and Peter alone. Paolo looked at Peter, his broad, kind face streaked with rain, worried and helpless.

Peter knew there was nothing else to do. By the time the truck pulled away, he was back on the roof, murdering nails in the rain.

When he was beginning the last row on his side, he saw another carpenter mount the slick wood on Anders's side. It was Steen himself. Steen had shucked his coat, changed his shoes, pulled his leather carpenter's belt right around his dressy pants, and climbed up to finish off what Anders hadn't been able to.

They both worked along the ridge, nailing home the last plank. Steen looked at Peter while they worked, hammering, scuttling to the side, breathing water. He looked as though he wanted to talk, wanted at least a nod of understanding. But Peter kept his eyes down on the work that had to be completed.

Two days later the roof deck was dry, and Peter began laying felt under a sky so bright and blue and clean that it hurt his eyes to look into it.

. . . .

The second time Peter went to visit Anders in the county hospital, he took in some figures and a sketch of the motel roof that he was going to raise the next day. Anders was laid up in the middle of a narrow ward, a long white room with tall windows darkened by thick roll-down shades. His bed had a pipe frame over the top, and pulleys and lines and counterweights kept his legs pointing upward.

Peter stood by the foot of the bed and put the papers on Anders's chest. Anders held the first one straight out in front of him at arm's length.

"Petey," he said, "can you get my spectacles? They're on the nightstand, but I can't reach them."

"Sure." He handed over the glasses, but when Anders took them one of the papers slipped onto the floor.

"Damn." Anders clawed toward the floor on the side of the bed opposite Peter.

"I'll get it," Peter said. "Don't hurt yourself."

"Yesterday I dropped a piece of the newspaper I was reading," Anders said. "Couldn't finish an article until I caught a nurse's attention."

Peter handed him the sketch. He blinked behind his lenses and studied it, then passed on to some of the numbers laid out.

"Double-pitch roof, no cornices," he said. "Twelve-foot run and a six-foot rise. One-fourth pitch. That should be easy for you now."

"Sure."

"Just measure twice and cut once. You'll do fine." He stuck the papers out to the right, still looking dead ahead.

"So what's the doctor say, Anders?" Peter looked at the legs aimed at the roof, the man upside down.

Anders covered his face with his hand.

"They say one leg will be shorter than the other. What do you think of that?"

Peter touched his shoulder, but he didn't move.

"I just wish I was back at work," he said. "I just want to be working again."

"You'll work again," Peter said.

He shook his head. "You can't be a roofer with a game leg."

. . . .

Peter spent most of that summer alone on top of the motel. One of the other carpenters, a thick man named Casten, helped him get the ridge into place, but Peter dropped the plumb bob from the end rafter to the plate to make sure it was true. Once the ridge and the rafters were in place, Casten went back to the ground, and Peter was alone placing the sheathing boards on the twelve-unit building, then walking through the sky laying down the courses of shingling with galvanized nails. He finished around the time the apricot harvest was winding up, around the time his last year of school was to start.

Pirelli's Motel and Roadside Café opened before Thanksgiving, on time and on budget. And Steen announced one morning that he was going to trade in the old Jordan for a new Buick Century. "When you see me come back," he bragged, "you'll see me in a brand-new blue touring car, with whitewall tires."

But two hours later, he came back still driving the Jordan, frowning and not talking to anyone.

At dinner that night, while Betsy was trying to get Peggie and Jenny to sit down quiet, Peter asked Steen what had happened to the touring car. Betsy gave him a look, but Steen was too angry at the dealer in San Jose to bother being angry with Peter.

"Why," he said, "they won't give me but fifty dollars in trade for the Jordan. Fellow claimed that because they don't make them anymore, they aren't worth so much. 'Why, it's only eight years old, isn't it? It still runs, don't it?' I ask. 'Sure,' he says, 'but it's out of style now.' I'd rather not get a new car than be taken advantage of that way."

"The Jordan still runs fine, Steen," Betsy said. "We don't have to have a new car."

"That's right. We don't."

"We can just keep driving the old one. If that's the way you feel."

"Sure that's the way I feel. Now don't you start too."

Then Peggie started to cry, head down toward her empty plate. She was only six, and whenever she cried, everyone in the house turned to her to find out what the matter was. Betsy asked if she was hungry.

"No," Peggie said.

"We're going to eat right away."

"It's not *that*."

"What is it, then?" Betsy dipped her hand gently into Peg's golden curls.

"It's, it's . . ."

"Yes?"

"I wanna new car, too," she sobbed.

Steen slammed his hand flat on the table and made the dishes jump. Then he swore in Danish under his breath, and Betsy looked at him hard.

"Not at the table," she said.

Steen looked blackly at Peg, which made her cry even more.

"I have an idea," Peter said suddenly.

"Oh, yes?" Steen said. "So what's your idea?"

"Give the Jordan to me. For my wages."

Peter saw Steen's mind go to work. Thinking about what

he'd done that summer, figuring out what he'd really have to pay him if he meant to keep his word. Maybe Steen was also thinking about what he owed for Anders's fall, how much better he'd be able to feel if he paid Peter off. And he'd still be able to drive down the road in a new Buick Century.

"All right," he said grandly. "Done. It's yours."

Steen gave Peter his hand. Peter took it, then added, "I want the pink slip."

Steen looked at him suspiciously. "What do you want the pink slip for?"

Peter didn't have everything worked out yet, didn't know exactly what his plan was. He just knew that he wanted it to be really his car, one hundred percent his, so that when he drove somewhere, he wouldn't carry the name of Steen Denisen with him.

"If I don't have the pink slip, I won't really own it. It will just be a privilege you're giving me."

"So? What are you planning on doing to make me take back the privilege?"

"Steen," Betsy said. "He earned it, didn't he?"

Peter knew then that his mother was on his side. This time, anyway. And so he kept quiet and listened. Steen said something to her in Danish, and she answered back in a stronger tone. They went back and forth a little bit, until Steen rolled his head toward Peter.

"All right," he said. He pulled out his billfold and handed Peter the pink slip that had come back with him from San Jose. "Now we're square."

He looked at Peggie, who was still sniffing and rubbing her eyes.

"Come on. Come sit on Poppa's lap," he said.

Peggie hesitated and looked at Betsy.

"Come on." Steen patted his knee with his hand.

Late that night, Peter studied the pink slip by lamplight alone in his room, and he saw that his mother was the one who had signed it. The Jordan was registered to her under her maiden name, Moreberg. That had been Peter's last name too, until they made him change it.

"Peter Moreberg," he said aloud. "Peter Me. Peter Me."

Peter drove with Steen into San Jose the next day and stayed with him until he'd made a deal on a new Buick Century. Then he let Steen drive right home to show off the new car, while he took a slow turn through downtown and passed by all the places he had been taken by his mother and stepfather. There was Hart's, where they bought him overalls. The Owl Drugstore with the fountain where they would all go for a soda. The five-and-dime where they let him pick out pencils and erasers at the beginning of every school year.

The wheel of the car felt good in his hands as he glided down South First Street. At a stop sign, just on the edge of downtown, a group of boys looked up at him. About twelve years old, about the same age he had been when he first worked carpenter for his stepfather. He waved at them through the window, and in a group they waved back.

Peter pulled out fast and left skid marks, and he thought he heard the boys cheer.

On the road back to San Natoma, he saw Paolo Pirelli's place coming up. A big sign swooped down into an arrow pointing to the motel parking lot, and on the café the word "EAT!" was painted in fancy red letters. Paolo was working back in the glass windowed shop at the gas station, and Peter pulled in.

"Mr. Pirelli," he said, "how do you like my new car?"

Paolo whistled low. "*Your* car now, eh?"

"For building your roof," Peter said. "I even have the pink slip."

"Your stepfather pay you with this car?"

"Yeah!"

"Is that all he gave you?"

"Well, yeah."

"Tell you what," Paolo said. "Why don't you start it and put it in neutral? We'll take a look at your car together."

He folded back the hood and watched and listened while Peter turned over the engine. Together they watched the fan turn and the fan belt spin the generator, listened to the roar of the engine.

It all seemed perfect to Peter. But Paolo stood upright and frowned and tapped his ear.

"A little bit of a rattle," he said over the engine noise. "Your valves need to be adjusted."

He motioned for Peter to turn it off, and then he leaned back down under the hood.

"And look here," he said. "Oil leak around the front seal. Not bad now, but it will get worse. You see?"

Peter looked where he was pointing—a black ooze where the shaft that turned the fan came out of the engine block.

"Your stepfather couldn't have known about this. Steen barely knows one end of a car from the other."

"Yeah, I guess," Peter said.

Paolo patted him on the back.

"If you want, bring it in on Saturday. I'll show you how to fix it. Free for you, Petey."

"Really?"

"Sure, you bet. You built my roof. It's the least I can do."

"Thanks, Mr. Pirelli."

"You don't gotta thank me. I'll see you on Saturday." He folded the hood back down.

While Paolo worked on the car that weekend, showing Peter what to do, it seemed normal for Peter to break off and pump the gas for anyone who came in. Paolo found a few more things wrong with the car, and so Peter came in the following Saturday, and the Saturday after that, pumping gas, washing windshields, and checking the oil and water for anyone who pulled in. Little by little, they were taking the Jordan apart and putting it back together again, until everything was just right.

Then Peter started coming in and helping with whatever car Paolo happened to be working on. Pumping gas, handing him the tools, and learning all about what goes on inside an engine. Paolo started paying wages after the turn of the year, regular hourly wages, so he could feel free to leave the gas station to Peter and look after the motel and help his wife and daughters in the café. And Peter always got all the gas he wanted in the bargain.

When Peter told Steen that he didn't care to work for him the next summer, that he had another job he liked better, Steen said he'd regret it.

"Oh, yeah?" Peter said. "Tell that to Anders."

"Anders is back to work now."

"Not roofing."

"And did you know that I paid every penny of his hospital bill? Every penny?"

But Peter didn't care. He was already through the door, in the Jordan, flying out the driveway and spraying gravel behind him.

28
· · · · · · · ·

The Language of Birds   February 1939

Albin Roberts remembered wandering through all the empty, hidden places of the big house. The long white hallway upstairs was lined with bland and mysterious doors, always closed, always the same. One room downstairs had a fireplace so big he could sit inside of it. The kitchen was filled with square chair legs and chipped round table legs to hide behind; he would hide and giggle until Mrs. Madison finally discovered him and gave him a treat before chasing him away.

Always he remembered sidling into the red-tiled sunroom in the southeastern wing of the house, where his mother sat for hours every day in front of an easel. She wore a long white smock, and her hair was tied in a thick black rope that curved down her back. A vase of flowers would usually stand on a small table in front of her, and a half-finished image of the vase on her canvas.

Here, at the end of his wandering, he would stand as quietly as possible until his mother noticed him. It was a game he had invented. To stay in the room with his mother for as long as he could.

When she discovered him, she called him to her side to look at the painting. "It's the lasting quality of art," she said. "The flowers come and go, but their beauty is saved in the painting."

She held both his hands and looked him in the eyes. "Albin," she always said, "you're a very gifted child. Very special. I know you'll do wonderful things."

Then she turned back to her canvas and left him to wonder at what wonderful things he would do.

Once, his father caught Albin standing secretively in the sunroom, and he lifted him up laughing and carried him to his mother's side.

"Your mother," he said, "is become a devotee of the true and the beautiful. And I'm the one who has to pay for it. Don't you catch the same disease."

He kissed her good-bye behind her ear and strolled out of the room. His mother smoothed down her thick braid of hair and picked up a brush.

"Don't pay any attention to him," she said.

She pointed the brush toward the painting, and her face sharpened.

Albin backed out of the room and caught up with his father at the front door. "Where are you going, Poppa?"

"To town," his father said.

"Can I go, too?"

"No, no," his father laughed. "I have to turn some land into money. Stay here and play with Olivia." And he shut the door behind him.

Albin's older sister had decided that she would be a great dancer. He usually found her in the ballroom with the chandelier and the piano. She stood in front of a long looking glass that Wong Sing had mounted on one wall. Sometimes she would move around, but other times she just stood there and looked at herself.

When Olivia caught Albin watching her, she threw a shoe at him.

"No little brothers allowed," she said.

He threw the shoe back at her and ran out of the house.

When he couldn't be in the sunroom, and couldn't be in the ballroom, and couldn't be in the kitchen, Albin went up into the hills to study the language of birds. He walked through the orchards of Ida Valley, the sections that hadn't been sold off yet, and up into the tall grasses on the part too steep to clear. In the zone where oak trees gave way to pine and redwood, he'd dug a little fort with a trowel he'd borrowed from the garden shed when Wong wasn't looking. Nobody knew where the fort was except for him. There he sat and listened to the birdsongs cross over his head.

The first bird he'd called was the mourning dove. He could recognize the low, faraway sound of loss and sadness, traveling through the still air in early evening; he thought it was speaking to him. He discovered that if he cupped his hands in front of his lips, he could make a whistle echo, change its pitch, and die off slowly. He whistled into his hands whenever he heard the dove call, and he came close to being able to imitate exactly the same variation in pitch and length.

One evening, just before heading down from his hill, a bird called and he returned its call. There was a pause in which he heard nothing but crickets, and he turned slowly toward where the bird had spoken and whistled again, long and slow and sad. Then the bird answered him. He was sure it was answering him, because its call seemed to have changed to fit his. He brought his hands together again, touched his lips to his thumbs as delicately as a kiss, and called out.

Cooooh - Aaaoooh - Coooo.

The dove answered again. Another bird joined in from the wood to the northeast, and Albin spoke to both of them, through the cupped hollow of his hands. Then he saw the first bird fly up against the deep sky to the west.

In the following years, he began to repeat the calls of other birds, each in its season. The single-pitched trill of the junco. The rattling note of shorebirds. The distant click from the back of his throat for the long-legged egrets and herons in the wetlands. He reached out for the songs he heard in the wilder places around the Valley, and he was sure the birds answered him. He couldn't read exactly what they meant, but he thought they were all trying to tell him a story. And he didn't say anything to anyone else about it.

· · · · · · · ·

When he was fourteen, Albin walked into the brilliant green hills of winter. The trees on the Valley floor were still bare and dormant, but the grasses quickened with the rains of December and January and greened all the slopes rising up from the orchard land. Albin passed through thigh-high stalks bent with arrowy seed pods and came to the knoll where he'd dug his fort.

He looked down at the plain of trees stretching out toward the silver bay, with spiderweb-thin roads cutting across it. Where roads intersected, groups of houses and buildings cut into the orchards. Close to the bay, the naval air station occupied a huge plat of land, with massive domelike hangars for the dirigibles stationed there.

Albin leaned back, closed his eyes, and listened. He heard the burbling quick whistle of the meadowlark. He stretched his neck out and answered it in its own voice.

The meadowlark called back to him, sounding like a bright flute playing. It was early in the year for the lark to have built a grass saucer and laid eggs among the tall stalks in the field. But Albin thought that perhaps it was choosing a place now to nest, making in song the normal and miraculous decision of where to lay its eggs.

Albin stretched forward as though reaching for something with his lips, and he sang once more.

Then Albin heard a human tramping below the knoll, and the birdsong stopped. He knelt down in his fort, but the sound of footsteps came right toward him. The grass stalks around him began to swish aside.

A stocky and square-built woman heaved into view as the grass parted, and she looked down at Albin.

"Albin Roberts," she declared.

"Hello, Miss Russell," he said cautiously.

Diana Russell wore long riding pants, high leather boots, and a broad-brimmed hat. A pair of brass binoculars hung around her neck, and she carried a notebook in her hand. She looked knowingly at Albin, then lifted her binoculars to her eyes and scanned the trees.

"Eighty years ago," she said, "you wouldn't have been able to sit here all alone."

"Why not?" Albin asked.

"Grizzly bears. Or if not bear, then mountain lions. But the last bear was hunted out of the Coast Range when I was just a girl."

She lowered her binoculars and looked at Albin.

"Can you do other birds besides the *Sturnella neglecta?*"

"The what?"

"The western meadowlark."

Albin didn't want to answer. Miss Russell sat down on the rim of his fort and smiled.

"Every year, when I make my observations, I find that the flowers are fewer than before. The toyon is stripped from hill-sides for Christmas decorations, and the wild lilac is cleared to build houses. Poppies, lupines, mariposa lilies are picked by people who don't care. And I don't hear as many birds as I used to. I can't remember when I last heard an Oregon junco."

She held her binoculars up to her eyes, and Albin pursed his lips and made the quickly tinkling call of the junco.

Miss Russell lowered her binoculars after he had finished. "Thank you, Albin."

She stood up. "Do you know where I live in town?"

Albin nodded.

"Come by tomorrow, if you can. In the morning. And we'll talk about birds and bird calling. All right?"

He nodded again.

"Then I'll leave you alone. I'm going to seek out some poppy fields I know. Have you ever heard Joaquin Miller's poem?"

She began to recite:

This Golden Poppy is God's gold;
The gold that lifts, nor weighs us down,
The gold that knows no miser's hold,
The gold that banks not in the town,
But careless, laughing, freely spills
Its gold far up the happy hills.

She raised her hand in sign of farewell, and she walked with strong, stocky strides up the hill through the pliant grasses.

. . . .

Miss Russell wasn't the kind of person you could say no to. She had a way of making it seem that what she wanted you to do was

276 *The Blossom Festival*

the most important thing you could possibly be doing. Besides, Albin always kept his promises. But when he left home that morning, he didn't tell anybody where he was going.

As soon as he arrived, Miss Russell dragged him into the room she called her study. It was a musty old room with yellowing windows, and books and maps stood in piles on the floor. A projection screen hung down at one end of the room, and a black Magic Lantern sat on a table surrounded by metal boxes of transparencies. On top of a rolltop desk, a line of bird skulls lay amid dried flower petals.

Miss Russell lightly brushed a fingertip across the tops of the skulls. "This is Roland, and Bard, and Jeremy. I found them all in the hills and brought them here."

She sat down in a bentwood chair. "Now, Albin. You can test me. Do a bird call. Any one."

Albin called the first thing that came to mind, a song he had heard on the way over. Miss Russell stopped for a moment with her head cocked in concentration. Then she sprang up and seized a heavy folio-size book from her desk and threw the book open. She piled through the colored pages until she suddenly thrust her finger down on an image.

"There," she said. "Is that the bird you're imitating?"

The thick paper felt like linen. Albin looked up mildly. "I'm not imitating," he said. "I'm calling."

Miss Russell nodded. "Of course, Albin."

He looked down at the reproduction of a brown bird with a short seed-cracking beak and a buff-colored throat.

"That's the one."

"The towhee. *Pipilo fuscus*."

She got him to repeat the name.

Albin called every birdcall he could think of in the close room. Miss Russell recognized most of them, and from somewhere she was always able to find a drawing or a photograph or a painting of the bird. She was surprised that he didn't know the names of many of the birds he called, even though he could recognize them when he was shown them, and she tried to persuade him to memorize the names, if not in Latin then at least in common English.

Afterward, she tested him by asking him to repeat a call by the name of the bird, without showing him the picture.

"Stellar's jay."

He repeated the clipped chirp and caw of the jay.

"Western tanager."

Albin turned his face up and sang the quick repeated note, halfway between a chirp and a whistle. He sang it several times, varying the pitch.

"Albin," Miss Russell said. "You sing beautifully. You have a real gift."

"Thank you," Albin said.

"No, I really mean it. It's a wonder your mother has never mentioned it to me. She must be proud of you."

"She doesn't know," Albin said. "Nobody knows. Except you and the birds."

"Really?"

Albin nodded.

"Well, she will. I know that I would love to have a son just like you." Miss Russell stood up and closed the blinds, then pushed some stacks of books and newsprint away from the Magic Lantern on the table.

"I want you to learn to run the Lantern, Albin. And I want you to do your calls at my Bird and Wildflower League talk next month."

Albin froze while Miss Russell busily looked through the transparencies. She turned out the desk lamp, then flashed on the Lantern.

On the screen at the end of the room, a male and female robin appeared, two feet high.

"Miss Russell, I don't think I can."

"It's easy. You just put the transparency in here and turn it on."

"I mean I don't think I can call birds in front of a bunch of people."

"It's for a good purpose, Albin. The league is to protect birds and nature."

"But I can't. Not in a closed room with just pictures of birds."

"You can do it, Albin. You just did for me."

"But you're different," Albin said.

An intense white light leaked from the Magic Lantern into the darkish room. The birds on the screen were enormous.

"Sometimes I think the birds talk to me," Albin said. "That's why I call them."

"Albin. You can't keep your gift just for people who are already close to birds. You have to share it with everyone."

The room was quiet except for the whirring of the fan against the bright lamp.

"I believe you can do it. Trust me."

Suddenly a gaping white hole melted into the red breast of the robins on the screen, and a stink of melting stock smoked from the Lantern. The birds on the screen burned away while Miss Russell fumbled for the switch.

. . . .

Albin led Miss Russell past the staircase and into the hall between the dining room and the library.

"She'll be in the sunroom," he whispered.

He paused when he stepped onto the red tiles. His mother sat still and quiet before a blank canvas under soft, filtered sunlight, and her thick braid of hair was settled in a fold of her white smock.

Then Miss Russell clattered her leather boots across the tile, and his mother turned. Albin had to fall in behind.

"Diana," his mother said. "This is a surprise."

"Hello, Eugenia." Miss Russell looked with interest at the easel and at a finished painting propped against the wall. "Your work is better and better."

"Thank you." His mother looked curiously at Albin; he thought sure it had been a mistake to come.

"And how are you, Diana? Ready for your talk at the festival?"

"That's why I've come. I want Albin to help. He can run the Magic Lantern while I talk."

"Oh. Well, that's fine, I suppose." She smiled at Albin, and he felt his knees stop trembling.

"He can do one more thing for me. Something special. Albin?"

Albin looked from Miss Russell to his mother. They both had their eyes on him. His mother's face wasn't smiling now, just expectant.

"Go ahead," Miss Russell urged.

Albin closed his eyes. Then he cupped his hands, brought them to his lips, and whistled into them slowly. The sad and longing call of the mourning dove.

He opened his eyes and looked at his mother.

"Isn't that wonderful?" Miss Russell asked. "He can do some birdcalls while the Lantern shows the picture."

"It is wonderful. Yes. Of course he can."

"One last favor. Theodore Wores is going to show some of his landscapes at the club during the talk. I'd love to have some of your paintings on display there as well."

Miss Russell smiled engagingly.

Albin left the sunroom with her, and he looked over his shoulder at his mother's back recomposing itself, the dark, shiny hair falling in a line across textured white cloth.

He couldn't rid himself of the idea, for a long time after, that when he'd opened his eyes, his mother's face had been beautiful and jealous.

29

The White-Limbed Girls   March 1939

In the first week of March, the prune orchards that cover the
Santa Clara Valley are in green tip. The trees break dormancy,
and the little bumps on the lateral branches swell up into
hard, tightly closed buds standing out green from the branches.

Soon, the buds come into the popcorn stage. They grow
rounder and fuller, and cracks of white appear overnight in
the hard surface. Then, if the sun is fair and steady, the trees
break into blossom all at once. The orchards turn white with
full bloom, a bright clear white above the cover crops of yellow mustard or volunteer oat. And in the middle of every
blossom is a tiny prune, tender and pale, smaller than a
child's fingertip, ready to ripen and grow.

While the trees are still in green tip, the growers meet with
the businessmen of San Natoma and decide when to celebrate

the Blossom Festival. They look in their almanacs, study their trees, talk about the sky, and choose the weekend they think will be closest to full bloom. Then programs are printed, the newspapers are informed, the speakers and dancers and musicians are contacted. And everyone watches the weather and tries not to think about the three inches of rain that fell on festival day in 1915.

Full bloom can last as long as three days. Then the orchards take on a brownish cast. Five days later, petals are already falling to the ground.

Of all the white blossoms that shine under the bright sunlight of late March, and all the pale green bulbs that begin wrapped in flower petals, less than 15 percent grow into fruit.

. . . .

"Look," Olivia said.

Spread out across her bed was the long white tunic, the rust-colored sash for her waist, the short, blunt-edged sword that Bert the blacksmith had made of iron and painted with gold leaf.

Fumiko looked at the costume. "You're lucky to be able to dance, Olivia."

Olivia picked up the tunic and held it to her shoulders. She had sewn it of shiny, hard-finished cambric cloth, and it shone a little in the light. She swayed left and right.

"Don't I look like a rustic king?"

Fumiko touched the smooth cloth, and the seam where the material was gathered under the yoke. "It's beautiful. You should be proud."

Olivia laid the dress back on the bed and brought over her wicker sewing basket and two small embroidery hoops. "I already traced the design," she said. "It's simple. Just tiny flowers to match the sash. You can start down by the hem, and I'll start on the yoke."

She drew a couple of chenille needles from her pincushion, handed one to Fumiko, then brought out a skein of English crewel wool of the same rusty shade as the sash. She doubled the wool around her needle, creased it tightly by squeezing it between her thumb and forefinger, then pushed the crease through the needle's eye. She cut the wool and handed it to Fumiko.

Fumiko threaded her needle in the same way and pulled the material taut into her hoop around one of the light blue patterns Olivia had made with the dressmaker's carbon. A simple four-petaled flower with a little stem. "What kind of stitch should we use?" she asked.

"Use a chain stitch for the outline, a satin stitch to fill in," Olivia said. "Then we can put some French knots in the middle of the flower."

"You'll have to show me how to do the French knot."

There was a polite knock on the door.

"Yes?" Olivia said. "Come in, Wong."

Wong opened the door and carried in a tray with a tea set. He placed it on the marble-topped table beside the bed.

"Would you like anything else, Miss Olivia?"

"No, thank you, Wong."

Olivia poured the tea, and Fumiko took the delicate porcelain cup into her hands. She liked her family's fine tea things, textured and flecked with black and gold. But she suddenly wished they also had cups of smooth, almost translucent porcelain.

"You have so many beautiful things," she said.

Olivia showed Fumiko how to make a French knot on a stalk, a little knob growing from the middle of the petals. Then they both moved their hoops and began on the next flower.

"I had to ask my father if I could come tonight," Fumiko said. "If I'd asked my mother, she would have said no."

"Really?" Olivia took a sip of tea.

"Since my little brother was born, she always complains that she has to have help to take care of four men."

Fumiko didn't mention the way her mother looked when she went to her father to ask permission. Her mother had kept silent, unwilling to speak against what her husband was deciding, but her eyes had narrowed.

She began to run her needle up and down very quickly and precisely, building the chain stitch link by link along the faint blue outline. Needle up, form a loop, needle down, then back up through the loop.

"Old Mrs. Madison used to sing a song when she helped me sew," Olivia said.

"Do you remember it?"

"She sang it in a foreign language. She just said it was something women sang when their men were out fishing, to make sure they would come back."

"It must have worked," Fumiko laughed. "She got married." She took another stitch, then added, "It's funny she got married so old. Usually only young people get married."

Olivia threaded more wool through her needle and began on the satin stitches. "I don't want to get married."

"Never?"

"I want to dance. Besides, Isadora Duncan never married."

"Oh." Fumiko couldn't think of anything good to say about marriage after that.

Olivia moved her hoop again and watched the cambric ripple between her and Fumiko.

"I'm so glad you could come," she said. "My mother is too busy with her painting to help me."

"I'll be proud when I see you," Fumiko said. "I'm sure I'll be able to come after church."

"Of course you'll be able to come. You can't miss this."

They worked together around the dress and embroidered a rusty flower over each blue outline. When they finished, Olivia held the dress up to her shoulders again.

"I think I have to go home now," Fumiko said.

"But you can't leave until we try it on," Olivia said. "Let's try it on."

Fumiko did want to see Olivia wearing the dress she'd helped embroider. The white sheen of the cloth suddenly appeared to be the same color as the blossoms unfolding in the orchards around the valley.

. . . .

Albin Roberts walked out of Diana Russell's house into the night. The sky above was clear, and there was still a wintry chill in the air. He pulled his scarf around his neck and fastened the top button on his coat. Mrs. Russell had told him to protect his throat, to be sure not to catch a cold. There would be a large audience for their presentation on Sunday morning, and he had to be in perfect voice for his birdcalls.

Halfway home, he stopped on the corner to let a car go by. But the headlights caught him, and the car slowed down.

"Hey, Al. Need a lift?"

It was Peter Moreberg, who was a couple of grades ahead of Albin.

"Sure." Albin climbed in on the passenger's side and closed the door. He was flattered that Peter had stopped to pick him up. Not only was Peter a senior, but he also owned his own car. Plus, he worked at the gas station and could fix cars, so the few other boys who did own cars all looked up to him.

They drove down paved roads toward Ida Valley. The land around them was filled with fruit trees blooming in the darkness. Here and there, a newly built house pushed into the orchard land.

"What are you going to do for the Blossom Festival?" Albin asked.

"I don't care much about the festival anymore," Peter said. "It's mostly for kids. Or out-of-towners."

"Yeah." Albin didn't want to disagree.

"When I was younger, it was okay. Now I think there's more to the world than San Natoma."

"That's what my sister thinks," Albin said. "She says she wants to go to San Francisco. Or even New York."

"Oh, yeah?" Peter looked interested.

"To be a dancer."

"If you really want to do something, you can do it," Peter said.

"She's dancing on Sunday." Albin decided not to mention his own part in the festival. "She's the star. You could see her dance."

"Huh. Maybe I will."

Peter pulled the Jordan onto the long gravel lane that led to the big house at Ida Valley. The house was well back from the main road, still surrounded by orchards. Peter drove between the lines of cypress trees that ran alongside the gravel lane, then pulled into the large open space in front of the house.

He cut the ignition and set the hand brake. A window in the house was glowing with light.

"Look," he said.

Olivia unzipped the dress she was wearing. It slipped from her body and fell into a heap on the floor, and she stepped forward, suddenly wearing only a teddy, sleeveless and loose-fitting around her thighs.

Fumiko watched everything Olivia did. Her friend held the tunic against her now bare shoulders, turned to the mirror, and smoothed it over her body with one hand. Then she lifted it over her head, and the shining cloth glided down over her, fitting snugly about her shoulders and blousing out below the yoke.

She took up the sash, a long, flowing rust-colored streak, and fastened it around her waist. The long lines of her body were revealed as she drew the sash tight and knotted it. Above the sash, the tunic rose up and out over her breasts, then back to the point of her shoulders. Below the sash, it spread out over her hips, then ended. Her dancer's legs rippled with muscle as she went up on her toes.

She held up the golden sword and turned from the mirror to Fumiko.

"Don't I look like Oberon?" she asked.

"You do," Fumiko said. "You do."

"Kneel down," Olivia said.

Fumiko went to her knees, and Olivia touched her two shoulders and then her head with the sword.

"I hereby dub you a knight of the fairies," she said.

"Can't I be a princess?"

Olivia moved the sword again over Fumiko, then brought it to rest on her head where her hair was parted.

"I make you a princess of the fairies, then."

Fumiko stood up smiling. "It's sad you only get to wear this once," she said. "It's so pretty on you."

"Try it on?" Olivia asked.

"Oh, Olivia, it's too big for me."

"You're a princess, you should get to wear the tunic." She was already unknotting the sash and lifting the tunic over her head.

Fumiko unbuttoned her shift and laid it on the bed. She was

wearing a simple white cotton slip underneath, which hung straight from her shoulders to her knees.

Olivia handed her the tunic, and she poked her head into it, found the armholes, and let it fall. It was much too large, as she had known. The hem came down almost to her ankles, and her thin body seemed lost in all the cloth that ballooned out from the shoulders. She tied the sash around her waist, but it didn't make the tunic conform to her body gracefully. The material just bunched up at the knot and stuck out everywhere else.

"That's no good," Olivia said. "Take it off, I have another idea."

Fumiko glanced at herself in the mirror. It looked like she was wearing a flour sack. She quickly took off the tunic and stood again in her slip.

Olivia drew from her dresser a long silk scarf, aqua blue, with tassels on each end.

"I love this scarf," she said. "It feels so smooth."

She placed the scarf around Fumiko, drew it snug, and tied it off. The plain cotton slip suddenly revealed the graceful lines of Fumiko's slender body. Fumiko looked in the mirror again, and ran her hands over herself, as Olivia had done.

"You look pretty, Fumiko."

Fumiko lifted the end of the scarf and rubbed it against her cheek.

"Here," Olivia said. "I'll show you a secret." She pulled a chair up to her vanity table and picked out a large square-cut bottle. Then she found an octagonal box, a brush, and a saucer in the drawer.

She took the stopper out of the bottle and passed it under her nose. Then she offered it to Fumiko.

"Rose water," Olivia said.

Fumiko breathed in the faint sweet scent of roses.

Olivia poured the rose water into the saucer. Then she opened the box. It was filled with white powder. She scooped the powder into the rose water with a spoon and carefully stirred it with her brush. The powder swirled into starfish shapes before dissolving. Olivia added powder until it was as thick as fresh cream.

"Zinc oxide," she said. "When we dress in these tunics, Miss Johnson wants us to look classical. Like Greek sculpture. We have to brush this on our arms and legs so that we look like marble."

She dipped the brush into the whitened rose water and began to brush down her left arm. Her ruddy skin paled, and she dipped the brush again rapidly.

"You have to keep working from a wet edge," she said. "Otherwise it looks uneven. But if you work too fast and you're not careful, you can streak."

Fumiko thought about a time her father had taken everyone to see Japanese dance in Nihonmachi. Fumiko didn't like it very much, because the dancer didn't move around, and only fluttered her hands. But she remembered that the dancer's face was made up pure white with rice powder. It made her eyes seem like black jewels, glittering and passionate and alive.

Olivia finished her left arm and waved it slowly in the air.

"Can I try?" Fumiko asked.

She took the brush and ran it down her left arm, using the same technique she had seen Olivia use. The rose water was a little cold, but the brush felt soft against her skin, like a cat rubbing against her. When she finished her arm, she dipped the brush again and ran it over her cheek.

"Fumiko, what are you doing?"

"It's all right. I want to see how I look." She brushed white onto her forehead and down her jaw to the point of her chin and up the other side. Then she closed her eyes and carefully ran the brush over her eyelids.

When she finished, her face was as pale as the moon. And her eyes were just like the dancer's, black and glittering.

She turned to Olivia and smiled with her eyes.

"Fumiko," Olivia said, "you're beautiful."

"Let me paint your right arm," Fumiko said. "Then you can paint mine."

Fumiko laid the full brush against Olivia's shoulder and watched the bristles spread out. She moved it down the upper arm and around the crook of the elbow. The skin gave slightly under the pressure of the brush, then sprang back as it passed. Down the delicate inside part of the forearm, around the wrist, to the tip of each finger, Fumiko covered Olivia's skin with brushstrokes.

Then Fumiko turned and gave her own arm. Olivia moved it with her left hand as she brushed with her right. She worked very carefully, kept a wet edge, didn't allow any streaks where the skin could show through. When she had finished, Fumiko's two arms matched her whitened face.

"Shall we do our legs too?" Olivia asked. "I'm going to have to on Sunday."

Fumiko held her arms up by her face and looked in the mirror. "Okay," she said.

Each girl painted one leg for herself. Then they painted the second leg for each other. "I like it when you're painting me," Fumiko said. "It just feels nice. Nicer than when I paint myself."

Olivia began to jump up and down to dry her legs. She landed with her feet about twelve inches apart and her heels pointed in toward each other. "That's an échappé," she said.

Fumiko tried to imitate her, but she couldn't make her feet land in a straight line like Olivia could.

When their legs dried, Olivia put her tunic and sash back on. "Let's go to the ballroom where the mirror is," she said. "So we can see what we really look like together."

Fumiko ran her hand over her shoulder strap. "Olivia, all I'm wearing is a slip."

"It doesn't matter," Olivia said. "Nobody's up at this hour. Come on, you're a princess."

She took Fumiko by the hand and led her down the curving staircase and into the front room where the piano was. She pushed a button, and the chandelier overhead suddenly blazed with light. Then she stepped to the high velvet curtains along the side wall and drew them back. A dance bar of polished oak ran parallel to the floor, and behind it was a series of tall mirrors.

The two girls looked at themselves. They were both dressed alike, in white with colored sashes, and they both had skin the tone of marble. Fumiko looked like a smaller version of Olivia, except that Fumiko's face was paler.

"We look nice together," Fumiko said.

"We make a nice couple," Olivia answered.

They both laughed. Then Olivia stood behind Fumiko and placed her hands firmly on either side of her waist. "You can help me practice my pas de deux. I'm the cavalier, and you're the ballerina."

"Okay." Fumiko looked in the mirror and saw Olivia's head growing out of her own. "What do I do?"

"Go up on one toe and cross your arms in front of your chest. Then I'm going to use my left hand as a pivot to spin you to the right, and I'll stop you with my right hand. Okay?"

Fumiko rose up on her right toe.

"Try sticking your left knee out to the side," Olivia said.

Fumiko nodded and rested her left foot against her right calf. She was sure she would be off balance if Olivia were not holding her.

"Ready?"

Fumiko nodded again. Then suddenly the room spun around in a great flashing whirl, and her arms flung out as she tried to catch herself, and Olivia was holding her, keeping her from falling to the floor.

Olivia helped her back to her feet. "I lost my balance," Fumiko said.

"You have to trust me and let yourself go," Olivia said. "Trust is the main thing in partnering."

Fumiko stood once again in front of Olivia. She went up on one toe, and she felt Olivia's hand press against her, strong and solid, as though it were meant to be there.

"Are you ready?" Olivia spoke softly down into Fumiko's ear.

"Ready." Fumiko crossed her hands in front of her chest with the elbows down.

Suddenly, brilliantly, she was spinning.

. . . .

"Look," Peter said.

Peter and Albin got out of the Jordan and stood silently before the large bay window at the front of the house. The window was brightly lit, and they could see the two white-limbed girls dancing and leaping inside. One girl spun across the window and disappeared. The other posed for an instant with her arms curved gracefully before her, then turned and threw her legs high in the air. The two girls came together, one in the arms of the other, then whirled apart again. They sprang upward and landed on one foot, joined in many poses and fell into separate movements, disappeared and came back again into the bright window.

Peter and Albin watched them dance and play inside. Neither spoke. They turned their collars up against the evening chill.

Today I see the orchard's myriad blooms,
Ten thousand acres as a garden plot.
Thus Magic hides Utility's stern brow
Makes poetry of prune and apricot.

A golden cycle and a thousand years
Man's struggle upwards from the soil to God
Is typified in every mystic bloom
Which bursts the bonds which tie it to the sod.

Oh, Santa Clara, with your wealth undreamed
And joy and happiness and gifts untold,
Give thought to those whose vision blazed the trail,
Their faith was boundless, and their spirits bold.

—R. R. Stuart, "Blossom Day from John
Brown's Mountain"

30
. . . .

The Blossom Festival   April 2, 1939

The clear night sky was suddenly alight with a white flower bursting open. It hung glittering above the earth, spread wide, then broke apart and dropped in diamond fragments. The little pieces of light flickered down and fell one by one into darkness.

The crowd standing in the Festival Glen sighed.

Another thin tracer snaked upward and exploded into a giant red star. Streaks of light arced across the sky and spanned the grounds for a moment before dwindling.

A blue burst followed, then another white, then a bright-green cascade of sparkling shards fell over the glen like shining leaves.

The crowd watched the rockets scream upward, sighed happily as every brief display fell apart in the sky.

Peter stood at the edge of the road at Pirelli's Associated Gas Station and watched a little explosion arch above the tree line. A moment after the flash, he heard a little pop come from the Festival Glen.

He shrugged. There had been posters around town touting the Shell Pyrotechnics "Battle of the Clouds" as the kick-off to the Blossom Festival, but it didn't seem so great to him.

Headlights pulled into the gas station, and Peter went back to his pumps. It was one of the new Chevrolets, with the aerostream-style bodies. The driver rolled down his window. He was dressed in a fine dark suit, and the woman next to him wore a coat with a fur collar, and a hat that tilted down over one eye.

"Fill 'er up?" asked Peter.

"With ethyl," the man said.

Peter unscrewed the gas cap and put in the pump nozzle. He was glad Mr. Pirelli had finally gotten rid of the old "visible supply" gas pumps. The new ones kept track of the gasoline with little clock faces, accurate to one tenth of a gallon.

He opened up the hood and checked the oil on the dipstick. The engine was beautiful, a big six-cylinder with valve-in-head engineering, so new that the valve cover shone under the hanging lamps. Peter kept the road grime off his own engine, but it had never looked as clean as this.

He took the dipstick on a rag to show it to the driver. "Oil's fine, mister."

The gas pump bell dinged as the clock ticked off a full gallon. The driver smiled up at Peter.

"Must be tough to work when it's fireworks time," he said.

"Too busy to think about it," Peter said. "So many people from out of town. Where you folks from?"

"Berkeley. Just down to see the blossoms."

"If you grow up here, you've already seen plenty of fireworks and plenty of blossoms."

"Maybe," the driver said. "Then again, maybe you can't see things for what they're really worth when you grow up with them all around you."

While Peter cleaned the windshield, he sneaked looks at the woman sitting in the dark interior of the car, her face half hidden by the sweep of her hat. It was easy for the driver to talk, but Peter would have been glad to change places with him, and drive back to Berkeley. Except maybe Peter would have rather driven his own Jordan. And maybe he would have had Olivia Roberts beside him.

Mr. Pirelli came back soon after the fireworks. "How was business?" he asked.

"I pumped a lot of gas today, Mr. Pirelli."

"And the motel is full," Mr. Pirelli said. "All twelve rooms. I wish it were blossom time twelve months a year."

"Mr. Pirelli? Can I get off from work tomorrow at noon?"

"Sure. You worked twelve hours today. You going to watch the baseball game?"

"Oh, maybe."

"It should be a good one," Mr. Pirelli said. "San Jose Merchants team against the Bear Photo team from San Francisco. First game of the year."

"I guess I should go," Peter said.

"Sure, go out and enjoy yourself. I'll hold down the fort tomorrow."

Peter filled up his tank before he left. With ethyl.

. . . .

Albin stood with his head tilted back and his face to the sky and watched another "triple-bursting" rocket explode. Three expanding wheels of light suddenly glittered overhead in red and white and blue.

"Airplanes," he heard someone say.

Olivia tugged at his coat sleeve. "Come on, Albin," she said. "We have to keep looking."

"There must be a thousand people here, now."

"But if she is here, she must feel completely alone."

Olivia led the way through the Festival Glen. Some families had brought food and spread blankets out, and now lay flat on their backs, looking up at the fireworks. Other people stood in knots, leaning back, commenting on each display. Olivia stole a look down the glen. The earth spread out like a natural bowl, and at the bottom, in darkness, lay the stage where she would dance tomorrow.

They turned back uphill and met Diana Russell bearing down on them. "Albin," she said, "what on earth are you doing here? You'll wake up with a sore throat."

"Sorry, Miss Russell." Albin adjusted the scarf around his neck.

"Promise me. Tomorrow morning, until you come to the clubhouse, you won't speak a word. Save your voice!"

"Have you seen a Japanese girl, Miss Russell?" Olivia asked. "A friend of ours?"

"There are some Japanese over there." Miss Russell pointed to the lower fringe of the glen.

"We looked there."

"Promise," Miss Russell said. "Your singing is so important to me. No, I haven't seen her."

"Okay, I promise," Albin said.

Another round of fireworks exploded overhead, and Diana Russell sailed away.

Olivia and Albin threaded their way toward the strings of paper lanterns that marked the food booths. The plywood booths were bright and glary from naked lightbulbs. Plates of cakes and cookies and strudel lay displayed on the counter, and giant blue-speckled coffeepots percolated on some gas stoves at the back.

Olivia knew all the women working the booth, Mrs. Finney and Mrs. Gordon and Mrs. Hogg. Mrs. Gordon was laughing while she talked.

"That's how I got fat, licking the spoon too much learning to bake cakes. But like they say, 'Kissin' don't last, cookin' do.'"

The women all laughed together. "That's so. That's so."

Olivia caught Mrs. Gordon's eye, and the large, smiling woman came to the counter. "Can I tempt you with something, my dear?"

"No, thank you, Mrs. Gordon."

"Sure, you have to dance tomorrow. Time enough to be getting fat when you're older."

"Have you seen a Japanese girl around? About so tall?" Olivia held out her hand.

"A Japanese girl?" Mrs. Gordon stopped smiling. "I don't think I've seen any Japanese at all. Have you?" she asked the other women in the booth.

"Is she supposed to have done something?" Mrs. Finney asked.

"No. It's just a friend I was going to meet here."

"Oh." Mrs. Gordon pursed her lips. "Well, we haven't seen her."

"Thank you." Olivia turned away and went on looking among the people in the glen, taking Albin in tow. She stopped in an open space, and they both looked around.

"I just don't think she came," Albin said.

"But why wouldn't she?" Olivia asked.

"Maybe she didn't come because of me," he said.

"Silly. She hardly knows you."

"But maybe she doesn't want to get to know me."

Olivia continued to look around. "Well, she wouldn't have not come because of that. Not after she told me she was coming."

Three rockets streaked simultaneously upward and burst into great round patterns crisscrossing against the sky. Another two rockets followed and broke into sparkling fountains. Then three more rockets howled into the night.

"Lindbergh," a man in a straw hat said.

Albin looked at the explosions that filled the air.

"I don't think we'll ever find her," he said.

He let himself be dragged along while he kept his eyes turned toward the sky, as though Fumiko might be found there.

. . . .

"Fumi-chan. You may pour the tea now."

Fumiko left her baby brother's crib and went into the front room. Her mother sat in an overstuffed armchair with her feet up and her hands folded across her lap, facing the radio. The everyday tea set was on a low black-lacquer table beside her, and Fumiko knelt down and picked up the small teapot by the handle.

The music coming from the radio was bright with horns and clarinets, and a muted string section played in the background. Fumiko poured the tea, green and fragrant, carefully into a small cup without handles, offered the cup between her two hands to her mother.

Her mother took the cup and sipped it critically while Fumiko remained on her knees. "When the tea is poured," her mother said, "it should make a pleasing sound in the cup. But I couldn't hear because of the radio."

The song ended, and the announcer said, "That was Louis Armstrong playing 'Struttin' with Some Barbecue.'"

"What does that mean, 'Struttin' with some barbecue?'" her mother asked.

"I don't know, exactly."

"It's a foolish song. Yesterday there was a song that went 'Zaz Zuh Zaz' and 'Hidey Ho' over and over again. I asked Kenji what it means, and he says it means nothing."

"Do you want to keep listening?" Fumiko asked.

"It is the only program on," her mother replied. "Go heat up more water, the tea will grow cold quickly."

Fumiko rose from her knees and walked toward the kitchen. She paused to wiggle her fingers in the air above little Ichiro's nose. The baby grabbed at the wiggling fingers with his chubby hands.

Fumiko then began to flick her fingers hard toward the boy's forehead, as though she were trying to make a coin spin. Her fingertips shot out toward the baby's skin, came within an inch, a half an inch, a quarter of an inch. She came deliberately closer to hitting Ichiro with each darting strike of her sharp nails.

The boy smiled and reached for her fingers. Fumiko left him in the crib and went into the kitchen.

She put the kettle on to boil and walked out onto the back porch. The sky was dark and filled with stars. She stood very still and listened carefully. In the distance, she thought she heard the explosions of the fireworks.

Then she heard her baby brother begin to cry. "Fumiko," her mother called, "see what Ichiro wants."

She came back inside to her brother's crib, picked him up, and brought him into the front room. The radio was still playing swing music. Fumiko turned her brother toward the music and bounced him on her knee until he quieted down.

Her mother looked at the two of them. "I was too old for this baby," she said. "Too old to have another baby."

Fumiko tickled Ichiro's belly. "When is Father coming back?"

"He is on men's business."

"And Kenji and Yoshi are probably watching the fireworks."

"It's no matter where your brothers are, or where your father is. You are where you should be. You are helping your family."

"And I have to help tomorrow?"

"Don't I need your help every Sunday after church?"

"Yes."

"Didn't you disappear from the house one whole evening this week already?"

Fumiko didn't answer.

"You are worried about your friend," her mother said. "Listen to me. One day, you will marry, and she will marry. And her husband will not like your husband. And then you will not be friends anymore."

From the radio, the slightly strained tenor of Cab Calloway began to sing.

Now zaz zuh zaz was handed down—from a bloke down in Chinatown—

"Here's that foolish song again," her mother said.

"Do you want me to turn it off?"

It seems his name was Smokey Joe—

"Of course not. But you can bring some more hot water for the tea."

He used to Hidey Hidey Ho.

Fumiko stood up with the baby in her arms. She had forgotten about the kettle.

"Give me Ichiro and go get the water," her mother said.

Fumiko thrust the baby toward her and ran into the kitchen.

Zaz zuh zaz zuh zaz zuh zaz—

She heard Ichiro begin to cry. Again.

. . . .

Knots of people wandered along the streets in San Natoma, on their way home from the fireworks display. Peter drove the Jordan slowly and watched for Albin again, or better yet, Albin and his sister together. He didn't find them in town, and he cruised out toward Ida Valley, but he didn't come across them along the road either. Once there, he stopped the car and looked at the big house set back among the orchards.

The house was quiet now, and all the windows were dark. He turned the Jordan around and headed for home.

Peter found his stepfather alone in the house, sitting asleep in the big Morris chair. A *Saturday Evening Post* was open over his chest, and his pipe still smoldered slightly in the pipe stand beside him.

Peter listened for a moment to a dull snore whistle through Steen's dentures. Then he went to the kitchen and pulled a bottled beer from the icebox. Steen didn't like it when he did this, but since Peter was now contributing something to the household, his disapproval didn't hold.

Peter cracked open the beer and went back to the front parlor. Steen was shaking his head to wake himself, and he looked at Peter through blinking eyes.

"Are your mother and the girls back from the fireworks yet?"

"Don't think so. I just got back myself."

Steen picked up his pipe and began to tamp down the tobacco. "So. How was work with the Italian today?"

"Fine." Peter took a small sip of beer. "He's a good boss."

"You may think that now, but you watch out for him. Those Italians always take care of their own people first."

"Unlike the Danes," Peter said.

The back door opened, and Peggie and Jenny tumbled into the house, bringing their mother with them. Steen brightened at the sight of his two daughters coming into the parlor. He put down his pipe and opened his arms.

"Come and give me a kiss," he said.

The girls scrambled up and kissed him on the cheek. Peggie made a face.

"You're all scratchy," she said.

Betsy followed them in, loosening her scarf and hanging up her coat in the front closet. "Tell Poppa about the fireworks."

Peter stepped back as both girls fought for room on the footstool in front of the chair.

"Was it pretty?" Steen asked.

Both girls nodded. "Beautiful," Peg said. She was older than Jenny, and she liked to use bigger words than her sister when she could.

Betsy looked at Peter. "Did you have a chance to see any of the fireworks?" she asked.

"Too busy at the gas pump. Lots of people from out of town this weekend."

"A couple of your friends from school stopped by. Nick Burrell and Victor McCracken?"

"Yeah?"

"They wanted to know if you were going to the ball game tomorrow afternoon, so they could ride with you."

"I don't think so," Peter said. "I'm going to be working tomorrow."

Betsy came close to her son and looked in his eyes. "You work so much, I hardly see you at home," she said.

"Ah, Momma." He leaned forward and kissed her on the forehead.

"So was there a grand finale?" Steen asked.

"Was there ever!" Peggie said.

. . . .

The following morning, Olivia woke up early to put on her costume and make herself up. She thought about Fumiko when she was brushing on the zinc oxide and rose water. She wasn't sure why they hadn't found each other at the fireworks, but she knew Fumiko would be there to see her dance. And afterward, they could walk through the flowering orchards and talk about everything, about how well the dance went and what was next.

She left Ida Valley for a final rehearsal at nine o'clock, about the time the church bells began to ring.

Albin kept a scarf around his neck while he ate breakfast, and he didn't speak. Miss Russell's talk was to begin at eleven, but Albin's mother wanted to go earlier. To mingle, she said, with people who cared about nature and art.

Albin dressed in the good clothes his mother had bought

for him. The light-colored wool coat, the long pants, the tan shoes, the stiff collar. His mother said that he had to make a good impression on people. His father was away on business, so Albin had to represent the family name.

As he stood in front of a mirror slicking back his hair, Wong knocked and opened the door.

"Mrs. Roberts wants to know if you are ready," he said.

Albin nodded his head yes. Wong looked at him.

"You are handsome," he said. "Mrs. Roberts will be proud of you."

Albin smiled. Wong looked back at the door. Then he spoke more quietly. "You know the Japanese girl? The one who was here with Miss Olivia on Thursday? The one you watched dance?"

Albin shook his head. Wong ignored him and continued to speak.

"You know her? You like her?"

Albin wasn't sure what Wong was getting at, or how he knew that they had watched Olivia and Fumiko dance. But he decided to nod his head. Yes, he knew her. Yes, he liked her.

"Good," Wong said. He disappeared, and Albin straightened out his coat once more and fussed with his tie.

Suddenly, the door opened again, and Fumiko stood there, wearing a fancy peach dress with puffed sleeves, and shiny peach shoes.

"I caught her in the house," Wong said.

"Albin?" Fumiko smiled uncertainly. "I had to sneak away from church to see Olivia in the festival. Can you take me there?"

Albin pointed to his throat and blushed. "Mr. Albin cannot talk right now," Wong said. Then he left and closed the door behind him.

"You can't talk right now?" Fumiko asked.

Albin bit his lip and shook his head.

"I don't want my father or my brothers to find me. If I can just stay with you until the dance."

Albin pointed at his head. Yes, he had an idea. He left Fumiko in his room and raced down the hallway to his mother's door.

"Yes?" his mother's voice said.

He found her sitting in front of the mirror, placing a comb in her hair. She turned and inspected him.

"You look fine, Albin. Ready to go?"

Albin pointed out the window and jumped up and down on one foot.

"You're anxious, aren't you? Do you want to walk and meet me there?"

Albin nodded vigorously.

"All right. Make sure that my painting, the one with the Mariposa lilies, is right there at the entrance."

Albin turned to go, and his mother added, "Be careful that you don't get dirt on your shoes."

Albin hurried back down the hall. He paused for a moment at the floral arrangement below the oval wall mirror and plucked out a bright yellow flower that he had seen often in his mother's paintings. He stopped in front of the door to his room, straightened out his coat again, and hid the flower behind his back.

Fumiko stood up when Albin opened the door. "Is it all right? Can we go?"

Albin took one step into the room. Then he began to edge nervously to the right with his arm hidden. Fumiko watched him curiously.

"Are you all right?" she asked. "Is anything the matter?"

He continued to shuffle sideways, and Fumiko followed him with her eyes.

"What do you have behind your back?" she asked.

He circled around the edge of the room with his back away from her until he reached the open window. He sat down carefully on the windowsill and let the flower drop out behind him into the yard. Then he jumped up and held his empty hands in front of him.

Fumiko looked at him with a puzzled smile.

They went quietly out the back way and paused at the edge of the lawn. Albin thought about Fumiko's father and brothers, patrolling the roads, searching for her, and he led her out into the orchard toward the Foothill Club. They walked through volunteer oat that grew waist high, and Fumiko ran her hands through the oat stalks and looked up at the canopy of white fruit blossoms that arched over their heads.

"It's a beautiful time of the year," she said.

Albin heard an Oregon junco call. He looked up to point it out to Fumiko and stepped in a patch of mud.

. . . .

Miss Russell, dressed in khakis and high boots, set the Magic Lantern and the two boxes of transparencies, one for birds and one for wildflowers, on a stand in the back of the room for Albin. Then she checked one last time to see that her speech was indeed in her shoulder bag.

The Blossom Festival talk was the most important of the year. She gave talks frequently to schoolchildren for enrichment, she gave talks to social and literary clubs, to sewing circles and fraternal lodges. She talked about wildlife and wildflowers anyplace people would listen. But at the Blossom Festival, she would speak to the most important sort of people, the ones who actually supported the California Bird and Wildflower League, descendants of forty-niners who had pride in California and, more to the point, people who could still afford a hundred-dollar honorary membership.

At times she had to browbeat them into coming, or appeal to their vanity by displaying their paintings around the club. But they came—the old landowners, the men in public life, the writers who were in the valley for blossom time, the Athertons and the Norrises. They came and listened; they paid, and her work went on. And this time, they would have something special and different to listen to.

As Miss Russell was pulling down the heavy screen behind the podium, she heard the door to the vestibule open and a voice say, "Don't worry, it's not that bad."

She opened the door to the vestibule and found Albin wiping mud off his shoes, and a young Japanese girl watching him. "How is your throat? Did you keep your promise?"

Albin nodded. "My throat is fine. Miss Russell, can Fumiko stay? We're going to the glen together afterward to see Olivia dance."

Miss Russell hesitated. The girl's dress was so bright and

cheap, such a noticeable shade of peach. "Of course she can stay. But she can't be in the auditorium with us."

"But I want her to hear me sing."

"There's no room for her. And she might upset some of the people who have paid to come." Miss Russell saw in Albin's face that he didn't hear what she was saying.

"There is a motion picture projection booth that has an opening into the auditorium," she said to the Japanese girl. "If you can sit quietly there, you can stay during the talk. You can even open the square window when the lights are out. But you must sit quietly. Nobody must know you are there."

"I don't want to upset anybody," Fumiko said.

"Neither do I," Miss Russell said.

"I've been learning to sit quietly my whole life."

"Good. Then you'll be just fine there. Now Albin, do you want to help me finish getting ready?"

. . . .

Eugenia Roberts came into the Foothill Club late enough so that she would not be the very first but early enough to see and approve of the placement of her painting. The Mariposa lilies canvas stood on an easel at the entryway, just as she had intended. And she had chosen her dress, a wide-collared dress that came down to just below her knees, in a shade of blue that went well with the muted background she had brushed in behind the vase. She smoothed her dress and went to look for her son.

Albin was leaning against the wall underneath the projection booth. Eugenia looked at him critically; his shoes were more scuffed than they might have been, but he was more or less neat and presentable.

"Stand up straight, Albin. People will be looking at you."

Albin straightened up, still staying close to the wall.

"Do you want to come and greet people with me? Your name is on the program."

Albin shook his head violently and pointed at his throat.

"Oh, Miss Russell still doesn't want you to speak?"

He nodded.

"All right. You can meet people with me after the presentation. But try and stand like a soldier, so that you look well. Are you nervous?"

He nodded.

"Well, don't be. There will be lots of important people here, so you must do well. And don't slump."

She looked pointedly down at his shoes, and he quickly buffed the toes against the back of his pants legs. Then she went to stand near her painting.

Miss Russell was standing in the vestibule of the club, greeting her guests, when a large man with silver hair and small eyes came through the doorway. "Diana!" he boomed. "You're still here, trying to rescue the birds and flowers."

"Stephen, it's good of you to come. We see you so seldom."

The man smiled and took off his hat. "When one spends half the year in Washington, one doesn't have enough time for friends. But I wouldn't miss your talk on Blossom Day."

"And you're going to speak yourself, in the Festival Glen?"

"Yes, they've invited me to speak there. Something after the manner of James Duval Phelan."

"Well, come in, I've saved a seat for you." She led him to the front row, to a large chair covered with green leather.

Albin watched as the men with shiny hatbands milled around in one area, laughing heartily through their beards. The women stood in another area, dressed in blues and grays and pinks, their language a low buzz. Then Miss Russell closed the main door and pointed to him. Albin turned on the Magic Lantern and stood ready with the first box of transparencies.

Miss Russell went to the podium, adjusted her thin glasses, and cleared her throat. The crowd gradually took their chairs and fell silent. She cleared her throat once more, then began to recite:

Hast thou named all the birds without a gun;
Loved the wood-rose and left it on its stalk;
Unarmed faced danger with a heart of trust;
And loved so well a high behavior in man or maid,

That thou from speech refrained,
Nobility more nobly to repay?-
O be my friend and teach me to be thine.

"Welcome, friends all, to the California Bird and Wildflower League," she said. "And as Emerson said, I am here to call you to a high behavior: to safeguard California's natural beauties against the coarse passion that delights in destroying flowers and killing birds. Twenty years ago—even ten—one found acres upon acres of our state flower, the golden poppy, adorning the open fields of our state. And now one must actually seek them out, as one looks for rare things, in certain sequestered places. It would be a high behavior, and indeed simple wisdom, to protect our irreplaceable natural assets against foreign vandalism and native gluttony."

Miss Russell gave a signal to Albin. He turned off the lights from the back of the room, and while he did, he kicked the wall below the projection booth as a signal to Fumiko.

Only a small lamp attached to the podium remained lit. Albin flashed the first transparency on the screen, a field of bright-orange poppies. From behind him, he imagined he heard the square window open.

"Of course, many promising hillsides have most necessarily been cleared of wild lilac and other shrubby growths. But I am sure there must always remain enough of it to give its distinctive color and charm to our mountain regions."

Miss Russell talked about creamcups, and coneflowers, and the toyon, which urgently needed protection. Albin's hands were sweating, and he was half blinded by the projection lamp. He wished she would finish with the flowers.

"We have all loved the songs of birds on our walks through the hills of California," she finally said. "They remind us always that we must safeguard the natural world for ourselves and our children. So for my talk on birds, I've invited a good young friend to accompany me with his imitations of birdsongs."

Chairs scraped slightly on the wood floor as people turned their heads toward Albin. He couldn't look back to see if the square window was open. He slipped a transparency into the Magic Lantern, and suddenly a meadowlark appeared on the screen, with bright-yellow breast and barred wing feathers.

"A winter visitor to California, the western meadowlark comes from as far away as Saskatchewan," Miss Russell began.

Then Albin sang the long, flutelike notes of the bird and heard the expressions of surprise and pleasure. He sang the quail's rapid three-part call, and the staccato chatter of the ruddy turnstone. He sang with the images of juncos, and jays, and towhees, and he sang to Fumiko. The Magic Lantern flashed, went dark, then flashed again. More bird images, more bright-colored feathers, and more birdsong. Albin sang fluidly and perfectly, and he heard murmurs of approval after he finished each call. But he cared only for Fumiko. He wanted to touch the quick, flitting world of birds, the world that lived overhead and out of reach, and offer it to her.

"I might have chosen to finish with our state bird, the California quail," Miss Russell said. "But instead I'll finish with a particular favorite of my special young friend. The bird he first learned to call. The mourning dove."

The dove shone on the screen, a dusky body with a pointed tail, and eyes that were dark and glittering.

"Our most widespread wild dove, a lover of farmlands and towns as well as coastal scrub and grasslands."

Albin pressed his thumbs to his lips and blew into the hollow of his hands. The sad, searching note echoed in the open beams of the club, hovered for a moment, then faltered.

People began to applaud. Albin turned and saw that the square window was shut, and that it was safe to turn on the lights. When he did, he realized the applause was directed toward him. The old men in dark suits and the women in blue-silk dresses were looking his way, clapping and smiling. Then his mother was beside him, hugging him and petting his slicked-down hair.

"I didn't know your son had such a gift," one woman said.

"Albin is just shy," his mother said. "He doesn't want anyone to make a fuss over him."

Miss Russell came and shook his hand. "You did splendidly, Albin. Flawlessly. Eugenia, you should be proud of your son. He is very gifted."

"I am proud. I always told him to find the genius he'd been given. I found my calling with flowers, and he has found his with birds."

People were standing up and beginning to circulate. Albin looked back at the closed window and wished everyone would leave. But they all gathered in small circles to speak with each other, and Miss Russell grasped him by the elbow and steered him amongst some men and women who smiled at him.

Stephen Ironsides said, "So, this is the new star of your show. Where did you find him?"

"Where I discover all beautiful things," Miss Russell said. "In the hills."

Ironsides took a cigar out of his vest pocket and smelled it. "I bought this cigar at the Lindstrom Hotel," he announced. "It cost a nickel. And the clerk said to me, 'Why, Mr. Ironsides, your son always smokes these twenty-five-cent stogies.' And I said, 'Ah, my son has a rich father to pay his bills for him. I don't have that luxury.'"

He laughed heartily, and everyone in the circle joined him. Then he looked down again at Albin.

"Well, my boy, you put on a fine show."

"Albin, this is Mr. Stephen Ironsides, the congressman. Stephen, Albin Roberts of Ida Valley."

"Of course, I knew your grandfather. Did you know that this area was once known as Robertsville?" Ironsides put out a meaty hand with hair on it and squeezed Albin's firmly.

"Not much of a grip yet," he said. "Your grandfather had a grip like iron. If a horse misbehaved to Abraham Roberts, he'd walk to the front of the plow and smash the horse across the teeth. Why, he'd bring blood from the horse's mouth."

"Didn't he hurt his hand?" one of the women asked.

"Perhaps. But the horse knew who was master."

Albin saw his mother talking with four other women, and she beckoned him. "This is my young artist who knows the language of birds," she announced to the group.

"You must truly love birds," Mrs. Jackson said. "It's too bad your father couldn't be here."

"I think," Eugenia said, "that when I'm finished with my current series of *natures mortes*, I'll have Albin take me into the hills, and I'll begin painting birds."

"Mother? Is everyone going to the pageant soon?" Albin asked.

"Are you anxious to see your sister? My other artist," she explained to the group.

Albin glanced toward the square window. He nodded.

"You could go now and save us some good seats. Halfway down and toward the center?"

"I'll go right away."

"Darling. You can't wait to be in the open air with your birds. You belong in the sky." She kissed him on the cheek. "I'll see you at the Festival Glen."

Albin ran out of the club into the still air, warming now toward noon. He paused for a moment, to make sure that no one was coming out behind him. Then he walked quietly beside the flower beds and manicured shrubs that ringed the clubhouse and came to the back door.

He walked through the kitchen, gleaming with white enamel stoves and sinks, and white painted cupboards. Then down one little hall, paneled with dark wood. And one more door, unmarked, set into the wall.

Albin opened the door quietly and closed it behind him. He whispered loudly, "Fumiko?"

There was no answer.

He went up the narrow ladder that led to the projectionist's loft, expecting to see the bright peach of Fumiko's dress shine through the shadows. She wasn't there. He whispered her name again, and looked in all the corners, behind the garbage can, in the tall storage closet. He peeked out the square opening onto the main clubhouse floor, as though she would suddenly be out there among the audience that had heard him sing. But he saw only the same men and women, well dressed in suits and ties and dark-blue dresses.

Mr. Ironsides waved his arm around and laughed hoarsely.

Albin whispered again, "Fumiko?"

No answer.

. . . .

The young dancers in carnival colors swirled across the broad, grassy hillside. Some were dressed as flowers, and their heads emerged from floppy petals sewn around their collars. Others were flying things, birds and dragonflies, and they ran about with their arms outstretched so that shining cloth rippled in the air like wings.

A little girl in pale blue tugged on Olivia's tunic. "Olivia?" she asked. "You ever get scared?"

"Do you have a little stage fright, Vikki?" Olivia asked.

The little girl nodded. "Everybody's going to be here. My gramma and everyone."

"Just remember, they all love you. And they'll love you no matter what, right?"

Vikki nodded.

"So just dance and be happy, and you'll do fine. They'll tell you so afterward. And remember, you've got lots more festivals ahead of you. Okay?"

Miss Johnson, wearing a long dress and a hat with flowers around the brim, called to Olivia. "Can you get the girls together into organized groups? It's almost time."

"Of course, Miss Johnson." Olivia went near her teacher and clapped her hands. "Please, can we have all the lady slippers here? The trolls? Trolls here." The dancers all gathered before Miss Johnson, staying together but still stirring slightly, like a flock of painted birds ready at any moment to burst into flight.

Miss Johnson tapped her cane on a stone until all faces were turned toward her. "Now," she said, "there will be the invocation by Reverend Walters, then the Sousa marches, then the speech by Mr. Ironsides. Then, our music will begin. When Mr. London begins playing the piece by Romberg, the selection from *Blossom Time,* we will sweep over the hill and down into the Festival Glen until we reach the stage. Do you remember which groups go first with King Oberon?"

After a moment, the sweet williams and bluettes and drag-onflies raised their hands.

"Good. And then with Queen Titania? And the rest with Silverheels? Very good." She looked at her watch. "Please stay in your groups now, the music will begin soon. And I'm sure all of you will dance beautifully."

She bowed her head to them. The brightly colored groups of birds and flowers and sprites made an uneven *revérence* in return, bowing down row by row and then springing up.

Miss Johnson smiled at them all, then turned away with Olivia. "I'll depend on you to send things off when the music begins."

"Of course," Olivia said.

The music that preceded the invocation began to come from the glen. Miss Johnson walked slowly and stiffly over the low ridge, marking steps with her cane.

Olivia imagined that just on the other side of that ridge, the natural amphitheater was filling with thousands of spectators. Elegant men in dark suits and ladies in smart dresses were waiting to watch her race down toward the stage at the head of a rainbow of dancers. And she felt a little stage fright, because they didn't love her no matter what. A little scared, because this was her last festival.

She hoped that Fumiko would be there.

. . . .

Peter looked up in the sky. A pale-blue box kite floated high above the grassy schoolyard, along with a dozen other diamond-shaped kites.

He wandered over to where a line of children controlled the kites. Mr. Hogg, the drugstore owner, was talking with Finney the newspaperman.

"How many prizes you give out?" Finney asked.

"Just two," Hogg said. "Prettiest and best flying."

"Get the names of the winners for me, will you? Might sell a few papers if they're from in town."

"Hello, Mr. Finney, Mr. Hogg," Peter said.

"So, Paolo let you off for the day," Finney said. "You going to watch the ball game?"

"Petey," Hogg said. "Which kite you think is the best fly-ing?"

"The box kite. It's the prettiest, too."

Finney looked at Hogg. The drugstore owner shook his head.

"Oakland," he said.

Finney shrugged. "Too bad. Come on, Petey. Help me judge the races."

Across the field, a checkerboard of picnic blankets spread out on the grass. Parents and children sat among large wicker baskets, bread and cheeses spread out on cloth napkins, last year's apples, and dusky green bottles of homemade wine. A thick circle of men and women stood around a pit barbecue, and a dense cloud of smoke and steam rose up among them. Peter smelled vinegar and pepper along with the roasting lamb and rabbit and chicken.

Two fruit boxes had been set up as a starting line, and a group of young children were putting their feet into flour sacks. One mother instructed her boy, "You have to hold the sack up to your waist and hop. If you try to run, you'll trip."

The boy hopped a couple of times, then tried to move his feet separately and fell forward onto his face.

"See?" his mother said.

Finney put one foot up on a fruit box, took a tin whistle from his vest pocket, and blew it. "The first race is a sack race for eight-year-olds and under," he announced. Two other fruit boxes were set up at fifty yards down the field. "Hike down to the finish line, Petey. And get the name of the winner for me, will you?"

Peter watched the children hop up to the starting line. A crowd of adults stood just outside the fruit boxes, clapping and calling encouragement. Peter signaled that he was ready, and the newspaperman put the whistle to his lips and blew.

Immediately, half the children fell down. Parents laughed and shouted as their children floundered about. The children in the lead hopped forward before falling one by one and being overtaken by the others.

Peter watched one boy break ahead of the pack, hopping

deliberately with a look of cold concentration on his face. Then he too stumbled forward but made no move to get up. He lay still while others passed him by, until his mother rushed out to him.

"Get up," she shouted at him. "Get up and try."

They all struggled across the green field, chased on by shouts and hoots and howls of laughter and ridicule. When they fell, they awkwardly raised themselves and continued on for another ten yards before falling again.

At last, two furious boys approached the finish line. One of them attempted to walk by keeping his feet in the extreme corners of the bag and rocking from left to right. The other made quick, short jumps forward, being careful not to jump so far that he would trip. The group of parents and spectators had moved down the course with the racers and now screamed alongside these two.

They came close to the fruit boxes, angry and determined. The boy hopping saw that the other was slightly ahead. He gave two strong leaps forward, then lunged ahead and fell to earth with his head across the finish line.

"Winner! The winnah!" people shouted.

The boy shed his flour sack, sprang to his feet, and danced around with his hands in the air, dirt smudges on his face and elbows. Peter got his name before he was led off by his parents. The boy was from nearby Los Gatos, so Mr. Finney would be pleased.

Peter watched the three-legged races, the broad jump, the relay races, and a game of steal the bacon. Mrs. Finney offered him some barbecued rabbit, but he said he had to go meet some friends.

"Well, take some with you, then." She piled a few crispy pieces on top of a cloth napkin for him, and told him to bring her the napkin back any old time.

Peter ate the rabbit as he walked and threw away the bones. It was nearing two o'clock, and he decided to cut through some orchard land to the Festival Glen so that he wouldn't have to tell somebody else that he was thinking of going to the baseball game. He didn't really have a good reason for giving up a ball game to see Albin Roberts's sister dance. But since he had seen her through the lighted window, he hadn't been able to think of anything else.

Once he entered the orchards, the smell changed from the hot grease and smoke of the schoolyard to the musky scent of the white fruit blossoms that formed an unbroken roof overhead. It was a warm, still day, and the perfume of the flowers settled and hung in the air. This orchard was one of the oldest, one of those near the center of town that hadn't yet been sold off to builders. The trees here had been planted back in the 1890s on twenty-foot centers, and now their trunks were thick as a man's body, and their branches had to be pruned back where they met over the ground, and their crowns rose higher than a two-story house.

Peter moved quietly among the gnarled, flowering trunks and branches. The only sound he heard came from the bees flying from blossom to blossom. He angled away from that corner of the orchard where he knew the beehives were stacked up in white boxes.

Suddenly he heard a woman's laugh. On the other side of a thick tree, he found a man and a woman leaning together among the branches. Their arms and bodies touched each other, supported against the smooth bark of the fruit tree, and their feet and legs dipped down into the volunteer oat growing green around the roots of the tree, as though they too sprang from the same stock.

The woman noticed Peter first, and she giggled and buried her head on her lover's shoulder. The man looked at Peter calmly, as though he were seeing him from a great distance.

Peter held up his hands in apology and went silently on his way. He suddenly felt very alone. But as he approached the road that separated the orchard from the Festival Glen, he tried to imagine himself, somehow with Olivia, somehow with these people in the trees.

Along the road, shiny black cars glided up to the entrance of the glen. A boy on stilts dressed as Uncle Sam directed traffic. He waved the cars with a windmill blue sleeve into a rutted vacant lot, where other boys guided them into spaces.

Peter knew this lot. It was an orchard that his stepfather

had bought and cleared, and allowed the festival to use. Houses were going on it later this year.

He wandered into the glen and took a program from a girl in a frilly white dress. On the far side, a hillside still freshly green from the winter's rains sloped down to the stage. On the near side, dozens of rows of folding wooden chairs were rapidly filling up. Above the rows of chairs, planks were set into the natural incline of the glen to serve as benches.

The very first row of chairs was being occupied by a line of veterans, wearing their full dress uniforms with rows of medals above their left pockets. There were other men in uniform too, young soldiers from Moffett Field. Peter recognized Howard Jackson among the veterans. He had more medals than anyone else, the most decorated soldier from San Natoma. People said that he wasn't respectable these days, that he tended bar at a joint in San Jose. But to Peter's eye, in his crisp doughboy's uniform with his ribbons and medals, he still looked impressive.

Two white trellised pillars, hung with garlands of flowers, stood at the corners of the stage, and a long white arch stretched from one pillar to the other, spanning the entire platform. Gilt letters one foot high spread across the arch, proclaiming WELCOME TO THE BLOSSOM FESTIVAL. A podium stood near the left pillar, with a microphone suspended above it. In front of the stage, the Union High School Band stood before music stands and warmed up their instruments as the audience settled into place. The band members were dressed as Mexican caballeros, with wide sashes and shiny black trousers and fancy sombreros.

Peter stood near the top of the glen and listened to the band play "March of the Pioneers." Then Reverend Walters took the stage to give the invocation. He gripped both sides of the podium, and his voice quavered through the loudspeakers.

"The flowers appear on the earth; the time of the singing of birds has come; and the voice of the turtledoves is heard in our land . . ."

Peter looked at his program while the reverend spoke.

There were speeches, hymns, and more band music. The ballet was last.

"We thank Thee for leading us to this beneficent land," the minister's voice went thinly on. "This favored place, this valley of heart's delight. To subdue all things to Thy glory. And to use all things for the good of Thy children." Peter wandered out of the glen, the reverend's voice fading behind him. Back in the cleared lot, he noticed the ten-foot-tall Uncle Sam still stalking unquietly around the sleek black cars. A half circle of boys stood at his feet, waving their arms and chanting.

Yaaah-yaaadh-yaaah.

Curious, Peter came closer. Then he saw that in the middle of the circle, backed up against a Buick, Olivia's brother was standing.

"Hey!" Peter sailed in among the boys. He found Albin standing beside Fumiko, who was crouched beside a curved black fender, still wearing her bright peach dress.

"You hurt?" Peter asked.

Fumiko shook her head. She looked around her with frightened eyes.

The half circle of boys had closed in around them.

They were short, thick-faced boys, with red hair and freckles, and they all looked like they came from the same family. Peter didn't recognize them; out-of-towners, maybe from San Francisco.

Uncle Sam loomed above, constantly moving on his long striped legs.

"What's the problem?" Peter asked.

"She wants to go to the show," Uncle Sam said. He had a wad of cotton pasted to his chin for a false beard, and it waggled around as he spoke.

"So what?" Peter said.

"Japs steal our land," a boy said. "Don't you?"

Fumiko didn't answer, and the boy continued, "All the Japs steal our land and take our jobs."

"Come on," Peter said. "She's just a girl."

"She worships the emperor in Jap School," another boy said. "Plus, she invaded China."

"She's never even been to China," Peter said. "She was born here."

Uncle Sam hovered above them. "She's a Jap before she's anything else," he said. "And you're a traitor."

As he spoke, his false beard loosened and fell off his chin. The white wad of cotton spun down into the circle, and Peter snatched it out of the air.

"Hey, give me that!" Uncle Sam said.

Peter waved the beard in the face of all the boys. "Here," he said. "Take it."

One boy grabbed at it, but Peter pulled it back out of reach.

"No, you don't," he said. "If you want it, you have to catch it."

He tossed the wad of cotton into the air, then walked forward with Fumiko and Albin while the boys darted in to try to catch it before it hit the ground.

"Just keep walking," Peter said quietly. He looked back and saw the group of boys standing and watching them go, unsure what to do now that they were outside their grasp. Uncle Sam was staggering around, using both hands to try to reattach his beard while balancing on his ungainly cartoon legs.

Peter shepherded Albin and Fumiko toward the Festival Glen. "You still want to see the show?" he asked.

"That's all I wanted to do," Fumiko said. "All I wanted to do was see the show."

"Out-of-towners," Peter said.

"Everywhere," Fumiko said.

"We'll be safe here." Peter guided them onto a bench, and Fumiko sat between the two boys.

On the stage, the reverend had been replaced by a large man with gray hair, speaking in the round tones of a politician. "Who's that?" Peter asked.

"That's Stephen Ironsides," Albin said. "The congressman."

"Preparedness, then, is the watchword of the day." Ironsides spoke into the microphone, and his voice carried out over the glen. "I would prefer to speak just of nature and the land. Consider the scene before us. The works of man are tawdry compared with the works of nature. And it is a triumph to combine the beautiful with the useful, the aesthetic with the practical. We may well celebrate the arrival of the blossoms. They produce the fruit; there is purpose in their luxuriance; their mission is to feed man. There are fifteen million fruit trees in the Valley, truly enough to supply the markets of all the world.

"But we cannot speak of the land without speaking of being prepared to defend it. Even on this glorious day, forces are on the march throughout the world which threaten our native soil, both from without and from within. Armies are on the attack which devour all in their path, and when they have finished with the old, tired worlds of Europe and Asia, they will inevitably turn their lustful and greedy eyes on our golden state, on our land and our people.

"Within our very gates, too, we must be vigilant. We must protect our soil with a jealous hand against a silent invasion. I speak of the alien occupation, insidious and stealthy; low wages which make competition well-nigh useless, and an uncanny thrift which permits of such low wages. It is this which we must overcome and combat. The land is the foundation of all things, and we must keep it and hold it and cherish it if the great life of the Republic is to endure."

Fumiko put her head down to be less conspicuous, and Albin and Peter edged in on either side of her to protect her from notice. Albin looked down over the descending arcs of spectators. He couldn't see any other Japanese people in the entire glen.

"And we can overcome and combat these threats, both the internal and the external, if we are vigilant. And if we are prepared.

"I see in the audience before me the stouthearted young manhood of the nation. War is the most terrible of the inventions of man. And yet, when we are threatened, we must not shrink from battle. The youth of this nation, these boys who sit in this audience today, are ever ready to go at the call, eager to fight for the cause of right, of liberty, and of humanity."

As the congressman spoke, Howard Jackson stood up from the row of veterans and walked toward the stage. He walked straight and tall as a young soldier, medals shining on his chest. When he passed by the bandleader, he took a last swig on a hip flask and cast it to the ground. Then he mounted the stairs.

The audience ruffled their programs, searching for his name. Jax was well known. People still remembered his letters from France published in the newspaper during the war, and everyone had seen him march many times on Armistice Day. But they couldn't find him scheduled to speak on this day.

Ironsides fell silent as Jax crossed the stage to the podium. The ex-soldier looked the congressman in the eye and said, "I feel called on to add a few remarks to what you've said."

The microphone picked up Jax's words and broadcast them to the crowd. Ironsides stepped back from the podium. Howard Jackson was still enough of a public figure that the congressman didn't want to cut him off in front of thousands of voters.

"You all know me." Jax spoke too close to the microphone at first, and his voice was loud and distorted. He backed up a bit, gave a half smile to Ironsides, and spoke again. "You all know me, when I talk about war. And I say, whenever someone tells you that you're brave, you can be damn sure that they want you to do something stupid and dangerous. Something they'd rather not do themselves."

Jax paused to clear his throat. "I remember going over the top, many times. But I remember the first time best, because we were all so excited, and we ran laughing out of the trench, and none of us thought we could die. We were going forward with a rolling barrage to clear the path, the sergeant swearing at us to dress right. And suddenly Jimbo, who shared cigarettes with me and slept by my side at night, staggered out of line and went down. Preston, to the left of me, went down too. They were brave boys. But they're lying asleep somewhere in the fields of France, and they'll never wake up again."

Jax looked at Ironsides, daring him to make a move. "I'd like to say that we who were left alive made good on those deaths. But who can say to Jimbo or Preston or a million others that it was worth it? Who can justify it now?"

Jax paused again. In the audience, his wife stood up and talked to his brother, Albert. Then his brother began to walk down the center aisle toward the stage.

Jax began to speak hurriedly, as though he were saying things he had long thought through and knew that time was running out. "It's been twenty-one years since Armistice Day. Long enough for a baby to grow up and be a man. So let me tell all you out there, all you kids too young to remember the Great War. It won't be the bankers and politicians who end up in the trenches. It will be you and your buddies. It won't be a politician like Ironsides here. It'll be you."

Ironsides came back to the podium and tried to shoulder Jax aside. "That's too much. That's a personal insult," he said, his voice floating out into the glen.

Jax held on to the podium and wouldn't let Ironsides back to the microphone. They rocked back and forth on the stage, then Albert Jackson climbed the stairs and grabbed his brother from behind.

"Come on, Howie. You've had your say."

He pulled Jax back from the podium, and Ironsides straightened his coat and tie and prepared to say something to smooth over the incident. But Jax broke loose from his brother and his wife and bulled into the congressman, knocking him to the ground.

The line of veterans in the crowd stood up. So did many of the young soldiers behind them. On the other side of the glen, the Democratic Circle rose to their feet, along with the Knights of Columbus and the Modern Woodsmen.

Albert grabbed Jax again, and when Ironsides scrambled to his feet and saw Jax stationary in front of him, he threw a right fist into his stomach.

Jax doubled over, and the crowd roared. Everyone was standing up to see. Then one veteran began walking straight toward the stage, cutting through the band. Two other men in uniform followed him, then five more.

The first veteran scaled the stage. A group of Oddfellows

came down from another part of the glen, shouting for calm. The Masons and the Foresters of America began shouting for calm too, while the Knights of Columbus moved toward the podium in a mass. Some boys in their teens also ran down the aisles so that they wouldn't be left out.

Jax grabbed Ironsides and pushed him back into the podium, which crashed down on the stage like a fallen monument.

The bandleader saw some of his musicians looking toward the stage as though ready to throw down their instruments and join in. He rapped his baton on the music stand. "Stay in your places," he shouted. "Stay in your places."

Congressman Ironsides scrambled to his feet and saw people rising up and coming toward him. He quickly ducked off the back of the stage and circled around toward the benches. Masons and Modern Woodsmen and Oddfellows crowded onto the stage and surrounded the fallen podium, shouting at each other to be quiet. Jax felt himself being pushed left and right, so he began to push back. The stage was filling up, with people clambering on from the two stairways as well as over the apron. Somebody pushed Jax again, and he shot out a big open palm. He couldn't tell if he'd hit the same person who had shoved him or not.

The groups on the left side of the stage massed against the groups on the right side. The men in the center snarled at each other, forced together by all the men at their back. Jax and his brother were crushed against each other, and Jax grinned at Albert.

"Some shit I started, eh?" he said.

Suddenly, one man in the middle threw a clenched fist, and another man went down. The audience still arrayed around the glen cried out like one large wounded beast. More punches were thrown around the podium on its side, and the men whipped back and forth across the stage, now the left side gaining the upper hand, now the right, while more men and boys from the audience joined in.

Reverend Walters went to the bandleader and clutched him by the arm. "Play something," he implored. "Maybe they'll stop. 'Music soothes the savage breast.'"

The bandleader shouted, "Ready now, and play as loud as

you can." He brought his baton up, and then down sharply, the band began to play, loud and ragged, the music that was on their stands, the selection from *Blossom Time*.

. . . .

On the other side of the ridge, Olivia heard the music and began to count measures in her head. *One — two — three — four. Two — two — three — four.* She had heard the shouts and roars as well, but once the music began, she heard just what her training had taught her to hear.

Three — two — three — four. Four — two — three — four. She remembered saying to Miss Johnson that sometimes she just didn't feel like dancing, and her teacher telling her that was the reason one learned technique—to carry the dancer through the times when she didn't feel like dancing.

Olivia looked around at the flock of young girls behind her, dressed as toadstools and birds and trolls and flowers, to make sure they were aware of the count and were ready to go. She exchanged glances with Titania and Silverheels, who would lead their own groups down a few measures after her own.

Six — two — three — four. Seven — two — three — four. Olivia raised her hand as the music played on, loud and raucous.

Eight — two — three — four. Nine . . .

She cast down her hand. "Now!" she cried.

And she sprang toward the ridge, followed by the throng of brightly costumed girls.

In the audience, Fumiko stood up when she saw the first troupe of dancers fly over the hills and begin down into the glen, led by the tall girl in the white and rust-colored tunic. The group approached the stage in neatly ordered rows, each row a brilliant shade of blue or yellow or red. Then the rows hesitated, broke apart in confusion when they found the stage filled with milling, fighting men.

"There's Olivia," Fumiko said. "There's Olivia."

The music continued, and another group of dancers came over the hill in neat rows of color, led by another figure in white. Four measures later, a third group raced down into the glen. The last two groups ran into Olivia's group and collapsed into a motley, disorganized crowd before the mass of men on stage.

The entire audience screeched and howled on its feet. Many of the musicians in the band had stopped looking at the bandleader and were watching the fight. Then one tuba player laid down his instrument and ran toward the stage and climbed up. Three trumpeters and a clarinetist followed him.

Fumiko grabbed at Peter's sleeve. "Come on," she said. "We have to help Olivia."

All three of them ran down into the glen and tried to circle toward the back of the stage. More band members were abandoning their seats, leaving the bandleader moving his baton emptily in the air.

When Olivia led her troupe of dancers running over the ridge, she saw that the stage was filled with men. But she heard the music continue, she kept the count, and she raced down the hill. It seemed that at this moment, being the first over the top, being at the head of a band of bright flowers and sprites, seeing the audience of five thousand waiting for her and the Festival Glen ringed by flowering trees, nothing really could stand in her way. She roared down the hill, driven forward by the girls behind her and carrying them along with her. At this moment, in her last Blossom Festival, the stage would magically clear, and she would be able to dance.

Twelve — two — three — four. Thirteen — two — three — four. At the end of fourteen, she should first leap upon the stage and make a series of small steps describing an arc to downstage right. There, with her troupe arrayed behind her, she would await the arrival of Titania and Silverheels.

But at fourteen, a wall of men closed the stage off to her. Olivia stopped short while the music played on loudly and unevenly while all the little sweet williams and dragonflies piled up behind her. She looked around for Miss Johnson. If her teacher was trying to come, she would have trouble getting through the crowd around the stage. Olivia looked back up the hill and saw the other two bands of dancers sweeping down to join her.

The men blocking her way pushed and shoved at each other, or just stood with wide, excited eyes, and their lips drawn back so that their teeth showed.

Little Vikki tugged at Olivia's costume. "Does this mean we don't get to dance?" she asked.

"I don't know, Vikki," Olivia said.

"But everyone wants to see me dance. My gramma helped me sew my petals."

"I don't know," Olivia shouted. The little girl quailed and fell back to her group.

One of the men on stage, a burly young man in a red-and-black sweater, suddenly leered at Olivia.

She drew the short, blunt golden sword from her sash and held it in both hands like a club. The young man laughed, and licked his chapped lips, and blended back into the crowd.

Titania's group barged into Olivia's group and stopped in confusion. The girl dancing Titania came over and said, "What should we do, Olivia?"

The third group fell down the hill and joined with the other dancers. The music was petering out, barely recognizable as *Blossom Time.*

"What should we *do*?"

Olivia waved her sword in the direction of the crowd of men on stage.

"Abra-ca-dabra," she said. "Abra-ca-dabra."

31

. . . .

The World's Fair   April 2, 1939

One trumpet shrilled a last harsh note. Then the band fell
mute, and the air was filled only with the hot cries of angry
men and the roar of the audience, while the flowers and
birds and insects of the Enchanted Forest followed the
King of the Fairies trudging back up over the hill.

Olivia pulled on a pair of riding pants in the dressing shed.
She found Fumiko, Peter, and Albin waiting for her outside, and they walked aimlessly through the end of the festival crowds. Everyone wandered with a vague, dissatisfied
air, as though they had come looking for something they
hadn't quite found, as though they might still discover it if
they just lingered a bit before they had to climb into cars
and buses and trains and return to their normal lives.

The four of them came to the edge of the lane that led
back to Ida Valley. Olivia looked at the rows of trees in deli-

cate blossom, the yellow heads of mustard spreading out below the branches.

"I hate this," she said. "Let's go somewhere."

"Where can we go?" Fumiko asked.

"I've got a full tank of gas in the Jordan," Peter said. "We can go anywhere."

"Let's go to San Francisco," Olivia said. "That's where I'm going to study dance, someday."

"I should go home," Fumiko said.

"Come on," Olivia said. "Do you want to go out and be something, or do you want to be stuck in San Natoma your whole life?"

Peter led them to where his car was parked. On the way, Albin looked back at the Festival Glen.

. . . .

The Jordan sailed north on old Bayshore Boulevard, through the towns of Sunnyvale, Palo Alto, Redwood City, along the pewter tidal flats marked by restless herons, past gas stations and Dairy Queens and shuttered fruit-and-vegetable stands. All along the way, they saw billboard signs for the San Francisco World's Fair at Treasure Island. The signs promised a Pageant of the Pacific, the Glories of Civilization, the Wonders of the World.

Peter drove with one hand on the wheel, singing a song under his breath. He wanted to be gallant for Olivia, to save her from something, to fight for her and please her. But she sat in the back seat and refused to talk. Fumiko sat beside her, still wearing her peach dress, quiet and sober-faced. Albin sat next to Peter, sometimes watching where they were going, sometimes looking out at the bay.

Peter took the Jordan into San Francisco past Potrero Hill, then mounted onto the skyway. North of the skyway, the downtown buildings were blocks of tan and gray and off-white, with tall glass windows. The hills climbed up from downtown, crowded with houses and flats. On top of the hill nearest the bay, a slender fluted tower rose into the sky.

Fumiko touched Olivia and pointed. "What's that?" she asked.

Albin followed Fumiko's gaze. "Coit Tower. On Telegraph Hill."

"I've never been to San Francisco before," Fumiko said.

The Bay Bridge, completed only three years earlier, stretched out over the water before them. Peter stopped at the toll plaza and paid two bits to a white-jacketed toll taker. Then they drove out onto the broad concrete roadway suspended in the air by silvery cables and left the older city behind them.

Peter drove through a wide tunnel bored through Yerba Buena Island, turned off the bridge at the next exit, looped back over the bridge on a thin roadway, and joined a line of cars heading down the causeway.

"There," he said at the peak of the causeway, with a touch of pride in his voice, as though he and his Jordan had somehow brought into being what lay before them. "Treasure Island. The World's Fair."

At the end of the causeway, a four-hundred-acre artificial island rose from the waters, wrought with a city of glittering towers, and broad-pillared avenues, and flowered fountains and lakes. The flags of nations snapped over the separate pavilions scattered along the curving pathways to the east. It appeared in that moment like a better version of the world, a landscape formed by an artist for human delight, unlike Lone Hills they had lost or Festival Glens that ended in deception. From a distance, the island promised that the blank between desire and fulfillment would be bridged, that wholeness would be found, that memory and regret would vanish.

They drove down the curving boulevard lined with palm trees, past the western walls of the exposition buildings, and parked on the northwest corner of the island. The four of them stood for a moment and looked over the bay at the new Golden Gate Bridge soaring between the steep headlands of Marin and San Francisco. Alcatraz, crowded with thick, square penitentiary buildings, squatted down in the choppy salt water. Above it, the span arched gracefully between twin towers of an earthy orange hue. The towers tapered off as they grew higher, until they seemed to meet

the sky in a single thin edge. Beneath the bridge, the beck-
oning rim of the Pacific led out toward Hawaii and China and
Japan. Already some fingers of fog were ghosting through
the Gate, twisting around the base of the north tower.

Then a small open car appeared around the corner, topped
by a paisley howdah and sprouting an elephant's trunk
from its hood. The car pulled a string of tallyho wagons with
striped canopies and open seats.

"Elephant train!" the driver called through a small loud-
speaker attached to the howdah. "Elephant train to the Por-
tals of the Pacific!"

At the main entrance, barkers shouted about guided tours
and maps for sale, and a souvenir seller with a straw hat
and a tray hanging from his neck planted himself in front
of Olivia. "Badges. Banners. For a day you'll never forget."
To the right, Chinese men in red-satin tunics and round
black caps stood waiting for fares beside rickshaws. "A
rickshaw tour of the fairgrounds!" one driver shouted.
"Takes you right to the Mysterious East!" He looked at Fumiko and joked, "Not for you, sister." A man wearing a sandwich board advertising Sally Rand's Nude Ranch was laughing at Peter and Albin. "You two aren't eighteen. Too bad,"
he laughed. "Too bad."

"What's the Nude Ranch?" Albin asked.

"Where your dreams come to life," the man said.

"Not my dreams," Albin said.

"Haw haw," the man laughed at him. "Haw haw."

"Let's just go in," Olivia said.

They walked through the entrance and found themselves
at the foot of the Tower of the Sun, a slender beige tower
with tall open arches, surrounded by the fluttering flags of
all the nations with exhibits at the fair.

Suddenly, a marching band sounded a great fanfare, and a
man in a green suit rushed up and gave them all green ribbons to pin on. "Come join the parade!" he shouted.

Peter asked, "What are these?"

"Free! Everything's free! Just join in!" the man shouted
over his shoulder.

Olivia looked at the ribbon. On it was a large yellow drawing of an artichoke and the words ARTICHOKE DAY AT THE FAIR.

The marching band played a bright martial tune, marked by shrill trumpets and the steady rap of drums. The band filed past the Tower of the Sun in red-and-blue uniforms with shiny rows of brass buttons, following a drum major-ette who wore a tall white-plumed shako hat and carried a silvery baton. Olivia and the others fell in behind them, along with the rest of the crowd, and they marched up a long concourse. The man in the green suit appeared again, this time handing out mimeographed sheets of paper to ev-eryone following.

"Just join in," he shouted. "When the band starts, just join in!"

He disappeared into the crowd, scattering more sheets of paper. Then the horns stopped, and they marched to the simple beat of drums. A few moments later, the band be-gan to chant in a loud, certain voice.

What's the best with mayonnaise?
Artichoke! Artichoke!
What tastes good both nights and days?
Artichoke! Artichoke!

Some of the people walking along began to chant good-naturedly with the band, reading lines in praise of the arti-choke from the mimeo.

Olivia turned away from the parade. "This is stupid," she said. "There has to be something more beautiful than this."

Doesn't cost much when you're broke
Artichoke! Artichoke!
Favorite with all kinds of folk
Artichoke! Artichoke!

She walked back down the concourse, and she felt the others drag along behind her.

"Come on," she said to them impatiently. She felt she was being awful, but the others couldn't understand what she was going through. She was afraid that coming to the fair was a mistake, that she wouldn't find anything here.

They wandered under a massive arch into a flower-filled courtyard, where a slender statue of a woman stood on a pillar. To Albin's eyes, everything they saw was artificial and false. The flowers they saw everywhere hadn't grown here, he knew. They must have been forced in a greenhouse and brought out to this man-made island. The trees had been transplanted. There were no birds but seagulls and pigeons, scavenger birds. And the walls that looked like stone were painted plaster.

Olivia stepped back to look up at the statue of the woman, who was dressed in a long classical garment, similar to the chiton she still wore. Albin touched the elegant pillar with the tips of his fingers. Then he tapped on it. The pillar sounded hollow.

"How were your imitation birdcalls?" Olivia asked suddenly. "You never said."

"They were all right," Albin said.

"Did people applaud afterward?" she asked.

"Yes."

"And did they say you were wonderful?" When Albin didn't answer, Olivia added, "At least you got to do them."

"We're sorry you didn't get to dance," Peter said.

"I don't care," Olivia said. "In front of all those stupid people who would rather fight. Who cares?"

"We care," Peter said.

"No, you don't."

"Can't we at least be kind with one another?" Fumiko asked.

"Even if everything else is awful?" Olivia asked. "Come on."

They wandered to the Lake of Nations, where the countries that touched on the Pacific Ocean had constructed buildings. From the bridge that crossed the lake, they could look over the water and see the pavilions of the Philippines, French Indochina, Australia, and Hawaii, just as though they were standing in the center of the Pacific. The Japanese exhibition had a three-story pagoda and a stone garden with a rich red bridge that extended out into the lake.

"Fumiko," Olivia said, "do you want to visit Japan?"

A small Hawaiian war canoe, with six half-naked paddlers, shot under the bridge to the sound of chanting.

"I think I like America better," Fumiko said. She felt Olivia testing her, and she remembered what her mother had told her. *One day, you will marry, and she will marry. And her husband will not like your husband. And then you will not be friends anymore.*

"Come on, let's go see where your parents came from." Olivia knew she was being awful again, but she couldn't help herself.

"All right," Fumiko said. "We'll go together."

They walked into the the Japanese Pavilion and heard the plucked notes of a samisen, each note reverberating simply and singly, surrounded by silence. Fumiko had seen places like this in Nihonmachi, with landscapes of distant mountains and waterfalls painted on heavy paper screens, and flowers in a vase, set alone in the tokonoma, and an exquisitely small central courtyard, open and sunlit, holding a few tiny evergreens and a stone lantern. But the women she saw in the pavilion wore traditional kimonos, with the bright-colored obi wrapped tightly under their breasts, restricting their movements. These were not like the women she had grown up around, not like her own mother when she had worked beside her father in the fields, not like the woman she wanted to be. The men wore Western-style suits and ties, and they walked about with ease, greeting visitors and answering questions.

A man in his twenties came up to Fumiko and bowed politely to her, ignoring the others. Fumiko saw very clearly the precise line where his glossy black hair was parted before she returned an adequate *ojigi* to his. He straightened up and smiled, and fixed her with a glittering look.

"Greetings," he said in Japanese. "You are *nisei*?"

She knew that he could tell, from her bright peach dress, from some flaw in the way she had bowed.

"Where were your parents born?" he asked.

"Yamaguchi-ken."

"And are they here today?"

"No. Today I just came with my friends."

"Ah. Do the *gaijin* treat you well?" He used the contemptuous word that meant "foreigner," or "outsider."

His black eyes made her think about the parking lot, the red-haired boys. "Why do you ask?"

The man smiled. "The emperor is concerned about the treatment of our people in California."

Olivia broke in, "What's he saying, Fumiko?"

"That he welcomes us. And he is pleased I can speak Japanese."

The man smiled again at Fumiko's answer, and he spoke in flawless English to the group. "Come, and I will show you our pavilion."

He took the four of them into a darkish room where some women behind a low barrier were spreading green leaves out carefully on broad sheets of paper. The women paused in their work and bowed to the young man, who returned their bow. "Silkworms," he explained in English. "The young will eat fresh green leaves five times a day until they are ready to spin their cocoons. Later in the year, these women will give an exhibition of silk weaving."

They went to a display of Japanese art, and he pointed out the simple black lines against a white background of the Muromachi period, and the plum blossoms against a burnished-gold background of the Momoyama screens. He was most proud of the heroic paintings of Mount Fuji by Yokoyama Taikan, the glorious painter of modern Japan.

Fumiko had heard about these artists, these times, in Japanese school. But she had learned about them abstractly as something distant or mythical. They had always seemed very separate from her real daily life in her father's pear orchards in San Natoma. Now, this man from across the ocean seemed to be offering her a version of home, with everything he showed her, where being Japanese would give her a place in the world. This is your true heritage, he was saying. This is where you belong. Even if you don't know it yet, this is in your Japanese blood.

After the art display, the man said to Fumiko, "Maybe next time, you will come with your parents."

He glanced at Peter and Albin, who were studying a suit of Japanese armor. Olivia stood near Fumiko.

"I'm sure they will enjoy hearing how much you've learned," he said.

Fumiko bowed politely. The man returned the bow and smiled.

"I'd like to tell you a traditional tale about an artist and his daughter. A tale from your home, about obedience. But I have to tell it in Japanese. All right?"

"Of course," Fumiko said.

"In times past," he began, "there was a famous artist who lived for his art. He cared about nothing else, except for his very beautiful daughter. Now, a great Japanese lord commissioned him to paint a 'hell screen,' which should depict the horrors of the damned and so inspire all who saw it into obedience.

"This lord took the artist and his daughter into his house, and as soon as he saw the artist's daughter, he fell in love with her. But she told him she could never love him. And so the lord was angry with both the daughter and the artist.

"The work on the screen, however, continued. You might wonder what he chose for the torments of the damned. Well, he showed the damned doing little very differently than what they did in their lives. It was like the world. But the horror was that they would do it endlessly and without love.

"However, the artist had trouble deciding what image should go in the very center of the screen to give the highest sense of horror. And he weighed this in his mind for many months.

"Finally, he decided that a woman trapped in a carriage, forever trying to flee a wildfire that would overtake her should go in the center. And he demanded that the lord burn a carriage for him to paint. To the artist's surprise, the lord ordered that the most ornate and precious carriage he owned would be burned for the artist; the lord himself would witness the burning.

"When the artist was prepared in the central courtyard with his brushes and paint, and the unfinished screen before him, the carriage was brought out and set ablaze. Only after it was on fire did two servants roll up the curtains from the outside and reveal the artist's own daughter within the carriage, struggling to get out.

"The artist stopped in horror. Then, a kind of glow came over him. And he began to paint. He would paint for this lord for the rest of his life."

Fumiko stared at the man, trying to grasp the story. Without love, her place was at the center of hell. But how could she love only being Japanese?

Olivia watched her friend's face and suddenly felt she had pushed her too far in making her come with them from San Natoma, in making her come here. She put her hand on her shoulder.

"What did he say, Fumiko?"

"He said . . ." Fumiko began. Then she stopped and took a deep breath. She reached up and covered Olivia's hand with her own and looked at the man as she spoke. "He said he hopes you and I will be friends always."

Outside, twilight was beginning to fall over the fair. The Tower of the Sun was already softly glowing with hidden mercury vapor lamps. They went back across the bridge over the Lake of Nations and stopped in the middle.

"Always," Olivia said quietly to Fumiko. "Friends always."

Suddenly Peter pointed to the sky and shouted.

"A Clipper! Look there, a Clipper!"

In the fading light, a large four-engine plane with a hard chine hull for a body was descending for a touchdown in the waters of the bay. The girls watched it, holding hands.

"A real Clipper," Peter said. "I've only seen them in news-reels."

"That's not fake," Albin said.

It was one of Pan Am's China Clippers, one of the mighty aircraft that skipped like a stone across the entire Pacific Ocean, touching down at Guam, and Midway, and Wake Island, originating in Hong Kong, where, the newspapers reported, war was near.

· · · · · · ·

In the brash white lights of the Gayway, Peter watched the two girls walk hand in hand.

They walked slightly ahead of him and Albin, past the double Ferris wheels spinning couples high into the air, past the cotton candy stand, Madame Titti's Nudist Colony, and the Tilt-a-whirl, down the central asphalt thoroughfare surrounded by the smells of french fries and corn on the cob, the glare of the attraction signs, the shouts of barkers crying, "This Way! Last Chance! See It Now Or Never!"

They walked and held hands, and it seemed to Peter that they were in their own private circle, a magical circle they had created about themselves, and he felt as separate from them as when he had watched them on a chill night from outside the window.

It was late, and the rest of the fair was closed, but the Gayway was still filled with flash and noise. There was no place to stop and rest among the booths. They drifted from light to light, pausing here and there, the two girls together and Peter and Albin trailing along behind. Peter was jealous of them, as though they had found something he hadn't. While they wandered, he felt strangely that he didn't have a real home to return to. There was only this wandering now, through this place that was no place at all. He felt grown-up and rootless.

Peter made everyone watch while he shot a rifle at a shooting gallery, knocking over small metal buffalo and Indian braves that whirred along drawn by a chain. But he felt the others grow impatient and bored behind him, and he put down the rifle without winning anything.

Outside the Odditorium, they saw a woman with no arms play the piano with her feet. The barker shouted a promise that they would see even greater freaks inside. Then they came to a low platform with a sign reading ROCKO WILL GUESS YOUR WEIGHT running over the top. A little man, only three feet high, caught their eye and began to sing out in a high, scratchy voice, "Have fun with your weight. Men by palpation, women by observation. Win a prize if I'm not within three pounds. Only twenty-five cents."

Peter looked at the rows of fuzzy blue bears lined up on shelves. "Do you want your weight guessed?" he asked Olivia.

"Have fun with your weight," the little man sang.

"You shouldn't ask a girl that," Olivia said.

The man wore a bowler hat and carried a crook-handled bamboo cane, and his face was yellowed and wizened with dozens of fine shallow lines. He looked at them wisely.

"How about you, sir? Maybe the lady would like to see *your* weight guessed."

"Okay," Peter said. It was worth twenty-five cents just to have Olivia's attention on him.

He stepped onto the platform and sat in a large square chair next to a meatpacker's scale. "Have fun with your weight," Rocko cried to the passing crowd. "In ancient India, a rajah would be weighed once a year, and his subjects would balance the scale with glittering diamonds, and precious rubies, and gold."

He turned to Peter, and poked at his leg under his pants, and grasped his ankles with hands that felt like claws. "Gimme your arm," he said. Peter laid out his right arm, and the little man felt it with bony fingers, stroked the wrist, then looked cunningly at the flesh around the chin, the fullness of the cheeks.

Fumiko, standing beside Olivia in the audience, glanced across the Gayway.

"Look, Olivia," she said. "It says there is a talent show tonight."

Olivia turned away. "Stand up!" Rocko said.

Peter stood up distractedly, trying to see what Olivia was looking at.

"I guess the weight of this fine young man, this sterling example of virile youth, to be One Seventy-five—no, One Sixty-eight. Please take your seat under the scale."

He sat down on a steel seat slung from a meathook under the scale's large dial. Olivia was watching him again, but her face looked blank. The others in the crowd who paused to watch also looked at him without expression, a line of anonymous blank faces, waxen in the white lights, witnessing him being weighed like ground beef.

The needle swung around then came to rest. Rocko smiled knowingly.

"One Sixty-five. So no prize for the young gentleman, we're sorry. Who will be next? Everyone! Win a prize if I'm not within three pounds!"

Peter tried to grin as he stepped off the platform. "I'm no rajah," he said.

Olivia was already drifting toward the brightly lit stage strung with banners across the way. "Let's see when the show starts," she said.

Albin watched them walk over to a woman dressed like a pirate who stood near the sign announcing the talent show.

He wanted nothing more than to go home. The others kept moving, as though there were still something to discover on the island.

"Hey, you."

A hiss slipped toward Albin from near the stage.

"Yeah, you. I'm talking to you."

He turned to where the voice came from, a ticket booth in the shadows of the Gayway.

"Come over here."

Albin walked a few paces over to the booth. A ticket seller with a lumpy face covered with red blotches peered out at him from behind thin green bars.

"Are you eighteen years old?"

The ticket seller began to work from side to side in his seat, and Albin heard a metallic squeaking and the whir of a bicycle chain. Then the seller stopped and coughed.

"You don't quite look eighteen."

"Well . . ." Albin began.

"But I'll believe you. If you say you're eighteen, that's good enough for me. You've got an honest face. Tickets are a dime."

He began to writhe in his seat again, seemingly pumping bicycle pedals that moved some squeaky machinery in the small building behind him.

"Only a dime, come on, business is lousy. You think Sally Rand or Madame Titti is going to believe you're eighteen?"

"What is it?" Albin asked.

"It's My Little Chickadee."

"What's My Little Chickadee?"

"Something your mama don't want you to see."

Albin glanced over at the stage. Olivia was talking with the pirate woman, who pointed toward an upright piano.

"Something you've wanted," the seller said. "Really wanted for a long time."

"Will it take long?"

"Naw. Not for you."

He pumped the bicycle pedals a few more times and the machinery squeaked. Albin suddenly fished two nickels out of his pocket and pushed them into the brass bowl under the bars.

"Enjoy yourself," the seller said. "Life is short."

Albin walked up into a narrow corridor hung with heavy plush curtains. A record player hidden somewhere was playing the end of a song, and he heard the music fade, then the tone arm lift and move back to the beginning and drop again on the same record. He turned a corner and walked into a larger open space, like a small theater lit with smoky red lights.

Against the back wall, there was a large painting of a woman wearing only a black brassiere. The woman was a giantess, twelve feet long, lying down with her knees open and her head thrown back, and her eyes were closed, shuttered by thick black eyelashes. One stub-fingered hand rested red fingernails on her thigh.

One other man was in the room, wearing a long dark coat. "Damn," he said, "you'd have to strap a two-by-four to your butt to keep from falling in."

A darkly shaded woman's voice started from the scratchy record: "All of me. Why not take all of me?"

Albin heard the whir of the bicycle chain and the squeak of machinery, and the painting started to move. The legs churned slowly. The lips parted to show a crimson tongue, then shut, parted and shut, as though she were mouthing the words to the song.

"Take my lips, I want to lose them. Take my arms, I'll never use them."

"That's so fake," Albin said. But he stood and stared.

The man in the long coat chuckled. The machinery continued to scrape.

As the mechanical legs pumped, open and shut, Albin wondered what his mother was like. He couldn't help seeing her now, painted on top of the monstrous painting, a representation on top of a representation, nothing real underneath.

"Oh, baby, take all of me."

The man in the dark coat turned sideways to look at Albin. Then Peter was in the theater with him, taking him by the arm. Peter stopped to gaze at the mechanical painting, then walked Albin out with him into the glary lights of the Gayway. Albin blinked and lowered his head.

Fumiko ran up to them. "Did Peter tell you?" she asked. "Olivia is going to dance!"

She pulled them into the crowd that was forming in front of the stage. "Olivia asked if the piano player knew her music, and he said that he knew everything and anything, and played it right there. It's so wonderful."

The Master of Ceremonies mounted the stage, wearing a shiny tuxedo. "Albin?" Fumiko said.

"Yes?" Albin had his eyes to the ground and was turned half away from her.

"I asked him if you could do your birdcalls. I told him that you had done them for the California Bird and Wildflower League, and he was very impressed. He said he'd be glad to have you do them."

"My imitation birdcalls," he said with regret.

Fumiko asked shyly, "Do you want to?"

"I don't think so." His voice was husky.

The Master of Ceremonies announced the first act. They watched a boy who could walk on his hands and do cartwheels. A very young girl was pushed out on stage by her mother and sang "The Good Ship Lollipop." She curtsied very prettily afterward. Then a magician pulled a stuffed rabbit out of a top hat.

Between each act, the master invited the public to throw tips into a basket he had placed in front of the stage. To support the arts, he said, and to encourage young performers.

Finally, there was a flourish of music from the piano, and the master stepped center stage.

"For our grand finale tonight, we present the talented young *danseuse* from the garden spot of the South Bay, the Siren of San Natoma, Olivia Roberts."

Olivia stepped out on the stage. She had shed her pants and was again dressed just in her chiton and rust-colored sash. The pianist began playing *Blossom Time*.

She danced the part of Silverheels, the dance of the fairy princess who was to be married, the solo she knew she could do better than anyone. She had memorized the steps during rehearsals, practiced it by herself at home, and now it came to her easily, naturally, hers by right. She didn't notice the small stage, the tinny music of the single piano, the audience made up of vague women holding children by the hand, curious girls clutching kewpie dolls, tired gray men heading for the ferry home. She danced as though moving through a landscape of rounded hills covered with thick green forage, herds of shaggy goats trailing out from fenced pastures and well-tilled fields, shepherds blowing pipes.

In the audience, Peter watched Olivia under the concentrated white light focused on the stage. She leaped gracefully, landed and went down to her knees and drew her hands to her heart. Her head and shoulders dropped, she was mourning something. Then effortlessly, she was back on her feet, joyfully spreading her arms out toward something gained.

A woman with a coat draped over her shoulders moved against Peter in the audience. He started when he recognized her as the woman without arms, the woman who could play piano with her feet. Close by her was the man in the green suit, the artichoke man, and Rocko the midget with the scale, and the dark-coated man from the giantess. Further off, the representative from Japan hovered, moving around the fringes of the audience, never still.

They were all around him, and Albin, and Fumiko. They pressed in, just as the dark waters of the bay pressed in on the island city, just as the more obscure waters of the ocean pressed against the shore.

Albin still looked blindly downward with his hands in his pockets. But Fumiko's brilliant eyes watched her friend.

Peter followed her gaze, shared this moment of Olivia dancing in shadowless splendor.

She spun on the stage and came down to one knee, and she flung her arms out behind her.

Epilogue To 1942

The spring of 1940 arrived, bright and insensible of human
sorrow. The orchards came into blossom again, the cherry,
the apricot, the plum, and the pear, fecund and heedless,
meaning nothing to themselves but everything to the people
who gathered once again in the Festival Glen. Miss Hampstead Johnson, crippled and caned, dressed the young girls
of the town as lithe sprites and fairies, dragonflies and
butterflies, sweet Williams and asphodels. She created a
ballet of redemption, where a young princess strays away
into winter, spends six months in exile before finding her
way home again in time to bring the sweet promise of new
life. And those who watched from the rounding slopes of
the glen, who followed the dance under the long white arch
between the garlanded pillars, who smelled the orchards
in full bloom surrounding them, could believe that the sweet

and blessed place had been glimpsed and was within reach.

Olivia Roberts was not among the dancers that spring. She had left San Natoma during the previous summer, to study dance, she said, in Los Angeles, and to study acting. She told Peter that there was nothing for her back there. Her family had sold much of the land that had been the Ida Valley Ranch, some to Peter's own stepfather. And now her mother and father were talking about selling the house itself, though it wasn't clear if there would be a buyer. She thought she would have to make her own way. The name of Roberts meant less now than when a crossroads had been called Robertsville. But she could enroll at UCLA, live with an aunt and uncle, and make a start for herself that way. And it was natural, wasn't it, that they should grow apart some now that they were all graduating? She was sorry if he was disappointed.

The World's Fair at Treasure Island opened for a second year, a Fair in Forty, with brighter lights, lower admissions, more of everything. Billy Rose's Aquacade was there, with Esther Williams, and big names played at the temple compound stage: Benny Goodman with his singer Louise Tobin, the Count Basie Big Band, Hoagie Carmichael, George M. Cohan, Irving Berlin. All free for those on the island, all free for those who had sought out the glittering city that promised the best of all nations.

Peter was already at Camp Roberts in San Luis Obispo when the fair opened again. He had stayed on in San Natoma for a season, working at Pirelli's garage. While the fruit was still in the trees and the summer seemed endless and good, he dreamed undisturbed by loss. But when the harvest came in, and school began without him, he raised his eyes and saw the fallen leaves, and the bare, pruned branches. He saw definitively that whatever ripeness he thought he had gained for himself was already behind him. It was not for him to hold, but would fall away when it would. He joined the army soon after the turn of the year, and left regret behind him, left it for Betsy to feel. Steen, however, praised the decision. His hometown in Denmark had been overrun by the Nazis, and his brothers and sisters were living under a government of occupation.

The 1941 Blossom Festival was, many said, the finest ever.

Thousands came for the Ballet des Fleurs, the concert by the Union High School Band, the opening remarks by Major General Grant Hutchinson. Diana Russell again spoke of saving the natural landscapes of California for the wild birds and flowers, and she raised money to support her work with schools and community groups during the coming year. Albin Roberts was not there to help her by doing his birdcalls, as he had done previously. Earlier that year, the last of the land that had been called Ida Valley was sold off, and the family had moved to a house on Nob Hill in San Francisco. Most of the orchards were still standing during the festival; when war broke out in December and any destruction of food sources was held to be treasonous, only half the trees had been bulldozed.

In the spring of 1942, Akiro Yamamoto took special care of his pear trees, and he intercropped them with strawberries for the first time in years. The Department of Agriculture had stated that Japanese farmers could best demonstrate their loyalty by making sure that crops were not lost due to sabotage or neglect, and Akiro thought to show that he was doing more, not less. All the family worked with him, spraying the trees after they had blossomed and watering the tender berries. His wife came out into the fields for the first time in years, tended young Ichiro when he was awake and restless, worked when he was asleep. Fumiko also worked alongside her brothers every day, as she had wanted to when she felt excluded as a young girl. But in May, when their plants and trees were thick with life, they boarded the train for Santa Anita, and then were sent to a camp far from the coast in Wyoming's Heart Mountain.

Betsy was one of those women who helped serve donuts, coffee, and milk to the Japanese at the Southern Pacific station in downtown San Jose. Then she drove back to San Natoma. A battalion had taken up temporary quarters in the town and was camped in the midst of the Festival Glen. Betsy had to stop twice on her way into town for sentries to allow her to pass.

It seemed to Betsy then that all her capacity for wonder had left her. In the trees, she saw nothing but trees, in the fruit nothing but fuel for the wars.

At home, she sat down at the old secretary, the same desk at which she had once written checks for Moreberg Construction, and she began her daily letter to Peter. She wrote to him of the evacuation, because she knew he had been friends with some of the Yamamotos, and she wrote about the fruit crop, which looked good. Peggie and Jenny were both collecting scrap metal for the school's scrap metal drive, and they both wanted to win. The prize would be a collection of warplane photographs. She didn't mention in this letter that she had heard that Albin Roberts was missing, that his Army Air Corps plane had been lost in the sky. But she wrote that Olivia Roberts was now dancing for the uso and she hoped Peter would have a chance to see her perform someday.

She ended by promising him that he would have whatever he wanted when he returned, but she did not truly believe her own promises. She knew he might not return. Some boys, already, would never return. And she knew that his return would not bring a wholeness, but only a change.

She addressed her letter with the name and number of his battalion, and walked it herself to the post office. She didn't know where in the world his battalion might be. It was up to the apo to know and to locate it. But at least, she thought, she could walk it part of the way there.

A book such as this one is not written alone. I owe much to the archives and oral histories preserved in many small but priceless institutions, and also to those who generously shared their stories with me—members of my own family as well as many others from the Santa Clara Valley.

I would like especially to thank Willys Peck, Susan Elizabeth McClendon, Sheila Stanfield Heid, Peggy Stanfield Stuart, and Arch Brolly. I also offer warm thanks to Lisa Christiansen of the California History Center at De Anza College, and to Rich Azevedo of Sunsweet. I spent valuable time at the Saratoga Historical Museum, the San José Historical Museum, the Bancroft Library, the Oakland History Room of the Oakland Public Library, the Los Gatos Public Library, the Saratoga Public Library, the California State Railroad Museum, and the California Room of the San José Public Library.

While writing the novel, I received support from the Eisner Prize Committee of the University of California, Berkeley, the Utah Arts Council, the Adamson Fellowship of the University of Utah, the Writers at Work conference, and Villa Montalvo. I also received help and guidance from many other teachers, writers, and friends. My thanks go out to Dorothy Solomon, David Kranes, Kristen Rogers, Ron Molen, Pam Carlquist, Franklin Fisher, J. B. Hall, Deborah Foss, Elizabeth Goodstein, Bharati Mukherjee, Elyse Lord, M. L. Williams, Margot Schilpp, Sophie Corbeau, and Alison Bond. And always, for everything, to Kimberly.

. . . .

Acknowledgments

Lawrence Coates grew up in El Cer-
rito, spending many happy days with
his relatives in Saratoga, the small
California town upon which San
Natoma is based, and his grandfather
was Saratoga's last blacksmith. Coates
has served in the Coast Guard, in the
Merchant Marines, and aboard an
oceanographic research vessel. He
holds a bachelor's degree from the
University of California at Santa
Cruz, a master's from U.C. Berkeley,
and a doctorate from the University
of Utah. Coates is a past editor of
Quarterly West, a member of the
board of Writers at Work, and he
teaches at Southern Utah University.

About the Author